THE LONGEST NIGHT

ALSO BY LAUREN CARTER
Lichen Bright
Following Sea
Swarm
This Has Nothing to Do with You
Places Like These

THE LONGEST NIGHT

A NOVEL

LAUREN *f* CARTER

© 2025 LAUREN CARTER

Thank you for buying this book and for not copying, scanning, or distributing any part of it without permission. By respecting the spirit as well as the letter of copyright, you support authors and publishers, allowing them to continue to distribute and create the books you value.

Excerpts from this publication may be reproduced under licence from Access Copyright, or with the express written permission of Freehand Books, or under licence from a collective management organization in your territory. All rights are otherwise reserved. No part of this publication may be reproduced, stored in a retrieval system, text or data mined, used for training of artificial intelligence or similar technologies, or transmitted in any form or by any means, electronic, mechanical, photocopying, digital copying, scanning, recording, or otherwise, except as specifically authorized.

Freehand Books gratefully acknowledges the financial support for its publishing program provided by the Canada Council for the Arts and the Alberta Media Fund, and by the Government of Canada through the Canada Book Fund.

This book is available in print and Global Certified Accessible™ EPUB formats.

Freehand Books is located in Moh'kinsstis, Calgary, Alberta, within Treaty 7 territory, and on the traditional territories of the Siksika, the Kainai, and the Piikani, as well as the Iyarhe Nakoda and Tsuut'ina nations.

FREEHAND BOOKS
freehand-books.com

LIBRARY AND ARCHIVES CANADA CATALOGUING IN PUBLICATION

Title: The longest night : a novel / Lauren Carter.
Names: Carter, Lauren, author
Identifiers:
  Canadiana (print) 20250229811
  Canadiana (ebook) 20250229838
  ISBN 9781990601958 (softcover)
  ISBN 9781990601989 (EPUB)
  ISBN 9781990601996 (PDF)
Subjects: LCGFT: Novels.
Classification: LCC PS8605.A863 L66 2025 | DDC C813/.6—dc23

Edited by Naomi K. Lewis
Design by Natalie Olsen
Author photo by Jason Mills
Printed and bound in Canada

FIRST PRINTING

**FOR THE SURVIVORS,
TIME-TRAVELLERS ALL**

"Everything is determined, the beginning as well as the end, by forces over which we have no control. It is determined for the insect as well as for the star. Human beings, vegetables, or cosmic dust, we all dance to a mysterious tune, intoned in the distance by an invisible piper."

— ALBERT EINSTEIN

"No one created the universe and no one directs our fate."

— STEPHEN HAWKING

PART ONE

"...in a black hole, no one can see you disappear."

—STEPHEN HAWKING

1

ASH BLINKS, tearing her sticky eyelashes apart. She's nearly at the end of the road, the start of the trail to Ore Lake Beach. Through the forest she can hear the groaning of the newly forming ice; spinning around, she walks fast for home.

Although it was home that pushed her out in the first place. Her parents screaming at each other. Nothing new, but she can't take it, not when their seeming hatred lashes against all of her grief.

For Frank.

For Goma, her grandmother.

Her throat burns. Maybe they're in heaven, she can childishly hope. Their souls seeping into the web of fathomless dark matter, entwining with the particles of her long-dead older brother, Zach, a baby she never knew.

Alive up there like intergalactic angels, drifting through distant galaxies where the Borg roam, those silent, eerie cubes floating in space, or Reavers intent on murder and rape, or the USS Sulaco.

Aspects of all the old science fiction shows—*Star Trek, Buffy the Vampire Slayer, Doctor Who* and so many others—that Frank had shared with Ash and her best friend, his daughter Leigh, when the two of them were young. Younger than now, than eighteen.

Why not? In Ash's mind, Goma recites the *Hamlet* quote she'd loved: "There are more things in Heaven and Earth, Horatio, than are dreamt of in your philosophy."

A gust of wind slams through the tree boughs by the road, twirling snow like smoke. Frigid air pushes under the hem of her flimsy nightgown, into her parka; the cold is an ache in the exposed skin of her face and legs. Her boots crunch fast over the icy gravel, but in front of her house, she stops.

✶

It's dark. Back light turned off. Christmas tree's shimmer extinguished. Music gone silent; upstairs TV no longer flickering in her mother's bedroom.

The just-past-full moon means she can see, thank God, because the streetlight installed after too many kids started partying at the beach is broken, the glass dome shot out. Still, her foot hits the steps of the verandah along the side of the house before she knows they're there. Clumsy from the cold, she stumbles up to fish a hand toward the doorknob. The heavy wood clunks against the deadbolt.

Her mother will have earplugs in, her father out cold in the spare room. They would have thought she was in bed, asleep under her grandmother's quilt, the pink and green patchwork ruined long ago by a spilled cup of tea.

They probably haven't even checked on her. Why would they? Too caught up in their own shit. Her father's thudding baritone, her mother's shrill panicked pitch. Occasional heavy banging, books thrown across the room, fists slamming through walls, wine glasses shattering. Noise and chaos that twist Ash's stomach into complicated knots so this night, this night—one week since Frank's terrible death, the night before his funeral— she'd had enough. Climbed out of bed, slipped downstairs to the mudroom to pull her parka over her flannel nightgown printed with images of sugar skulls, stuck her bare feet into her fur-lined Sorrels. Shut the back door at the exact moment her mother had slammed her own bedroom door, the booming percussive crack erasing the quiet click.

Now, she knocks.

Nothing happens. Nothing moves.

She strips off a mitten and hammers on the hard oak until her knuckles hurt.

Silence. Only silence.

She turns away, trying to think.

The side door is the only entrance they've ever used; the front door hovers five feet off the ground, the porch never finished. The garage, across from her, is also locked, the key hanging up on the brass pineapple screwed into the mudroom wall. Beside it, the spare house key that Ash put there a couple of nights ago instead of returning it to its nail on the back of a verandah post. Exhausted after a somber late supper with Leigh and her aunts.

And her cell phone is upstairs. On her bedside table, plugged in, charging the battery that drained as she and Leigh were texting about the next day. Frank's funeral. Ash has to be there early, to bring the 1940s cocktail dress she wore to Goma's memorial last spring so Leigh can wear it instead of the one from Barb's wedding to Suzanne, which is bright yellow and floral. Too cheerful. Black is needed, the darkest shade.

Because it's Frank.

Her best friend's father.

The man Ash secretly loved.

Unrequited, of course.

And dead now, because of her.

A howl rises into her throat. She hollers and yells and screams, but it does no good. Her voice is swallowed by the forest; the yard and her house are cast in a heavy, grey light. Freezing Moon, she'd learned back in high school. Waning now, one day past full.

Her spent breath hangs around her face.

Cold pulses in the bone of her nose.

In her boots, her bare feet burn; she curls her toes, clenches them, twists to look toward the road. A veil of snow billows across the gravel, coils up the trunks of the hulking white pines.

The night around her, cold as walls of glass.

2

IT MIGHT BE funny if she wasn't so scared.
Shit, shit, shit, think, Hayes.
She wraps her arms around herself, trying to take deep breaths, to stop her body from shaking.
Can she break into the garage? Her father's terrain, where he works on his 1978 Pontiac Firebird, drinks, and plays video games for hours on an old laptop when they aren't in the coldest depths of winter. Stuck in who he used to be, Goma once said. Seared to the moment in time when his son, her unknown brother, had died.
Just died.
That could happen to babies.
From mewling, hungry life to nothing, in an instant, for no reason.
Over the years she put together what happened: her mother gone away for a few days after 9/11, her brother dead in his crib while in her father and Goma's care. Cue a lifetime's worth of guilt. Although Goma hadn't seemed to carry it. Regret, yes, but not the black tar of shame that no amount of alcohol can wash away from her father.
He will be passed out after his half dozen beers, the usual for a weeknight. Her mother with ear plugs and eye mask, drifting off on a full dose of Zopiclone. If Ripley were still here, she'd be barking her head off, but the dog disappeared last spring.
Probably wolves, her father theorized.
Hungry after a hard winter.
Dread spreads through her like fast-moving ice. Ash plunges toward the wood pile, messily heaped beside the veranda, covered in freezing rain before they could properly stack it. She tries to pry loose a log, but her hands are so cold she can

✳

barely feel them, and a sharp pain shudders into her ankle when she kicks and kicks at a broken edge of wood. Any rocks or hammers or useful car parts are buried in snow or locked inside the garage, whose two windows are small, multipaned, and covered with thick plastic to trap the woodstove's heat. The windows on the house are thick, triple-paned, replaced in the summer with part of Goma's estate. Ash squeezes her hands into fists in her mittens, feels the throb of cold in her finger bones, hears the ice on the lake creak and pop.

Terror stills her breath. She moans around its cold mass as she presses her body against the icy surface of the solid door. With both fists, she hammers and hammers and hammers. Will she die here, right here, her mother tripping over her frozen legs, spilling her coffee, as she rushes out for work at the veterans' home? A wave of fear crashes through her, and she stamps her feet, hunches, tries to think, shaking harder.

A light. A throb of amber. There, in her peripheral. She tears her frosty eyelashes open as an electric crackle snaps through the air. The streetlight flickers on, its warm, sulphur light spreading suddenly over the pale gravel road. *How is that even...* In the yellow pool, she sees a fox. Bushy red tail twitching like a lure in a deep current.

Their eyes meet. It stares straight at Ash, then turns, trotting east toward the intersection with the road into town, and before that, their only neighbour's place. Of course!

The house isn't close. Nearly a half mile away. But getting there is her only hope. Ash grits her teeth, pulls her hood up to protect her face from the biting wind, and forces her sluggish, cold body to move.

3

THE FOX IS far ahead, an orange blur against the dark hem of forest on the side of the road. Swiftly, as fast as she can, Ash walks. She pulls her coat tight around her and marches, not even noticing as she begins to bend forward. At the neighbour's driveway, she's nearly kneeling, then almost crawling on her hands and knees up the slope, past an enormously tall inflated Grinch, its wide, toothy grin a bright, wobbling smear in the shadows, its internal pump humming. Toward the square of inky black Ash plods, finally stumbling up the steps onto the concrete porch. Somehow she has lost a mitten. Her hand burns. A trembling sensation grows inside her, like throbbing lava, writhing under pressure, building to release. Its molten, welcome heat.

If no one comes, if no one can help her, she's done for. The fox has vanished, disappearing into the woods on the other side of a life-sized manger set up to the left of the house. Mannequins dressed as Mary and Joseph catch Ash's hopeful eyes until she sees that they are frozen, too, stuck in time, peering into a crib. She could climb in there, curl up, pull some straw over herself. Go to sleep.

Her hand trembles as she presses the doorbell. It glows the thin green of a distant satellite. Her family has a doorbell, too, but it doesn't work; it did work once, sang "The Star-Spangled Banner" until the night her father threw a fat glass ashtray at the box on the wall issuing the sound. What had set him off that time? She can't remember. He slurred a slight, fuzzy apology as Ash and her mother stared at him, startled by the sudden violence.

If she dies, it will be their fault. But if by some miracle she manages to live, she'll be gone on the first ride out of town. Even

✳

if she has to double mask and wear a Hazmat suit to go back to university in Minneapolis, to the observatory, the planetarium, she'll be there.

She presses the doorbell again, then knocks. No sound, nothing but the creaking of pines in the wind. Breath gushes out of her, a heaving, frightened gasp, and its thick fog lifts around her face. She closes her eyes. No one comes.

Her face throbs. Her cheeks; her neck. Sweat at the roots of her hair. She thinks of Leigh, the bright flare of her best friend's face when she sobbed and sobbed, talking about her dad, what had happened to him, and Ash thinks now of one of the last times she saw Frank, how she woke up in Leigh's room, on a hot July night, the old-fashioned alarm clock glowing 3:33 on the dresser. She got up to pee and found him in the living room, watching a black-and-white movie on TV, petting their cat Yoda, whose purring filled the room over the low murmur of a couple on the screen.

"*Casablanca*," Frank said. "Seen it?"

She shook her head.

He smiled and patted the couch, then pressed a button to flip the movie back to the beginning. She sat, and eventually Leigh came out and crawled under the blanket, head against Ash's hip, bare feet pushed against her father's leg, as the movie spun along — "... the problems of three little people don't amount to a hill of beans in this crazy world, someday you'll understand that" — and morning came with Ash and Leigh curled into each other, asleep, and when they woke, they found that Frank had made coffee, but was gone.

Just last week, he killed himself.

Her fault. She'd asked him for help. She moans, sinking down, finished now too. She clings to the hope that she'll see him — somehow, somewhere — as the lava flows freely, spreading its heat. And what about Leigh? Leigh needs her. She can't die now, she thinks, as she pulls her arms out of her parka sleeves, kicks her boots away to cool her feet, smells the suddenly fragrant air. Sharp and rich as mud after rain, the tang of hot tomato leaves, and a warm current catches her, carries her away.

4

PAIN. ASH ROLLS over, curls around a searing sharpness in her hand, feels softness beneath her. Is she home? But there's a weird smell, musty, and strangely sweet, and from far away a piano plays, a foreboding melody that coils her stomach in trepidation. Slowly, she opens her eyes. A haze of sepia-tinted lace, a curtain surrounding her. She shoves aside the weighty blankets: a plaid sleeping bag with a rattling zipper, a yellow wool blanket with a satin hem. Her fingers tangle in an unravelling knitted afghan as she struggles to push her feet through the curtain hung from a canopy.

Only one of her hands is operational. The left. The right is mittened with white gauze wrapped in dull silver duct tape whose edges are fuzzy with lint. She stares at it. Fear sharpens as the night comes back: locked out of her house, the knife points of the stars, and the cold, so cold, that delicate snowfall that had seemed so lovely, drifting over her face like a hundred fairies promising good things before the welcome slide into heat.

After that, nothing. Yet here she is. Her whole body hurting. Thighs aching, everything aching, and the hidden fingers burn. Her head swims. She stands, then realizes she's naked.

Fear slams through her. Who undressed her? She pulls a pillow over her breasts as her gaze scrapes the messy room. A window covered with a heavy grey curtain. No clock, or none that she can see within the chaos of stacked cardboard boxes, wooden chairs, a dresser piled with objects: a tangle of plastic hangers, a toy horse with a rainbow mane, a stuffed brown teddy-bear missing one beady eye. The smell deepens. Rot and mildew, the dry, astringent odour of old paper. In the corner, something shifts, and she jerks her gaze toward the movement to find a white cat staring at her from atop a heap of clothing on

✺

a rocking chair. The animal watches with its yellow eyes, irises huge black bowls. Ash wraps herself in the afghan and stands, steps closer, reaching out her unbandaged hand.

"Kitty, kitty, kitty," she murmurs, but it leaps to the ground, streaks through the hoard to the cracked-open door and disappears. The piano music goes on and on alongside a steady engine-like hum that Ash feels through the soles of her bare feet.

She was wearing her parka, she remembers. And that baggy, denim-coloured nightgown with the Day of the Dead print designed by a Latina artist that's been her favourite since Goma gave it to her for Christmas a few years ago. Neither of these are on the chair. Instead, she finds a frilly black taffeta dress, a stretched-out red bathing suit, a fur stole, even an acid-green wig that's a surprisingly sharp match for the coloured streak in her own black hair. At the bottom, finally, she discovers plain underwear, a white bra, a grey T-shirt and a pair of pink jogging pants, all neatly folded. The bra clasp is impossible with her bandaged hand, so she leaves it, quickly pulling on the T-shirt and the jogging pants with a drawstring she can't cinch. She still feels cold, though, so she hunts further, digging through the drawers of the dresser, pushing past cassette tapes, a tartan tie, and five music boxes that each tinkle a few notes when she nudges open the lids. Dirty Tupperware containers, a plastic bag full of stinky vitamins, a dried-out wand of blue mascara, a dozen or more half-burnt candles.

She finds nothing useful—no socks or sweaters—so, instead, she wraps the fur stole around her neck for a frail bit of warm even though it feels repulsive to her to wear a once-living creature's fur. The slippery lining against her skin makes her cringe. The head, a fox's sharp whiskered snout and small ears, is still attached, bouncing when she moves as if the creature's lanky body is stretched across her shoulders like a companion. A familiar, Goma might have called it. "Look for familiars," she said sometimes to Ash's rolling eyes, "if you ever need help." Well, she did that, she thinks, as the beady amber eye glints up at her, reminding her of the fox on the road that had led her here, that probably saved her life. If she's actually alive, that is, and not dead, frozen amongst the Christmas decorations spread across the front lawn of the neighbour's house, waking into what might be a strange afterlife.

At the bedroom door, she hesitates. Beyond the piano and the deep hum, she hears a low gurgling as if she's deep underwater, and then, a voice. Lilting, like a child playing pretend, like her and Leigh when they were little, puppeting their Barbie and Ken dolls. Only a few words come clear: breakfast, friend, finally, mom . . . Maybe there's a mother here? Someone who can give her back her clothes, tell her how they saved her, get her back in time to bring the dress to Leigh, to get to Frank's funeral, tell her what's happened to her hand. Ash pulls in a deep breath, feeling a sudden wave of relief to be alive. She pushes the door open, eager to start making her way home, and steps into the hallway's shadowy light.

5

IN THE HALL, she turns toward the sounds. The first door to her right is a bathroom: mint green fixtures, the window above the toilet glowing a dull grey, the outside view obscured by white swirls on a hazy plastic coating. She quietly closes the door. Awkwardly, using only her left hand, she pushes her pants down to pee, and when she's done, she turns to the window. She'd like to climb out, run home, not have to face these strangers— emphasis on strange, she thinks, based on what she's seen so far—but it's sealed shut. A thick line of transparent caulking threads the border.

Her head feels fuzzy, thick, like it's the morning after too many gummies at a party, and underneath is a strange sense of dread. Illogical. These people helped her; they saved her life. Probably just the after effects of hypothermia. What she needs is to find the whispering girl, the piano player, thank them, ask them for her parka and boots, a pair of socks, and then run home. But she's afraid. Why did she wake up naked? Why is her hand wrapped up, strangely numb? The bandage is like a mitten. She pinches a corner of the duct tape and tries to loosen it, but it doesn't budge. She bites the edge and pulls, but it's as if her hand has been dipped in glue. Her teeth ache from the effort.

Ash stands in front of the sink. There's no mirror, so she can't see what she looks like, and this, too, is strange. She focuses on her breath: *In, one-two-three-four-five. Out, five-four-three-two-one.* A calming technique Goma taught her which she uses all the time.

Everything will be fine. She's alive, and soon, she'll be exactly where she should be: in her own room, explaining to Leigh why she disappeared, getting ready to go into town. To support her best friend, to say goodbye to Frank. Her stomach clenches.

✳

"Twinsies!" a shrill voice blasts from the doorway. Ash turns fast to look, and a flash explodes. She hears the grind of a machine and when she can see again, a woman is there, holding a boxy camera, flapping the Polaroid picture that it's spat out. She swishes it toward Ash's pink pants, which are the same as the ones this stranger is wearing. Grinning, the woman twists, nudging her butt cheek with the camera. Satin letters arch over her behind: PRINCESS. Ash tries to look down at her own rear end, but sees only an obscure silver glint.

"Trust me," the woman says. Blonde hair thinning at her temples, shot through with grey threads. Wrinkles around her eyes and her mouth. Her lips are shiny, as if smeared with grease. She has glasses on, and the lenses are smudged and oily, the frames a glaring shade of orange. A tattoo trembles on her upper arm: a dark blue hummingbird with tiny red eyes, iridescent feathers that seem to vibrate. Ash lifts her good hand to touch her own tattoo, only a few weeks old and still tender, hidden on the back of her neck behind the veil of her hair because she didn't want to deal with her parents' disapproval and, anyway, that's where Ash had wanted it: a single blue eye, watching everything. Meant to keep her safe. Like the nazar amulet Goma had given her for her sixteenth birthday that she had carelessly lost.

Hummingbird woman steps closer, her eyes creeping over Ash's face, hair, her body. She reaches out and lifts Ash's hand.

"I couldn't find my clothes," Ash says.

"You were near frozen."

Ash flinches, wishes she could remember, but all there is after the swarming heat is blackness.

"You saved me," she says. "I don't know what . . ." It's too much, too big. "Thank you, but now I need to . . . My friend's dad . . ."

The words sputter out, like there's air trapped in the tap of her voice. Hummingbird woman watches, standing weirdly close. Her smell is strange too, like overturned earth, like leaf mold. In the photo she's holding, Ash looks normal, if a bit wide-eyed from the shock of the flash, and pastier than usual: dark eyes, black hair with that wide streak of parakeet green on a lock beside her left eye.

"I need to go home," she says.

"Breakfast first," Hummingbird says, turning away.

A cup of coffee. Maybe some toast. Her stomach is empty. It growls, suddenly, painfully, bringing with it a memory of Frank making pancakes on Sunday mornings, wearing the too-small apron meant to be Leigh's.

"Do you know the time?" Ash asks at the end of the hall. The front door is to her right. Tall windows on either side glow a dull, deceptive grey that could be early daylight or an overhead porch light.

"In here," says Hummingbird, and Ash turns to follow her into a large living room crowded with more boxes, mismatched antique furniture, a silver and brass chandelier sitting on its side on the floor, and a large hunk of bleached driftwood, branches snagged with ribbons of dust.

An enormous aquarium stands against the wall. Half a dozen fish roam the murky water—the swish of their feathery black tails, the glitter of their orange and white scales as they swim and circle—and then the woman is beside her, holding out a mug. Ash realizes only then that she could have just left, could have slipped out the front door. But her feet are bare, and she needs her stuff, and, anyway, this woman saved her life.

"Tea?" she asks. Ash hesitates. Didn't Goma always warn her about not accepting food or drinks from strangers? And, this past fall, the dangers had been discussed in a frosh week seminar.

"Aren't you thirsty?"

Yes, she is. She feels the sudden dry ache of her throat, and besides, it smells delicious. Cinnamon and apple and honey.

THE LONGEST NIGHT

Gratefully, she takes the mug, sips, and the flavour combusts in her mouth: sweet, salty, spicy. She drinks deeply, tasting, then, a subtle bitterness, an earthiness that reminds her of the chestnuts her mother sometimes roasts at Christmas. Ash pictures her vividly: moving efficiently, humming as she packages the nuts in a pocket of tinfoil and sets it on the blazing wood stove. Sometimes singing along to a CD of old-fashioned carols, Nat King Cole crooning "Silent Night" or that creepy "Baby, It's Cold Outside," encouraging Ash to join in. When she was younger, Ash usually had, hoping to soften any hard edges in her parents' moods, help everyone get along. Not this year, though. This year she just went to her room. Put on her own music, dark and loud, old bands Leigh had discovered, that her Aunt Barb used to listen to. PJ Harvey, Siouxie and the Banshees. Soon she heard clattering, not of Santa's sleigh but of her parents, arguing about the chestnuts (her father insisting they'd cook faster on the coals) then escalating into a blur of accusations and hostilities. It ended the way it always did, the way it had last night. Doors slamming, and a heavy silence like a churning sea after a violent storm has passed.

Thinking about it tightens Ash's stomach.

Usually.

Not this time though. This time she feels okay. Better than okay. Soothed. Comfortable. Calm. Whatever this drink is, it's the most amazing thing she's ever tasted. She lifts the mug to her mouth again and is surprised to find she's finished.

"More?"

Ash nods. Head bobbing up and down almost despite herself, despite a distant, slim crackle of a warning in her head. But Hummingbird is already back, and as Ash takes the refill, she says, "I'm Lucille."

Ash swallows the delicious, silky liquid and introduces herself.

"Like, ashes to ashes?"

"Ashley, but everyone calls me . . ."

"Oh, well, then," says Lucille. "Ash it is. And you can call me Luce. Short form, what my friends call me."

Ash nods. Again Lucille is standing so close that Ash can smell her breath, pungent but not unpleasant, like ripe apples turning soft. She steps away, toward the only clear space: two recliners at the end of the room, that face an old-fashioned cabinet TV. At her house, it'd be on, her mother ever vigilant to CNN churning out the news of what feels like the end of the world: record hurricane season, California wildfires, the manbaby former president refusing to accept his loss, hundreds of thousands of pandemic deaths. Ash's gaze travels from the blank screen to the chandelier and the many boxes, one spilling an unravelling ball of baby blue yarn.

"Are you moving or something?"

"Aren't we always moving? Do we ever stop moving?"

Lucille spins around on one foot. Some of her tea sloshes to the floor. The amber liquid soaks into the filthy carpet as Ash holds her own warm mug against her chest with her good hand. She looks down at the shiny surface of red-brown tea, which holds a light. It's shifting, changing, as if its tiny pond contains its own circling current.

"What time . . ." she murmurs, and makes herself set the mug down beside the aquarium before walking to the front door. The tile floor in the foyer is so cold it stings her bare feet, and there's nothing to help her get warm. No boots heaped on a dirty mat. No parkas hanging on hooks. She opens a closet to find only a pillar of cardboard boxes marked with heavy black marker: 1918, 1847, 2002.

The front door is studded with half a dozen deadbolts that she awkwardly turns. When she opens it, the seal releases with a sucking sound, like it's been closed for a long time. Outside is nothing but blackness covered in the static of a heavy snowfall. The cold catches her breath, pulls it from her lungs like she's stumbled into an unfamiliar atmosphere, tumbled out of an airlock without her spacesuit on.

Quickly, she slams the door, and turns around to find Lucille standing close. Nervousness fizzes in her chest.

"Can I use your phone?" Ash asks.

Lucille looks at her, face blank, mouth hanging slightly open. She blinks, then glances back at the mess like she isn't sure, like Ash has asked for something very strange. A potato masher. A narwhal horn. In the living room, she starts digging through a box, tossing items aside: a cheese grater, a studded dog collar, an old-fashioned bottle of paste with a red rubber top. Ash takes in every piece of the puzzle, but dully, detached, as if she's watching the blur of a landscape moving by.

Suddenly Lucille straightens and holds up a single finger—wait—before scurrying past the aquarium, into another room where there's a table. Three places set and ready. Thick curtains on the wall, hiding another invisible window. Near Ash, there's an oval-framed sepia portrait of a man with a pipe and eyes that look almost white, probably a pale blue in real life. Other pictures, too, half a dozen or more, tipped at various angles as if they are at sea, as if nothing can stay straight. Some black and white, some in bright colour, but all the same man, the same shade of irises echoing over and over.

Lucille pulls open the top drawer of a hutch, digs inside, then turns to Ash. A flip phone is nestled in her palm like an egg. It looks the same as her mother's old one, and as she reaches for it, Lucille pulls it back.

"I'll dial for you," she says. Of course she's right. Because how can Ash do that with her bandaged hand? She needs help. Lucille presses and holds the button to turn it on. The familiar chime sounds, the same as her mother's.

"What's the number?"

Ash hesitates, struggling to remember, then slowly recites the number for their landline. It's the only one she can pull out of her head, the one she'd memorized as a little kid. That cream-coloured phone with push buttons that hangs on their kitchen wall, that's been quiet since Goma died, except for telemarketers. Lucille presses the tiny buttons firmly, with exaggerated concentration, as if she's never used a phone before. When she finishes, she holds it up to Ash's ear. Ash takes it, but nothing happens. No ringing. Only silence, throbbing, slightly staticky.

"That's weird," Ash mutters.

"Try again?" Lucille takes the phone back and the second time there's a recorded voice, tinny and robotic: we're sorry, your call cannot be completed . . .

"You're sure you got the number . . ." They recite each together, voices sagging into silence.

Confusion makes Ash's head swim. "Can we try a different one?" she says.

"This is the only . . ." Lucille holds up the cell.

"A different number," Ash says, and Lucille dials what Ash thinks is her mom's cell phone as Ash watches, but the same thing happens: that robotic voice. She stares at the phone, wishing she could dial herself, thinking Lucille must have gotten the numbers wrong. She doesn't know what else can be happening; she turns away, lifts her tea off the table awkwardly, automatically. Did Lucille give her more? Is this her third cup? There's a flutter in her chest like a trapped bird. Ash sets the cup down with a clunk.

Maybe they forgot to pay the bills? But that is not like her mother, the woman who so carefully organizes their lives, trapping the chaos of their family within walls of organization. She's even learned how to repair the holes that Ash's father occasionally makes: cutting away the rough edges, plastering in neat squares of drywall, then painting over the patch. Humming as she works or singing along to nineties music on the radio.

Ash's head is swimming, but she pulls in a breath, tries to strengthen her resolve. With the right clothes she can tunnel through any blizzard.

"I appreciate your help," she says, holding up her hand. She isn't sure what's beneath the bandage, but she'll find out, on her own, with her mother, a receptionist who at some point gave up on her dream of being a nurse but still has skills.

"But I need to go. If you can just give me my boots and—"

"Are you hungry?" Lucille asks, as if Ash hasn't even spoken.

Has she?

Maybe she only said the words in her mind. She shakes her head. Her thoughts branch crazily, moving fast, and Lucille's face is flickering. The grey hair at her temples turning brown, the wrinkles around her eyes spidering then fading away.

Ash stares.

"I've made eggs. With bacon and the chicken mushrooms the doctor collected last week. They are delicious. You're in for a treat!"

The doctor?

"I have to go," Ash blurts. "My house isn't far." She lifts her hand to point. The flash of the white bandage snags in her peripheral vision, the fox on her shoulder seems to blink. Is that even the right direction?

"Oh, of course," Lucille says. "How will you eat like that?"

She tilts her head, hair a rich brown now, the white totally gone—was it ever there?—and glances around as if she's looking for something that's vanished, maybe the cat who disappeared into the hoard. Ash looks again toward the front door, those dull windows on either side. Dawn will come. Whatever happens, the sun will go on rising and setting, as Leigh sometimes says.

Leigh!

She should be with Leigh. She should get the dress to her. She cannot miss Frank's funeral.

"He's very excited that you've come," Lucille says, and for a brief, crazy moment, Ash thinks she means Frank. Her head snaps up. He's here?

"He wants to meet you. Properly, I mean. Last night doesn't count."

A shiver of terror surges through her. Hands on her while she slept. Her belly churns, fear rocking her out of the numbing haze brought on by the tea, and she turns toward the living room and takes a quick step in the direction of the front door, but Lucille grabs her arm, holds tight. Close again, Ash can see the hollowness in her eyes, like looking at an impassable spread of wilderness from far up in an airplane. But Ash has never been in an airplane, has never travelled anywhere except, once, a road trip to Disney World when she was ten. Did that actually happen? Her father laughing so hard that Coke foamed out of his nose. Her mother napping in a chair by a man-made lake with a baby alligator only a few feet away. There are pictures. On the internet.

The internet! She can message her mom through Instagram! Are there any computers in this house?

But Ash's head rocks with sudden dizziness. Stars spark in the darkness. Her whole self is only her heartbeat, hammering.

Lucille's fingers circle her wrist.

"Don't you want to meet the doctor? He did save your life, after all."

Ash struggles to breath, frozen in a blizzard of fear.

"Don't be frightened," Lucille whispers. "Today is the first day of the rest of your life."

6

LUCILLE LEADS ASH through the kitchen, past an avocado green stove with a clock that says 9:10 (a relief since the funeral isn't until two), and a white fridge crowded with magnets. A polar bear, a couple of palm trees, the Eiffel Tower.

At the top of a flight of stairs, a closed door is straight ahead, but Lucille turns them to the right, her hand tight on Ash's elbow. As they descend, the piano music grows louder, and Ash doesn't resist.

I mean, he's a doctor, right?

He can help her. He *has* helped her.

And it won't take long. Find out what happened, even eat a good meal—the aromas are making her stomach growl again—get to know the neighbours, and then she'll be on her way.

And, anyway, it doesn't seem like she has a choice, like she didn't last night. She remembers how she felt: caught in a flow of lava that wasn't lava, that obviously couldn't have been lava, that was actually creeping hypothermia. Last winter, a girl died that way: the search party followed her footprints through the woods, found her abandoned clothing—scarf and hat, jacket, boots—before locating her body, curled up under a ledge of stone. Of course, Ash didn't see her, but she imagined her: skin whitened by frost, silver eyes staring into the low branches of a pine tree, almost naked. As Ash herself could have been.

She shudders.

I'm alive, she reminds herself. I'm safe.

And in a few hours, everything will be all right. She'll be sitting in front of the fireplace, getting warm, until it's time to drive into town. Her parents attentive, available, thinking about what they'd almost lost.

Maybe it will even be a new beginning.

✸

Like she's longed for, for years. Wishing for a new baby brother as a kid, or a new start in that beautiful (if beat up) house with the second-story turret near her old elementary school, that had housed Planned Parenthood before they lost their funding. And more recently, to win the lottery so Leigh can join her at school in Minneapolis or do what they've always said they would: move together to New York City.

"Every fellow needs a man cave," Lucille says, breaking into Ash's drifting thoughts. The hum in the long basement room is louder, the eerie piano music plunking away. Across from them, an enormous painting hangs on the wall above a white couch. A mandala in black, grey, and white, swirling, alive as if with static; it drags on Ash's eyes. She peers right inside the centre as they get closer, into a miniature painting locked at its heart. A field, a girl on the ground, her body twisted to look back at a tiny, distant house.

It's like gazing through a monocle, as if she's a sailor seeking land, and she hesitates, drawn into the tiny scene before Lucille pulls her away. The frame, golden, etched with tiny symbols, streaks in her peripheral.

The room's other details fill her gaze: an enormous glowing pillar of pink stone in the corner, past a neatly sheeted massage table. A shiny cabinet holding a stereo that plays the moody piano music. The notes plunk and trill, the same song, over and over. Beyond all of that, on the far wall, there's a wooden door beside a window with red curtains roped back on either side. Through the glass panes, she sees the night sky, a jagged edge of distant trees. The moon hanging above, and pinpricks of stars.

"Tomorrow, I'll..." she starts to say but then loses her train of thought.

Tomorrow? Isn't it already the next day? Her head aches; her lips feel thick and fuzzy. She pulls the fur stole tighter;

the fox head flops as if to nestle closer to her neck. She already feels like she'd miss it if it left. Like she misses Ripley. Like she misses Leigh and the life they planned all through high school. They couldn't wait to leave their small town with its single traffic light, its tiny main street with a few stores amongst the vacant buildings, its summer rush of tourists.

 Dollar General. True Valu Hardware. The Taconite Tavern. The bakery. Judy's coffee shop. Four liquor stores. Three rock shops.

 Her life will be more. Meaningful, exciting even, although everyone knows that the future seems bleak. She and Leigh were part of a climate action group that skipped school on Fridays for Future until the honks and shouts of aggressive drivers, probably miners, wore them all down. They took the #NoFutureNoChildren pledge. It wasn't hard for Ash—she never had any particular desire to have babies—but Leigh had thought about it for days and then they did it together. After, Leigh cried, wiping her tears before they had a chance to drop.

 "We're going to have great lives," Ash assured her, and believed it. They hadn't thought much about money. Leigh would study art while Ash went to NYU for astrophysics. That had been the plan.

 "Best not to make plans," Lucille says. "Clear your schedule. Give yourself time to heal."

 "What?" Ash says. Her mind spins. Leigh's face is solid in her mind, and Ash wishes she could grab onto her, let her best friend's gravity pull her away, but how?

 "You'll see," Lucille says, and snaps off the overhead lights. Above, a thick spread of stars appears.

 Is all of this actually happening or did she crawl across the snowy front lawn after all to climb into that pile of straw in the manger and sleep? Is this how the story will end? *And it was all just a dream . . .*

Above her, the stars glitter like a thousand eyes, so realistic she can pick out the obvious constellations: Orion's Belt, the Big Dipper. A clunking sound stops the delicate, eerie music. The hum deepens, coming from the other side of the wall, through that door to the outside, the red-curtained window.

"Lights on, please, Luce?"

And then there's a man, smiling. Sandy blond hair combed in a thin wave over his wide forehead. A white button-up shirt, neatly tucked in, the first few buttons undone to reveal a gold chain. Khaki pants with lots of pockets. He's tall, nearly a whole head taller than Ash, and she's five-foot-six. He must have to stoop through doorways, crouch under shower heads, pretzel himself into cars.

"Ashley Hayes," he says, stepping close. His blue eyes glow. Eyes like in the upstairs photographs. He touches her arm; her skin shivers.

"It's okay," he says. "I won't bite." He lifts the fox head, then lets it drop. The lower jaw bounces off her breast. She tries to move back but the hard edge of the massage table stops her. "I haven't seen that old thing in a dog's age. Where on earth did you find it?"

"In the room," she says. "I couldn't find my clothes." Up close like this, she can see into his gaping collar, spots the edge of a pendant. It's mostly hidden by the button band of his shirt, but gives off an opalescent sheen that reminds her of a gemstone inside the curio cabinet back home in her living room. It's held in its own small glass box amidst other heirlooms and items: fossils, antique coins, an intact blue jay wing, and Zach's ashes in her great-great-grandmother's black-and-orange glass vase, like an artifact they can't part with.

"So many treasures," the doctor says, pinching the stole. "The world is full." A thatch of fur comes away in his fingers, and he chuckles.

"Deep breaths," he tells her, and draws one in as if to demonstrate. When it releases, she smells citrus spiced with clove. Her tight belly relaxes. Lucille coos reassurance, squeezes her elbow.

"Let's see this hand, then," the doctor says. "Assess any permanent damage."

No permanent damage. A term her father uses when she hurts herself, stubbing her toe or nicking a finger, his tone flat and distant, very different from this doctor who beams concern. He pats the surface of the massage table. "Hop on up."

Ash hesitates. Behind her the cat pushes through the flap of a cat door at the bottom of the wooden door and, glancing back, Ash realizes that the scene—the wooden door, the window, the outside view—isn't real; it's just an incredibly realistic painting that the cat sits in front of, staring at Ash.

"Her name's Zeuxis," the doctor says. "Now, come on." He pats the table again, and awkwardly, one handed, Ash climbs up. Her legs swing, like she's a little kid. Lucille grins, hand at her mouth, thumbnail stuffed between her two front teeth. "Give us some space, my dear," the doctor says to her. Quickly, she steps away, as he clicks on a circular fluorescent lamp that stands at the end of the table.

"Quite the night last night," he says, sitting on a tall stool to face her. "Must have been something very bad at home for you to run away like that."

The doctor gazes at her, and she sees striations of laugh lines around his eyes, a faint grin on his thin lips. She piles her hands casually on one knee, the bandaged one on top, afraid of what's beneath the gauze. Tenderly, he lifts it.

"Lucille," he barks toward the surrounding darkness. Ash jumps.

"Can you please see to breakfast." He gazes into Ash's eyes as he speaks.

"It's all ready."

"Coffee?"

"You told me the tea . . ."

Tea. Saliva floods Ash's mouth. That sweet, nutty flavour, slightly bitter, like really good chocolate, the barely sweetened stuff Goma liked to eat, studded with almonds and candied ginger.

"I think I'd like some coffee this morning. Nice and creamy. A treat. You, Ash?"

His eyes pulse.

Cold blue, like the big lake, Lake Superior.

"Tea," she says.

His eyebrows pop up. He looks pleased; relief settles in her tense shoulders.

"All right, then." He glances back. "Got the orders?"

"Yes," Lucille says.

"We'll be up shortly."

"Okay," she says, but doesn't move. The doctor taps Ash's bandage, the sound like patting a diapered bottom.

"Okay then," he says, and Ash feels Lucille's gaze on her. Strangely guilty, she holds her breath. Like on the playground years ago, part of a gang of girls turning their backs on the one who wasn't welcome.

But this is not that. This is not some mean girl conflict. This is only a friendly neighbour. A neighbour who's saved her life. She forces herself to focus as the doctor picks up a pair of silver scissors from an array of instruments spread across a metal tray. Lucille's footsteps clunk up the stairs.

"She means well." Gently, he turns her arm so her wrist is facing upright. "Trauma. Too much loss." The cold blade slides under the bandage.

"Relax." She tries to let her arm go limp, stay as still as she can, aware of how quickly things could turn, one twist and she'd be done for, blood soaking into the clean white sheet that covers the massage table. But it isn't that clean: beside her, there's the ghost of a stain, as if someone once wet the bed. He's cutting now, the thick gauze and the silver tape crunching as the blades bite, and what might she see? Dead skin gone blue black, fingers wizened? She thinks again of the phone calls, the strange dead signal, the operator's canned denial.

"After this I can go?" she mumbles. The words feel mushy in her mouth.

"Nobody gets very far on an empty stomach."

His eyes stay focused on the task.

"After breakfast, I'll drive you myself. That way if they're not home—"

"You mean, if they're out looking for—"

"Sure," he says, but his eyes jump up, drop down.

"What?" Ash asks.

The scissors pause. His gaze tips up to meet hers. Less than a foot apart, she sees every small detail in his face. A dark mole on his left temple, slight spider veins in the corners of his nose, a scar like a starburst on the underside of his chin. And she can smell him too—fresh air, the forest, something else she cannot define: the crackle that lightning leaves in the air. Vivid and clean. She has a sudden urge to lean her forehead into his chest and rest there, succumb. An awareness passes between them, but she isn't sure what it is or if it's something to which she should cling.

"What?"

"Would they care enough to look?" he asks.

She blinks. She opens her mouth to insist but his eyes have dropped to the splitting bandage. It opens, revealing her skin, waxen like she's been in a bath for hours, like her hand has been wrapped for days, much longer than a single night. The split silver tape and gauze tumble to the floor; Ash stares at her hand.

"We couldn't save it," he says. "We tried, but it was frozen solid, and that ice would have crept right up inside..."

Is that how frostbite works? Like a fungus, like gangrene? A moan comes; she hears herself as if from far away.

"I did what I had to," the doctor says, and the sutures glare up at her like winking eyes where her little finger was sliced away as she slept.

7

ASH IS FROZEN, perched on the table, staring down at her hand. Past it, the carpet, peppered with spots of dried blood. If they'd woken her, she would have said no and asked them, told them, right then, to drive her home. Surely her mom would have known what to do or could have called someone for advice, looked it up on YouTube, bathed her hand in warm water or massaged it beside the crackling woodstove until the blood began flowing. She stares down, head swimming, eyes strangely dry. She is so tired. All she wants is . . .

"Sleep will help. Lots of sleep. You must be exhausted," the doctor says, and suddenly, they are walking up the stairs, his arm curled around her, his elbow hard against her spine.

Her eyelids droop; she feels the wobble of her neck.

In the kitchen, the white cat sits on the counter, licking her paw. Her gaze settles on Ash, indifferent. The doctor lifts the animal up, and her legs dangle before he sets her down on the linoleum floor. His movements are gentle and slow, but the cat hisses, quietly, like an opened valve, before she scampers down the hall toward the room where Ash woke up.

Her room.

She looks longingly after the cat, wanting to go there, to her own bed, or what feels like her own bed. But it isn't. She has another house, where she belongs. Somehow that other place feels like it's disappearing, shrinking back in time.

She can pull the lace canopy curtains closed, lie still in that mottled darkness. Sleep.

She tries to resist. "I have to go . . ."

"I'll have Lucille save you some food."

Ash blinks. Her eyes feel gritty and dry. She smells it, tantalizing grease, and hears Lucille humming in the dining room.

✳

She is hungry, but tired, oh so . . . and a thought occurs to her, a question she knows she should ask. "Then you'll drive—"

"Of course. Go have a nap, and then we'll put you back where you belong."

He smiles. Ash hesitates.

"Doctor's orders," he says, and she nods. Her fingertips graze the corner of the kitchen island, the doorjamb, the walls as she wanders. Past the front door, down the hall. From behind, she hears Lucille—"but what about . . ."—then the mumble of the doctor's reply.

Finally, Ash arrives in the silence of her room.

Exhaustion tugs her toward the mattress, that heap of blankets and pillows, but she curls a hand around the canopy post at the end of the bed, pushes off it to go to the window. Heavy grey curtains cover slat blinds. She pulls the fabric aside, leans close to squint through a narrow gap. It's still snowing, a fractal drift sliding sideways. Beyond that, a black mass. The forest. Thick boreal spotted with mushy swamps and mixed forests where trappers set their lines to snag bobcats and fishers.

Another theory of what killed Ripley.

Ripley.

A struggle to draw the dog out of her memory and form her: shiny black fur, brown eyes, the grin she'd give when Ash promised a hike, how she pranced around, tail wagging hard, impatient to set out.

She looks away from the window, toward the bedside table. No clock. No idea what time it is, if time is even a thing in this house. The only clock she's seen so far was that digital one on the stove in the kitchen, but the numbers were the same when she came upstairs: 9:10.

Outside, nothing has changed. Dark for hours now, since she'd slipped out of the house the night of the winter solstice, the longest night. When? Yesterday? It feels like much longer than that. She shakes her head, pulls her fingers free from the blind, feels in the motion a slight, distant sensation in the place where her little finger used to be. She stares at the gap, the sutures. A smear of rust crosses her knuckles, and she licks her thumb, rubs at it, then touches the stitches, presses down. A roughness like frayed rope, but that's all. No other feeling, only the washing in of heavy fatigue. Shock, probably. The need to blank out what's happened. A nap, the doctor had said. Cradling her hand, she burrows through the gap between the lace curtains to tunnel into sleep.

8

ASH WAKES TO fragrance, treacle-sweet like cotton candy. She opens her eyes to a drift of steam, beyond that a body, a pair of eyes. Lucille, holding a mug. White with a curved rainbow comprised of arcing bands of colour.

Purple, blue, green, yellow, orange, red.

"Rise and shine."

Ash squirms, struggles to sit up. Moments ago, she was dreaming. She and Goma out in a field, near a hedgerow of trembling aspen and burr oak, in a place they'd once visited on a trip west into the plains. Goma stood, pointing across the tall grasses and wildflowers—big bluestem, false sunflower, purple aster—at something Ash couldn't see. Her form flickered, like the hologram of Princess Leia in the first *Star Wars* movie, which Ash had seen more than once with Leigh and Frank. How Leia turns away at the end, alert to coming danger, then hunches to press a button on the droid and end the recording.

In the dream, Goma seemed sharply present, and Ash felt a wash of relief. Like everything would be okay. But that isn't unusual. She dreams about her a lot. Once they'd gone flying, had soared over the big lake alongside a pair of bald eagles. Will she dream about Frank, too? How long has she been sleeping? She looks up at Lucille, who is coiling the curtain around the canopy post near her head.

"What time—"

"You slept all day!"

Ash sits up fast. The funeral!

Tea sloshes out of the mug in her hand, but she doesn't remember picking it up. It smells amazing, like brown sugar and butter cooking in a pan, turning to caramel, and she can have some, can't she?

✺

Just a little bit.

But what will she say to Leigh? She hasn't been there for her, hasn't even delivered the dress, the one she could wear because they are the same size, the same build, similar enough that Ash's favourite high-school teacher—Mr. Schmidt, physics—had always called them "the twins."

Ash shakes her head, trying to clear her mind, orient herself. Frank; she's missed it. Missed his send off. How can this be? She groans, and the movement in her mouth makes her taste the tea she's been guzzling down, despite herself. Sweet, earthy, slightly salty. More than that: it helps her, will help now, to calm the flood of remorse that's moving through her. She takes another drink.

"Good girl," Lucille says. "You'll feel better after that."

"I don't . . . Frank . . . My best friend . . ." It's hard to release the words; she has to pull them out like extracting slivers as her hands lift automatically to her mouth, driven by her body's craving. As it soothes, the dream of Goma pulls away from her like a broken web, taking with it the memory of her grandmother's explicit warnings about exactly what brought her here, about leaving the house in the night in cold winter, those stories she'd often told about kids who died this way, once a toddler on Christmas morning.

But Ash is alive, isn't she? She's survived; she has not frozen to death. She is one of the lucky ones. Unlike Frank. Frank is dead. Stupidly, terribly, dead. She tries again to speak.

"His funeral," she says. "I've missed . . . Frank. My friend—"

"If he's truly your friend, he'll understand," Lucille says, moving around the bed to tie the rest of the curtains to the posts. She picks up a pillow and slams her small fist into its heart, shakes it out by the corners, then sets it down and stares at Ash, head cocked.

"Ashley May. Is that your boyfriend? Frank?"

"No." The word is a moan.

"Have you ever had one?" Lucille holds the woollen square of a folded blanket against her belly, breath held, stroking the satin hem.

"Once."

"And his name was?"

"Roger. Roger Boyle."

"Boil?" Lucille blurts.

Ash looks at her, sees Lucille's smudged lenses, oily with reflected light. Why are they talking about this when there are more important things—

"Did he get all red and engorged?" Lucille asks, swivelling her hips, thrusting out her groin. Ash can't take the weirdness, drops her gaze to her mug, but it's empty, the bottom covered with tiny shreds of leaves, like pine needles, like those black sutures. It clatters onto the bedside table as she sets it down, quickly stands. Stars burst from the movement.

"He was your first?" Lucille asks, moving to the rocking chair, folding socks.

"What?"

"You know," she says. "Are you a virgin?"

"Are you?"

Ash expects a giggling confession, but instead Lucille drops her gaze. Cowed. Trauma, the doctor had told her.

"We did it a few times," Ash says, reaching toward Lucille, surprised at the fuzz of light that seems to surround her arm; she avoids looking at the strange, slight nub of her missing pinky. Lucille drops a pair of socks into Ash's outstretched palm. "Why?"

"Just curious. Just wondering what kind of girl has wandered in here."

"Woman," Ash says, sits on the bed to pull the warm wool over her cold toes. At least she didn't wake up naked, is still dressed in the grey T-shirt, the pink jogging pants. Her hands fumble, and she has to focus to draw the socks on.

"Can he... home. Take me now?"

The words are all disjointed; the dizziness from getting up has stayed; her head feels like a cold wave is gushing through her brain. She wants to lie down, forces herself to say upright, waiting for Lucille to answer. But she ignores Ash's question, and when her voice comes again it's deep and resonant, emerging from the base of her throat.

"And man was not made for woman, but woman was made for man," she recites, staring up at the ceiling. A shiver flies up Ash's back.

Lucille blinks. "Corinthians."

Is she one of those? Will they try to convert her?

Ash draws in a breath, forces her words to come clear.

"Is he ready?" she says. "To take me—"

"Yes! Supper is ready, and you do not want to miss his mushroom medley!" She presses her finger and thumb together in a chef's kiss. "Magnifique!"

Ash's stomach rumbles. She can't remember when she last ate. One meal and then...

"Luce?" Ash breathes.

"Yes." Lucille stands in the doorway, Zeuxis spiralling around her ankles, also ready to be fed. Ash holds up her hand.

Lucille nods. "Frozen solid." She flickers her fingers over her right hand like she's scattering seeds, casting a spell. "All white and dead."

Ash looks down, the mug in her hand once again, tilted against her knee. Empty.

"Come on now," Lucille says. "Turn that frown upside down." She extends a hand. Her fingernails are painted a sparkling turquoise blue, the same shade as the sky over Goma's panicked face in Ash's dream.

9

IN THE LIVING ROOM, the television is playing *The Wizard of Oz*, frantic orchestral music accompanying the spinning of the black-and-white house. The doctor is seated at the head of the dining room table, his arms outstretched, palms up, pointing toward Lucille and Ash's places. The three plates are covered in dull silver domes, and yet the smell of the food has filled the room, salty and meaty, and Ash can hardly speak around the flood of saliva in her mouth. She swallows it, nearly chokes, and stands her ground, holding the edge of the table to keep herself upright. For Leigh's sake, for her own need to be there for her best friend, even if she has missed the funeral. She can't imagine what Leigh's going through now, worried about Ash gone missing when she should be focused on grieving her father. Behind her, the jagged music softens, the film transitioning, she knows, to garish Technicolor. Bright yellow of the brick road, the cotton candy pink of Glinda the Good Witch's dress, the puff of red smoke as the Wicked Witch of the West arrives, those ruby high-heeled slippers that Leigh has always coveted . . .

"Turn that off," the doctor says, snapping Ash back into the room. Again the crisscrossing thoughts. She was going to ask for something, but what? As Lucille stands, he says, "I don't know what you see in that childish film when there are so many stories with more grit, more meaning. *Laurence of Arabia*. *Chariots of Fire*. Even John Wayne."

He swivels his gaze to Ash. "I bet you have more sophisticated tastes."

Her stomach rumbles loudly.

"Well, then!" The doctor chuckles. "Time to taste something, anyway!"

Lucille lets out a trill of a giggle, then pinches her bottom lip.

✳

She's seated across from Ash, in front of a swath of thick velvet curtains. When did she return to her chair? When did Ash sit down? She can't remember. Just the snap of the button on the old TV when Lucille turned it off. The back of her neck prickles, as if all those men in the array of images on the wall behind her are watching her. They might be, but so is the doctor. Carefully.

"Ah, yes," he says. "The ancestors."

He leans forward and lifts the lid off her plate. It's full: scrambled eggs, fat slabs of bacon, thick toast spread with butter, and a glistening brown heap of mushrooms.

"Breakfast for supper," Lucille says.

Ash sucks in a breath, tries to clear her head. "You can't keep me here," she mutters, but her mouth is full. Egg and salty bacon fat melting onto her tongue. The fork in her hand.

"Bon appétit," the doctor says, but Ash's plate is nearly empty. Grease-smeared, scattered with crumbs, a few pulpy tomato seeds stuck to the white porcelain. He beams at her: concern, compassion, humour in that slight, kind smile. She prods the remaining mound of mushrooms.

"Try them," Lucille says.

"Shhh." The doctor lays a hand flat on the table between himself and Lucille, but his eyes don't leave Ash's face. "How are you feeling?"

Ash knocks the fork against the side of her plate again and again, anchoring into the clatter. What is there to say? Her head hums, or is that the sound from the basement, the constant interior rumble?

"I remember when I —"

"Hush," the doctor snaps, staring at Ash, waiting. Ash hunts through her head, through her scattered thoughts, lifting them, piece by piece.

"I don't get —"

"Yes?"

"Why . . ." She takes a sip of water. "Why I'm—"

"Of course. I'd feel the same way."

"Why you haven't—" she starts but he speaks at the same time.

"Why they haven't come, beaten down the door to—" he lifts his hands, makes air quotes, "rescue you."

Ash stares at him. His gaze drifts toward the velvet curtains behind Lucille. "I mean, how hard would it have been? Couldn't they simply follow your tracks in the snow?"

Ash does not speak. His logic is stunning and clarifying. They'd let her go; they wanted her gone. She lifts her hand to wipe a tear from her eye, but there are no tears. Her heart feels numb, nothing but dead wood in her chest, nudged along by the channel of her blood.

The doctor leans forward. "The thing we're wondering is why. What sent you off like that, into the coldest, cruellest night, maybe of the whole entire year. Things must be bad. Things must be very bad, and no one . . ." He reaches out, clutches Ash's wrist, easily embraces her small hand with his own. All she feels is warmth, no pain, no irritation of the severed digit at all. As if its removal was meant to be, as if it hadn't belonged to her at all.

"No child," he continues, "should have to live like that."

"Oh, honey," Lucille coos. The doctor hands Ash a cloth napkin. She presses it against her face, breathes through the weave. It smells sour, like cheese, she notices, as it absorbs a sudden spring of her tears.

"Here you'll have a new lease on life. We'll get you all straightened out. You'll learn your truest destiny. We'll help each other. Okay?"

She's crying now. Her tears splashing out like an opened faucet while part of her watches, distanced, unsure. It's true, isn't it? She's learned how to swallow her feelings, how to shut herself down, ignore her own pain. Move through her family home like she's made of glass, a hard skin bottling her emotions. She'd never broken like that before, run away, had enough, tried to escape the aggression in the middle of the night. She broke the rules. No wonder they locked the door and went to bed. No wonder.

"And why should you go back to that?" the doctor says. "To parents that lose their children. First Zach, now you."

Ash stares at him, squeezes the napkin.

"Small town," the doctor says. "Common knowledge."

That makes sense. Her eyes feel tender, newer, like she can suddenly see better. Lucille's face seems to glow; the hummingbird on her arm flickers as if alive. The smell of the food rises to Ash's nose, and she feels suddenly emptied out, dug hollow, even with the rest of the meal settling in her stomach. Ravenous. She gobbles the mushrooms in three bites. The flavour explodes on her tongue. She feels a rising surge of hope.

"Good, huh?" the doctor says.

Ash nods, chewing a last wedge of toast.

"We should have given her some jam."

"I can still fetch it."

"Our own garden strawberries," he says, clutching Lucille's forearm to keep her in her chair. "And blackberries and fireweed. Did you know you can make jelly out of fireweed? Nothing but a simple weed." He clicks his tongue, shakes his head in amazement. "There is abundance everywhere. If you just know where to look. If you can simply surrender to the gifts the world wants to give us, my girls."

My girls. Ash and Lucille look at each other. Lucille beams with joy, and as if she were nothing more than a mirror, Ash reflects that pleasure back. It's only later, in her bed, feet warm in the wool socks, that she thinks — like glimpsing a solid form through striations of murk — *if it's such a small town, why have I never heard of you?*

It does not make sense.

None of it does.

She needs to get out, get away.

She pushes back the blankets, but her body can't move. No matter what the tiny insistent voice says in her head, she stays where she is, and gradually, slowly, despite her tiny internal self, twisted to stare back at her lost home, she slides into the delicious, dark warmth of sleep.

10

A CUP OF tea each morning.

Honey-sweet or nutty like pecan pie with a slight bitterness, barely discernible, a little bit like orange pith or too much clove.

Softened with cream that Lucille says they get from a local farmer, freshly skimmed off the milk that very morning, the doctor leaving through the door at the top of the stairs, into the garage, then the sound of an engine firing. A way out? Yes, if she could ever clear her head enough to try to get away. Even waking up on her own is hard because the nighttime tea—which Lucille watches her drink, refusing to take no for an answer—sinks her down, so far down, adrift on a delicious warm ocean until morning comes, and with it, another drink. Always the same mug: the rainbow arching over a blank white plain as if floating, with no earthly context.

She tries to resist, but as if it were a real rainbow made only of water droplets splitting light, her hand has no power to push it away. Quickly, the tea is in her mouth, sinking fast through the thin skin of her tongue—*I remember once licking the post of the chain-link fence around the playground, that sensation of being held fast, then the sharp hard pull, and pain*—into her blood.

To her heart, her lungs, her head.

What might it be? Rohypnol?

There is a sort of amnesia, a growing sense that her life has been fragmented: before and after, inside and outside, alive and dead, multiple versions of her own self. Like the unfortunate cat in Schrodinger's thought experiment to illustrate superposition.

Superposition.

Just a term for something we don't understand, she'd read once.

Is it magic, she wonders.

✳

An alternate reality. A place where it is always night, always winter, every window in the house hidden by slat blinds, thick curtains, revealing only darkness, sometimes snow when Ash peeks through. Here, the doctor rules like in some twisted version of Narnia. Did she collapse the back of a wardrobe in her effort to escape what now seems so ordinary, so innocent: her parents' terrible marriage.

Why did she leave her house? She can't help but blame herself. And the muscular regret, the rippling shame, becomes a gestating self, growing fast, demanding that she drown it, that she drink the tea...

If there is a rhythm to her days, this is its foundation.

Time flows past; soon she can't remember when she was last outside. The chattering, panicked voices in her head — the Tin Man and Scarecrow trying to shake Dorothy awake in the poppy field — gradually fade away.

They watch a lot of TV. Turned down low so as not to disturb the doctor, practising his meditation, his mysterious arts, downstairs where Ash hasn't been since the bandage was removed, however long ago that was. Movies on fat black video cassettes slid into a silver box of a machine. Never Netflix, never the news, and, gradually, the world outside the house grows very far away. A pinprick of light in a vast, black expanse. A distant star; unreachable.

Occasionally, in the flicker of clarity before her hand reaches for the first drink of the day, Ash sees it, her old life.

Tiny recollections: her parents' miniature faces, her friend Leigh. And wasn't there something important, something she had to do? She tries to grasp the memory. It's like a rope that will lead her through a blizzard, back to her old life, to safety, but she can't. It slithers from her grip. She's here, now. The doctor and Lucille are kind to her. So very kind.

They're her family now. This is her home.

THE LONGEST NIGHT

Like the glimmering carp in the giant tank, Ash swims through the main floor, from her bedroom to the kitchen, the dining room, the living room recliners. Her eyes snag on items: the knife block, knitting needles, a sharp horn that fits in the grip of her hand until Lucille takes it away from her. She is not wearing enough clothing to hide anything on her body, yet she tries. Even when she doesn't know what she's doing, some sliver of her sees clearly, attempts to harvest things she might use later on.

For what?

To defend herself.

Is that really necessary? The doctor's voice in her head, something he says often when tears roll from her eyes at the supper table or the few words she needs to say fall out of her mouth like loose teeth. *Home. Take me.*

But her mind always blurs. It's impossible to hold onto anything for very long.

The days spread like this, like steady waves grasping and releasing a sandy shore, a knife's edge of sweet jam on toast.

Until they change.

11

"**WHERE ARE YOU** in your cycle?" the doctor asks her.

Cycle, Ash thinks, reaching for her orange juice. The idea of a cycle is strange in this life that's been pressed flat, into predictable routines. Lucille bringing her the morning tea, as usual, although it was different this morning, not the taste of nutmeg and honey. Something new, and Ash reached again and again for the rainbow on her bedside table even while a distant, tiny corner of her brain said *no, don't don't don't*, and then she swallowed it all, and then Lucille had climbed in bed with her, spooning her, her odour—lilies, sickly sweet, past their prime— making Ash's nose run as Lucille's fingers crawled all over her, threaded through Ash's own, lifted her hair to look at the eye tattoo while Ash dropped into a drowsy dark cave.

"I'm so excited for you," Lucille said. "For us! But it's okay to be nervous, too."

Excited, Ash thought, from far away, then, *Nervous. Why would I be —*

"Come on," Lucille said, shaking her awake. "Breakfast first. It's the most important meal of the day!"

Cycle, Ash thinks now. She dimly remembers Lucille giving her an odd cloth belt with clips to hold a pad between her legs. The pads were kept under the sink, in a box with Lucille's Private Things written on it. Only a few other items inside: a pink spray can labelled Lehn & Fink's Feminine Wash, a brown glass bottle in a box marked Wizard Oil Women's Tonic, and a bar of Wright's Coal Tar Soap.

The doctor leans forward, his face the colour of dried glue.

"Your period," he says, annunciating, but Ash doesn't have an answer. In part because she can barely get her lips to work.

✸

Her mouth has managed to mash some scrambled eggs, but she has to focus to swallow. They watch her: the doctor and Lucille.

"You know you've come to me for a reason, Ash."

"There are no accidents," Lucille murmurs.

"Come so yoush could cut . . ." It's hard to talk.

"Precisely. Guided by the divine hand of fate."

Fate. What had Stephen Hawking said about fate? The words drift into her mind then melt away before she can grab them, soaking fast into the cloggy earth of her brain. Head wobbling, Ash clutches the table so she doesn't tip over.

"Did you give her—"

"Tincture of Bainsblood, yes," Lucille answers. Ash squints, sees the doctor nodding, his face a blur above the steady glow of his pendant, the large opal. He's smiling at her, and Ash lifts her heavy chin, feels her lips tremble, trying to smile back, but why?

Why?

He pats the table's edge, pushes his chair back.

"Give me ten minutes," he says, and leaves. Lucille stands and starts to clear the dishes. Minutes, Ash thinks. Minutes and hours and days and months and years. All of it an arithmetic she can't grasp; she can't locate herself in the equation. She pushes her plate away and starts to stand, an urge from her body telling her to go somewhere, do something, but she can't read it clearly, and then Lucille is back.

"Oh, dear," she says. "You should have told me you needed the toilet."

And then they are downstairs.

And the table, when she reaches it, is a relief.

Like the back of an animal she decides she can trust. She lets it take her, sinks into the darkness of its warm, velvet hide.

12

ASH WAKES, breath sputtering, pushing up from fathom's deep. She's in her bed, the curtains pulled to make a cozy box. Under the covers, curled around her core, with the cat beside her like a heap of soft white ash piled against her belly. When Ash touches her fur, Zeuxis's yellow eyes spring open like twin searchlights sliding over Ash's face, trying to tell her something. What?

Ash cannot think. Cannot look at what's happened. Lets the pieces scatter like a giant puzzle swept off a table, a hundred bits of disconnected scene.

She squeezes her eyes shut, sinks down. Into the Marianas Trench or the farthest reaches of the cosmos, slipping through an Einstein-Rosen bridge to another point in space-time.

Anywhere.

Anywhere but here.

✳

13

ASH WAKES, and for one blank, searching moment, she doesn't know where she is. There's only silence. And inside that silence, a monster, rising up. She bolts upright, struggling to push the heap of heavy bedding aside.

"Shhh," says a voice, so close she can smell it: sweet and chemical, like fake sugar.

Lucille, beside her, stroking her bare arm.

"There, there. The first treatment isn't easy, but just think of what—"

Ash twists away, kicks her legs through the lace curtains. Her body feels weird, like something's been hidden inside of her. The jogging pants are heaped at the end of the bed as if Ash herself kicked them off, but she didn't, did she? Her head swims, a tightness stretching into hazy distortion with pain at its edges, and she tries to remember what happened, but the last thing she can recall are hands, so many hands, moving her, turning her this way and that, before she slipped down into blankness, like going under inside a vat.

"He can fix you," Lucille says. "It's nothing out of the ordinary. The cauda equina seizing up. That's all he's doing; massaging it, loosening you up, making space for . . ."

She keeps talking, but Ash tunes her out, drawing in a long, tremulous breath. Pain ricochets between her temples. Her stomach flips, and she leans over the edge of the bed, sees a bucket, and vomits.

"Let it out," Lucille says. "I'll get you something to settle your tummy."

Ash gags and heaves, and it seems to go on forever before Lucille returns with the rainbow mug and a damp cloth that she uses to dab at Ash's mouth.

✳

"This will make you feel better," she says, but Ash only glances at the mug. She curls her fists against the mattress. She shakes her head, and the movement disturbs her belly. She holds her breath, counting backwards, and Lucille strokes her face, tucks her hair behind her ears.

"The doctor said it won't even take very long."

Ash squints. "What . . . long?"

"To fix you. It's normal. How the nerves in the spine get all tangled up, especially in women. Because of the monthlies, how we tense and release, tense and release, and that can frazzle the nervous system making it impossible to—"

"Thash fushing crazy," Ash murmurs, her voice a mushy slur.

Lucille pulls back.

"His expertise doesn't come from nothing, you know. He's been all around the world, twice, probably more, studying shamanism, Ayurvedic. The doctor who mentored him in Bali was so jealous of him that he sent him up here, into the hinterland, and aren't we so lucky for that? If it weren't for him, I—"

"Shava normal life?" Ash says, and eyes the tea; her hand twitches toward it, but Lucille pulls it away, and speaks, forcing Ash to listen.

"I would be a cripple. I had polio; I was in a steel lung."

Ash stares. Polio? Who had polio anymore? A steel lung?

Questions wobble in her head—*how, why, where did you come from, what do you want from me*—but they tip away so quickly she can't grab them. They do not seem like part of her, but rather a screen, like the constant, chaotic unrolling of Twitter. Her eyes scurry around the room. She's trembling as if she hasn't eaten in days when, in truth, she's been stuffing her face. All those delicious eggs and mushrooms and jam wildcrafted from weeds. The thought of it makes her hungry, and her stomach rumbles, but it isn't hunger. Nausea pitches her over the edge of the bed again, hand catching the curtain so she hears it tear as she lets out another stream of foul-smelling bile. When her body is finished forcing it up, she whimpers; Lucille rubs her back. The mug floats toward her.

"Now drink it," Lucille says, but Ash waves it away, the smell roiling her stomach.

She just needs to stay still, keep breathing. *In, one-two-three...*

No.

No, she needs more than that.

She needs to run.

She flings her arm out. The tea geysers, soaking the bed.

"Oh, now, look—" Lucille starts, but Ash is up. Her head like a water balloon, like the water pillow her mother uses, sloshing this way and that as she lunges toward the doorway, thrusting her heavy body in that direction, the direction of Out.

Already behind her, Lucille grabs her wrist. Ash shakes, hard as she can, then kicks her, in the shin, in the ankle, ignoring the rising urge to puke, swallowing, swallowing, swallowing. She stumbles forward as Lucille falls back, nearly trips and crashes to the carpet but manages to catch the doorframe, the wall, the bathroom doorknob, before she rounds the corner into the front foyer and tosses herself against the door.

The locks. The brass deadbolts so cold they burn her fumbling fingers. Behind her, Lucille shouts her name, and then Ash hears the doctor's feet rumbling up the stairs, but she's done it. She's twisted the final lock, and the door flies wide, and there it is: a blast of icy air in her face.

14

ASH RUNS. Like a launched rocket she pulls away from the gravity of the house. Adrenaline pitches her forward; her bare feet barely touch the driveway's ice as she plunges into the darkness like diving into a hole. Her whole body propels her, driving her without conscious thought, driven by the escape velocity of panicked flight.

It's only when the fuel is spent that she stops, and the cold sucks the air out of her. The sweat on her body turns instantly to slush. Snow starts falling, blinding her, and beyond that it's so dark that she can't see her hand in front of her face. Everything burns: the soles of her feet, her bare arms and legs. Her heart pounds hard as she looks, eyes bulging, pressing hard in the direction—she thinks—that home is in, but she can't be sure. It would be like swimming upstream, led only by instinct, and if she's wrong...

Zeuxis lets out a long guttural croak. Ash spins toward the sound. Her eyes push into the darkness to try to make her out but there's nothing, not even a slight smudge of white. She doesn't know what to do, and then there's another meow, a few feet farther on.

"Zeux," she calls. The cat responds, its voice sharper, higher pitched. Calling Ash to follow. Will she lead her like the fox had that long ago night? Back to the only guaranteed safety, the doctor's? Or home? Her real home? Maybe Zeux wants to escape too. Should she follow?

She's cold, so cold. Can feel the soles of her bare feet adhering to the ice, the prickle of early frostbite on her bare skin. And Zeuxis persists, calling, calling, and finally, with a frustrated cry, Ash pushes herself forward to follow. She has to risk it.

✺

THE LONGEST NIGHT

She stumbles forward, and soon the house appears, a long black box against the blacker night.

Seams of inner light around the blocked windows.

She stops. *No no no.*

Part of her wants to lie down and die rather than go back inside. But if she does that there are no more chances, and here she is, having escaped. Maybe another day will be different. Maybe another day will be spring.

She grabs the doorknob, but it's locked, and she snatches her hand away, palm seared by the cold metal. She doesn't have much time. Will she be found like this? Dressed only in a pair of baggy underwear and a T-shirt, the fox fur stole that she sleeps with, that she carried with her, leaving a trailing of red hair all on the ground, like a detail from a fairy tale, she imagines, as she sinks, collapses against the rough wood of the threshold. Maybe she'll get her wish: to die rather than be imprisoned.

Beside her, Zeuxis scratches frantically at the door, claws scrambling.

They're in there, listening. The doctor — she knows, she isn't stupid — is teaching her a lesson.

"I'm sorry," she calls out. "I shouldn't have . . ."

The cat howls furiously, a guttural groan from deep in her throat. Ash runs her fingertips over grooves and pits that have been carved into the wood, feels brambles, cursive twists, symbols she doesn't understand.

Look for boundaries, Goma used to tell her.

Marked thresholds.

There you'll find doorways.

Doorways to what?

I mean, if you're ever lost.

Lost, Ash had wondered. Why would she ever be lost?

Images flash in her mind: Goma, her parents, Leigh, the life she wanted, school.

"Any particle that crosses the event horizon of a black hole is doomed, since it must fall toward the infinite crush at the centre," one of her textbooks said, a quote she'd used in a final paper before Christmas break, seven-hundred-and-forty-seven years ago it feels like. Maybe more.

And that's her now, the particles she's made of losing shape and form, tumbling to annihilation. Slowly, she rises to her feet, ready to stumble forward, to meet her fate. She doesn't have to die here, begging for salvation. She'll find her way into the woods.

The outside light snaps on.

The door flies open.

Lucille and the doctor pull her inside. Zeuxis scampers past, a brief softness against her throbbing skin. She's safe.

15

AFTER THAT, they lock her up. She roams through the hoard in her own room, hunting for anything she can use as a weapon, as a means of escape, but finds only clothing—a poodle skirt, a pair of beaten-up leather moccasins, a felted hat with a veil of torn lace like a cobweb—and other mostly useless items. Lucille sits by her bed with her knitting, intending to supervise Ash drinking the tea, but Ash refuses. Twice she backhands the mug out of Lucille's hand, sending it spinning, the ruddy brown liquid a sparkling wave that sinks into the carpet, drying into sticky patches Zeuxis digs at as if they're peppered with catnip. The sickly sweet aroma fills her room and fires her craving, but she hardens herself against it, against everything they offer when they guide her to the dining room: eggs and salty, buttery mushrooms, spaghetti with meatballs, slices of chocolate cake, garbanzo bean curry, creamy and sweet with coconut milk, green salads.

All of it, she refuses. Keeps refusing, despite the apparent futility. Despite deep hunger, dizziness, pains in her body she's never felt before. Her father is—was—a fan of the reality show *Alone* so she'd seen people suffer like this before, watched them roast tiny mice and snared squirrels. That sounds like a fine meal to her right now, but instead of setting traps, she searches, digs through the boxes while Zeuxis watches lazily from the bed.

In one, under a stiff and yellowed wedding dress, she finds a dusty candy, an ancient Halloween treat, so old that she can't unstick the black-and-orange wrapper from the caramel, so she pops the whole thing in her mouth. The hit of sugar makes her every molecule dance, gives her energy to keep looking. For what? She does not know. But it's better than doing nothing.

At the supper table, the doctor chews, watching her as she sits with her hands tightly clasped in her lap, her right palm still

✳

stinging, raw and red from freezing to the metal doorknob. He wipes his mouth, the napkin spotted with the grease of whatever roasted creature he's eating.

"I wonder how long you can last, Ash. What's it been so far, three days?"

She shrugs. "Wouldn't know. Can't tell days." She clears her throat, lifts her chin. "I can't tell how time is passing in here."

He cocks his head, takes another mouthful. He chews, he chews, he chews, and swallows, and Ash swallows with him: a trickle of empty saliva.

"Do you need to?" he asks.

She stares at him.

"What if you could let go of all of that, live in the diaphanous . . . What if you let me teach —"

It's her chance. She sees it, seizes it. Swallows down any discomfort. "I wish you would."

She squeezes her hands into fists as she sweetens her voice, attempting to seduce, entice, get him to tell her things so she can figure out how to get home.

"Teach me."

He smiles, lips like a trip wire. Ash feels the coldness in her empty belly. "Honestly, Ash, I would if I could, but I'm afraid it isn't for you. You're of the world, born of the world, harnessed to it." He looks down at the gravy congealing on her plate, at her body. "But there is another way."

"Oh yes," says Lucille, voice breathy. "The honour."

A prickle of fear spreads across her collarbone. She pretends it isn't there. Sits waiting as the doctor gazes at her, like he's considering. He picks up a scrap of bread, soggy with sugary red jam, and stares at her as he eats it. Saliva rushes into her mouth as the back of her neck — the eye, looking out for trouble — tingles. It's as if she's transparent, as if he can see her scrolling thoughts, intended manipulations, even the pounding of her heart's demanding fist.

Finally, slowly, he shakes his head. "I'm afraid you aren't yet ready," he says, and leaves the room, dishes abandoned, left for the women to clean up.

SHE LASTS A couple more days, anger building, irritation, desperation. The door of her room so secure it's like a wall, the knob immoveable when she gets up in the night to try to escape, the window behind the thick curtains nothing but a dull sheet of black glass. Finally, when she refuses to leave her bed — too hungry, too dizzy — the doctor has had enough. He stands in the doorway as Lucille delivers a plate of spaghetti and meatballs, the sauce a matte paste on top of the noodles, and sets down a slice of chocolate cake by a mug of festering tea.

"Come on, Ash, come on," she whispers. "You're not helping yourself, he's getting—"

Meat thuds against the doctor's chest. She wants to laugh, but she's afraid. He looks down, knocks a hunk of hamburger off the opal pendant, then lifts his cold gaze.

"Still acting like an animal, I see."

She doesn't respond. Wipes her greasy fingers on the bed and burrows under the blankets as he crosses the room in two strides, stares down at her.

"Do you know the story of the two wolves?" he asks.

The fleshy, crimson splatter on his chest makes him look like he's been shot, and Ash thinks suddenly of Goma's ladylike revolver with the pearl handle that she'd tried to give to Ash before she went into the hospital last winter, but which Ash had refused. She's only handled a gun once, when Frank took her and Leigh to a shooting range and she hit the paper man's heart on the first try and he praised her, surprised. If only she had it now. If only she could pull it out from under her pillow and press it against his clavicle, pull the trigger, watch his chest cave in, the bright light in his blue eyes die fast.

All this time he's been talking. "Whichever one you feed," he says, and his hand blurs quickly. He stuffs his finger into her mouth, pushes it deep, so far back she gags. Bile gurgles up, burns the back of her throat, but then there's the taste: salty meat, tomato sauce, his skin, something else. The flavour hits her like a shockwave, and her whole body melts. In an instant she's ragdolled, him over her, on his knees on the bed. The pendant swings a streak of light as he swishes his fat finger around in her mouth.

Ash claws at him; it does no good. He yells for Lucille to bring a spoon and the metal clangs against Ash's teeth as he scrapes sauce off his shirt, feeds her hunks of stale chocolate cake. The food weighs her down, satisfies her growling stomach, as the poisons ease her every pain and fear, settling her into a floating bed of moss. It's a relief to be fed. A soothing relief, even if it means giving in, abandoning the fight.

Who cares, Ash thinks, letting go.

"There, there," the doctor soothes, as her legs kick as if by instinct. As if she's died but her nervous system doesn't know it yet. Only when the motion's spent does she crack open her eyes. Lucille stands, staring at her, holding the rainbow mug. The room stinks of puke and tomato sauce. Ash is held in the doctor's cinching embrace. She focuses, tries to find words even though she doesn't want to speak, wants only to sleep, relax, watch movies, pet the cat, listen to the gurgling aquarium, let the sound of Lucille's knitting needles carry her easily through the invisible movement of time.

She swishes her tongue around in her mouth, sucks in a breath.

"Why . . . you doing this—"

"Doing what?"

More words; she needs more—what are the—"Holding me . . . keeping prisoner."

"Prisoner!" the doctor scoffs. He lifts his greasy, sauce-stained hand to gesture to the ceiling, orating: "Oh God, I could be bounded in a nutshell, and count myself a king of infinite space." Recognition flickers in Ash, but she can't grab it; the poisons pull like an underwater grip even as the doctor speaks.

"You are keeping yourself imprisoned, my dearest. When you surrender you will see. What I offer is far beyond your own impressive yet puny intelligence, beyond your wildest dreams, and far, far beyond a simple nutshell. There's so much more . . ."

Tenderly, he pushes her hair out of her sweaty face. She feels his oily fingers on her skin, the sharp edge of a flinch that quickly eases away.

"So much more," Lucille repeats. "Your very own—"

"Hush," the doctor says, now holding the mug. The aroma of cinnamon, oranges, a tinge of tannins rises into her face, and she tries to squeeze herself into resistance, but she can't help it: her hand lifts. It curls around the warm vessel. It carries the mug to her mouth despite her own desire to stay the course, not give up, and she guzzles. Greedy, ready, eager for the numbing drink to pull her into the warm, friendly ocean on which she only has to drift. Not think, not resist, not plan, not fight, not feel. Her body a fleshy length of kelp buffeted beyond her control.

But then a thought intrudes like a bright little fish.

Bad dreams.

Didn't the thing the doctor said about a nutshell end with "if only I didn't have bad dreams?" Isn't it from *Hamlet*? Leigh playing a guard one summer. The Lighthouse Theatre. That scene where the players swear secrecy about the ghost of Hamlet's father in order to plan their revenge. Revenge, Ash thinks, from somewhere deep inside.

But the doctor pulls her away from all that.

"Hush now, hush now, hush now, hush," he whispers, and her thoughts fall away as she sinks, taken under into the vast, relieving nothingness of sleep.

16

WHAT ELSE CAN she do but submit? If she doesn't, the doctor will make her, so she does what she needs to. Descends into the basement every day, having greedily drunk the tea because it helps. It blurs her head, allows her to let her body go, separate from it as she lies on the table. Lucille strokes her forehead during the difficult bits, muttering endearments.

"There, there," she breathes, as Ash drifts, floats through the room, levitating in front of the painting with those strange, black scratches in the gilt frame, the complicated mandala in black, grey, blue black, pale yellow circling the central scene.

She looks like that tiny figure, doesn't she?

Isn't there a resemblance? Couldn't they be twins? The same black hair, the same square face, the same height.

Oh, no, dearest. You are much prettier.

She looks so lonely, doesn't she?

She won't survive very long in there without help.

In there? Where's there?

The world she's made for herself.

What will happen to her?

Perhaps she'll melt like a snowman.

The doctor chuckles. The painting seems to move, to pulse and rotate, like an aperture.

A trick of the eye, he tells her. Yet, still, it's an opening, and the only glimpse of the outdoor daylight she's had in . . . however long she's been here. The perspective tunnelling to that far distant point, barely visible: a tiny patch of dark green forest beyond the house, blots of grey storm clouds above the field, sometimes even flea-sized specks of stars, a low hanging crescent moon. That's where Ash wants to be: in that field, having escaped, where time passes normally. Beyond the chasm in which she's trapped.

✳

THE LONGEST NIGHT

You always have the ability to escape, the doctor tells her. Close your eyes and drift, drift, drift. With me, you can be anywhere: any time, any place. You'll see.

Like some demented librarian, Ash thinks, reminded of Goma, who gave her so many books: slim novels about kids who slip through portals into strange landscapes and have to find their way back home, or black-covered texts philosophizing on the supernatural, the importance of talismans, walking counterclockwise, and, later on, books explaining things like string theory, quantum tunnelling. All that learning muddled up in her head, inaccessible except as bits and pieces, like an unreadable collage.

Like a puzzle.

Start with the pieces you know, Goma used to tell her. So, she does try. Tries to focus during those wispy lucid seconds before the tea comes in the morning, to remember who she is, her old life. Blurry, faded images, like old photos with blank backs, no identifying scribbles. Her family, her friends, the dark planetarium in Minneapolis, her new school, her old high school, which was not so long ago: the clamour of the cafeteria, smokers gathered in a clutch out back, the dances where somebody inevitably drank too much and puked in the washroom.

Do they remember her?

What do they think happened?

Maybe that she walked to the lake and fell through the ice. She can envision that scenario so clearly, it's like it actually happened: wandering onto Ore Lake, past the ice-fishing shacks, until the surface gently gave way, delivering her into a frigid, inky blackness, never to be seen again.

It happens. Bodies go missing.

Everyone who lives here knows that.

November storms on the big lake swallowing ships whole.

Steel freighters cracking in two.

No survivors.

She nods to herself.

That's what happened.

She's down there, her skull-print nightgown stretched like a flag, snapping in the grey-green currents as hungry pike nibble on her flesh, nose open her ribs.

And this person, here—this individual on the basement table under the doctor's kneading hands, watching from a long way off, pulled so far inside herself that she's like a star in another galaxy, blinking from the distant past—is only the flimsy remains of her soul.

He talks while he works. He tells her about the constellations on the ceiling while she says nothing. She knows every single one, even knows the mistakes he's made in his positioning of the glow-in-the-dark stickers.

In the beginning, she said that. "I know," she told him. "I know."

But he ignored her, kept talking. Mansplaining.

"They aren't even real," she wants to tell him sometimes, but she doesn't speak. Even though she knows all about it, knows everything or, at least, a lot.

There are eighty-eight constellations.

Icarus is the farthest star ever seen, its light taking nine billion years to reach Earth.

Stars are made of hydrogen and helium, the lightest gases, and form around fusion in their hot core.

When super massive stars die, they collapse into gravity, creating a bottomless pit, a black hole.

The boundary of a black hole is called the event horizon.

No one knows exactly what would happen past the event horizon except that you wouldn't survive.

None of this she says out loud. Instead, she drifts, rising fast and far, as far as she can. Into the dark universe beyond that distant veil, the farthest that space telescopes can see: the surface of last scattering.

"If you say so," the doctor mutters, and a jolt of fear surges through her as she drops, hard, into her body.

"A little pressure." She braces and then his hand, his fingers, finally numbness as he does his work. His face floating over the cold steel stirrups like a fat white moon, his cold eyes open but unseeing, gazing toward the trompe l'oeil wall, the window with the red curtains, a pot of pink geraniums on its sill, the cat flap cut into the door, beyond which the furnace—Ash assumes it's the furnace—hums.

"Relax," he instructs, scolding.

Then: "There's a good girl."

When he's done, there's an inrush of cold, a vacuous opening, the sensation that she is suddenly empty and she doesn't like the gaping pit, to have to stare down into it, alone. She turns on her side to drift into sleep, to once again escape.

"No, no, no," he says, cupping her knees, forcing her onto her back. "Stay," he tells her, finger wagging. "Let the nerves straighten out. You don't want to twist them all up again, do you?"

She's not allowed to move for at least an hour. Lucille pulls the plush grey blanket over her, and the pink glow of the salt lamp pulses through Ash's eyelids like the rush of blood under the thinnest, palest skin. She does what she's learned to do: freezes herself into a shell of hollow metal or something harder, titanium or tungsten. Like the Tin Man, her favourite character from *The Wizard of Oz*, which, by now, she's seen half a million times.

Maybe more.

If only escape were so easy—tapping the heels of those magical shoes while muttering *there's no place like home, there's no place like home, there's no place like home.* Dumping a bucket of water on the evil forces so they all just melt away.

At least I'm alive, she says to herself every morning as she pins her memories like butterflies to the wall, tries to make a plan, but her mind does not do what she needs it to. It does not want to focus, to look at the predicament she's in, to see the truth. It wants only to go blank, to usher her away, to spare her the vivid reality.

And that is how her life unfolds, day after day after day.

Until finally, there's an alteration.

A proposal. A new horrendous plan.

17

"**did you hear** what I said?" the doctor asks her one morning. Ash is deep in her drugged state, her mind tripping along on waves of nothing. Fractals of light, crests of colour. Her heartbeat crammed into the underside of her jaw, jumping like a creature rattling its cage. She swallows a mouthful of spicy tea sweetened with maple syrup. Lucille leans toward her, the twin moons of her glasses hovering over her breakfast plate.

"Ashley Ash, Ashen Ash, Earth to Ash," she says.

"Hush," the doctor scolds, and Lucille shrinks back, pulls her knitting off the table, into her busy hands. He reaches out to shelter the narrow stump of Ash's little finger, gazes at her over his unfinished breakfast. She looks down to see what's left on her own plate: a ground beef hash, it's supposed to be, but when she lifts a spoonful into her mouth it isn't succulent and salty but dry and bland. Her throat aches as if she's swallowed fibrous leaves, jagged stems. The doctor's smile is razor straight. He takes a sip from his mug. Clear glass so she can see the wobble of the liquid when he sets it down.

"How do you feel about that?" he asks.

About what? Whatever he's said has been swallowed by the vacuum in her ears, and all she's left with is her body's reaction. Her stomach churns. She shifts her gaze to Lucille, whose hands are working the needles to build a constant weave. The last of the diminishing ball of yarn is coiled in a figure eight on the table, like a Möbius strip, Ash thinks, that infinite, confusing coil.

"A gift," the doctor says. "A life-changing, world-changing gift for me and for you."

"And me," Lucille whines, but the doctor ignores her.

A howling starts in Ash's ears. It builds on the hum from the house's core, the piano music set on repeat, the chatter of the

✳

television set playing a show Ash has seen so many times it's now embroidered into her life. *Where the fuck am I?* her head suddenly spits up.

"To serve us both," he says.

"Us all," says Lucille.

"Us all," he mutters, hands cupping Ash's shoulder blades now, and when had he moved?

He strokes her cheeks, her jaw, her neck, lifting her split ends, the filthy strands of her hair. It's longer than it was, isn't it? There are no mirrors in the house, so she doesn't know what she looks like anymore. The back of her neck itches, and she reaches back, rubs it, feels the ridge of her tattoo, presses the round eyeball then realizes her hands have not moved at all. She feels a tugging in her scalp.

"Would you look at that," the doctor says. "Not only smart, but creative to boot. The perfect match. Doesn't life just have a way of working out?"

Lucille's eyes pulse. There's a glow of happiness in her face as she lifts her knitting, pinching the tiny shoulders, a baby blue sweater.

"That's a sweet colour," the doctor says, as Ash's belly bottoms out with fear.

"For a sweet new life," Lucille answers.

A howl starts in Ash's ears, a screaming rising from her every nerve ending. *A baby?* She leaps up. The back of her chair knocks hard against the doctor, but he catches himself. He grabs her, holds her as her head rocks back and forth, a boat pitching, pain the sharp crest of choppy waves, because she stood too fast. She hauls in a breath and tries to shake him off, to wriggle out of his grip, but he's got her arms pinned to her sides. Darkness shifts and whirls in her peripheral, cluttered with exploding stars. She pinches her eyes shut, tries to breathe . . .

"... a shock," the doctor is saying. "But you'll eventually see..." His voice rattles on as he muscles her back into her chair. "... a win-win really. That steady bearing down... help your spine... a weight to make you straight..." He chuckles; Lucille joins in with her trilling giggle. "You will be so very happy you found me, Ash, once you are looking into the bright blue eyes of your own little magician..."

She holds her hands over her face, presses hard, breathing into the curve of her palms. A band of white light, orange splotches like the burning of a setting sun.

His voice ebbs and flows: legacy, apprentice, heir.

A boy, he says. Of course a boy. She feels him move away, hears a drawer in the kitchen open, then close. When he's behind her, she opens her eyes and sees through blurred vision what he sets down: a turkey baster on top of her plate.

"No contact," he says. Her heart clogs her throat. No contact? All he ever does is touch her, handle her, shove his cold fingers all over her, inside of her. When he speaks again, his breath is hot in her ear.

"No sexual contact. No intercourse. Nights spent in my silk sheets." He touches her neck. "Unless, of course..." Her stomach flips right over. Lucille stares, hands stilled. All the food Ash has gobbled down without awareness churns back up in her throat. She twists away and, in her head, right then, sees Leigh's face. Vivid and clear: the freckles on her nose, the scar on her cheek from the time she fell out of a tree, the silver hoop in her eyebrow piercing, and her mouth, moving, saying something. Ash clutches the table's edge, remembering the details of her life before. The black dress. Frank's funeral.

How Leigh had looked over FaceTime when she told Ash about Frank, how he'd written Leigh eighteen letters, one for every year of her life so far. That he'd pinned a note on the cabin door: Do not come inside. Call the police.

Maybe I'm in a coma.
The shock of it all.

Maybe Leigh is with her, standing over her hospital bed, trying to communicate. She closes her eyes to look at Leigh's face in her head, to try to listen harder to whatever's coming out of her mouth, but the doctor pokes at the hollow spot on her throat with the baster's plastic tip.

"We can get started right away," he says. "But before we do, you need to say it out loud. Nothing happens without your consent. No means no."

No.

The shape of the word on Leigh's lips.

Is that it? Similar, but not quite.

No purses the lips and this word opens them, stretches them wide as the tongue hits the teeth. Ash jolts in her chair when she realizes, jerks like she's waking from a dream of falling.

Run.

Not a denial, but a command.

Ash snaps awake. Leigh cracks into focus. She hears her now, clear as day, hollering: Run, run, run!

She leaps up, and turns hard to bolt. Twisting to the left as the doctor stumbles back and Lucille stays in her chair, stunned. Only the advantage of surprise, that is all she has. And Leigh, and Ash's body coming back to her, the numbness parting at least a little to reveal panic, fear, the need to flee.

She's at the front door by the time they come after her, trying to undo the locks, one, then two, but there are too many, so she twists to run into the kitchen. The doctor is blocking the door into the garage.

"Ash," he says, head cocked, arms open, like she's overreacting, like she just needs to do her breathing exercises. She senses a shadow slipping close and lifts her left arm, jabs her elbow sharp behind her. Lucille cries out. Ash spins around, runs back to the dining room. The sight of the turkey baster rocks her stomach, but she can't, can't do that, can't be sick, must stay sharp, even as her head swims and rattles and lurches so she has to grab the table, follow its edge around to the other side. Moving is like pushing through deep water, all she has is the instinct to kick and thrash. She drops to her knees, scampers under the table and into the living room. The doctor's fingers slip over her wrist, but she shakes him off as she squeezes into the gap between the wall and the aquarium. At least this, she thinks. She's become so skinny. She can now fit where she needs to be. Back pressed against the wall, chest heaving against the cool glass, she catches her breath as the fish nose at the grey plain of her T-shirt.

"There's no way out, Ash," the doctor says. He stands on the other side of the tank, face smeared and wobbly, and she thinks of him as a bubble, nothing but a bubble she needs to pop, as she gathers her strength, as she braces her back against the wall.

"What do you think you're . . ." he shouts as she starts to push.

Lucille screams as it tips, as Ash runs, bolting away from the sudden combustion of shattering glass and water, so much water. The beautiful fish smacking against the sodden carpet, gasping for breath, behind her. She spins left in the foyer, powers through the kitchen to the door into the garage. It takes a second for her eyes to adjust, to delineate the dark bulk of a van from the rest of the space. Only the big door, the garage door, and how to open it? She leaps down the few wooden steps to the concrete floor and runs to it, tries to tug it up, but it doesn't budge.

"Ash," the doctor growls, voice low like a threatened animal. He's already in the doorway, one arm crossing his belly, blood on his elbow, shirt soaking wet. He repeats her name, calmly, soothing, like she's a runaway cat to be enticed back home.

"Let me go," Ash screams. Her voice echoes, pulses in her ears, feels like it's emptying all of her breath. She sucks in more air, shakes her head to clear it.

"Where? Where will you go?"

"Home. Let me go home." A whisper now, the words. She sobs, but she can't sob; she can see that pitying smile on his face, the one that, ages ago, a hundred years ago, made her think that he cared. Water drips from his hair. She wishes for cold, that searing cold of her last night in normal time, that it would come and freeze him solid. He stands straighter, newly confident, believing he's got her, that it's she who has frozen, because there's no way out. Is there? She creeps around the end of the van.

"You are home, Ash. I wish you'd realize this, that you'd understand what you've left behind. If you'd just stop fighting, just trust me. Trust me like you did. Do you remember how you did? How you let me save you? You've got no idea what I can offer. Together we will make miracles. I have gifts to give you that you won't even . . ."

His voice drones on. Through the driver's side window, she sees the keys in the ignition, dangling like a pendant, a talisman, a charm.

"Ash? What are you—"

Engine fired. Deep breath in. Frank taught her to drive. Frank, because her own father was too impatient, easily annoyed with her mistakes. Shift into reverse. Foot on the gas before she can stop to think, and she leans into the wheel, twisting to look as the van blasts backwards, crashes against the metal door.

Not enough velocity. Mass plus velocity produces momentum. She pulls the gear shift into drive, lurches toward the doctor's sneering grin as he looks down at her from the landing. Confident, cocky, the prison guard holding the keys, speaking, saying "You don't know where you're going, Ash, you've got no idea" as she sees it: a box stuck to the passenger's sun visor, three silver buttons. She presses one before she can think about it, and behind her the door grinds up while the doctor pounds down the hollow steps, reaching for the passenger door, opening it as Ash throws the van into reverse, stomps on the gas pedal to speed wildly down the driveway. The sun's sudden dazzle blinds her, and the boxy vehicle veers off the gravel so the back end slams down into the ditch. The tires spin uselessly, one of them hung up on the culvert, she sees when she climbs out and—*can't stop, won't stop*—in her sock feet, in the fragile yellow light of either early morning or near dusk, the welcome heat of a new season, she runs.

PART TWO

"And you cannot move at all in Time, you cannot get away from the present moment."

—H.G. WELLS, THE TIME MACHINE

18

IT IS NO LONGER winter. Snow gone, birds singing. Ash's feet hurt in the thin socks. She stumbles, pushes hard, running away from the deflated Grinch, a smear of lime green on the lawn like a toxic spill, a plywood Santa flat on his face amidst a bunch of straw, probably from the manger where she almost lay down to die.

Ages ago, months, maybe even years? In the daze of the house, the days had become an indiscernible flow. Enough time for the season to change, but how long, exactly?

On the gravel road—rough and needing to be graded—she tries to run faster, lurching forward, emotions swirling as she breathes in the spicy aroma of forest, the freshness of the open lake. She's always been a good runner, but she's weak, and her head is thick, and there are other things as well: fear, a sticky panic like part of her is still caught in the doctor's house, entangled. It's all happened so fast, but what did he expect? *A baby? No fucking way!*

She's almost home. Just needs to round the corner, and her house will be there. Her parents, overjoyed, relieved, and Ash can almost feel her mother's hard embrace. They'll take her to the police. Still, her nerves prickle, anxiety surges in her gut. What if he wasn't lying? What if her parents are disappointed to see her, have moved on, maybe even moved away?

Ash pushes harder, needing to get the reunion over with, but a strange frothy wave smashes through her head. Sudden dizziness makes her stop. She bends forward, hands cupping her knees, the ridiculous fox stole still with her, dangling around her neck. Breath tears into her lungs; her heart hammers. From a far distance, she hears a sound. The doctor, yelling. Her name, drifting through the oily pink-gold light. Dusk? Dawn? She hasn't a clue.

✺

She hauls herself up, forces herself to move. As soon as she's home, they'll go to the police. And she'll take them there, to his house, show them all of it. The blocked windows, the basement room, the treatment table.

He cut her finger off. She's been held against her will. Told it's for her own good. Told she's being healed.

Assaulted with his treatments—even the name of which is intended to gaslight.

The Freedom Technique.

"Freedom, my ass," she mutters, then sucks in a long breath and straightens to round an outcrop of granite at the curve in the road, sees the fat white pine on the left of the driveway . . . But there is no driveway.

There's nothing.

Nothing but trees, and a blue and red real estate sign hammered into the ground at the edge of the road.

No house.

No evidence of any house.

No heap of blackened rubble from a fire or the skeleton of her father's broken-down truck. Not even a clearing.

Nothing but the woods.

Like the house has never existed.

Again, her name, rising like a howl in the forest's silence. The doctor, closer this time. Right behind her, blocked only by the jutting stone.

She plunges into the trees where her house should be.

These woods, she knows. She's explored them, mapped them, built forts, camped out, she and Leigh, fingertips orange from Cheetos dust, reading to each other in the tent. After half a mile or so, she stops in a shallow cave cut into a slope of granite where they once built a winter shelter for an outdoor education assignment. Her lungs burn. She breathes hard, feeling the rock against her back as she tries to calm down, tries to think. Two acres, the real estate sign said, exactly the size of their property. And yet it wasn't there; it never has been.

Panic churns. Her heart beat leaps in her neck. She pulls the fox stole into her hands to worry its fur. Sucks in breath.

One-two-three-four-five.
Steady, Hayes. Steady.
Five-four-three-two-one.
Where the hell am I?
One-two-three-four-five.
Where am I supposed to go?
And again. *Just breathe.*

Has her mind been warped by whatever it is they've been feeding her? The poison teas, the straw-like roots cooked into stews and scrambled eggs, churned into green smoothies.

She moans, drops to the ground. She wraps her arms around her knees and rocks back and forth, back and forth.

Where are her parents? Leigh? A lump burns in her throat, but there isn't time for tears. She swallows, tries again, breathing into the swarming panic.

In and out. In and out. In and out.

Goma comes to her. Her hands busy on a tabletop, doing a jigsaw puzzle. Ash can see her, her eyes attentive, serious in her instruction. "Start with the pieces you know," she'd say.

Ash needs to find some pieces.

Leigh. Of course, Leigh.

Even though she's missed Frank's funeral, just didn't show up. Not her fault but still . . . What is Leigh thinking? And it *was* her fault, wasn't it? She brought it all up, retriggered him, sent him back down into another tailspin, fatal this time.

Ash whimpers, lifts the stole from where it's fallen to the ground, strokes the fox's small ears, ratty but still soft, then pushes it against her face to cover her eyes, to look inside, to try to come up with a solution, make a plan. Around her the forest shifts and crackles, never still, reminding her of the nights she and Leigh slept out. How nervous Leigh was. How Ash woke once to see her friend's face lit by her phone because she was texting Barb. Barb who's always been like a mother to Leigh, taking care of her after Frank went overseas, and also an aunt to Ash. Concerned, cornering her once in the hallway when Ash emerged from the washroom to return to Leigh's room at Barb's and Suzanne's place, where they were watching a horror movie on Leigh's laptop. She touched Ash's arm, face pinched with concern.

"Everything all right at home? It's just Leigh told me . . ."

Ash pulled back. She appreciated the question, it was just . . . She couldn't talk about it. Her parents. Icebergs bobbed through the ocean of her house, hard and huge, burning if you got too close. Just there; just reality. She'd learned how to navigate, how to read the signals, how to stay safe.

"If you ever need to talk," Barb said.

Ash never took her up on that, but she knew Barb was there for her.

Steady Barb, and her partner, Suzanne.

And Suzanne is a cop.

Ash drops her hands from her face. Daylight, still startling, floods her sensitive eyes.

"That's it then," she says, and stands. There's blood on the dirt from her feet. Her big toe pokes out of the torn sock.

She'll go into town. Find Barb and Suzanne. Get help. Report the crime.

Locate her parents. Return to her life.

Loosen the gravity of this dense dark hole.

19

ASH CREEPS THROUGH the forest, staying low, heading for the main road. Through the trees across from the doctor's house, she holds her breath, moves through the spruce and pine like a nervous animal, alert to scent. But it's only herself she can smell. She needs a shower, clean clothes, shoes.

She needs help.

Her head hurts, too; a kind of crackling sensation intermittently sparks in her temples. When she moves her eyes too quickly, pain throbs in her forehead, and her belly surges like she's going to be sick. Still, she keeps moving; if she gives in to the nausea, she knows that the doctor and Lucille will find her like that, on her knees, emptying her stomach. Easily captured, dragged back to the house, locked up again, drugged. The cycle repeating.

She sinks lower, crawling like an animal dragging a gored leg, a missing limb. The garage door is a black gap. The van is in the ditch still; she sees it as blue spots through the dark blur of the trees.

Steadily, as quietly as she can, she moves. From far off, down the road where her house used to be, she hears him still calling her name. As if his voice is thunder, she counts: one-one-thousand, two-one-thousand, three— He's not far away. When she gets to the main road into town, she climbs down into the ditch, which is full of jagged hunks of blasted granite. Crouched in the shadow of an enormous hunk of stone, she watches the road and waits.

"YOU OKAY, HON? Where are your shoes?"

Ash is trembling, sitting on the front passenger seat, the fox fur spread across her lap. One knee of her jogging pants torn open from when she scrambled out of the ditch, over a jagged granite boulder spotted with dynamite holes, to wave down

✳

the minivan. Now, she's strung tight between the safety of this stranger's vehicle — burgundy, not blue, with rusty fenders and a sticker in the back window that says Gore for President — and the threat of the doctor.

"Please," she says, jerking her hand. "I'll tell you. I'll tell you. Just drive!"

Because any second now. Any second she'll see the blue van roaring up to the bullet-pocked stop sign behind them, close enough that he will spot her panicked gaze in the side mirror. The woman doesn't move.

"Please," Ash bleats, begging, and the driver hits the gas. Stones rattle off the wheel wells as they accelerate. Slowly, Ash breathes, as questions come at her.

"What's happened? Are you hurt? Do I need to take you to . . ."

But Ash barely hears her over the humming of her adrenaline. It rushes in her ears. She works to settle it, picturing a shaken snow globe calming. A quiet scene: frosted spruce tree, little house in a field. The painting in the doctor's basement. The girl inside. How it had seemed to spin, ratcheting into motion, the girl's skin flickering as if she was moving very fast. A trick of the eye, the doctor had said, but how?

"I'm Tammy," the driver says, jerking Ash out of her thoughts. They are passing the cemetery where Goma is buried, and Ash's grandfather, and her older brother.

"You scared the shit out of me, jumping out like that."

Tammy's hands clench and unclench the steering wheel. She's wearing a T-shirt, and the thick flesh on her arm wobbles as she reaches out to snap off the mumbling radio, reminding Ash of Lucille, of the hummingbird tattoo that sometimes seemed nearly alive, fluttering on the flesh of her arm. But this isn't Lucille. Too alert, too awake, her eyes a deep, steady brown instead of Lucille's shifting shades of green. Too present, too real. Was it real?

The white numbers on the dashboard clock say 7:31. Morning or evening?

"Is that the—"

"And where are your shoes?"

They're passing the convenience store now, where they—Ash or her mom or dad—would often stop for milk or chips, where the silver-and-blue shell of a phone booth was turned into a little free library. As they drive by now, she sees someone half inside of it, holding open the bifold glass door, a black handset held up to his face. Ash stares, then crosses her arms, tight, protective, holding herself together as the store disappears behind them.

"My house is gone," she says.

"What?"

"My house. The house my dad built."

"Oh," says Tammy. "Did it burn? Did you run away from . . . Has anyone called the fire . . ." She hits her blinker, readying to pull over. "I can stop."

Ash shakes her head. "Can I borrow your cell?"

"A car phone? I don't have . . . I have a pager."

Ash blinks. Tammy veers onto the gravel curb.

"No!" Ash says, and Tammy accelerates again.

"Obviously you need some help. I think I need to get . . ."

"The cops," Ash says. Suzanne.

Tammy nods. "Yes."

They drive. Her head swims; she realizes how good the soft seat feels under the soreness of her body. Tammy pulls a water canister from behind Ash's seat, hands it to her. She takes a long drink—it tastes good, fresh and uncomplicated by strange flavours, quick-acting invisible agents that she was unable to say no to. When she's finished, she flips the visor down to look for a mirror so she can see herself. Her face is streaked with dirt and sweat, her hair a tangled mess. The last of the green streak colours the split ends that reach below her shoulders.

"I've got a kid of my own," Tammy says. "Not far from your age. You can talk to me."

Ash opens her mouth, but where would she even start? It is summer—late spring, fall—when before it was deep winter? It is either morning or night. Her house does not exist anymore. Her parents are missing? Where are they?

Where is she?

Over the rainbow, somewhere where there isn't any trouble. When all she wants is to go back home.

"We can start with your name."

Ash lets out a long breath, digs her fingertips into the soft red fur of the stole.

"Ash," she mutters.

"Your feet. That looks painful."

The socks are filthy and smeared with blood. Ash's stomach lurches. She flips the door handle open in time to lean out over the blur of grey asphalt. Hot bile spews out of her mouth. Tammy veers onto the gravel edge; they shudder to a stop. Ash heaves again, but nothing comes up. Once more, she grabs the canister that Tammy nudges against her arm, cold metal, painted with a chipped camouflage pattern, and gulps.

"Take it easy," Tammy says. The container gushes as Ash lowers it to her knee, drops her head back against the seat, breathing slowly. *In, one-two-three . . .*

"Maybe the hospital would be better?"

Ash shakes her head; pain stabs at her temples. This is withdrawal, she figures, and right now what she needs more than anything is a familiar face, and one who can act immediately to go after the doctor. So, Suzanne.

"Cops," she moans.

"Okay, then," Tammy says, and accelerates. Ahead of them, the pavement ripples in the day's heat. Another illusion, Ash thinks, as they pass her old high school, a clutch of smokers right outside the front door where they aren't supposed to be, then the parking lot beside the black train museum, where Leigh said goodbye to her last September before Ash left with her mom for Minneapolis, hating the severing of their friendship just because Leigh couldn't afford college yet and was too worried about her dad to leave. Ash refused to go to New York without her. Chose somewhere closer to home instead, and anyway, it's a good college, with its own observatory.

Her throat burns. She wants to see Leigh, to give her a hug, to say sorry.

Gently, Tammy touches her knee.

"There's a bag of clothes back there," she says, jabbing her chin toward the rear of the van. "Some stuff I was bringing to the charity shop. My daughter Bonnie's. Bonita, I should say. Gone goth now. If it isn't black or midnight or onyx . . ." She clears her throat.

"But for right now you should stay in what you're wearing," she says. "Grab anything that strikes your fancy though. For later. There's a pair of shoes . . ." Her gaze slides up from Ash's feet, over the ripped and dirty jogging pants, Ash's filthy T-shirt.

Carefully, mindful of her rocky stomach, Ash turns to climb into the back, squeezing the shoulder of the front seat as her head wobbles. Through the windows the town passes by: the equipment yard, the ice cream parlour. When she sees Jack's Pool Hall—freshly painted a bright teal when she remembers it as a sickly flaky green—she drops her eyes to the garbage bag, digs into the clean clothes.

20

IN THE PARKING LOT of the police station, Ash removes her torn, dirty socks and slips her feet inside a pair of silver, sparkling sneakers. She ties the laces, then looks around, tense as she watches for the approach of the doctor's face, his tall body, his blue van, certain it can't be this easy. She can't have simply escaped after all this time. Gently, Tammy wraps an arm around her shoulders and guides her forward. Her heart is beating hard, and there's a feeling like sloshing water at the base of her throat, but she's eager, too. Eager to speak, to tell them what's been done to her, to get this over with, to get justice.

Ash doesn't recognize the man sitting at the desk who buzzes them in. Commercials mutter on a boxy television set hanging from the corner of the room, the noise buzzing in Ash's head as she approaches the scratched-up plexiglass shield, trying to figure out where to start. Not with her missing house. That's crazy.

At the beginning. That's what Goma always said. Begin at the beginning. Find the recognizable pieces. One wave at a time, and you can cross a whole ocean that way.

"Can I help you?" he asks. Yang says the nameplate pinned to his light blue shirt.

Ash nods. Her fingers grip the counter's edge. She sees the space where her little finger once was, and her breath fogs the plastic shield when she begins to talk. She isn't far into the story—locked out, last January—when a blonde-haired officer comes through the door behind him, and their eyes meet.

Ash expects instant action, for Suzanne to rush around the barrier between them, give her a hard hug, then pull back. Hands on Ash's shoulders, examining her face, assessing. Expects immediate, no-nonsense care. Frozen in the moment,

✳

her hand lifted to press on the glass as if trying to push through, she holds her breath, but nothing happens. The two officers stare at her, faces deadpan, waiting for her to speak. It's a scene in a weird dream. Ash's mouth goes dry. *What is happening?*

Does Ash look so different? She was at Barb and Suzanne's wedding the summer before; she danced with Leigh; she even danced with Frank, his warm hand on the small of her back giving her a forbidden shiver.

But then she realizes how different Suzanne looks. Her hair long and poker straight instead of short and curly, the way it grew in after she shaved her head for a charity fundraiser. And her face . . . skin smooth, mauve eyeshadow on when she never wears makeup . . . thinner, too, Ash realizes. And how is this . . . she presses a fist against her fluttering chest.

"It's Ash," she says loudly, needing her voice to get through the foggy barrier.

Suzanne's gaze shifts to Tammy, then back to Ash. Finally, she steps around the desk to come through the door, to talk to them directly and a bolt of hope slams through Ash. Suzanne touches Ash's wrist, looks at the blank spot where her finger was cut away, the crimson scar.

"Ash," she says. "Do you want to tell me what's happened to you?"

Suzanne's face is flat, attentive, steady in its seriousness. Ash remembers the width of her smile, the flush of her cheeks after too much wine, her hair held in place with glittering combs, her brother Terry walking her down the aisle.

"Barb," says Ash. "Can you call Barb? Can I speak to—"

"Who?"

Ash flings a glance at Tammy as if Tammy can help. As if Tammy will know what the hell is going . . . Suzanne touches the fox stole draped over her shoulder, then gestures to the metal door into the back.

"Let's go in there and talk." A hallway, Ash imagines. A room with no windows. A place to let it all out.

"Room Two," Officer Yang says, as Suzanne guides Ash toward the door, but another officer bursts through, nearly knocking them over, his eyes flashing.

"Are you seeing this?" he shouts and grabs a remote control off the desk, points it at the TV. Ash's gaze jumps up to the screen, and there's a familiar silver skyscraper, next to its twin.

A jagged gash cut into the metal, smoke billowing out.

A collective gasp goes up in the room, and Ash looks at each face. Tammy holds her fingers over her lips. Suzanne's eyes are wide and focused, her face gone pasty white. Officer Yang's mouth is hanging open as his hand fumbles for the ringing phone.

What is this? Some sort of reenactment, a historical cosplay? Preparation for the twentieth anniversary that's coming up in a year?

"Did you see what happened, sir? Did you see what happened?" a reporter asks someone on the street in New York as sirens wail.

Plumes of black smoke pump into blue sky. The local time at the bottom of the screen says 7:59. It will be 8:59 on the east coast. The start of the work day.

The start of the day that will change everything.

Images that Ash has seen her entire life are being born on the television screen.

Pictures that have floated over the white board in classroom lessons, that sit flat and glossy in history textbooks. Ash sees them appear as the seconds tick past, imagines what is to come: the confetti storm of papers, people leaping to their deaths, the Twin Towers sliding into terrible nothingness, to dust.

Then, the war drums.

The war that will start.

THE LONGEST NIGHT

The war which will eventually, many years later, claim Frank.

"Oh my God," Suzanne breathes, amidst another collective sharp intake of air. Ash isn't looking, can't see anything beyond her shock and fear, but it must have happened: the second plane, plunging into the second tower in an explosion of orange.

Stumbling, afraid—terrified, actually—Ash spins around; she runs.

21

SUCKING AIR. *How how how.*

Her new sneakers' thin soles pound, jarring her body, as she rounds the corner onto Main Street and nearly crashes into the blue, red, and white barber pole that's now in the town museum. Or, will be: up ahead, in the future, where she belongs.

Is the doctor's house a time machine, the humming at its core a kind of quantum drive pushing particles faster than the speed of light, his own sort of Tardis?

She plunges into the protective cove of an alley. She bends over, one hand clutching the gritty brick wall, the other on her churning stomach, to throw up.

Her head feels like it might crack open, spill something essential onto the dusty asphalt. Withdrawal, yes, but also shock. She did not see this coming. How could she have? The eye on the back of her neck aches, no good for warning her of any incoming danger, she thinks as she sinks to the ground, realizing only as she feels the grit of the pavement through the thin fabric of her jogging pants that she hasn't checked for needles. But that disaster — opiate addiction and poverty, rife in her hometown — waits up ahead, in the future, as does Ash's own life, which has been — what? — ticking in reverse for twenty years?

She moans. Cups her face in her hands as her mind fires.

The towers will crumble before lunch. Thousands will die. Bush, Cheney, Rumsfeld will set their sights on Iraq. Eventually war will start and then echo and echo and echo, and in her own little town a peace group will gather every Sunday afternoon near the lighthouse for years and years and years.

Her grandmother was part of that group. They held placards that said things like No Blood For Oil and Don't Attack Iraq and Bush Lied, People Died. Then, later, when the group

✳

dwindled to just a few, before it finally disbanded, they held images of doves and one single word: Peace. She found some photographs in Goma's old albums. She used one for the cover of an essay for her freshman writing class. Who is your hero? Goma, yes, but also, Frank. A veteran would make more of an impact, she'd thought, so she chose him.

Made him sit there and spill it all: how he'd turned eighteen a few days after the attack and signed up in the recruiting office that is now—then—will be—his therapist's office. The irony, he'd said.

First, Afghanistan, then Iraq. Three deployments. He tried to keep it simple as he spoke to her over FaceTime because they were in lockdown.

This, then that.

He didn't talk about PTSD. But she knew, and so she brought it up. For the rest of her life, she will remember his face: the flicker of that grin which is—was, will be—his armour. How he thoughtfully extinguished his cigarette in an ashtray out of the frame of the call while she waited, asking him to *go there*. Her finger on the trigger.

Is that why she's here? Is she supposed to fix this, somehow stop it all from happening? Head to D.C. and spout her truth, sounding like a crazy person, hoping somebody will listen?

Or is her arrival a random accident, like the accident of her own existence, soon to combust into being in her mother's womb—her parents seeking comfort from each other, Goma's told her. She'll go unnoticed for several months, her parents lost in their grief, her father drinking, her mother keeping busy, ignoring her body. They'll only become aware in the new year, five months before her birthday.

June 21, 2002. A Cancer. Sensitive and loyal.

Just ask Leigh. Leigh. Who shares the same sun sign as her but with a moon in Gemini.

Leigh, who doesn't exist yet either. Not here, where Ash is currently sitting, struggling to think it all through.

Or is this a punishment? For what she did to Frank, how she got him to talk about his trauma, to bring it fully back to life, so that he'd gone and killed himself?

It isn't your fault, Leigh told her. But how did she know?

Her heart aches underneath the churning, churning of her head. Memories coming at her fast, like she's trying to anchor herself in her own timeline, stitch together what she knows. But what good will it do? She's here, in an alley, on September 11, 2001. Somehow. She drops her face to her knees, giving in to all of the grief. For this trap, for Frank, for Goma, for everything the doctor has done to her. The enormity of the whole situation swells inside her like one of those inflatable decorations, the Grinch looming over her that first night on the doctor's front lawn. She must focus to pull it back under her control, let the air hiss out, manage the tethering lines until it's something she can hold, that won't overpower her.

She has to think. She breathes, and feels better. Lighter, clearer, ready to start figuring out what to do next. Across from her, Y2K is spraypainted in fat balloon letters above an image of a face in a gas mask on the wall. In her time, in her own far-off existence, the brick is covered with stickers of local amateur bands that play up and down the North Shore, images of neon-yellow citrus and black-and-white sketched squirrel skeletons. Her head swims as she relocates herself again, and then a thought springs into her mind, accompanied by the sudden leaping of her heart.

Frank! Alive and well in this time, but oh my God, he'd be younger than she is! But if he's here, then also . . .

Goma.

A fit and active sixty-year-old widow in her house on the edge of town, backing onto Devil's Fork Creek, probably glued to the television set right now with Ash's parents, who were living with her in 2001, Ash remembers, to save money as they looked for land. The three of them, plus baby Zach. Zach! Her whole family, a ten-minute walk away.

All the rules from a glut of science fiction clutter up her head. The prime directive. Don't interfere in the normal development of a society or the unfolding of a timeline. She'd give anything for Jean-Luc Picard to be in charge right now, to arrive with his fatherly authority and tell her what to do.

"Got a smoke?" someone asks. Ash looks up and there's the doctor. He stands in the mouth of the alley, eyes hidden behind sunglasses, hands stuffed in the pockets of his jeans, the height of his body blocking the clear September light.

22

ASH SCRAMBLES UP, ready to run. A wave of pain floods her head, that familiar sudden tipping sensation, and she has to reach for the brick wall to stabilize herself.

"Just kidding, of course," says the doctor. "Who smokes anymore in this day and age?" He shuffles closer. She tries again to bolt but then retches, doubling over, spits a gob of bile on the ground. Is he doing this to her? His proximity? Or is this still withdrawal?

"That day and age, your day and . . ." He heaves a sigh. "We're all just stardust anyway, so what does it matter where we float?"

His hand rubs her back, the other shackling her wrist. How did he get to her so fast? Ash shakes her head, a quick jerk to try to clear it, and focuses on pouring her weight into her feet to stand straight, to get ready to . . .

"I've got to say, Ash. Interesting choice!" The doctor tightens his grip, standing so close she's pushed back against the wall, pinned there. The strip of sky above him is a perfect blue, unmarked by clouds. A beautiful day, Frank had told her, and everyone on the documentaries she watched said the same thing: one of those pristine mornings in late summer, edging into fall, when the light seems to glow.

"I might have thought broken heart, maybe even just a slight rotation back to when your poor grandmother passed. But this . . ." He clicks his tongue. "The gravity of this situation must mean something to you even if—"

"Choice?" she croaks.

"What's that, dear?"

"Choice. You said choice. I have a choice?"

The doctor shrugs, leans his shoulder against the brick wall. Young, then not. His face lined, then not, wrinkles sketched,

✳

then furiously erased. Like Lucille that first morning. Both of them a kaleidoscope of ages. Ash's eyes hurt.

"In a manner of speaking."

"What manner?" She hears the sharpened pitch in her own voice, the rise of a panicked hysteria, and pushes her fingertips against the rough brick. *Focus, Hayes.* The doctor smiles. His eyes are hidden behind the black-brown lenses of aviator glasses. If she has a choice, then — "Can't I just choose my own time, my own place, and find my way home?"

"There's no place like home," he says, in a strained falsetto. "But that's not really true for you, is it?"

Ash doesn't answer. He isn't wrong.

"The most authentic choice is the one we aren't even aware of. That comes unbidden" — he wiggles his fingers beside his temple — "from our minds, like a dream, like how your dreams tell you the truth, even if they don't seem to make any sense. You are blessed with knowledge beyond your comprehension. Have you heard of the law of attraction?"

She stares at him. Feels a sudden urge to laugh. Under that, a crackling surge of terror. Is he right? Has she unconsciously wished for all of this? Did her vibrations move her into this time, this place, instead of where she should be, where she belongs? But then, in her head, there is Goma, urging her to Stephen Hawking rather than *The Secret,* that dusty DVD that Barb had played one day for her and Leigh. Goma had scoffed when Ash told her about it, saying, "As if we can sum up all the mysteries of a vibrant, complex, random universe into a simple tool to give ourselves a steady income stream."

"You probably don't understand, and that's okay," the doctor says. "All you have to do is trust me. I've lived my whole life tethered to this mystery, my forebears, too, and I long to share it, to pass it on, to fully fulfill my legacy — with you." He pulls off his sunglasses and stoops to look intently into her face.

She shuts her eyes, tight, feels a rumble in her hollow belly, suddenly ravenous. He smells like spicy incense, like aromatic herbs—first in the pot with the onions, Lucille had taught her. Ash twists her head away, trying not to breathe him in.

"What an honour it is that I've chosen you! That's the only choice that matters. Trust me, and you will see that visiting your crappy little backwoods town from twenty years ago is the tip of the iceberg!"

"What do you . . ." she starts, but her mouth has gone numb, the words melting fast on her tongue. Turned to syrup. Cue a piercing desire for the treacle-sweet tea, her favourite, like burnt caramel, that subtle bitter note rounding out the sugary flavour. Her lips feels gluey and thick, as though the memory alone is powerful enough to drug her. She worms her hand under the waistband of her pants, squeezes the soft skin of her belly, trying to ground herself, but the dazzle of him—his height, his eyes like the widest sky, the opal swirling with some inner light—tips her equilibrium, and she slumps back.

"This must all be so overwhelming, my darling," he says, arm looped tightly around her shoulders now, overtop of the fox stole. Its yellow eyes glint from inside the dark bend of his elbow as he leads her down the alley. She does not want to go with him, but she is, that's what's happening, she's like a well-trained dog on a leash. Collar too tight. Barely able to breath.

His van is parked on the far side of street, one side of the rear bumper smashed in. Did she do that? She presses her hand against the warm metal, uses its mass as a guide as he leads her, his bulk muscling her along the passenger side. Before he opens the door, she looks toward the turn at the end of the street that would take her to Goma's house. A police car is pulled up to the stop sign, and she stares at the silhouetted head in the driver's seat, wishing the cop would turn around, look in her direction so she could send some sort of signal. But then the doctor is behind her, opening the door. She climbs inside. Is she frozen? Must be. Her ancient brain, the amygdala, shutting down, seizing, because where else is her head? Her fighting spirit? Where's Leigh when she needs her?

"Everyone you love is still alive, still living their lives. You're one of the lucky ones."

She doesn't know what he means, but she supposes he's right. No one she loved was sipping their morning coffee above the ninety-third floor when the first plane hit. When the second tore through the neighbouring tower.

"Trust me," he says, behind her now, opening the door. "You'll be okay."

Will she? But the picture of running from him, escaping, is only that: a picture. A flimsy flip book that can just as easily move in reverse, landing her always right here, with him, time cycling backwards toward his house.

Anyway, where could she even go?

"There's nowhere to go," the doctor says.

But in some other universe, another her has gotten away.

Her sparkling sneakers pounding up the street. Her body pitched into the velocity of flight, the jolt of concrete in her ankles.

Or else the cop arriving in the mouth of the alley to ask after her, to check in on the confrontation between her and the doctor.

She can see it, can unfold the scene in her head.

The doctor claiming her as his daughter, his arm around her shoulders, hand on her neck.

"She's derailed," he says. "I mean, this day—"

"Tell me about it. Terrorist attack it's looking like. Crazy towelheads."

"They're called turbans," Ash mutters. "And it's not them."

The cop's lips crack open in surprise.

"It's Al Qaeda. Muslim. Sikhs wear turbans."

Alarmed, the officer's gaze swings to the doctor. "How does she..."

"She has these theories," the doctor says, and the men stare at Ash who stands silent like an automaton, an android from the future. "Darling, I told you no one knows. No one knows anything yet."

But people did know, didn't they? The FBI, the CIA. You just wait, she wants to say, but her entire body feels too heavy, too tired, and the doctor and the cop gaze at each other in agreement. She is only a stupid girl.

Did that happen? The doctor squeezes the nape of her neck. The tattoo of the eye, trying, trying to see danger, now pinched shut by the doctor's fleshy palm as he pushes her into the van. Locks the door, goes around to the driver's side.

Ash leans back into the soft headrest. Light refracts on the inside of her eyelids. There's a blurring, a confusion, like drowning. Her stomach rocks with the movements of the van, which feels more like a boat than something that travels on roads. It wobbles down the street, and she looks out to see the drug store, the Taconite Tavern with the Ladies and Escorts and Gentlemen entrances, still there in her time, but more a novelty than anything that's enforced. He takes the corner sharply and revs the engine to go as fast as he can and Ash opens her eyes and there's her grandmother, right goddamned there, standing in her front yard as they drive past her house. Ash swivels to follow the soft auburn cap of her hair, those pale blue polyester pants, a blouse patterned with tiny pink and yellow flowers. Her dead grandmother, last seen in her rosewood coffin. Cheeks lightly rouged, smiling lips tinted coral, stitched closed like her eyes. The inside parts that made her who she was forever sealed. The single bubble window on the side of the van washes the view with a tint like sepia, like age, like an impossibly distant photograph. Her gaze crawls back to the doctor's face.

He glances at her, winks, and Ash knows that he knows that she's seen Goma.

Her belly lurches. "Schtop!" she shouts, the word mushy. He doesn't. He pushes harder on the gas, and they accelerate past her high school to start the climb up into the hills. She squeezes her hands into fists. "Stop the goddamned van!"

"You'll have to get a handle on that mouth of yours, Ash, if you're going to be the mother to my—"

"I want out!" she says.

"Out where? Into a time when nobody even knows who you are? How lonely you would—"

"How are you doing this?"

The doctor shrugs. He takes his left hand off the wheel and adjusts his pants, tugging the seams away from his crotch. A shudder spreads through her. The turkey baster, the return to that foggy oblivion, the basement where her own body is not hers. She hits her fists against her knees, trying to jolt open her numbness. No. Her whole body screams no as the outside world blurs by.

"Maybe you aren't even here, huh? Maybe you're back at your house, all cozy at the heart of your oh-so-happy family. Maybe this is only one version, one collection of particles . . ." His hand thrusts in front of her face, and he scoops at the air near her nose as if catching something she can't see. She pulls back, head bouncing against the headrest. "You've heard of the double slit experiment?"

"Yes."

He starts explaining anyway. "Given two options, quantum particles don't choose. They move between both openings at the same time. Seemingly impossible, but—"

"But I'm not a single particle; how can—"

"You," he spits. "Clearly the product of your age, all this lust to know everything, lay it all out in black and white. Hey, Google."

He scoffs. "Even Einstein didn't have all the answers, even he admitted that imagination meant more than knowledge."

"But knowledge feeds imagination," she says, plucking bits of knowledge from her hazy brain. "And what about entropy?"

The doctor sighs loudly, the sound ragged and strained, nearly a growl. "See? You're my smart girl. Always asking questions. Heat only flows from hot bodies to cold, never the other way around, and that is why we move forward in time."

"Time's arrow."

"Yes, and that's why eggs can't be unscrambled, and cream can't be removed from your morning cup of java."

"I know! Then how . . ." She waves a hand, gesturing at the world around her, the blur of forest outside her window as the van's motor revs hard.

"Well," the doctor says. "perhaps when you nearly froze . . ."

Ash stares at him, at the flat look on his face, his lips tightly smiling. "Oh my God. You don't know, do you?"

"Better than knowing." He slaps a palm hard against his solar plexus. "I trust. I am a servant of faith. I didn't invent this universe or its rules. I was led to this cosmic collage and simply given the proper spells."

"Spells?" She thinks of the threshold of the front door, carved with symbols, the weird painting, the teas, all of it a kind of enchantment. His power over her.

"Why do you need to know?" he asks.

That's obvious. To escape. To find her way home. The convenience store slides by, with its working phone booth. She tries to remember Barb's old landline number, the one from Leigh's late grandparents' place where Barb and Suzanne now live, but she can't. In her time that old rotary phone was repurposed by Leigh for an art project.

"So you can pull away the veil? Reveal me to be powerless and then all will be well? Like Dorothy. Tap your sparkling shoes." His gaze drops to her feet, and then his voice rises in a mocking high-pitched imitation. "And you were there, and you were there, and it was the most wonderful—"

Abruptly, he stops speaking. There's silence except for the rush of the vehicle, the hum of the tires carrying them up the mountain. Ahead, the cemetery appears, a smear of green and grey, spotted with bright red roses.

"This isn't a dream," the doctor says. "The truth is, if there is another version of you cozy by the fireplace as your parents try to annihilate each other, that isn't the you that I'm interested in. This you, my you, my Ash, has been invited into the wonder of my reality, of what can be *your* reality. And you should be grateful for that. Grateful that despite all of the strikes against you I am willing to offer you the keys to the kingdom."

The words boom out of him; he wipes the spittle off his lips with the back of his hand. His blue eyes crawl over her like water that can go anywhere it wants. Ash turns away, afraid of him but also needing time to think. Time to try to balance what's clearly some sort of sorcery with the science in her head, to make some sense of the impossible and develop a hypothesis. Her head is clearer from exercising her intellect, but he does not know that. She clutches her stomach, bends forward. "I think I'm going to be sick . . ."

But of course the doctor does not stop. Will not stop until they're in his garage. Will not stop unless she makes him. Fight like hell, she remembers Leigh screaming on the final day of a self-defense course Frank and Goma enrolled them in when they were eleven. They used the blades of their hands to snap hunks of lumber in half like warriors. Now, she reaches for that same focus, the strength she didn't even know she had. She grips the armrest on the door with the hand he massacred, pulls in a breath, and swings her feet up fast to kick him hard in the side of the head. The van veers. The doctor scrambles for control of the steering wheel, and Ash gets up on her knees and leans over him to hit the lock release. But he cares more about keeping her than preventing a crash, and he grabs her forearm and twists it hard, and Ash screams but doesn't let him stop her. She plunges a knee hard in his balls, and he collapses around his core, the opal pendant swinging, flashing light into her eyes as she pulls back, launching herself out the opened passenger door to skid onto the road, rise up despite broken skin and blood, and run.

"Where are you planning to go, Ash?" the doctor hollers behind her. Anywhere, she thinks, plunging into the forest. *Anywhere away from you.*

23

BREATHING HARD, pushing forward, grateful—so grateful!—for the shoes. She heads deeper into the woods, drawing a route in her mind: behind the convenience store, through the forest, up and over the water tower hill, and between the turret house and her old school to run through town, heading for Goma's. That's the only place Ash wants to go, even though she doesn't know what she'll do or say when she gets there, or if the doctor will already be there, waiting for her. How did he know about Goma? Easy. He knows everything. He's probably watching her even now in his magical crystal ball, but she hopes he can't see her memories, Goma telling her that if she ever had a problem—even, especially, one that sounded crazy—she could go to her, she could trust her. So Ash is taking her at her word. After all, she doesn't have many options. At least she can have a cuppa with her dead grandmother, right?

Way to look on the bright side, Hayes, Leigh says in her head, and Ash nearly chuckles. Cracking up? Probably. Better that than focusing on the sting of her scraped-up hands and knees or the fear that burns in her throat. She reaches for the soothing fox fur, grateful she held onto it even as she tumbled out of the van. It's a kind of familiar that gives her comfort and helps her run harder, shove through the forest, ignore the young aspen snapping at her face. She tries not to think, only to move, only to exist inside her flexing muscles. Thoughts are the enemy, Frank had said to her during one of their video calls, and in the Notes app on her phone she'd thumbed the words *shut down,* because that's what it is, isn't it? Power through, don't think, don't feel. A coping mechanism she knew from learning about PTSD, about trauma, naively thinking she could help him. She shakes her head. More than anything, she cannot dwell on thoughts of Frank.

✳

Finally, she reaches the base of the water tower and nearly cries when she spots a bottle of Gatorade, half full, on the ground. She chugs the purple liquid, then wishes she hadn't as her stomach sloshes on the jerky jog behind the chain-link fence enclosing her elementary school playground to the street. Memories, everywhere, of her and Leigh skipping, of the turret house she's always loved, painted a bright yellow that in her time has faded and cracked. There's a sign posted in the window that she can't slow down to read, not with her eyes constantly scanning, looking for the blue van as she moves behind the stores along Main Street, past the Taconite, past the ice cream parlour where Leigh always orders disgusting Tiger Tail while Ash gets plain chocolate, and Frank's favourite is rum raisin. At last she reaches the right-of-way beside Goma's house. There's a bench on the rocky shore overlooking Devil's Fork Creek, where people can sit while their dogs swim in a nearby calm pool or just look at the water, the waterfall upstream, maybe even read a book. No phones in their hands, not in this timeline. Ash aches for her phone: that quick access, instant connectivity, her thoughts overlapping with Leigh's. How many texts have piled up by now on her iPhone, left behind on her bedside table so long ago? Is time passing there, or is it still the same night? She shakes her head to try to dispel the useless worries and plunks herself down on the bench's rough boards.

The wooziness, the nausea, has returned, not that it really ever left. Slowly she breathes in and out. It feels like something is trapped inside of her, a breathless wild thing, a feral cat, and if she lets it out even a little it won't stop, it'll tear her to shreds. Like Zeuxis, scratching madly at the door when they were trapped outside. Freezing, but if she'd just been brave enough to run, she might have found her way back home. Now that she knows how deep this goes, a few missing toes sound like a welcome trade.

THE LONGEST NIGHT

Ash taps, bouncing two fingertips off her collarbone like Goma taught her. Hours now, maybe eight, since she drank her last cup of tea, ate her last enchanted meal with invisible toxins threaded through the meat and veg. She remembers how her mother once tried to quit her anti-depressants, complained about the strange electrical twinges that raced across her shoulder blades, up the back of her scalp, for days and days. Ash feels strange, too: like there's a restless creature inside her, racing around the dizzying space in her head. Kind of like she's looking down from the edge of a cliff. She regrets drinking the salvaged Gatorade. What if it was a trap, but how could that be, how could the doctor have known . . . She shakes her head, focuses, narrowing her attention to just the one thing: her fingers nudging her hard clavicle, and eventually, her stomach starts to unclench. She feels the firm ground under her feet, smells the freshness and hears the sound of the rushing creek and, beyond, the hum of the distant refinery near the big lake. A sudden, piercing longing for her phone fills her once again: to slip it out of her jacket pocket, text Leigh, post a selfie of herself in 2001 on Instagram: #TimeTravel, #ExtremeThrowback. But of course that isn't possible.

"No time like the present, Hayes," she mutters to herself and stands. Slowly, she approaches the cedar hedge that runs along the side of her grandmother's backyard, a bedraggled wall, rarely trimmed, stretching to the river. At the shoreline, she grabs hold of the prickly boughs and stretches out her foot for Goma's yard. The sole of one sparkly shoe slides across a rock, and she grips the branches, hauling herself around, holding tight to the hedge's slippery fronds. Their tiny leaves come away in her fingers when she lets go and settles into a crouch. The smell of cedar oil, pungent, astringent, rises into her nose, reminding her of Christmas as she looks up the slope of grass to the house and sees, with relief, that it's there, the treehouse her father built in the fat white pine in Goma's backyard after Zach was born. Before. Back when they were still happy new parents. Just last spring, Ash realizes. Only a few months ago. The sap will still be seeping out of the wood.

Quietly, she creeps toward it, watching the house. Through the sliding glass door there's movement, and she stops when she sees her father. His face floating, lit by the light from the television in its wooden cabinet in the corner of the room. Young, slim. Sober. The sight of him stops her, ignites a craving. To be held by him, her mom. To be safe. It's impossible not to feel hope. But Ash has felt a lot of hope—that time in Florida when her dad was sober for a month, only for him to start drinking again when they got home, after he hurt his back shovelling snow. As a kid, she rode those waves willingly—singing along to Christmas carols, anticipating birthdays, eager for family closeness—but eventually the constant disappointment became too hard. So she stopped. Automatically, now, as a matter of instinct, she tamps down the optimism, crosses her arms, sees him as he is: separate from her, another body in orbit, hovering like a distant, pale moon as he stares at the images of the towers, the fires, the planes.

The muscling pillars of ash, the grey-skinned survivors stumbling through the streets, the Pentagon on fire.

A tragedy that will lead to more tragedy. Personal tragedy, too. Her mother going away to wait with her aunt for news of her cousin.

Her brother dead in his crib while in her father's care.

Her family sits in a line on the couch, staring at things they don't yet understand. They won't notice her, Ash realizes, crouched in the shade of the pine tree, even though she wants that, wants them to see her, recognize her right away, welcome her inside, help her figure all of this out, care for her.

But she knows the rules.

THE LONGEST NIGHT

She's learned it in a hundred stories: if you happen to find yourself back in time, don't talk to anybody, lest you rewrite the timeline, snap some vulnerable threads, change everything. It's a given. You roll your eyes if somebody's stupid enough to break the code.

But now look. Now look where she is. She understands the temptation.

She's about to break the rule.

But first she needs to rest. Exhaustion washes over her as she pulls herself up the ladder nailed into the wide trunk. Her body feels heavy, hard to haul, like she's fighting the gravity of Jupiter.

It's a relief: the shadowy, quiet box. She curls into a corner, but she can't fall sleep right away. Adrenaline courses through her body, and her brain spits up thoughts and memories, trying to attach meaning to her overactive nervous system. She thinks again about Frank. What would he look like, here, now, only seventeen years old, turning eighteen in a few days, growing into the adult who always treated Ash like she mattered, like he wanted to hear what she thought, what she felt. Like she had a right to her own ideas, emotions.

Desires.

Once he told her that he had watched her dad crumble after Zach died. That he'd actually driven him—totally shitfaced, wouldn't have made it himself—back to Goma's house from the bar several times. Before he went away for basic, before he found out he was also going to be a dad, that his new girlfriend, whom he barely knew, was pregnant from the first time they'd had sex.

But they weren't really friends, he and Ash's dad. If they had been they wouldn't have ended up with daughters with the same name: Ashleigh.

Still, they might have been: become buddies, gone ice-fishing together. If Frank had stayed. If life—as he put it—hadn't grabbed him by the balls.

Frank was trying to help her when he told her all this. They were driving in his truck, Leigh doing a shift at the Shoreline Motel where she cleaned rooms, Frank taking Ash home. One hand casually cupping the edge of the bench seat, the delicate drift of dark hairs on his forearm, the tattoo of a blue and silver light saber peeking out from under the sleeve of his T-shirt.

She reached out to touch him. He jerked away, glancing quickly at her, then out his window at the oily light on the lake's rotting ice. She expected him to say something. She was ready. I'm an adult, she intended to tell him. It would be weird for Leigh. She knew that. They could figure it out. The heart wants what the heart wants. But there was no room for any of that. Instead, Frank gripped the steering wheel with both hands and picked up where he left off as if nothing had happened.

"Not that I'm complaining, because where would I be without Leigh?" he said. Ash shrank against the door, cheeks burning. "Am I right?"

She nodded. She couldn't speak past the lump in her throat.

"Ash?" he said.

She looked at him; hope fluttered in her chest.

"Everything's going to be okay. You'll get free of this place. You've got your whole life ahead of you."

She nearly laughs at the memory. Little did he know...

She holds his face in her mind as she relaxes, finally, and sinks into sleep.

24

ASH WAKES. Face pressed into a pillow. The comforting scent of Goma's house, rose-scented fabric softener and slight mildew from the basement that sometimes floods in the spring. She snuggles deeper into the bed.

All just a bad dream, she thinks. Like one of the stories that she and Leigh used to write when they were kids, passing notebooks back and forth in class until Ash grew bored and chose to end it, except for the time that Leigh didn't let that happen.

But the dream wasn't the end for Caroline, she'd written. *When she climbed out of bed, and into the dark cave of the room, she realized that everything was different . . . Maybe it had been a dream, but the dream had altered everything, had switched into her REAL LIFE.* And then she'd spun off into a whole other story. At that point, Ash told her to write it herself, and they started being different: Ash into science, Leigh artsy, yet curious about the fantastical elements of physics. Still, though, for always and forever, best friends.

"Honey?" someone says, followed by touch. Warm fingers against her wrist.

Then, another voice. "Ask her who she is and what the hell she's doing—"

Her father, sounding angry. Her belly tenses automatically. She struggles to sit up, but the weight of her body holds her down like the gravity's too strong in this alternate reality. Sharp pain rockets through her head, and she once again enters that black room of dreamless sleep.

SHE WAKES TO the rattle of curtain rings. Warm light on her eyelids, the smell of sweet tea. Her mouth fills with saliva and she moves to sit up. Someone there—Lucille?—helping her

✺

arrange the pillows, but then it comes back to her in a rush, a haze, refracted, as if seen from underwater. Her father, finding her moaning and sick in the tree house after she'd thrown up over the edge, heaving bile that she kept wiping off her lips, muttering "I'm okay, I'm okay," trying not to scare him, down there on the ground, holding his fishing rod, knowing she shouldn't be there, she shouldn't be seen by him.

But then he was helping her, his body familiar and not because he was so young, so scrawny, only a few years older than her, smelling both the same yet somehow different: the musky aroma of his aftershave, the sour scent of cigarette smoke from the habit that came and went, the undefinable odour of his own skin.

He led her into the house, and then they were all there, her whole family, gazing at her as she fought hard not to weep, as she squeezed her eyes shut.

"Have you lost someone?" Goma asked, stepping closer, looking like she'd stepped out of Ash's first hazy memories. Intense confusion had swept through her, and, now, looking back as she slowly wakes up in the bed, she remembers allowing herself to tumble into unconsciousness. That had happened before; on the doctor's table, it had happened.

"That's right. Just sleep. Just let yourself sleep," someone said. And she did, because what else could she do? It was a relief, the darkness. The decision to simply leave. The right one? Who knows, but it's the one that's saved her in those overwhelming moments.

Now, though, she's safe. Sitting up, she leans back against the soft feather pillows but keeps her eyes closed. As if not seeing them — her family from twenty years ago — means that they might not see her. A child's logic. Because she's not ready. Not yet. Her heart hammers in her throat.

"Welcome back to the land of the living," Goma says with a familiar timbre and tone that cracks Ash's heart. All she wants to do is lunge for her, hold her, but she can't. She can't even look. If she looks the gap will yawn even wider, and everything might come spilling out. Grief, tears, elation, joy. Lots of tears. She breathes — *In, one-two-three-four-five. Out, five-four-three-two-one.* Then holds her hands out for the tea, still without opening her eyes.

"All right then," Goma says, but hesitates, and Ash figures she's examining the scraped heels of her hands, her amputated finger.

"Frostbite," she mutters, taking the hot mug. She sips, savouring the normalcy. The feeling of the nubbly ceramic rim against her lips. The nebula mug, she calls it — dark blue, speckled with white, grey, green and red spots — which is right now, in the future, where she belongs, in the cupboard at her parents' house because she took it off the table at the yard sale when they sold most of her grandmother's things.

"Are your eyes hurt, too?" Goma asks as her weight settles onto the edge of the bed. Quickly, abruptly, Ash shimmies away, remembering her grandmother in the oak casket, her once ruddy face pale and streaked with blush, her normally haywire silver hair neatly combed. Goma springs up, off the bed, and Ash says, "I'm sorry, I . . ." starting to explain, unable to explain. *The last time I saw you, you were dead,* but it's too late. Goma clomps hurriedly out of the room, and then Ash breaks her own rule and peeks and sees the spill, the tea soaking into the square of fabric with its white background, its pattern of tiny pink and green roses.

The room rocks, tilting abruptly sideways. She fumbles to set the mug on the bedside table as Goma returns with a towel to soak up the sloshed tea that is quickly settling into the stain that has always been there, on this particular patchwork quilt that covers her bed, back home, where her parents will be . . . Doing what? Worrying? Looking for her? Stapling posters all over town? Plastering her picture all over Facebook? Talking to the police?

No one will ever find her. She's down a long, dark tunnel. Somehow she has to crawl back on her own, find an opening, using all of the lessons that her grandmother has taught her: don't get locked out in winter, if lost look for animal familiars, secret doorways, symbols and hedgerows, talismans. Be wary of unwittingly ingesting poisons.

Advice Goma has given her all her life.

Because she knew.

Goma knew.

Will know.

Tried to help Ash prepare; will try . . .

"It's okay, child, it's just a spill. Nothing to get so worked up about."

She feels Goma press the towel against the spill, Ash's leg underneath it.

Is this fated then? Meant to be? A secured knot in the weave of space-time, a causal loop?

"My goodness, you look like you've been through the ringer. What's happened to you?" Goma asks, sitting close to Ash's hip. Ash hunts for words. If Goma's always known, that means . . . she's been here before? Another her, slipping through another slit? Her head spins. One piece at a time, she thinks. If Goma knows, Ash must have told her, but when and how? Goma sighs, and Ash says, "I'm sorry."

"Oh, it's no bother. This old quilt's been through a hundred things worse than a spill of strong tea."

But of course that isn't what Ash means. For not listening, she means. For not heeding all of Goma's quiet warnings that couldn't be fully explained. Goma would have sounded like a crazy person, like Ash will now if she . . . Hot tears surge into her eyes. If she could, she'd crawl right into Goma's lap. Instead, she covers her face with her hands, but when Goma leans toward her, arms opening, fingers tugging at her shoulders to pull her close,

Ash falls easily inside the warm circle of her embrace, wants to stay there forever. After being lost for so long, she feels like she belongs, like she isn't floating anymore, like she's more than just an object for the doctor's use, a ghost in a reality that isn't hers.

But it's only temporary. Goma pulls back and thrusts the hard edge of a box of tissues toward Ash, bringing with it the waft of lavender and wild bergamot from a dish of potpourri. The smell stirs Ash's memories. Napping in this same bed as a child, sleeping here after high-school dances, coming to stay with Goma when her father was in a particularly foul mood.

Ash draws in a breath and opens her eyes. Red-brown hair, lightly touched with grey, shallow crow's feet around bright brown eyes, although Goma's gaze seems guarded. Ash swallows the ache in her throat, knits her fingers together on her lap, taps the sensitive gap of her missing pinky, trying to find an anchor for the pitch of anxiety in her chest. People have always commented on how much Ash looks her grandmother, but Goma won't see that. How could she? *Well, this young woman certainly resembles me; I'm guessing she must be my granddaughter, come from twenty years in the future to seek my help.*

Goma's lips twitch into a smile. Insincere, Ash sees; her grandmother is nervous. She hands the tea to Ash. "Drink this. It will stabilize you. Now, we haven't been properly introduced, have we? My name is May Hayes, and you are . . . ?"

How strange to feel so at home but also know she's a stranger. Out in the living room, her parents are probably watching CNN while waiting to hear what Goma, Jim's mother, will say. Who this out-of-it teenager is, and how May intends to get her out of her house. Shame rises in her as she hides behind the mug, lets herself be soothed by the familiarity of its taste, strong and sweet and creamy. Nothing at all like the doctor's complicated, chemically manipulative brews, and yet she feels a pang of craving for those flavours, their deadening effects. Sweat prickles in her armpits.

She resists the urge to turn her head and smell herself. She's been wearing the same food-dribbled T-shirt and grimy, torn jogging pants for a long time. How long? No idea, but she must look like shit. She needs new clothes—wishes she'd held onto the ones from Tammy's minivan—and, more importantly, a plan.

"When something impossible happens, look for what's possible," Goma used to tell her. Another bit of preparatory advice.

Ash pulls in a deep breath. She has to start somewhere.

"Do you recognize me?" she asks.

Goma searches her face. "Should I?"

"I'm . . ." Ash starts. But how she can say it? How can she formulate an explanation that won't sound entirely mad, that won't get her driven straight to the hospital, checked into the psych ward. Maybe her grandmother knows, but surely she didn't find out like this, with Ash blurting it out. She needs time. She needs them to get to know one another. She needs Goma to start trusting her. She picks up a crumpled tissue with her left hand and worries its bumps and creases, picking at it with her thumb and pointer finger.

"Ripley," she says.

"Ripley," Goma breathes, her face relaxing, then leans toward her. "Is it the day, Ripley? Have you lost someone?"

Ash shakes her head. Despite the tea, her mouth feels dry. Goma has her palms pressed together, hands slid between her knees. Waiting.

"Who can I call? Where are your parents?"

Ash almost laughs. She says, "Far. They're very far away."

"And you came here? Why here? Why were you sleeping in the tree house?"

Now. Should she tell now? But the words feel unreachable; how to translate what she's been through, what the doctor's done to her, into those symbols of sound, into—what do they call it?— a disclosure. The perfect word. Opening the truth, ending its closure inside the dark, lonely vault of her body, her mind. But as soon as she tells, the momentum will turn toward accountability, justice—if she's believed, that is—when what she needs most of all is to figure out how to get back home. And, unfortunately, even though part of her hopes that her kick to his head might have somehow killed him, cracked open an aneurysm, the doctor holds the key.

No, she can't explain. If the police go into the house, if they arrest him, take him away, send Lucille back to wherever she belongs, back into that iron lung—*maybe she meant it metaphorically?*—she might never figure out how to find the passage, the portal, how to get home. As much as she hates it, she needs him.

"Too much to drink," she says. "With my friends. I've been staying with friends."

Goma cocks her head. The words *don't you fib a fibber* pop vividly into Ash's mind; her eyes widen. For a few seconds, they stare at each other, and then Ash's father appears in the doorway. She sees him in her peripheral but doesn't draw him into focus; she can't. Her mother arrives, too, leans her head on his shoulder, so they appear as one in her fuzzy, unfocused vision, like a double-trunked tree. Ash does not look, not even as her heart stutters. When was the last time she saw her mother touching her father like that? They stand there like a memory, adrift in the background—Jim and Teresa, married just over a year—and Ash lets them be a blurry background.

And yet, of course she can't help herself. Carefully, she shifts her gaze, squints as if looking toward a throbbing light, a forbidden eclipse. Beside her, Goma lets out a rush of questions—"What friends? Where? Why are you scratched up? What happened? Has someone hurt you?"—and there they are, her parents. Her father stares at her, no permanent furrow in his forehead, no dark shadows under his eyes, no tension in his jaw, no grey in his untrimmed beard, no beard. Her mother's hair is light blonde, when now she dyes it a warm dark brown. Her cheeks are splotchy from crying, and she's holding a blanket-swaddled baby who's sucking on a soother. Ash bolts up. "Zach!"

Her voice sounds strangled. It's emotion, because that's her brother, her big brother. Not only a character in the origin story of her fucked-up family, but here, right here: a bundle of flesh, blood, bone, not just cold ash in the orange vase at the top of the glass cabinet full of trinkets.

They stare at her; as if the tension is a physical jab, Zach lets out a loud cry. The soother tumbles to the carpet. Goma touches her closed lips. There's the glimmer of the emerald ring she bought for herself on her fiftieth birthday, that was buried with her because it wouldn't slip past her swollen knuckle.

Zach's sobs grow stronger, and Ash feels herself pulled to him, pitying him, this baby who has only days left to live. The helplessness makes her want to shrink away, crawl back under the covers, but she doesn't. Instead she swings her legs out and stands. Because maybe she isn't so helpless. She almost takes a step toward him, but she can't, of course she—

"Wait. How do you know my son's—"

"I heard," Ash says. "I heard somebody say . . ." Her mother, Teresa, stares at her.

"Bathroom?" Ash murmurs, and Goma points to the ensuite that Ash has already turned toward. Teresa jostles Zach, holding him close, as Ash crosses the room.

"I'll feed him before I go," she says to Jim, then leaves.

"Go?" Goma asks.

To Aunt Iris's, Ash remembers, listening to her father through the closed door. He explains how Iris's one-bedroom apartment in Chicago is small, how a wailing infant would be too much for her while they waited for news about her son who was at the Twin Towers that day, who went to work as usual.

Except he didn't, Ash knows. Knows that he took a week off work without telling his mother, and that he and his girlfriend went on a canoe trip upstate in the Finger Lakes. He planned to propose to her and didn't want to jinx it by telling anyone, so they simply slipped away, into the woods, and when they emerged one week later, the whole world had changed. Ash has only met them twice, and both times they told her the story while Ash's mother busied herself with something—slipping into the restroom or cleaning off the table—because what could she say? Because of you my baby died? Because of you.

"Are you okay?" Goma asks. Ash has opened the door to face them, but she's frozen in place. She opens her mouth, closes it, then opens it again. Her mother has gone to feed Zach, pack a suitcase, gather what she needs for the eight-hour drive south. Can she speak? Should she?

"She shouldn't go."

"What?" her father asks. "Who?"

"Teresa." The name feels strange in her mouth. "She shouldn't go." He stares at her. He's her father, and his face is softer, but beneath his youth she sees the hardness that will grow and take over, that engine of aggression fuelled by alcohol. Right now, it's directed at her, a stranger who's wormed her way into their lives.

"Why would you say that?"

Ash has to try. "A terrible thing—"

"It is a terrible thing," says Goma. "What's happened today."

"No," Ash says. "I mean yes, but no, that's not . . ." She squeezes the doorknob, feels its cool solidity. Goma steps toward Jim, bends over to pick up the soother. The two of them stand there, side by side, staring at her, Goma now aligned with her suspicious son. Ash wants to reach for her, wants to plead: don't leave me. An ache starts in her throat. Closing her eyes, she draws in a deep breath, then speaks.

"A feeling," her father says, repeating her words. "Who do you—"

"We're all a bit off," Goma says.

"Her cousin hasn't checked in," says Jim. "Her aunt has no one else."

"But she's leaving Zach?" Goma asks.

"I can take care of my son."

He sounds so sure. Ash knows that this is the thing that will break him: the collision between his conviction, his intention, and the terrible outcome. She wants to crawl into the bed again, let time vanish inside the soft flannel of her grandmother's sheets.

"Why don't you get cleaned up," Goma says to her. "There are extra towels in the blue cabinet. I'll be back; we're not done."

Goma turns, ushering Jim to go in front of her, following him into the hallway with a limp. In a few years, shortly after Ash turns five, she'll have a knee replaced. By then, Ash's parents will have built their house, but Ash and her mother will stay with Goma for three weeks. It will be Ash's job to bring a buttered scone to her every afternoon, a cup of hot Lady Grey tea—clear, with one small spoonful of honey—while the TV rattles with afternoon talk shows and documentaries on the History channel and news of the war. Ash's mother will say nothing to her about how she should go outside and play, breathe some fresh air, build a snowman, and she definitely won't do any of those things with her.

Gripped by depression. Complicated grief. At least your mom's still around, Leigh sometimes reminds her. Leigh's mom ditched her when she was a baby. Ran off, disappeared. Too much pressure, everyone said. Too young.

All Leigh had were Frank's memories and a quick sketch he'd done. A grey haze of graphite lines on a page torn out of a book. Black smudges around the edge; the woman's face disguised by a pillow or the folds of a blanket. A sleeping figure who could be anyone.

Ash doesn't dispute Leigh's loss, but her own mother is challenging. Distant, like the captain of a lost ship constantly looking for land, unless she's play acting her fake cheer. Most authentically alive when she and Ash's father are fighting, like the last night that Ash was at home. What were they arguing about? Something stupid: the recycling that had accumulated in the mud room, her father criticizing the way her mother kneaded bread dough, or something else? A final showdown? A last confrontation? It had seemed more aggressive than usual, but maybe that was just because of Christmas. The first one without Goma. The grief. The stress. The 'what's-the-points' her mother has called her overwhelming emotions, to which Ash has always wanted to respond, I am. I'm the point.

Why hasn't she left him? Ash has often wondered. Now, though, she feels like she might understand a bit more. She loves him. She'll soon be pregnant again but doesn't know it. She's about to lose her infant son, to plummet into a trough of time and tragedy that will trap them both.

But it could be different.

Because Ash has the power to change it.

And could it be that fixing things will send her home? Like in that other old TV show that Frank showed them. Dr. Sam Beckett, physicist, leaping around in time, jumping between eras with a flash of blue light, setting things right with his lecherous sidekick.

If Ash saves Zach, would that happen to her?

Doubtful, her scientific-self thinks. The universe doesn't deal in moral binaries.

But even if it doesn't save her, even if she isn't instantly sent home through a quantum ripple lit 1980s-neon-blue, how can she not?

How can she not save her baby-big-brother's life?

FROM SOMEWHERE IN the house, Ash hears the rumble of her father's voice, and the familiarity of his anger this time somehow soothes her. She creeps over to the bedroom door to listen: "... have to call the police, missing person, she might be a minor!"

For a moment, forehead pressed against the doorjamb, she imagines a different kind of minor, one tunnelling through dark rock like in the tour up in Ely, in the heart of the Iron Range. Those cool stone walls, the cold cave lit only by the lamp beaming from the guide's hardhat. The image is not entirely wrong. This is a sort of tunnel, out of sync with her proper present, holding her, lost, between past and future, on this single day when the world has changed.

And it will change even more.

She needs to get ready.

She backs into the bathroom and closes the door.

25

A BATH IS a good idea. It will buy her time to think, but, also, she really needs one.

No showers at the doctor's. Because she could have fallen and cracked her head, they said. Only fast baths with Lucille on her knees beside the tub, studying Ash's body, or prattling on about how much the doctor loved them, unreachable in her plasticized glee as she scrubbed Ash's back, told her to lift up her arms. And also, of course, no razors. Slowly, she grew a fine, dark pelt in her armpits and on her legs. She didn't mind. It made her feel like an animal, and if she was an animal, she thought in brief starbursts of lucidity, she would eventually chew herself out of the trap, which is exactly what she's done.

But what now?

She lies back in the tub, body scrubbed, greasy hair washed, letting the conditioner soak in, appreciating the soothing heat, the silence.

A knock on the door startles her. She sits up, scrambling to pull a washcloth over her breasts. The door cracks open.

"I brought you some things to wear."

A hole opens in Ash's chest, and it aches. Her mother, twenty-five years old, steps into the room and sets a pile of clothes beside the sink, eyes downcast to give privacy, but Ash can't help staring. Her mind hunts for words. To explain. To get help. But she and her mother have never been close. Still . . . shouldn't she try? Say something? She could save Zach and free her mother from decades of misery, but what about her? Won't that erase her existence?

Teresa lifts a hand to her own cheek.

"Those scrapes and bruises," she says. "Do you want to tell . . . Do you want to talk about it?"

✵

Yes, Ash thinks, aching to say it all; they could be friends, couldn't they? She could confide in her, tell her about the doctor, explain it all including how Teresa needs to stay here, not go, for Zach's sake, for all their sakes. But how can she? None of it will make any sense.

"You should see the other guy," she mutters.

"Who is the other guy?" she asks, and Ash seizes the edge of the tub as a wave of vertigo washes over her. Is this how Goma finds out? From her mother? Should Ash confide in her mother? Has her mother always known? No. If she did, if she does, she would have acted, and things would be different, will be, wouldn't they? Won't they?

"Well, they're arguing out there about what to do with you. They want to take you to the cops, but if you'd rather go to Chicago, if you have people there, you could come with me. My friend Juanita is coming to pick me up."

Chicago. What would she do in—

"Although I hear that you think I shouldn't go." Teresa's eyebrows lift, questioning, and Ash is suddenly a seven-year-old, her mother asking her about the Hannah Montana doll she'd stolen from a sleepover.

Her head hurts. She can't speak. Teresa smiles, awkwardly, then pulls open the top drawer of the vanity. "There's disinfectant in here," she says. "Make sure you wash those cuts well."

"You'd be good nurse," Ash says, knowing. Knowing that her mother had always wanted to be one, had planned to go back to school when her kids were old enough, but after Zach died, Jim was fired from his job and struggled to stay with anything for long. Plowed snow through the winter and took tourists fishing in the summer. Nothing that paid very well. None of this has happened yet, though, and her mother looks at her brightly, a happy shine in her eyes.

"That's the plan," she says, and Ash plunges underwater to rinse her hair. When she surfaces, Teresa is gone. She's both relieved and empty, aching, wanting to both weep and harden, never to see her again, not here, not like this, a mysterious stranger holding secret knowledge she doesn't know how to divulge.

She opens the drain and waits until the tub is empty, her skin prickling with cold, before she climbs out. Wrapping a familiar red towel around her body, she examines herself in the vanity's wide mirror. Her shoulder bones poke out; her skin is pasty, semi-translucent, like a ghost who's stumbled through the rift. All that's left of the dye in her hair is a bit of green on her dead ends, like a snagged feather from a tropical bird. She remembers applying the colour in her bathroom back home before she did the first video call with Frank. Something different, something extra, she'd thought, but he hadn't commented on it.

He's somewhere in town, too, as is Barb, unless Barb has moved away already, out to BC to work at a resort before she came back to help Frank with Leigh after his girlfriend took off.

Leigh's mother. She must be close by as well. Soon they'll meet, she and Frank.

Ash tries to remember her name. It doesn't come to her, which feels dangerous. She needs to be careful, stay hidden, do what she has to do—save Zach—then see where it gets her. Nothing else. Limit the awful chance that she could meet Leigh's mom, send her off in a different direction, away from Frank. So she can't look up Frank either. Even though they are the same age. In fact, she's older than him by half a year.

"Tread lightly, Hayes," she mutters, gripping the edge of the counter, leaning close to peer into her brown eyes. "Don't do anything stupid."

A knock on the door makes her jump. The towel falls off. She sees her small breasts, her pronounced ribs; she needs food, good food, her grandmother's pineapple upside down cake, with whipped cream and marasch—

"Ripley?" Goma calls.

"Yeah," Ash answers, crouching to pick up the towel.

"Are you okay? Were you talking to someone?"

"Just myself," she says, with forced cheer. A pause. Ash rolls her eyes at herself. Has she just given more evidence that she's nuts?

"Almost done?"

"Out in a sec."

Goma shuffles away; Ash bends over, winds the towel around her sopping wet hair, looks past the prickle of stars in the air when she stands, then turns to her mother's clothing. On top, there's a green wool sweater with tiny holes in the ribbing of the cuffs that Ash recognizes. Her mother still has it, those holes mended again and again. She wears it under a bright orange down vest when she piles wood on cold autumn days.

Ash holds it up to her nose, smells it, then hesitates. If Ash takes it now, will Teresa still have it? Will the memory pop in her head and vanish? What else might change? She leaves it, pulls on pleated jeans and a T-shirt and a plaid long-sleeved shirt. Very grunge, she thinks, looking at the floppy collar and cuffs, remembering the nineties dances she went to in high school. If this was the time she belonged in, that would be her era. The Backstreet Boys and Nirvana—probably Nirvana. "Smells Like Teen Spirit." What does that even mean? Doesn't matter. It's a good song. She's heard it a lot, cranked loud, at Frank's.

SHE'S LOOKING FOR the optimal moment to tell Goma who she is, what she thinks she's doing there, and this is not it: her father, alone in the kitchen, smoking. She nearly turns around to leave, but then he slides the pack across the table to an empty chair like they're buddies at the bar, waiting for a pitcher to arrive.

"I thought you quit," she blurts. His eyes widen.

"With a new baby, I mean," she says, sitting down. "I thought you would have . . ."

He had, hadn't he? Hadn't she once Googled that—secondhand smoke and SIDS—and then asked Goma and been told that, yes, he'd quit. Cold turkey, as soon as her mother gave him the news that she was pregnant with Zach. Before the horror of what had happened pushed him to relapse and he started again. Was that a lie? Or has her arrival altered this? Is it her fault Zach's dead?

It's hard to keep track. He's been quitting, restarting, quitting again for her whole life. She can tell where he's at by the tin cans in the garage, filled with either crushed butts or discarded blobs of sulphur-coloured gum. It's the same with the booze. How she navigates by signs and signals: counting empty cans, monitoring stiff patches of sobriety, feeling her way over the punky ground of her family's secrets. Is he at least sober now, she wonders, staring at the small red box as he stares at her. She's tempted, even though she doesn't really smoke, apart from random pilfered vape tokes at parties or the occasional stolen cigarette from when she and Leigh were kids, eleven years old, choking down hot, acrid smoke at the beach. Lightheadedness won't help her now. What she'd rather do is get up and go to the ceramic canister on the counter that says coffee but actually holds miniature candy bars.

"Here's the deal," her father says, crushing the butt in a glass ashtray.

"Where's Go—Where's May?" she asks, because the very last thing she needs right now is a lecture from him, this stranger-not-stranger barely older than her.

"We've all been there," he says, ignoring her question, and suddenly his eyes—the exact same dark shade as Ash's—are soft. "A few too many times, if I'm honest. And, I mean, good

God, who couldn't have used some day drinking on a morning like..."

"I wasn't drunk," she says. Coldly, as coldly as she can. She flicks a finger at the smokes, sends the box skittering. His hand plunks down, seizing it.

"No?"

"No." A warning ticks inside of her. But she's tired. If she's already altered things, why not tell the truth? She sits up straighter, lets the words out.

"I was poisoned."

"Poisoned?"

He pulls out another cigarette, then slides it back in.

"By a doctor."

"A doctor."

She nods.

"In town here?"

"Out of..." she starts, stops. Can she say that? Can she direct him to the country road where he and her mom will soon buy property to build their dream home? Was it her who helped them find it? Or would sending him there, to the monster's lair, ensure that they wouldn't want to live on that road? And then everything would change.

But what would be so bad about that?

Maybe instead they'll live in town, give the house across the street from her elementary school a much-needed paint job, do some renovations, and she could have the room in the turret.

"Somewhere else?" he asks.

Cautiously, Ash nods.

"Well, that narrows it down."

Her father waits, but Ash has stopped talking, already feels like she's said too much. She grips his lighter, runs her thumb over the rough wheel again and again, and they sit in silence, near total, except for the distant hum of the television set in the back room, detailing what is so far known. She wonders if Bush has given his speech yet, talking about the terrorists trying to frighten the nation into chaos, and how they've failed, his words in her mind from watching it on YouTube. She doesn't know what else to say to her father, how to even do this: tell him what's happened, ask for his help. She hasn't been taught how. Has instead learned to suppress herself beneath their needs, his and her mother's, who right then enters the room, carrying the red leather suitcase that's now Ash's, that she took to Minneapolis when she moved away, brought home soon after when they went into lockdown again. Jim glances at his wife.

"So, a doctor," he says, "somewhere has somehow poisoned you."

She nods, wishing now that she hadn't spoken. What good will it do?

"Can someone corroborate your story?"

Her gaze leaps to his face. She scoffs. What does he think? That she's lying? Making it up? Why would she—

Teresa steps forward. "Ripley, what are you saying? We need to go to the police then."

The police. Suzanne. A good idea? Try again. Buy time. Work it so she can stay here, be awake, save Zach. Slowly, she starts to nod, but then imagines it: him, arrested, dragged out in handcuffs, Lucille testifying against him. Justice. Like in a movie, on a TV show. *Law and Order: Special Victims Unit*. One story out of hundreds: how long has that show been on?

But it won't go down like that. Pretty sure there's a statute of limitations where time travel is concerned, says the voice in her head.

The doctor would charm the officers, work a Jedi mind-trick, wiggle free. Leave her here. Stuck outside her own time. She shakes her head.

"If what you're saying... If you were drugged and... then—"

"Never mind," Ash says. "Forget I said anything."

Where is Goma? Goma is the person she needs to be talking to.

Her parents stare at her. The silence stretches until her mother breaks it. "Juanita will be here any minute," she says. "And I'd feel better if I knew you were getting help."

She'd feel better. Ash crosses her arms, flicks the lighter over and over, her eyes on the sparks. When the doorbell rings, she jumps. It isn't Juanita. It's Lucille.

26

"HAVE YOU SEEN this girl?" Ash hears when Teresa answers the front door. She's on her feet, fast, as Lucille steps into the kitchen, dressed like she's come from a corporate office: black slacks, a grey blazer. The Polaroid flopping in her hand, Ash sees as she turns to bolt out the side door, run up the driveway, and flee to . . . But the knob is turning and then, there he is: a bulk blocking off the outside sunlight, ducking to fit through the doorway. Ash stumbles backwards. Her father—Jim—is right behind her. He grips her upper arm, and at first she feels relief, so powerful she could melt into him, but he muscles her around to face the room, the doctor behind her. All of them stare at her, even her own miniature self, stunned, gazing helplessly from the frame of the photo in which she's held.

"Sweetheart! We've been worried sick! Ever since you skipped out of the unit while we were watching . . ."

Lucille rambles while Ash feels the doctor, setting her spine on fire. She squirms in Jim's grip, wanting at least to turn around, to face the stalking animal full on, but she can't until Jim releases her to speak to the doctor. Panic roars in her ears. She pulls away, moves to the kitchen counter, its hardness pressing into her lower back, to face the situation full on. Lucille and Teresa are standing in a clutch she could easily blast through, but then Goma arrives, coming from the bedrooms, saying something about Zach before her voice fades away, and she stops in the doorway. Everyone is silent. Before anyone else has a chance to speak, Ash does. She jumps in, appealing to her father.

"This is him," she says. "The doctor. The one—"

"Pleased to make your acquaintance," the doctor says.

"She said something about being poisoned?" says Jim.

✳

Lucille tsks her tongue. "Silly girl. It's medication. Which she needs. All twisted up. Her psoas muscle is like . . ." She squeezes her hand into a fist. Ash's father nods like he knows what Lucille is talking about. "She's on a steady treatment regime, but if we don't get back to . . ."

The house.

The treatments.

The doctor's baby.

Will that be it? Her whole life spoken for? Becoming, like Lucille, part zombie, part wind-up doll pointed in the direction of his choosing.

"Are you all right?" Teresa asks, lifting a hand to her own cheek. The doctor imitates her gesture, flinching when he touches the vibrant purple bruise from where Ash had kicked him. She's surprised it's there, surprised she could make an impact on him.

"Occupational hazard," he says, with a deprecating grin. "She's a wild one, needs a constant eye. Some stallions take longer to break. But what can I do?" He lifts his hands, palms out. "The first rule: do no harm."

They all nod. A rational explanation. A chance to wash their hands of her. Except for Goma. Goma cocks her head, examining Ash. Their eyes latch and something transmits. Some knowing, some awareness, but then Goma moves her gaze to the doctor.

Please don't let her be taken in.

She should have told her when she had the chance, spilled it all, let out the whole insane story, come what may. But she didn't, and now it feels like it's too late. The towers have crumbled, the planes have crashed, thousands are dead, the whole world destabilized. Frank, somewhere, leaning toward a TV screen, preparing to march into battle, that fight which will never end. She sinks back against the counter, looking at the table where Goma will sit and play solitaire, drink endless cups of strong tea, listen to books on tape about physics and magic, help Ash with her math homework, slip in lessons on staying calm, assessing enchanted realms, seeking magical portals that could lead her home, trying to help her, because she knew.

Ash opens her mouth to speak, but the doctor's voice booms over her frail intake of breath. Assertive, confident, professional, when all Ash has—

"Trauma, you know," he says. "Triggered by today's awful events. Interesting that she found her way—"

—is the truth.

"I'm from the future. 2020. And I know things, I know—"

"Jesus Christ," Jim says, at the same time as Lucille leaks a patronizing, "Oh, sweetheart." Goma watches. The doctor smiles patiently, stuffs his hands in his pockets. Probably she should stop. Probably she's digging the hole deeper but the rush of words, the release of her truth, feels so good!

"Zach. I know that Zach . . . He'll—"

"Oh, honey, oh Ashley," Lucille says, beside her now, wrapping an arm around her shoulders. "You missed your meds this morning, and now—"

"Ashley?" Goma asks, and Ash's heart sinks. She's done for. Her parents will never name their new baby after the crazy girl who landed in their house on 9/11. What else is shifting and altering around her? What else is she destroying as she struggles, tearing at the web of space-time?

"You have to listen," she murmurs. "I know what I'm—"

The doctor grabs her, digging his fingers into her forearm. On her other side, Lucille squeezes her hand, sparking pain in the nerves of her missing pinky finger. "There, there, a nice cup of tea," she murmurs, "and your own cozy room." Ash struggles, writhing between them as her mouth continues to move, warnings gurgling out of her, stuttered and non-specific because she isn't sure of dates and times. Her mother looks terrified as they muscle Ash past her, so close she feels Teresa's breath on her cheek—"How can you say these things?"—and Ash realizes with a bolt of dread that she is not helping. She is making everything worse. Knowing they could have stopped it, they will hate themselves even more. She is simply planting a bomb in the heart of her family, setting the timer, possibly erasing her own life at the same time. She feels herself give up, go limp. Like a doll. Like a drained cyborg. Like a sedated mental patient with no other options. It's too late. The damage she's done. At the side door, the doctor turns them around.

"Thank you so much for your gracious help with our girl today," he says.

They nod. No one can speak. Too stunned, Ash knows, too disturbed. She wants only to leave, to stop standing there, the doctor's head nearly brushing the ugly brass light fixture on the ceiling, leaving his imprint on her family, her future life. She'll become a story, impossible to erase. Where were they on 9/11? They'll be telling it over and over again, and she'll grow up hearing it: the crazy girl, the giant man.

"Please," Ash says. But the doctor isn't finished.

"And can I just say, Goma"—Ash's gaze leaps up. *What is he*—"How nice to see you looking so hale and hearty, and you, Jim! Such a shame about your early demise in that drunk—"

"Stop!" Ash screams.

"I'm sure you didn't mean to kill—"

"Please," she begs.

"Please what?"

She forces the words out of her mouth like a magician choking up an egg. "Please can we go home."

The doctor nods. "Her delusions, you see," he says to Ash's family. "She needs to choose a path away from the past." He looks at her then, lovingly, protective; only Ash can see the horrible vacuum inside his black pupils.

"Good girl," he says, but before they exit through the door, Goma's behind her.

"You forgot this, Ashley," she says, and Ash feels the fox stole being pressed into her hands. There's a moment of hesitation, the soft fur binding them together, before the doctor pulls her toward the van.

It is the only way.

Later—days or months or years or decades—she can try again, search for another escape. She aches for it. For home. A yearning so deep she knows she'll do anything—whatever he asks—to find her way back.

"**WELL THAT WENT** well," the doctor says as they pull out of Goma's driveway. In the backseat, Lucille titters. "Did you see their faces when you—"

"Shut up, my sweet imbecile." He flings a cold blue glance at the rearview mirror; Ash feels Lucille shrink back.

"Don't talk to her like that," she mutters.

"Oh so you're intent on being everyone's saviour today, are you, Ash?" He chuckles. "Eighteen going on terrible two: me, me, me, me, me."

Rage fires in her. She clenches her teeth as she stares out at the terrain rushing past, the road she's travelled hundreds, thousands of times: high school, convenience store, soon the cemetery, the turn to her (future, past) family home and the doctor's. If that's what he thinks about her, that she's selfish, demanding, why not be that way?

"You said . . ."

"Yes?"

"No contact. You said no contact."

"I know what I said, Ashley, but I'm afraid it is not possible to make a baby without . . ."

"I don't want a baby."

"Babies are the future," Lucille mutters, her hot breath so close to Ash's ear that she jumps.

"There is no future," Ash says.

"Oh come now, there's always a future," the doctor says. "Like there's always a past."

"A future of pain and agony." In her old life, she would have meant climate change, collapse of democracy, pandemic, the kind of hopelessness that she and all her friends are used to coping with, but here she means something else: a life like Lucille's, a life as a prisoner, cut away from everyone she loves, in servitude to him.

The doctor glances at her. "Who did this to you? Who turned you into such a negative Nellie?" Ash ignores the question. She knows the trick: to lure her into those tender spots, then soothe her grief. He's done it before, during those first days when she was so, so naïve and so, so out of it. He'd made her feel like he only wanted to help, like he cared about her more than her own parents. She crosses her arms.

"Why do you want this so bad? It's not like I'm some sort of Sarah Connor."

"Who?"

"My kid won't save humanity."

"Who said anything about saving humanity?"

"Why then?"

The doctor hesitates. "It is the human imperative to propagate, to create a legacy. My forebears did it, yours did, too; now we must."

She thinks of the vow that she and Leigh took, of the world two decades from now. Floods, record tornado seasons, scientists screaming warnings only to be ignored. The sixth great extinction. Does he not know about all of that? Does he live on a different plane, outside of the truth? Of course. Of course he does. He has this incredible power. Power she needs. Power that will send her home.

"If I do this, if I act as your surrogate, will you put me back where I belong?"

"You'd do that?" Lucille hisses. "You'd give your own precious baby away like he's nothing but a barn cat?"

"Now girls," says the doctor, cranking the wheel to turn them onto his road. "Of course she wouldn't. She wouldn't be the Ash I know if she did that: an Ash who cares deeply, who deeply loves." He looks at her. "Never forget that you came to me for a reason, Ash. You have magic in you. You can see the bigger picture."

"Bigger picture."

He nods.

"Really big. Ever expanding. Impossible for most to grasp. That . . ." — he presses his thigh like his finger is a pin skewering a bug — ". . . bigger picture."

She does not know what this means, but it doesn't matter. She needs to focus. Bargain. Strike a deal.

"You said no contact. No . . ." — the word is like hot bile she has to throw up — "intercourse. You said."

"How clinical you are." He slides a sharp look at her, making the back of her neck tingle. The eye, doing what? Squeezed shut. Leaking frustrated tears. *Dry them, Hayes. Get sharp.*

"And no more teas," Ash adds as he powers the van up the driveway, presses the button for the garage door to open.

"Promise me," she says, "and I'll do what you want, I'll . . ." She can't finish the sentence; it's too much, too terrifying, the thing that she's agreeing to. The garage door closes, shutting them into the black maw. The doctor's face is pale, sulphuric under the dim interior bulb, but his eyes are gleaming. He lifts his hand, curls his fingers, extending only the smallest digit. The one he cut from her.

"Pinky swear."

Ash stares at him.

"Oh, how insensitive of me." His voice is flat and hard and not sorry at all. "But you know I was only joking. Where's your sense of humour, sweetheart?"

An upswell of rage. She swallows it. It won't do her any good. "Promise?"

Faintly he nods, a quick bob of his head. Ash doesn't move even as he and Lucille climb out of the van. They have to open her door. Lucille has to grab her hand, lead her inside. She can't trust him. Of course not. What was she expecting? She'll have to bide her time, attempt to stay sharp. She holds the soft fox fur close to her face. It's been cleaned; it smells like Goma's place.

27

ASH WAKES TO an oppressive odour. Soot and saccharine vanilla. It coats the inside of her nose, makes her mouth taste sour, stings her eyes.

She groans, turns over, feels her head swim, nausea rising.

". . . promised," she gurgles to the blur of a tall shadow as if her accusation matters. She chokes down the urge to vomit, trying to orient herself, to remember what happened. They came into the house; she walked directly to her room and closed the door. She felt in herself the clogging buildup of ice, a powerful need to sleep. Shut down, she knew. From this never-ending and overwhelming adversity. The feeling not dissimilar to the plunging down she'd done as a kid to get through her parents' frequent screaming matches.

Now, her fingers grasp at the rough lace curtains, locating herself. She's in her bed and there's Zeuxis, too, soft under her hand. She tries to kick a leg out from under the blankets — *To do what? Go where? There's nowhere to go* — but nothing happens.

The shadowy form moves closer. The curtain's pulled aside, and something hard is stuffed into her mouth, pencil-shaped, potentially skewering. She tries to convince her hand to lift, grab it, lunge with it; again, nothing happens. The beep of the thing startles her. The person — it's Lucille, Ash can smell her — pulls it from her mouth and withdraws to the doorway, where another shape is standing. The doctor, filling the doorway, the two of them like ghosts who can't leave, like the toxic air she breathes into the moist, dark corners of her lungs, her blood, her body, once private but not anymore. Not hers, either. She belongs to the doctor. He's made that very clear. No more teas, he agreed, so instead he's set up some sort of diffuser like the one Barb uses to pump lavender mist into her yoga room.

✻

Ash sees the geysering fog overtop her bedside table, grey and glittering as if with tiny sparks. She rolls over, back turned, her hand with the missing finger cupped against her chest; her tears leak silently into the slim, matted pillow that stinks of someone else's dirty head.
Her own dirty head?
How long has she been here now?
She hates him.
Hates him like she's never hated anyone.
But that doesn't matter.
Because there's nothing she can do about it.
He's her only way home.

THEY LET HER wander the house, except for the basement, which is the doctor's private space and where she's only allowed to go for treatments. The piano music drifts up when he withdraws for what he calls his "meditations." Sometimes Lucille accompanies him, but mostly she stays with Ash, watching her, carrying her knitting around, the small sweater now finished, tiny booties growing from her needles.

Drifting through the house, Ash hunts. She starts at the far end, the doctor's bedroom, dominated by a king-sized water bed with a mirror inlaid in its dark wood headboard. When he isn't home, when he's gone out carrying boxes, to return hours later with other boxes, she lies down on the end of his bed. Not because it's his bed. Because floating there like that, held by the rippling, gurgling bladder beneath, reminds her of happier times: bobbing on inflatable boats on Ore Lake, she and Leigh tethered together, or farther back to her earliest consciousness, cradled inside Teresa's body.

The hum rising from the house's core vibrates into the mattress, standing in for the sound of rushing blood. Sometimes Lucille joins her, spoons her, and they curl together like fetal twins, Ash too tired, still poisoned by the diffuser, to bother protesting.

Lucille doesn't protest either. She lets Ash do whatever she wants: try to see outside by lifting the curtains over every window and the sliding glass door in the dining room, which Ash examines, sees is blocked by a metal bar along the bottom track. Usually the glass shows night, or snow, or a sort of matte blackness so she gives that up and instead digs into the closets, hoping the back walls will collapse into tunnels. She peers under beds for drawn pentagrams, looks through boxes for books, magic manuals, spells written down that would end this enchantment, tries to smuggle a knife from the kitchen, but Lucille takes it away from her, and then they don't let her go into the kitchen alone. Mostly, she finds nothing useful. No weapons, nothing that could help her escape or kill him — and what would happen if she did kill him? She might be trapped here forever.

One day, though, she pulls a slim notebook of blank graph paper, its metal binding corroded with rust, out of the narrow gap behind her dresser. Using the nub of a pencil, she begins to write...

> My name is Ashley May Hayes. I'm eighteen (maybe nineteen, twenty, or even twenty-one by now). I was abducted...

The unravelling of her mind onto the page helps her. Soon, she's recounting what's happened to her, the time travelling, talking to her grandmother, what she wishes she'd done better. She presses her mind into her family history, trying to recall the specifics, to figure out exactly what night Zach died.

None of them ever wanted to talk about it. But sometimes Ash would push — not at her parents' silence, but at Goma, who was more receptive. Goma had found him, checking on him before she went to church. She didn't go after that. *Any reasonable God* . . .

So, then, Saturday night. And 9/11 was a Tuesday. So, the night of September 15, it must have been. Ash writes down the date. She stores the notebook in the gap between the wall and the headboard. If she dies, if she's buried under the manger in the yard, perhaps someone will find this, then find her parents, let them know what happened to her. Because by now they must have given up. She has, pretty much, almost totally. What choice does she have?

She outlines her options on the tiny blue squares, writing in dim light under the covers.

1. Do what he wants, get pregnant, initiate countdown, and at nine months: blast off (will he let me go tho?).
2. See #1, and then just keep trying to figure out the way home.
3. Kill him? How?
4. Run away again. Find help in whatever space/time I end up in. Goma???
5. Call it. The End.

Every choice is shit. It's a SNAFU, as Frank would say. She tears the page into tiny pieces, which she then eats. Maybe she'll give herself lead poisoning, maybe she'll go mad in a more interesting way than from trauma, assault, losing everyone she's ever loved, losing everything. The pulp of the paper feels like thorns in her throat when she swallows.

She's entered stasis.

Drifting in space.

Waiting for her oxygen to run out, the gravity of a planet to pull her into its incinerating atmosphere, tempted to do it herself, to see if, by dying, she might pop the bubble in which she's been encased. Suicide as a reset button, that YouTube cult leader had said, the one whose rabbit hole Leigh had fallen into until Barb initiated an intervention.

But in this case . . . maybe?

Maybe she would wake up where she belongs?

But she doesn't do it. She does nothing.

Nothing but waiting.

Waiting for the days of the week to pass on the yearless, dateless calendar in the kitchen that's mapping her cycles, her morning temperatures.

For the doctor to call her downstairs for another attempt to implant his child.

For all of this to somehow, someday, just end.

28

THE FIELD OF time carries her along, but if time is simply change, her days do not feel like true time. They hold her, caught, in the trough of a wave, in its crest, and she can never swim forward. Her body stuck in the loop. No way forward; no way back.

Mired in the cluttered crevasse of the doctor's dark and dusty hoard through which he pushes, a shadow pressing against her shuttered eyelids during the night. The prong of the thermometer marking dawn when it is slid between her dry lips. Under your tongue, the doctor tells her, as she slumps again and again into sleep, jarred awake by the beeping.

He mutters her number: 97.3, 97.1, 97.8; Lucille scratches the information onto a notepad. Ash watches it populate the calendar, that record of her body, like she's a caged creature under observation. She pictures herself that way, this her who the doctor and Lucille are so closely monitoring. She does not really believe it has anything at all to do with her, with her real, hidden self. It's easier that way.

LUCILLE BRINGS HER a cup of tea. The familiar rainbow mug, rim now chipped. She sets it on the bedside table and pushes aside the curtain to sit down.

"I know you hate it, but it will help," Lucille says, picking up Ash's hand. She lifts one finger at a time as she tells Ash that it's time, today's the day. Her green eyes sparkle behind her smudged lenses. "The first day of the rest . . ."

Ash tunes her out, listening instead to the hiss of the diffuser. Her head, as usual, is floaty and numb, but not numb enough. Soon, the tea helps her with that, its aroma triggering her craving, lifting her hand without her even noticing so that soon the mug is emptied.

※

THE LONGEST NIGHT

"Good girl," Lucille says, like Ash is a toddler. She stands and extends her hand, and like a lost child, Ash takes it. That is the beginning of what feels to Ash like the end, an end she accepts, feeling herself without choice, as she flies up to the ceiling. Drifts in the spread of incorrect constellations, flying all the way to the limits of the universe, the last scattering. Pressed against the final veil of cosmic microwave radiation beyond which nothing can be seen.

The core.

Those first few seconds of the birth of the universe, when light and matter coupled.

What might it be like?

Pure, solid light, she imagines. Like death. Like going into death.

THE ROUTINE: Lucille guiding her downstairs for 'treatments.' Ash goes like a sleepwalker. Sometimes that's what she is. The tea's sedation a blessing as she climbs onto the massage table, as they cheerfully proceed, saying things like, "This time. I can feel it. I just know . . .".

But she doesn't listen. Instead she floats up, up, up, barely aware of the pressure as she's penetrated, as his sperm is squeezed inside of her to die. Over and over again, it dies.

Eventually, he moves on to other techniques, the bite of the cold clamp, a long cold wire threading into her like a skewer.

How does it not kill her?

Maybe it does. Maybe she's a corpse, she thinks, as Lucille smooths her cheeks, plays with her hair, rubs the raised skin of her tattoo like she's blinding the eye. Then, after she's lain there for the required half hour, Lucille stretches open the gaping leg holes of Ash's underpants so Ash can step into them, then shed the crinkly pale blue paper gown the doctor makes her wear as if this is all somehow official.

As if she has asked for it, requested it.

As if Lucille is her eager partner, hoping the procedure will work.

But nothing happens.

Even as time passes. Daily treatments, changing teas. Notes of caramel and salt, astringent grapes, sour rhubarb. Another with an earthy taste and fizz like Suzanne's homebrewed kombucha, which makes her feel alert to every twitch and pang, the cold clamp, the damaged nerves where her little finger used to be.

When it comes, her period is a relief.

How it scours her out, that cleansing red tide.

She can breathe again. She bathes. Special baths: sweetly scented, extra hot.

This is how her life passes, Ash looping through frozenness, fear, quiet relief.

And the doctor's frustration grows.

He works coldly and quickly with her body, like she's only an apparatus of gears and levers to be shifted on and off, a container to be filled. He snaps at Lucille if she doesn't respond fast enough to his commands.

Maybe I'm infertile, Ash thinks. Maybe the grief over her brother seeped from her mother's blood into her own DNA, her own cell structure. She's heard of that happening, how trauma can become physiological. Epigenetics. Chromosomes coated with stress chemicals.

"How would you like that?" a teacher once asked them in high school. "To be changed from the inside out before you're even born, by circumstances beyond your control?"

Or maybe the #NoFutureNoChildren pledge was like a spell. It had felt like casting a spell. They had lit a black candle bought at the dollar store, shipped thousands of miles across the trash-cluttered ocean from China on freighters like the ones out on

Lake Superior. Cross-legged on the forest floor in the woods behind Ash's house, they read the words to each other from the lit screens of their phones. Her and Leigh. Leigh. Whatever the reason, nothing happens.

ONE TIME, after Lucille has recorded the symptoms that Ash methodically reports—cramps, bloating, sugar cravings—a mug flies across the room, hits the fridge, and shatters into rubble. Lucille freezes, her jaw tightening, her shoulders hunching so she's curled around her core. The doctor's face hovers over them like a spaceship staring down at a primitive planet. He, on the bridge, in command, the two of them scratching survival out of the dirt.

"Oh, Lucille," he croons. "You know you had your chance. What do you think I am?"

The doctor is looking at Ash, and then he's standing right in front of her, pinching her chin, pulling her face to force her to look at him. She tries to pull free, but he won't let her. His gaze penetrates hers. Lucille, beside her, pulses with fear and anger, glaring at Ash.

The doctor does not speak. The examination is not instructive. His eyes are twin beams of the coldest, analytical light, prodding for hidden thoughts. Her mind like night water, lit up.

Ash leans back onto the doorframe like an inflatable, leaking air as he leaves the room. She shuts her eyes. She pulls the blanket of her own interior darkness over her, tries to convince herself that he has actually left. It's hard. He's lodged inside her mind. He's still here. She pulls the fox stole tighter around her neck, pushes its softness against her face. Then Lucille's voice breaks into her head, hissing, cruel.

"Why are you doing this? All he wants is his baby."

Like it's a small thing: dishes not done, breaking a promise to knit him a hat.

And like she has any control. Can simply decide, force her body to enact his wishes, summon a new life to please him.

Lucille walks away, then returns with the broom to start sweeping up the mess. Ash takes a long breath, tries to pull in strength.

"Why not you?" she asks. "Why isn't it you? Why can't you just put me back and you can—"

"Why do you think?" she snaps. "Nothing took. Now I'm too old."

"But you're . . ." Ash starts, then spots a bright memory in the flat collage of past, present, future that is the house. Her first morning here: Lucille, an old woman, with greying hair. Twenty years in the future.

"Have you ever tried," Ash asks, "to escape?"

Lucille doesn't speak for so long that Ash wonders if she's heard the question. There's the opening of the garbage can, the rush of debris into the bag, the snapping lid. Then: "Escape? From what? His blessings? He cured me. Like he's trying to cure you. If you weren't so stubborn, so selfish, you'd see what he's offering you."

"And what's that?" She swings out an arm, gesturing at the dim house: corners crowded with dust and blackness, walls built out of boxes and piles of junk. "Imprisonment in this garbage dump? A baby I don't even want."

Ash inches closer to Lucille. "Help me escape and I'll—" But Lucille pulls herself up tall, the broom in both hands like a microphone stand. Her voice booms. "Glory of the highest kind!"

Ash stares at her.

"And you *should* want it," she says, more gently. "Your own son, your own tiny . . ."

"I don't!"

"That's the woman's path."

Ash shakes her head.

"Well, maybe that's the problem."

"What?"

"You haven't accepted it yet. Once you do that. Once you accept your destiny..."

Destiny. What had Stephen Hawking said about . . . But he's wrong, isn't he? Unless even this had been pre-determined, guided by the pre-written map of the universe. She knows the arguments. A pre-determined universe versus quantum strangeness. Quantum mechanics versus free choice. None of that can she explain to Lucille. All she can say is, "but I haven't chosen to be—"

"Do we ever choose?"

Fatigue sweeps over her. There's no point.

Is there a point to anything anymore?

29

TIME PASSES. Whatever time is.
Not a condition in which we live but a way that we think. Ash tries to move inside of it, the swath of sameness, to bolster her nerve, plan another escape attempt, but where would she go? Where would she end up?

Through the dim windows in her room, hidden under layers of thick and dusty velvet, the scene in her head is always the same: not winter, anymore, not night, but bright day. That perfect blue sky. Is 9/11 going on and on and on? Is it the nutshell in which she now lives? Would she crack it open if she acted, if she ran once again, into town, to try to save her—

"Oh my, I wonder where Ash has gone?" the doctor's voice booms. Play acting, like she's a little kid, like she's giggling inside the curtains, believing he can't see her. He always sees her. His form is heavy, leaning into her now, wrapping the curtains tightly around her so she's trapped in the dusty dark coil, black like a failed cocoon. Her arms squeezed at her sides, lungs constricted, suffocating so she kicks, thrashes, screams, until finally his grip falls away and his hands dig in to exhume her. She flops on her bed, breathing hard, playing dead. Him above her, tall so tall how is he—

"I wondered where our Ash's fighting spirit had gone." He grins down on her. He's happy. They both are, Lucille there, too, on the other side of her bed, cupping a gold vessel in both her hands. It releases coils of steam, the hummingbird on Lucille's arm fluttering fast and hard on the other side of its grey veil. Something's happening. Something's different. She's been sensing it for a little while now, a hushed excitement when they wake her, the beeping thermometer accompanied by eager muttering, "Still elevated, hopes up," that she ignores, wanting only sleep.

✳

Now, Ash mewls, crawls under the blankets, wishing they'd just —
"Leaving you alone is not the answer, Ash. You need me."
"Us," Lucille murmurs.
"We're your family. Why can't you let us support you?"
He's sitting on the side of the bed, fingers on her, stroking her temples, lifting the greasy locks of her hair out of her face. It's as if she's split in two: the servile, drugged and drifting Ash who does what he wants, drinks the teas, reports her symptoms, waits as they all do for the news to come, for her cycle to stop. That Ash is lying here, eyes dry—she doesn't even have the energy to weep—and enjoying his touch even as it clenches her stomach, as she wishes she could lash out, release the other Ash. The Ash she struggles to remember: the one who wants to get away, the one who had kicked the doctor in the face. Where's that Ash gone? Buried under several feet of snow. Frozen solid.

"I have something very special planned for us, Ash," the doctor says and snaps his fingers. Lucille steps forward, holding out the golden vessel, its steam fogging her glasses. She lowers it close to Ash's face. On the surface floats a scattering of black herbs that look like flakes of dried blood and a white chrysanthemum with pink-tipped petals. It smells like cat urine and cloves.

"You see, I had an epiphany," the doctor says. "I'm being tested. We can cross our fingers, but I'm not sure. You're holding back. You're testing me, young lady."

Ash's gaze jumps to his face. His steady, cold eyes.

"Playing hard to get."

Not good, Hayes, a voice shouts in her head. A twitch of life in her other frozen self. She kicks herself up to sitting.

"I'm not . . ." she starts, struggling to find words. But they won't help. He never listens. He doesn't care. He flips everything around. He makes it all her doing, her fault.

"Like equations can't show us the glories of the universe, my words are clearly failing. So, you're going to see for yourself. Perhaps then you'll decide, perhaps then you'll open yourself to accept my humble offering."

Ash stares at him. What is this... Then Lucille steps close, and the vapour from the tea stings Ash's eyes, shifts things around in her head. She lifts a hand to push the bowl away, but Lucille balances it carefully so that none of the hot liquid spills. In an instant, the doctor's opal jumps like a leaping flame as he grabs at her face, and Ash is guzzling, swallowing, sputtering, swallowing so she doesn't drown in the foul, bitter liquid. The doctor pulling on her chin, plugging her nose, while Lucille pours. It sears her throat, sinks down, spreading fast fast fast as black ink dropped in milk so she thinks *this is it this is it*, and under that cold snow the whole body of other Ash convulses and *finally finally finally* bursts free, knuckles smashing against the hard bowl as she's pinned under the doctor, who's straddling her. Too late, though. Too late. The blackness drags her under, drags her down
    down
    down.

30

SOFTNESS BENEATH HER. At first she thinks it's her fox fur, but it is spread out beneath her whole body, more like the skin of a bear. And there, in her shoulder blade, the thumping of another's beating heart. An arm roped around her waist. The smell of him: musky, sharp bite of sulphur, something else sweet and woozy making, stirring the soup of terror in her gut. She kicks free of the heavy blankets, scrambling to get off the bed, away away away, and cold hits her as she nearly falls over, head sloshing from whatever she'd ingested from the golden bowl. She looks down at herself: bare feet, flimsy negligee, her own pale skin glowing through its diaphanous black film. Her voice, when it comes, sounds choked and broken, and what is she even saying. What. What's. Happened. What—

"Good morning, my sweetheart."

The doctor. In the bed. Naked hairy chest. Thin, smirky grin. He lifts a flute of sparkling wine, pulls his other arm out from the blankets to gesture at the space.

"Amazing, isn't it?"

Where the fuck is she. Not that it matters. She could be four thousand fathoms under water, on the USS Enterprise, on a back street in Minneapolis, stumbling home at dawn. It doesn't matter because this crevasse of darkness has swallowed her whole.

Hold it together, Hayes. Please, just ...

She grips her fists at her sides. Feels the heat from a small woodstove behind her, the solid ground under her feet, and looks around.

She's in a clear dome. Above, the thick swath of Milky Way and a shimmering green aurora, feathery like raised hackles, like Zeuxis alert to danger.

✳

"Beautiful, isn't it? Such a magical place. I knew that you with your eye turned toward the heavens would truly appreciate the sublimity." He sighs. "Unlike Lucille," he says. "She wanted worldly pleasures. Fashion Week. Coco Chanel. Absinthe on the Left Bank. A suite looking out at the Eiffel Tower. The whole Parisian fantasy. I should have known then that she wasn't . . . Well, you and I. We are different, we're cut from the same cloth, we are kindred, and we have the whole cosmos to explore." He looks at her, and Ash shrinks from the naked clutch of his gaze.

"How extraordinary our lives will be. You, me, and—" He lifts a hand, palm out. "I won't jinx it. But how exciting, Ash. We'll go everywhere. We'll do . . . everything." He bites his bottom lip, his gaze dropping to her body, the filmy nightgown she has no memory of putting on. Vomit surges up her throat, but she doesn't let it out, swallows it, must stay sharp. She's already noticed the seams of what must be a door. Where it leads? Who knows. Anywhere is better than here.

"So this is our betrothal, of a kind, our ceremony, our . . ."

She runs, past the foot of the bed. The door opens easily under her heaved weight.

"Are you stupid, Ash?" the doctor howls. The cold grabs her, squeezes tight. She takes it, stumbling forward, bare feet already burning. Gaze dragged up into the writhing sky like she herself is nothing but charged particles swimming toward a magnetic field. Then, she sees more: the gradations of monochromatic light, the grey ice stretching far, popping as it shifts. It is stitched to the horizon and against that line: shuffling beasts. The slopes of their backs, their large, swinging heads, their bodies growing gradually bigger as they begin to lope her way.

"You know what those are?" the doctor calls from the doorway. Terror shivers across her shoulders. "They're hungry. They're hunting for seal holes. Or stupid, tender girls."

Tender. Ash has never been tender. She's tough. Had to be. Her parents made her like that. And him. Him most of all. She steps forward, gritting her teeth against the cold, the threat of wild animals. Once again, nowhere to go, unless she's willing to die, nearly naked at the North Pole. It's so insane it's almost funny.

She takes two steps, three, four, into the flat terrain, hoping. For what?

Could she send herself back? Has she done this? Brought them here, like the doctor said she'd sent herself to 9/11? Manifested the polar bears, endangered predators she heard a lot about after Barb and Suzanne's honeymoon to Churchill, Manitoba, where you can't even walk outside in some seasons. But no. This was his doing. His fault entirely.

"Ash," he calls, voice sharp with warning.

She should show him.

One of the bears is close enough now that she can make out the yellow tinge of its fur. She should do it. Just do it. Run into the beast's embrace, let it feed her flesh to its hungry babies. Let her soul—if she has one—drift free. Free of him, of this impossible bind.

Suicide is selfish, people say, but to face death, full on, seems courageous to her. To reach out and meet it because your options have run out. A permanent solution to a temporary problem, people say. This problem—hers—does not feel temporary. She stares at the bear. Its black eyes. Its enormous paws pad her way. She trusts it more than him, the man behind her, her torturer who then scoops her up, wrestles her back inside.

The doctor throws her on the bed, but she scrambles off it, retreating to the warmth of the stove. She sits with her knees up at her chin, thighs squeezed together, the nightgown stuffed down to cover her crotch. Eyes shut, ignoring the barrage of his hammering voice. Waiting. To be back in the house. As soon as she gets there, she'll . . .

"... kill yourself with this idiocy, and that's fine, but my primary concern right now is of the damage you are probably..."

Breathing.

In, one-two-three-four-five. Out, five-four-three-two-one.

Pleading that some kind of universal determinism—although quantum mechanics debunks it, but she won't think about that—will spin her in the right direction, put her back where she...

"... belong with me and don't you ever forget that! I will not sit back and let your pathetic limiting fears and childish longings bury my legacy beneath..."

The ground shudders, the ice shifts and booms. It seems like the whole world might crack open, dropping her—splat!—like a yolk onto the sizzling surface of another time and place where she shouldn't be.

Anything is possible.

Let the ice split, let the bears come, let the dark ocean swallow her whole. She is past caring. Like a dog, she curls beside the stove's warmth, drops into extinguishing sleep.

31

ASH WAKES TO the piano music — somber, a steady plunking — as Zeuxis's rough tongue licks her chin. She touches the cat's soft fur, assessing: hard floor beneath her, likely the basement; still wearing the black negligee, its rough hem scratching her skin; soles of her feet stinging from walking barefoot on sea ice. Sea ice! She rolls over, pauses to let the swimming in her head settle, to slow the lurching in her gut. Zeuxis stares at her from in front of the cat door in the trompe l'oeil painted door as if inviting Ash through, as if Ash could shrink to fit like Alice did after ingesting the contents of the bottle that said Drink Me. Would Ash follow the instruction from that story? She likes to think she would resist because she has been resisting, despite the terrible bargain she's made: let the doctor use her body in the hopes that once he has what he wants, he'll let her go. But it isn't enough for him, Ash is realizing. Their trip to the Arctic made that clear. He wants her to want this, to cave in to him entirely as Lucille has; to — she shudders — worship him.

Maybe even love him.

Never. That will never, ever happen.

Carefully, she stands, tipsy from that last special tea and the oncoming creeping nausea of withdrawal — how long since her last beverage in the rainbow mug? She uses the jagged pink stone of the tall salt lamp to help her up. It's as if she's just been tossed aside, left in the corner like the filthy sheets pulled off the treatment table now and then. She listens, hears nothing other than the music. No footsteps cross the floor above her, no rumble of the TV, no voices. Slowly, she turns to scan the room. On the massage table, there's a stack of folded clothes, the silver sneakers set next to them. She walks over, bits of light scattering her field of vision. Jeans, a red T-shirt, a pale purple rain

✳

jacket. On top, the fox fur stole circles an envelope with her full name written on it — Ashley May Hayes. A swooping cursive in watery black ink. It's sealed with a dollop of red wax that's been stamped: a circle, and inside it, a kind of line drawing that looks like an hourglass on its side. Ash tears it open.

> My dearest
> You puke on my power. You reject my gifts. You have your own stubborn mind. So go ahead, go out into the world that you have manifested and come back when you're ready to stop turning your nose up at my offerings and can receive your fate with the proper respect, devotion, and humility. I did not have to save your life, but I did. When that day comes, I will consider welcoming you home, once again.

Beneath that, a quote, scrawled in what must be Lucille's juvenile handwriting: *When you love something, set it free. If it comes back to you, it was yours. If it doesn't, it never was.* Beside the words, an *XO*, and a drawing of a frowning face.

Free, Ash thinks.

A rat in a maze is free to go anywhere, as long as it stays inside the maze.

And at the bottom, it's stamped. Property of . . . and then the doctor's name. He has a name. She stares at the pale pink block print until it blurs. Property. That's what she is to him, how he sees her.

She crumples up the letter. Tears off the hated nightgown, pulls on the clothes from her mother, the shoes from Tammy, the jacket. Pulls on the jeans. Slips her sore feet into the glittering sneakers.

Dressed, Ash looks around for anything else she can use, picks up a vial of essential oil from the cart at the end of the table, thinking she'll rub some into her arm pits, but changes her mind. Poisoned, probably. And the clothes? Could they be outfitted with magical trackers? She fishes through all the pockets, runs her fingers over the seams, then worries the fox fur in her hands. It's the one thing she found in his house. It has given her comfort, but maybe that's its seduction, and maybe it's actually been keeping her tied. A kind of familiar, but one that's designed to spy. She leaves it on the table, turns it over to blind its beady eyes. Looks at the balled up letter, then smooths it out and stuffs it into her back pocket. Evidence. Now she's ready to go home.

 Home.
 How to get there.
 Properly this time.
 Upstairs? Out the front door? Maybe he's ended a spell, put her back at December 21, 2020. She crosses the room at a clip, ignoring Zeuxis mewling behind her, then cautiously climbs the stairs. No one's home, it seems, and outside, blue sky, a few tamarack trees across the road turning gold like it's early fall. Fuck.
 Unless she's been here this long, held by him, but the letter had said something about the world she's manifested. Is 9/11 repeating over again?
 Zeuxis calls her. Ash turns and sees her on the stairs, halfway down, calling again as if asking Ash to follow. Another familiar, the cat, of a sort. Something, anyway, to trust. And she's got nothing to lose. She shuts the door, descends again to what is, after all, the seat of the doctor's power. Ash knows that but nothing else: not how to stop the spell, end the nightmare, wake up in the place she belongs.
 Where is her good witch?
 The painting catches her eye. The one over the couch, with symbols carved into the frame that seems to shift and change. She climbs up for a closer look. The kaleidoscope turns, the

centre widens, and there's the field, the girl on the ground, gazing back at the grey house. The grass in the foreground twitches in a breeze. A trick of the eye, the doctor had said, but is it? But that's just crazy, right? To think she can... She prods the aperture and it shimmers like water, circles rippling, but then her fingertip hits hardness like a sheet of water over granite.

A sound startles her. The rattle of the cat door. She looks to see Zeuxis, staring at her. Wide yellow eyes. Yes, Ash reads. Go. Get away. She spins around, jumps off the couch.

The house is silent. Even the ever-present humming from deep in the basement is stilled. Cautiously, she climbs the stairs. At the top, a side door to the outside is wide open, sunshine streaming through. Are they out there, waiting for her? Ready to smother her mouth with a poisoned cloth, knock her out? She slips past, turning into the kitchen. Still no one. Slowly, she creeps through the house, the aquarium back where it was, the dining room table set for three. Lucille's knitting sits in a heap of tangled yellow yarn beside her plate. Ash pauses, then pulls on one of the long metal needles, unthreading all the loops. She grips it as she pulls back the dark curtains to reveal the sliding glass door. This way this time. Will it make a difference? She doesn't have anything to lose.

32

IT OPENS TO the back garden. Tall cornstalks, tomato plants studded with ripe, red fruit. Sunflowers staring at her with their big yellow and black faces. She touches nothing, instead pushes into the woods behind the house. Woods she knows will lead her to—*there it is!*—the train track. To the east, the shiny rails disappear into the rosy pink of dawn, and that's the direction she turns, knowing it will take her to the end of her road, near the beach. Then, she can loop back and head for home. Which will be there. Because it has to be.

She walks for a long time. The wooden ties are sticky with creosote and not paced evenly to her stride, so she walks on the gravel, but the chunky stones hurt her feet through the shoes' thin soles. Still, she moves steadily forward, sweaty, overheating, increasingly thirsty, occupying her mind by thinking about Einstein's thought experiments.

Lightning hitting equidistant from two observers, one on a fast-moving train and the other on an embankment. Eventually arriving at special relativity.

Time is relative to position.

Tendrils of thought braid and tangle, but sifting through them helps her avoid giving in to the fear curdling her gut. Her position is ever moving, slowly moving, within the luminiferous ether of the day, the dusk, even the night comes, and she does not stop, cannot. Ignores the grief choking her throat—*this isn't right!*—because it is as if she's outside her body, holding the strings to march her along, despite herself. But to someone watching from a far distance, it might seem like she is not moving at all, just as a person caught on the edge of a black hole would not appear to enter it, but would simply disappear.

✸

Finally, as the birds start singing to announce a new day, she stops. Head spinning. For a moment it feels like her body's still moving. Would it look like that to someone on a platform up ahead?

No one is up ahead.

There's only her, caught here, eternally spinning.

She stumbles toward the woods, eyes stinging as the rising sun hits them. Did she really walk all night? Time sliding under her feet. She remembers none of it. Not the setting sun staining the foliage; not the moon or stars. Only the burning push of adrenaline, the compulsion to get free, find safety.

But her body is beginning to fail. She's had no water for what feels like days. Is this it (again)? Will she die (again)? This time from dehydration, heat stroke, another kind of exposure, exhaustion?

A blue jay screams at her from a nearby tree as she tries to calm herself—breathe breathe breathe—even though she's more lost than she's ever been.

Then she hears it. Distant, but clear: the sound of running water.

She pushes through the woods—a stream running to the lake, maybe?—and breaks through a curtain of poplars to see Lucille, holding a gushing hose.

Her heart plummets. How how how . . . All this time, she's been walking in a loop, like an ant on a Möbius strip. She wants to drop to her knees and scream, but she doesn't have enough moisture in her mouth for that. Lucille must see it on her face, the animal longing, the need, because she turns the hose toward Ash, and Ash takes a few steps to stand beneath its beautiful coolness, drenched and drinking. But then Lucille pulls it away, points it at the tomato plants and Ash smells the leaves and is suddenly ravenous.

"You want?" Lucille says.

She releases the nozzle to stop the water and crouches, pulls off a ripe, red orb, and holds it out in her palm.

"Come get," she says, softly, as if Ash is a feral cat, suspicious of humans, previously harmed. Which she might as well be. But she's still armed, the knitting needle threaded through the loops of her jeans. She pulls it out, reaches for the food. The sharp sweetness explodes in her mouth.

"You came back!" Lucille says. "I was so worried!"

"You'll never cease to amaze me, Ash," the doctor says, standing in the frame of the sliding glass door in the dining room, Zeuxis spiralling around his ankles. He seems sewn to the darkness behind him, but his eyes glow from the exterior light, pale blue, pulsing at her.

"Never the easy way for you, is it, my girl?" He clicks his tongue. "You'll cut your own throat with Occam's razor."

She knows what he's doing: goading her, attempting to draw her into an argument so that he can win, seize control. She does not speak. She won't fall for it, but she also has no idea what to do, where to go. Has she tested every exit, every threshold? Is there no way out but—

"What happens if it's a girl? Or trans? Non-binary?" she says.

"Non-bin . . ." His eyes swim back and forth in confusion and then he smiles, a sneaky spreading grin. "Not possible. Not with my . . . Well, you'll see."

They stare at each other. The light over the angular roof is soft and pink from the rising sun. Close by, Lucille is looking at her, the hose gone limp in her hands.

"Luce," Ash whispers. "Come with me."

"But you just got back. And where on earth would we go? There's no place—"

"Lucille," the doctor scolds, stepping outside. He has to stoop to fit through the doorway. Is he taller than he was? His head nearly reaches the eavestrough.

"Your letter said I could go," Ash says.

"So it did." He takes a step, his stride spanning several feet. "But as you see"—he spreads his arms, palms up—"all roads lead back to me."

She shakes her head and feels a streak in her temples. He might be the minotaur guarding the labyrinth, but she hasn't fully charted the labyrinth yet. She doesn't even know where she is, or when, if her house is back in position, up the road, her parents waiting for her.

What was it Michio Kaku had said about impossible things? That they aren't blocked by laws of physics; that they are only engineering problems.

That anything is possible; she just needs to figure it—

"There's no way out," the doctor says, stepping closer.

Ash lifts the needle, points it at his heart.

The doctor layers his hands on his chest. "Oh dear," he says. "You've found a weapon."

"I need that ba—"

"Hush," the doctor snaps at Lucille.

"Come with me," Ash says, her gaze flickering over to Lucille. "Leave him. We can find—"

The doctor bursts out laughing, his blue eyes sparkling. Lucille says nothing, and Ash can see, finally, how broken she really is. Nothing left of her but a hollow that the doctor fits his hand into. Is that what will happen to her?

She lunges, but he dances out of her way, moving like an inflatable giant outside a car lot. She pulls back, turns, and when he leans into the chase, she twists around and jabs, hard, plunging the needle at him. Feels it hit, hears him scream, sees a sudden spread of blood on his blue shirt. He's human after all! But all of it smears in her peripheral as she races around the corner of the house, kicks through the scattered straw from the manger.

"Ash!" the doctor yells. "Ash, get back here, you had your..." Chance.

She'll take her chances.

She sprints down the driveway, hesitating at the road. Should she run to where her house should be? If it isn't there, she'll have wasted valuable time and her instinct says... She turns left, breath tearing out of her lungs. Her body weighs five hundred pounds, but she forces herself to keep going, stumbling to a stop when she reaches the intersection. And then, as if prearranged, as if predestined, there it is: the maroon minivan, coming her way.

33

BRAKES SQUEAL AS Tammy stops. Ash wrenches open the passenger door, jumps in.

"Drive, drive," she shouts, looking back. The doctor's van should be in sight, fishtailing on the gravel as he comes after her. She's done it now. Surely he'll kill her. She can hear him saying it, that she's more trouble than she's worth. A logging truck rumbles close, blaring its horn when Tammy guns her vehicle out in front of it.

"Go, go!" Ash whips her hand at the windshield. Tammy clenches the wheel, looking at Ash, the road, Ash, the road.

"What the hell!"

But Ash just shakes her head, breathing hard, turns to look back.

"Get off my tail, you shithead," Tammy hollers at the huge truck in her rearview.

Zeno's paradox, Ash thinks. Distance can be infinitely divided. Thus, all motion is actually impossible, and Achilles should never catch the tortoise. Her thoughts wobble; sharp pains prickle at her temples. Her throat burns from the tomato acid. There's the familiar churning of her stomach. She presses a hand on her chest, breathes in, breathes out, braces her body in the seat. Did they give her . . . Oh, God, the water. Are his poisons in the water from the well? But she can't think about that now.

Up ahead, a turn, hidden by a crumbling log house. She knows the road, dirt, twisting up to the river where she and Leigh first smoked pot. They had even tried kissing before deciding it was too weird, then took a dozen selfies until Leigh's phone went skittering down the rock slope to splash into a pool at the base of a tumbling waterfall. Ash went after it, scraping her bare calves on the rough lichen and stepping in with a screech as the

✷

cold sank to her bones. She smashed a hand through the smooth blue sky, through Leigh's peering face, to pluck the phone from a fold of rock, hollering, "Get some rice," when she held up the dripping, ruined device with its shattered face, and that had sent them off, choking with laughter. Oh, God, how she misses Leigh.

"Here," she says, waggling a finger at the road, at a bullet-riddled stop sign twisted on its post.

"What?"

"Turn!"

Tammy cranks the wheel, and they lurch around the corner, slipping sideways on the soft dirt. Quickly hidden by the building and the trees growing up through its roof.

"Pull over."

Ash climbs onto her knees on the seat to watch through the back window. Past the corner of the cabin, she sees the logging truck fly past, but no blue van. Had she hurt him badly? Hit an artery? Killed him? Is she stuck here . . . ? It's too much. She squeezes her eyes shut, taps her fingers against her knees. She's okay. She's safe. She and Tammy are hidden by the trees and the building. She'll figure out the rest of it later. She fumbles for the water canister that she knows is behind the seat, but she can't find it, and then the door needs to open. She cranks on the latch and leans out, vomits onto a mat of pinecones.

"Jesus Christ," Tammy says, digging behind the seat to pull out the metal canteen. Ash wipes her mouth with the back of her hand, then drinks. Her head is starting to crackle; the pain in her stomach beginning to build. She moans, kicking herself for being so stupid as to eat and drink anything they offered. Even the tomato was probably enchanted, seeds genetically modified with his own DNA. She leans out again, and gags.

"Oh my God, are you okay?"

Tammy touches her leg. Ash leans back into the seat, trying to orient herself, calm her stomach. Just breathe, she tells herself. One-two-three . . . The window on her side is lowered, and the breeze feels cool against her hot face. She focuses on drawing in the fresh, sweet air.

"What do you need? The police? The hospital? What—"

Ash shakes her head, tries to connect her thoughts: a plan, she needs a plan, she needs her head clear so she can make a plan. She dials backwards in her mind, tries to think of things as if they are fresh, no assumptions.

"Have you seen me before?" she asks.

"No! Who are—"

"I'm Ash."

"Tammy. I can bring you—"

"What's the date?"

Tammy blinks, hesitates. When she says it, it's both a relief and an annoyance.

It's early. The green numbers on the dashboard clock say 7:39. Nobody knows anything yet except the people on the planes. The first one will hit in six minutes. They could sit right here, on this quiet country road, listening to the shriek of a demanding blue jay as everything alters irrevocably. "You don't want to tell me?" Tammy says.

Ash looks out her window. A red squirrel chatters angrily at them, and Ash hunts to locate it in the branches. Her hand lifts to touch the soft skin and fur of the fox, but it's not there. A shiver of panic rolls through her gut. She swallows, tastes her sour mouth, feels Tammy's eyes on her. "Long story," she says.

"I've got all day." Tammy is twisted sideways in the seat, staring at her, but Ash doesn't speak.

"What happened to your hand?" They both look down at the remaining hump of her pinky. The incision scar is flushed, irritated from pushing through the bushes. The amputation still bothers her. It throbs as if signalling her, as if there's something she can do to fix what's missing, what the doctor's stolen, when there's no solution except to learn to live with it. She pushes her hand under her thigh.

"Frostbite," she says.

"Frostbite in summer?"

"Haven't you ever heard of Narnia?" A laugh sputters up; she has to bite it back. Tammy stares at her. Her eyes drop to Ash's feet.

"Those shoes. My daughter had a pair . . ." Her gaze swings to the garbage bag in the back seat that Ash does not need to open since she's already looked inside, has already claimed Bonnie's — Bonita's — hand-me-down sneakers. Would another pair be in the bag still? Has Ash replicated the shoes? What other echoes are being built?

Tammy opens her mouth to speak, then closes it, aligns her body again with the wheel. Her fingers play with the keys before she twists them decidedly and the minivan rumbles to life.

"No shame in it," she says, as she swings into the cabin's overgrown driveway to turn around. "Shit happens to the best of us. I can help, if you need it. Been there myself. Been a lot of places."

You have no idea, Ash thinks as they drive toward town in silence. When they pass the convenience store, Tammy reaches to turn on the radio, but Ash stops her, claims a headache. Late summer, exactly the same, the sun in the leaves creating tangles of gold against the clear blue sky.

"Do you want me to drop you at the school? Main Street? Where?"

"The community centre?"

Tammy's forehead scrunches; eyes narrowed, she peers at Ash.

Balloon animals and hot dogs and free family roller skating on the lower-level rink. The grand opening. She was six, maybe seven, and the building was brand new. It hasn't been built yet.

"The end of Cedar Drive?" Ash says instead.

Tammy nods, tapping her fingers against the steering wheel. "By the new subdivision? Yeah, they keep talking about building a community centre there. Are you from the future or something?" She hits her signal, turns left at the bakery. Leigh's window right up there, a blank spot. Empty. Empty of Leigh, anyway. If only she could say it: yes, yes, I am. But what good would that do? You have to talk about things, people are always advising Ash. The guidance counsellor in high school, the shrink her mother had brought her to a couple of times like she was the one who needed help. Don't bottle up your feelings, they said. Why not? she wanted to ask. Speaking doesn't do any good because nothing ever changes, and her parents—the people she most wants—wanted?—to be honest with, do not want to hear it. They are too tightly bound in the lie.

The van's engine revs loudly as Tammy pushes on the gas to get them up the hill. They pass the turn to the seniors home where her mother works, the grimy old movie theatre advertising a triple feature, and then there's Ash old school, brown brick, the playground fading into forest and granite outcrops past the chain-link fence.

And beside it, the house she's always loved. The three-story Queen Anne with the turret that looks toward the lake. Clean and well-kept. The wooden siding painted yellow, shutters bright white against the sparkling glass. A woman sits on a wicker chair on the front porch, reading, one hand on the dome of her pregnant belly, and the curved windows in the turret glow, filled with blue sky, blue water, the wide horizon line. Another woman stands in the front garden, holding a clutch of orange marigolds and pair of scissors with shiny blades. She looks at Ash; she nods as if she knows her. Ash smiles back, gaze shifting to the sign in the window that she'd seen earlier but couldn't read. Mrs. Montogomery's Safe House, it says. Women Only.

THE LONGEST NIGHT

"What's that place?" she asks Tammy as the house shrinks behind them to fit inside the side mirror.

"Maternity home," Tammy says, and they drive the final few blocks into the new subdivision, to the place where Ash has decided, this time, to start.

34

BARB AND SUZANNE'S house—Frank and Barb's childhood home—looks pretty much the same, just newer. Same white siding, only brighter. Same brass house number, 11, beside the front door. The gardens aren't in yet: the wide flower bed that will snake diagonally across the front lawn, created by Leigh's grandfather after he retired, not long before he died. It will be crowded with perennials that she and Leigh will wander through in the summers when Barb sends them outside to help with the weeding. Black-eyed Susan's, bleeding heart, cone flower, Russian sage. It's so strange to see the place like this: freshly built, surrounded by a struggling expanse of brownish sod. The shiny Volkswagen in the driveway that Leigh will be given for her birthday in 2018 since she used it all the time anyway. Beat up and rusty by then, but it brought them places: around town, Bluetooth speaker blaring from the cup holder, and even the hour to Duluth, as long as they stayed under sixty on the highway to keep from shuddering too much. That was the Best. Summer. Ever.

Ash looks at it from across the road, where Tammy pulled over when Ash said, "Right here's good." They're near the fenced-in industrial lot where the community centre will eventually be built. The ground is covered in heaps of broken concrete and dusty rubble, rusty lengths of rebar sticking out—the remains of an old fish canning factory, which will soon be cleared away.

"Wait a minute," Tammy says as Ash moves to unbuckle her seatbelt. "Are you sure you don't need more help? You look—"

"No," Ash says. She can't meet Tammy's eyes, can't think like that: that she's a victim to a predator. If she does, she'll slide into immobility, and what she needs right now is to stay sharp, focused, flexible. Get where she needs to go. Follow the plan she's been hatching.

✳

THE LONGEST NIGHT

Settle into Frank's fort for a few days. Save her brother. Hope it's enough to send her home. She casts a slim smile at Tammy. "Thanks for the ride. I'm fine. Really."

Tammy sighs. "All right, then," she says as Ash kicks her feet out the open door. "But if you need help . . ." Her voice fades away as Ash walks slowly down the street, not wanting Tammy to see where she's going. She's relieved when she hears the minivan's tires crunch over debris, a quick blast of the horn before Tammy speeds off. Will she turn on the radio right away, Ash wonders. Will she forever associate where she was on 9/11 with the strange woman she rescued from the side of the road? Has Ash altered her future?

Above, the sky is blue and clear, no contrails crisscrossing its depth. History is happening out of sight. The towers collapsing into the only timeline she's ever known; that other plane meant for the White House or the Capitol slamming into a field in Pennsylvania.

She turns to face Barb's house. If she wanted to, she could sneak into the backyard, take the key from its spot in the repurposed plastic vitamin bottle in the garden shed. Let herself in while Frank and Barb are at school, their parents at the jobs they took in 1998 when the family moved from Pittsburgh for Frank Senior's new position. She could leave notes offering advice, alerting them to futures that haven't yet happened. Warnings.

How Frank's girlfriend will soon be pregnant, how he'll die too young.

Ash stares at the house. The driveway a pristine spread of asphalt without any of the eventual fissures and frost heaves, the oak sapling in the front yard that's a stump in Ash's time, killed by a blight. She recalls Leigh's waxen face suddenly, their first FaceTime after Frank died, how she couldn't stop crying, how helpless Ash had felt on the other side of the screen, so very far away.

Of course, she can't write those notes.

It would mean changing everything. Maybe she'd save Frank, but she might also lose Leigh.

She needs to be careful.

She needs to hide.

She shimmies through a gap in the locked gate, ignoring the No Trespassing sign, then picks her way along the edge of the rubble, between the wreckage and the woods. No one is watching her. Everyone's eyes are turned elsewhere right now. She enters the forest to follow the narrow trail.

ABOUT A HUNDRED yards into the woods, she sees it. The abandoned one-room trapper's cabin that Frank claimed as his hideout when his family moved to town. In the gloom, as its shape comes clear, she's reminded of that creepy movie, the fake documentary with the shaky camera. Three teenagers' optimism sliding into horror as they snapped and cracked through the forest looking for a legendary witch, got separated, got lost, disappeared.

Like her. So much like her: vanishing from her own time and place to become a madman's prey. She shivers inside the shade. Hopefully she'll find a blanket inside, maybe even a warm sweater. She's wearing the lavender jacket, but it isn't enough. Even her feet are cold, clad in the thin shoes which are now grubby and missing sequins from the previous 9/11, the time-looping train track.

Outside the cabin's crooked door, Ash hesitates. This is the place they found him, where Barb had known to look when Frank had been missing for a day and a night. Blood, Ash knows. A lot of it.

Grief rises, surges in her chest. Inside the forest's silence, suddenly dizzy, she clutches the corner of the building where the split logs overlap. The cabin's the only private place she can think of to go. Here, she can hide, if Frank isn't around, and she doesn't think he will be. Very soon he'll be at the recruitment office, asking his questions, preparing to enlist. Eventually, he'll be one of the soldiers on those old news clips she'd watched on YouTube, pulling down the bronze statue of Saddam Hussein. He was there, his friend up on the ladder pressing the American flag against the dictator's face. Frank had felt good about that, had celebrated with the Iraqi people, but then, months later, the rocks started flying, thrown by children, ringing in his ears when they hit his lopsided, too-big helmet. On one of their video calls, he held up a bit of twisted metal, moved it close to the camera so it blurred then snapped into focus. She knew what it was: a grimy piece of shrapnel that had been pulled out of the artery in his calf. A souvenir of everything he'd been through: the deaths of his friends, the many, many civilian deaths, his own foot nearly completely severed—right leg pumping blood into the dirt—by the IED that had sent him home.

And the war kept on. The ongoing war on terror. Not terrorism. Not a beatable action. An emotional state, Frank had said, slurping on a coffee. How can you win against that? She'd dropped her eyes to her notebook, away from the hopelessness in his gaze. She'd never seen him look like that. Lines deep around his lips, nostrils running so he pushed angrily at his nose with the back of his wrist.

He spoke reluctantly, slowly, describing the yellow and black rocks that lined the roads, the calls to prayer singing out five times a day, random explosions and bursts of gun fire. His face moved the most when he took enormous bites of an apple cider donut, a day-old from the downstairs bakery, she knew, from the bags they gave Frank in exchange for odd jobs like sweeping autumn leaves off the sidewalk. Then, he licked the sugar off his fingertips, yellowed by nicotine although he was always trying to quit.

In a flat voice, he told her about the lack of armoured vehicles and other proper equipment, his friend's death in the same explosion that injured him as they were clearing a road. A couple times she said, "It's okay, we don't have to," and he answered, "No, no, I'm fine," because he wanted to help her. He wanted to help her with her essay. He wanted her to do well at college. "Leigh should be doing this," he said, and Ash nodded, even though she knew that it was more than money holding Leigh back, keeping them from moving to New York.

When they were finished talking, Ash thanked him, told him how much she appreciated his help, and more than that: how he spoke to her like she was a real human.

"You are a real human," he said. She didn't know how to answer. She hid behind the cup of tea that had grown cold on her desk. Felt her heart filling her chest.

"You know," he told her. "I'm envious of you."

She started to ask why, but he spoke first.

"Your whole life ahead of you. No wrong turns. No regrets."

She didn't know what to say. He tapped the piece of shrapnel on the table, out of the frame of her laptop, but Ash could hear it clicking steadily like a heartbeat.

Now, she presses her hand against the surface of the door. It's rough with carved hearts and lightning bolts, gouged initials.

It hasn't happened yet, she reminds herself. None of it has.

Frank is alive and well. His future hasn't been written. He's a teenager, a kid, his whole life ahead of him. Like her. Exactly like her. But spin through the next eighteen years and here he'll be, she thinks, stepping inside the cabin. Intent on his mission. To stop the pain. Too exhausted to go on.

Dead on the single bed, neatly covered in a grey wool blanket. She hesitates, then strips it off, wraps it tight around her shoulders. No matter that terrible mental image of what happened—will happen? Not if she can help it—she's still cold, still has immediate physical needs. She's hungry, too, so she's stunned when she opens a blue Rubbermaid bin on the narrow counter beyond the pot-bellied stove. Inside, there's food: apples, saltine crackers, a couple of cans of salmon, candy bars, sour cream and onion chips, even a bottle of multivitamins. Next to that, a plastic-wrapped flat of bottled water, the kind she'd lobbied her mother to stop buying when she was a kid.

Maybe it's Frank's? Where else could this have come from? What will she do if he comes here?

But he won't. Not tonight.

Tonight and probably tomorrow he'll be glued to the TV. Everyone will.

She has some time, hopefully enough.

She pulls out a Fruit Roll-Up, chews the sweet leather, lets the sugar seep into her blood. Feels relieved to not have to sneak over to the school yard to dig through the trash cans for discarded oranges, black bananas, sandwich crusts. Her body feels sore, tired, and suddenly parched. The headache is starting to flood in, and nausea, like before. She'd rather drink rain water — eight million tons of plastic end up in the ocean every year — but it isn't like she has a choice. One bottle emptied, she cracks open a second, then hauls a metal bucket from the woodstove to the bed for when the sickness comes.

Five days. All she needs is five days. Four, really. The rest of today, then Wednesday, Thursday, Friday, and part of Saturday. Then, she can go to her grandmother's. Sneak into the house through the sliding glass door in the living room that isn't locked, she remembers her father scolding Goma for that, then buying and installing a security bar.

She'll save her brother.

She'll evaporate into a quantum blur of reconstituted time.

Stranger things have happened.

Spinning head set on the pillow, she lets herself sink into sleep.

35

ASH WAKES TO a weight on her chest. The doctor, heavy as a stone gargoyle squatting on her tender sternum. She lifts her arms, but her hands can't connect. And then he's gone. A bubble bursting. Had she popped him with the knitting needle? Slowly, consciously, she pulls in a deep inhale. The cabin smells of wood smoke, leaf mold. Nausea swells, and she turns over, leans out of the bed, throws up into the bucket. Again again again.

After the dry heaves, she collapses back into bed, counting her breath, putting her attention on the bottoms of her feet, until she falls asleep. When she wakes again, a beam of light is falling through the dirty window, holding a galaxy of swarming dust.

For a while, she lies there, watching the tiny fragments bounce and collide until she slips back into sleep.

When she wakes once more, it's night. She doesn't know how long she's slept, been sick, slept again. Anything is possible — days, weeks — but she decides to assume the logical. A few hours; the afternoon and early evening. Freshly over, at least the actual day, 9/11. She feels stronger. Head clearer, calmer. She gets up and goes to the box of food and pulls out a Granny Smith apple, nibbles a patch of its green skin. Outside, the moon glows through the dark boughs of a white pine, and she hears the neighing call of an eastern screech owl. Goma taught her that, too: birds, their types, their particular calls, through videos on her bulky, ancient laptop as Ash coloured at the kitchen table, listening, trying to imitate.

Ash thinks of Goma now, across town, jostling Zach as Jim talks on the phone to his wife, Ash's mom, but not yet her mom, not yet even aware that Ash is an entity on the horizon. By now, she'll be at her aunt's apartment in Chicago, waiting for news

✳

about her cousin, Mark. Ash's parents met through this cousin when her dad took an accounting course with him at college, and Mark invited him for Thanksgiving supper.

Her parents spent the meal sitting beside each other, staring down—Ash imagines—at their turkey and mashed potatoes and cranberry sauce and wild rice stuffing studded with raisins, asking each other questions, answering them, both single and attractive, so they eventually took their pumpkin pie and coffee into another room, where they could look one another full in the face, cheeks lit by firelight.

Ash knows the whole romantic story, and she knows where they are inside of it, as well. That it will soon be four—maybe five?—years since they met.

That her mother doesn't yet have her job as a receptionist at the veterans' home.

That it's been only about a year since they moved back to town, since Ash's grandfather, Alf, died and Goma refused to sell her house on the river. By then, her mom was pregnant with Zach, and Ash's dad got a job at the railroad shipping company where he had worked through high school.

And, of course, what will happen next, she knows, too.

How Zach will die. How neither of them will recover. How the knowledge of Ash's existence will arrive in a couple of weeks like an echo of grief. Another chance?

Maybe.

Maybe that's how they see it. See her. Her life.

She sits on the edge of the bed. The apple tastes sour in her mouth; its sickly sweet juice churns in her stomach. The remaining half sits on an overturned milk crate beside the bed, the exposed white flesh slowly oxidizing to brown.

Thinking about her parents stirs a flood of homesickness. She wonders how they are, up there, on the other side of the thick veil of years. If they blamed each other. If the loss of a second child will fully do her father in, if at least he might now get the help that he needs. If their marriage will finally be laid to rest. But she can't worry about them. She must take care of herself. Her headache has returned. Gently, she reclines back into the bed, succumbs again to the need for sleep.

ASH WAKENS, the weight of the doctor on her chest. This time she fights, swinging at him, jerking upright, and feels him fall away to vanish into a beam of rosy sunlight stabbing through the dirty window. There's nowhere to go, nowhere to be; she doesn't want to think about the doctor, but memories wash in whether she wants them to or not.

Be kind to yourself, Goma used to tell her.

You are your own constant companion. Treat yourself well.

She tries. Holds herself gently on the narrow cot, does the butterfly hug, keeps a knife beside her to help her feel somewhat secure. But she also feels stiff and distanced, her head a rock upon her body's frozen earth, and the constant ache and nausea from withdrawal don't help, either. She still isn't free, still not safe, still not back where she belongs.

When she does get there, she's going to need a ton of therapy, that's for sure.

To drain the doctor's toxins.

To hold what he did to her up to the light, examine it, separate from her like those fleshy fetal pig specimens in jars in high school that she and Leigh and a few others had protested. They hadn't gotten very far, except to almost fail biology.

She tries not to think about it, not to name it, but it's hard.

Four letter word, rhymes with escape.

She flips onto her side, squeezes into a ball, thinking she might be sick again.

Breathes.

Of course, she knows other women, other victims.

Heard stories during that session at the start of college. Drugged drinks, crazy frat parties.

"Be careful," a facilitator had said, and another woman with a buzz cut died half yellow, half red, had replied, "Why is it always on us? Where's the how-not-to-be-a-rapist workshop?"

And then there was Beth Martineaux, once in Girl Scouts with Ash, the lead in *Grease* in ninth grade. Passed out at a party at the lake, woke up in a sauna with no pants on. She and Leigh had seen the horrifying Snapstreak together. Beth's uncle a cop who knew what to do, so that story had a good ending, if you can call it that. An arrest, at least, but Ash doesn't remember the outcome.

Does it matter? Because Beth wasn't the same after that, and Ash hasn't seen her in what feels like years. Decades. Centuries.

If that's what it does, if it traps you, like that, then rules your life, she won't let it. She makes this promise to herself. Grips the fantasy of the life she'll have, the happiness yet to be, the wide expanse of the big city, her and Leigh inside of it. Eventually. Eventually New York. It swirls in her head like a mythical galaxy, and she lets it, because she doesn't want to be a prisoner to what's happened to her. She doesn't want the doctor to have power over her even once she's escaped and somehow found her way home. But she remembers what she's read about trauma: how it messes up the hippocampus from recording endings, so the situation seems to still be happening. A time traveller stuck in the literal past. Frank jumping out of his skin when a spoon clatters to the kitchen floor or that time at the beach when the wind whipped sand in his face as fireworks exploded, pushing him back to Iraq. He remained there for a couple of weeks, pacing the apartment, smoking too much, slumped on the couch binge watching *The X-Files*, and Leigh didn't know what to do.

Will that be her? On edge, shut down, overtaken by her body's primitive responses? She hopes not. It's over, she tells herself. I'm safe. Over and over, she says this, out loud, ignoring the shadow of doubt chilling her mind. Ignoring her deeper worry: *if I killed him, will I ever get home?*

OUTSIDE, she dumps the contents of the bucket behind a large boulder, then holds onto the hard stone as she squats to pee.

She finishes the apple she'd started hours earlier—the previous day?—eating around the soft brown bits, then digs into a bag of chips. Licking her fingers, she looks around the cabin for something to do, to keep her from thinking too much, help her pass the time before she can slip across town, fulfill her mission. Inside the milk crate by the bed, she finds a dog-eared copy of *The Chronicles of Narnia*, white cracks woven along its black spine, a golden lion with azure-tinted eyes on the cover.

"How thematic," she mutters, a shiver darting up the back of her neck at the coincidence of *this* book being here for her to read. It's an escape that isn't much of an escape. But it's all she has, so she stretches out on the bed, remembering her mother reading it to her, or maybe it was Goma, probably it was Goma. Perhaps she can gather some ideas for how to handle her own displacement from her proper time and place, her own struggle to get home. Before she settles into the story, excited to spend time again with Queen Lucy the Valiant, she makes a mark with her fingernail on the soft log by her head.

One day over. Three more to go. She opens the book and begins to read.

36

TIME PASSES. The sun arcs over the pines, shines on the cabin, stretches the building's corners into shadows. Venus pops up on the horizon like a bright button before the rising moon.

Ash eats the food in the bin quickly, too quickly, because she is overwhelmingly famished, and then she finds a raspberry patch growing on the edge of the forest, near the gravel parking lot where she will lose her virginity with Roger Boyle in seventeen years minus three months. They had sex a few times, less because she liked him and more because she just wanted to get it over with, gather some experience. He moved away the spring that they graduated, sent her so many texts she finally had to ghost him because it started getting weird.

Ash gorges on the sweet berries, collects as many as she can in a singed tin pot to eat as she reads.

Each night she scratches a line for the completed day into the patch of soft log. Soon there are three. Only one more — Friday — to get through before she'll mark it, then spend Saturday waiting. In bed, her mind fixates on the mission, running it over and over, starting with the walk down the hill, through town.

She'll stick to the shadows — wander through the residential grid, move between the trash cans and back doors of the stores on Main Street, past the alley where the doctor found her after her first escape. Or second, if you count the night she was locked out with Zeuxis. She'll use the right-of-way to creep into Goma's backyard, then silently slip in through the back patio door.

It'll be easy. In and out.

Open Zach's door, lift him out of his crib, rock him through the night until dawn. Put him back. Disappear into something like the brilliant flash of blue light that transports Sam, the quantum physics doctor in that old TV show, to his next reality.

✸

Her next reality.

Back home.

An ordinary night. Her own bed. A fight echoing through the rooms. But, her brother will be there too.

Her brother. Will she know him, or will they be strangers? She can't help it: she feels excited.

It's cold. An autumn chill has gathered in the dark forest. The single blanket on the bed is barely enough. For a while she tries to sleep, but then she heaves a heavy sigh and kicks her feet out to get up. The first night she found a flashlight in the bin, and she turns it on, hunting again for matches to light a fire in the stove to push back the chill. It reminds her of the doctor, this cold. The night he saved her, the night he locked her out, but worse than that: his freezing silver speculum. The way he pressed his cold knuckles against her thigh to get her to open her legs wider. Ash grips the wooden counter, swallows a bit of rising bile. Sometimes there's a scream there, too, a panicked shriek that builds and builds but that she won't let out. She can't let it out. She isn't sure what will happen if she does.

Of course, she has fantasies. Wishes he had melted away when she shoved over the aquarium like the easy death of the Wicked Witch, cackling "Who would have thought a good little girl like you could destroy my beautiful wickedness?" as she steamed into vapour. Wishes she could kill him. A violent, outrageous murder like in that episode of *Buffy the Vampire Slayer*, when Willow, good-witch-turned-temporarily-bad, stripped off a man's skin, flayed him alive. Ash would do that if she could. Wonders if she has. If the knitting needle skewered a vein, if his blood soaked the earth, but she isn't thinking about that, is she? She's here, now, pressing her fingertips into the hard wood, feeling its fibers rip under her nails, directing the flashlight with her other hand to illuminate a shelf crowded with tea tins and coffee cans, wondering if she overlooked a hidden book of matches.

A noise behind her. Creak of hinges, shuffle of feet. She spins around, beam swinging like a spotlight. And there he is.

"Fuck."

Frank squints, lifts a hand to block the light. "Sorry, I . . . Can you . . . ?"

She lowers the flashlight, casting them both into greyscale but she can still see the gleam of his eyes, his long hair, his face so fresh and shockingly young. Missing the creases around his mouth, the dark circles under his eyes, and more than that, so, so, so, much more: alive. He's alive. Her heart hammers in her chest. She presses back against the counter's edge, securing herself to its solidity, resisting his magnetic pull. He holds up both hands, palms out.

She doesn't know what to say. Wishes she could simply tap her heels together, disappear. That the gaps in the floor will open up, suck her in. Her mind hunts for words, for an easy explanation. Nothing comes, and now he is close, so close she catches his smell, that familiar aroma of sweat and cigarettes and the musky cologne from a dusty bottle in the medicine cabinet that he occasionally, very rarely, wears. It enters her, tips her fragile equilibrium so all she can do is ride this current until she—"Oh," he says, as she presses her forehead against the prickly weave of his shirt, his hard shoulder, squeezes the hem of his jean jacket that Leigh now wears even though it's slightly too small for her. She breathes him in—he's here he's here he's here, and feels his heart beating, its rhythm quaking loose her tears.

His backpack sags, bumping her elbow, as he shifts to awkwardly loop an arm around her, pat her back. They are silent, they've said nothing—even Ash's tears are falling without sound—and in the quiet she finally catches herself, pulls abruptly back.

"Oh, shit, I'm sorry . . ." She pushes the tears off her face, avoids looking at him. He's grinning, that soft, patient smirk she's seen a million times.

"It's okay. It's been a . . . But we'll get 'em. No doubt about that."

She shakes her head. "It's not that."

"Oh, I thought maybe you'd lost . . ."

Yes, she thinks. You.

He's so close she could kiss him. Tenderly. Just once. Far removed from the inappropriateness of that action now. But then he pulls the backpack over his belly like a shield, his cheeks darkening in the dim light. He's young, younger than her. She pulls in a slow breath.

"Not that you had to lose anybody, I mean. We all lost . . . It's fucked up. Like Pearl Harbor. A declaration of war."

How it happened. She remembers. Not the actuality but the images, pictures, stories from Frank. Patriotism like an adrenal response, he had told her, describing his reaction as the towers fell.

"Final night of freedom," he says now, and pulls a bottle out of his backpack. He cracks it open, takes a swig, then hands it to her. The bourbon prickles her tongue, flows through her body. The kick of pleasure is a welcome change, and she grins as he dips a knee and extends an arm like some sort of Shakespearean gentleman to gesture toward the cabin door.

"My lady." The same cheesy move that always made Leigh roll her eyes. "Won't you join me, Miss . . ."

Nothing comes to her. Everything is fraught. Ripley the name of his favourite female movie character. She longs to hand over her own name, hear it in his mouth, but she shakes her head, quick, curt, needing to hide inside silence. Dial back the danger she might have already done, but he's waiting.

"Nobody," she says. "I'm nobody."

He laughs, that familiar dry chuckle that settles a stone in her throat.

"Seriously?"

She shrugs.

He shakes his head, and his auburn locks tumble, his hair thick when she's used to his bald spot. He pushes it out of his eyes; the bottle sloshes in his other hand.

"Suit yourself," he says, and turns around to leave the cabin. For a while, Ash stays inside, listening, her mind stuttering as she tries to figure out what to do. Twigs snap; he kicks through the underbrush. By the time she goes outside, dragging the blanket, he's got a fire going, and he's sitting on a log. He takes a gulp, flinches, then holds the bottle out to her again. The liquid glows as if holding its own flame. Ash chugs back a burning mouthful. The fire crackles in the silence between them as they sit there, passing the bourbon back and forth, its warmth braiding with her blood, loosening her mind, and as it does, she wonders . . .

"Where's your girlfriend?"

He chokes, coughs, then clears his throat. "I'm between lady friends at the moment. You?"

She shakes her head, studies the fire, confused. Hadn't Frank met the Invisible Woman — Leigh's nickname for her mother — immediately after 9/11? Ash had always thought it romantic: the two of them tumbling into each other's arms in the midst of such grief and uncertainty. Like a black-and-white movie set during the Second World War.

Casablanca. Ill-fated lovers.

But how had they actually met?

"Are you gonna tell me your real name?" Frank blurts, fumbling in his jacket pocket to drag out his cigarettes. "Because I'm Frank, in case you're wondering. And I've never seen you before, which is weird, in this little shithole of a place where everybody knows everybody. Which can be good, I guess. People need each other. Especially now."

Now implies the altered world. Nearly three thousand deaths, Ash knows, although he won't yet. The count is far from over. All those people in the planes, the towers, at the Pentagon, lost within the ash drift in downtown Manhattan. The images from her research flutter and flap in her head.

His lighter flares brightly, illuminating his gaze. He takes a drag, and she remembers herself and Leigh, the handful of times they'd stolen his smokes to pass back and forth behind the old amphitheater by the lake. A long time ago. When they were kids.

"You know those things will kill you," she says, then flinches. For a second, she'd forgotten. About him, about where she belongs. For a moment, she was right here, not thinking about the future.

"Everything will kill you," he says. Then, "Are you sure you're okay?"

She almost laughs. *No, not really, because I'm your daughter's best friend, and you're dead, and if I alter anything, I alter all of it, and what are we left with then?* A choking giggle claws at her throat, and before she knows what's happening, she's bent over, laughing. He sits there, watching her, calmly smoking; she doesn't need to look at him to read his face: slightly annoyed, yet patient. She is, after all, a child.

Her heart jumps in her chest. If she could, she knows exactly what she'd say.

I love you. And you're alive, and you're here, and you're alive. And I love you.

She takes a drink. Frank stands and goes into the woods, rustling around in the underbrush, snapping sticks, gathering fuel.

After he died, she had dreams that she tried to stop him. In one, they were in his pickup, lurching down a dirt track but he wouldn't listen to her, didn't seem to see her or hear her. It was like she wasn't even there as she talked at him, telling him what he had done, trying to get him to agree not to do it. Now, she can't say anything.

Yet, here she is.

Living this impossible situation. But then so many things are impossible, aren't they?

Until they happen.

Ash jabs a stick into the coals, watches the blue roots of the fire tangle with the orange.

"So, come on," Frank says, when he returns. Sparks explode when he drops a birch log. "Who are you then? What's your story? What happened to your—" His fingers twitch toward her butchered hand which is resting on her knee. She curls it into a fist.

"Did you already enlist?" she asks, although the story has started to come back to her: the recruitment office in the strip-mall, his mother freaking out, his father proud, and didn't he go and get his tattoo—

"That's the plan."

She leans forward. "So not yet?"

He fires a yellow filter into the firepit. "Like I said, last night of freedom."

"And it's your birthday?"

He nods. "Officially an adult."

Ash fumbles for words. "You know you don't have—"

His eyes jump up. "Why not?" he says.

Ash shrugs. She taps her shoe against a rock, watches the silver sparkles streak with the fire's light. Why not indeed? What brave young man wouldn't answer an attack, a call to war?

So many others had—they've been engaged in this war for Ash's entire life, so long that she doesn't know a single unaffected person. No one who hasn't lost an aunt or a grandfather or a cousin or a son, a family member they maybe knew or didn't know, who stares silently out at the family from their place in a frame on a bookshelf, on a wall.

Or a friend.

Her friend. Frank. Who had told her—will tell her?—all about it in 2020.

"I got over there," he had said. "We maybe did some good in Afghanistan, in the early days in Iraq, but then..." He scowled, gave a quick shake of his head, and she nodded in response. From everything she's read, the films she's watched, she knew exactly what he meant.

Afghanistan, but then, too quickly, Iraq.

Everybody happy; then the chaos, the looting. Ancient artifacts stolen; thousand-year-old books burnt. The entire Iraqi military decommissioned; their government basically planting the seeds of ISIL.

What's ISIL? Frank will ask now if she tells him. Should she confess her situation? He'll ask more than that. She giggles again, turns it into a cough.

"Because you'll die," she says, the last word elongated, its hard edge softened into a slur. Quickly, she corrects herself. "You might die."

"Well, duh."

He pulls out another cigarette. The lighter flares; his exhalation hangs in a white streak, studded with rising sparks. She knows what he is imagining as he stares into the fire, now, this eighteen-year-old boy. Heroism, a higher calling. Knows because in twenty years he'll explain that too.

"You couldn't have known," Ash will tell him. "Nobody did."

Because of the lies. Weapons of mass destruction. *You're either with us or you're against us.* All those years later, Frank will tell her, "I never imagined how shit would slide sideways so fast." In the future, Ash's past, he will fight and fight and fight the suck of constant depression, of PTSD. That part he won't tell her, but she'll know.

A bottle of Oxy, dated 2013. Left over from his last prescription. A few spilled on the cabin floor but most of them swallowed. In case, Leigh will tell Ash. In case the cuts didn't do it, she'll whisper, as if hiding from the fact that she had to say these things out loud at all.

"You okay?" Frank asks. Ash nods, although she isn't. He heaves a sigh.

"Life's fucking random," he says. "Imagine going to work with your takeout cup of coffee and finding yourself in that situation? At least I can make a decision; I'm not some poor guy deciding to try to fly rather than . . ." His voice fades out. He gives a quick shake of his head, then drinks. The throb of his remorse comes to her through the dark, dimpled light, and Ash remembers the police station. Everybody stunned and scared, Tammy's hands stacked over her mouth. There's nothing Ash can say: no amount of knowledge can alter the initial blow. It's part of the story she's never learned: the impact of the actual day, the searing rip in the collective timeline. How that felt in the belly, in the bones.

Frank rustles around in his backpack. He pulls out a candy bar; the wrapper crinkles as he tears it open. When he hands her a square, saliva springs into her mouth. She feels a loosening inside her, tastes the flood of sweet chocolate as it melts on her tongue. It gives her a spike of energy, enough to help her realize that she has to gauge her position, figure out if she needs to find somewhere else to stay tonight. The treehouse, maybe?

"So, anyone else coming to celebrate with you?"

Frank shrugs, throws the wrapper into the fire. It combusts, the silver foil gathering into a tight shiny ball then vanishing.

"Everybody's got other plans. Except you." He winks at her, and Ash feels desire prickle in her belly. Oh no. Oh no, you can't . . . Leigh in her head, face stern.

"Want to hit the show with me?" He glances at his watch. "Triple feature, told my sister I might be there, that I can drive her home." He screws the cap back on the bottle, stuffs it into his backpack. "We could still catch the last movie."

Ash cocks her head, squints at him. The old theatre stayed open until she was eleven. Monthly triple features, not that she ever went, but her parents sometimes did, and they were always the same day. Saturday.

"On a Friday?"

"Somebody's been hiding out too long. Somebody named Nobody." He grins. "It's Saturday."

Ash's stomach flips. She's missed a day, lost track of time in those long hours of rest and reading. Is it too late? Is Zach already dead?

"If you don't want—"

She jumps up. The blanket falls. She kicks through its tangle to spring out of the circle of firelight, crashes onto the dark trail through the trees.

"Wait!" Frank calls.

If only. If only she could.

37

ASH RUNS THROUGH town. Her feet slam the sidewalk, her lungs burn, a stitch sears her side, but still she keeps going. All the streets are empty, the houses dark, and the only thing the sky tells her is night. It could be midnight or closer to two in the morning. She has no idea when Zach died: early in the evening when he was first put to bed or later. She needed to be with him for the whole entire night, and now it might be too late. All she can do is run as hard as she can, ignoring the slosh of bourbon in her gut, the swimming of her head, letting her panic drive her forward along the abandoned Main Street. She flies past all the quiet stores, until she reaches the end of Goma's driveway, races into the backyard, puts her hands on the handle of the sliding glass door.

It clunks uselessly in its frame.

Locked.

She steps back, surprised, trying to catch her breath. This is not how it was supposed to be. It's not how it had been when she was a kid. Back then, it was always open. Whenever she needed to, any time of day, she could slip inside Goma's house without having to hunt around for a hidden key or remember to bring hers. Has her father already installed the security bar? Has her earlier arrival altered things? She looks around, trying to figure out what to do, and sees a pale haze leaking through a crack in her parents' bedroom window, smells cigarette smoke. He must be awake. Should she knock on his window?

What other choice does she have? Her brother might already be dead, fading to the blue of an old bruise in his crib while her grandmother sleeps, her father smokes, and, in Chicago, her mother stays up late, sipping wine with her aunt, having probably called home earlier that evening to be told that everyone was fine.

✳

At least her great aunt's worry is almost resolved, Ash thinks, remembering how her mother's cousin had called on Sunday morning, fresh out of the woods, befuddled, shocked, full of grief for all the friends he and his new fiancée had lost. Ash remembers how he'd used that word once, in one version of the story that he shared with her. Befuddled. Like the old man who nodded off at the base of a tree and woke a hundred years later.

How the stories seemed to cleave apart even though they were inextricably linked: his shock, the aunt's relief, her mother's piercing loss. Same day.

"Hey!"

She jumps. It's Frank, sneaking up on her again.

"What are you doing?" he whispers.

She jogs over, grabs his sleeve and pulls him around the corner of the house to the side door, far from her father's window. His black Jeep, the one he'll still have in her future, is angled onto the curb. He should not be driving. Good Christ, if he crashed, if he—

"What are you doing here?" he asks again.

She stares at him, mind ticking, trying to remember. Had he met the Invisible Woman picking Barb up at the theatre? Should he be there right now? Has she messed that up? On the sidewalk, a crowd is approaching, people walking home from the bar. More eyes on her. She presses back against the dark house, pulls him with her. The sooner she's gone, the better.

"I have to get inside."

"Why?"

"You can't ask me any questions. Either help me or go get Barb."

He cocks his head, a quick startled movement. "How do you know—"

Fuck. "You told me. You mentioned her. The triple feature."

His gaze tracks over the siding behind her. Thinking.

"I don't have time for—"

"Do you smell that?"

All she smells is him: the sweet treacle of bourbon on his breath, the arousing drift of his aftershave, but she's been steeling herself against this feeling. Consciously, she shifts her mind. Looks past him at the garage as a memory stirs. A hidden key. In the garage? No, that's at her house. But the vague wisp of a memory remains in her mind. A jar? Lid like a gold coin?

"One condition," Frank says.

"What?"

"That you tell me about yourself, about your deal."

"My deal?"

"Who you are, why you're here, what's going on with the late-night burglary."

"It isn't . . ." But she doesn't have time to explain.

"Fine," she says, because she doesn't expect to be here. One way or another, she'll be gone, despite the temptation, the sweet tug to stay. Just stay. Here, with him. She steps closer. Their eyes lock. It would be so easy to lean into him, let him hold her, confess it all, but the voice in her head screams at her, reveals an image of Leigh like a frail bubble. She spins around, lets the anxiety propel her to the side door. It, too, clunks against the deadbolt.

"Do you know how to pick a—"

"My sister babysits here sometimes," he says, and an image surges into Ash's head: Ash dyeing Easter eggs at Goma's kitchen table with Barb.

He steps closer, opens a small white cupboard beside the door that was used for milk bottle delivery in another era, and pulls out a glass container. Gold lid. The maraschino cherry jar. The frail memory gathers to completion. Grinning, he shakes it; the key rattles loudly. She closes her hand around his wrist to still the movement and feels the beat of his pulse in her palm.

38

"THAT," FRANK MUTTERS, as they enter the kitchen. "Do you smell that?"

Smoke prickles her nose, but it's an intruder in the story. Her brother had simply died. Alive and snoring in his crib one moment, gone the next, yet she can't ignore the sneeze scratching at her nostrils as she creeps past the fridge.

"Stay here," she whispers, leaving Frank standing beside the stove whose digital clock glows 1:12. She moves into the hallway, holding her breath as she turns right, away from Goma's bedroom. In the nursery, a gritty yellow light falls through the window over the crib, from the streetlight in the right-of-way, and she reaches through it to find only empty blankets. Where is he? Have things already changed? Did they somehow hear her from the last time, the previous version of this day? The air swirls with smoke, like the quick gathering of a ghost.

In the hallway, she looks right, then left. All the doors are closed. She makes a decision, presses her ear against her parent's door, then turns the crystal knob smoothly, easily. Her heart pounds. The smoke inside is thicker. She sees its root: a thick grey coil rising from the carpeted floor. Beside it: Zach, asleep in his car seat, chin dropped to chest, hands gripped in perfect, tiny fists.

Ash lunges forward. Smoke and sparks billow around her shoes. She grabs the handle of the car seat, spins around to carry him out of the room and nearly collides full on with Goma. She stumbles back, dread filling her. Goma's eyes are wide. She clutches her housecoat closed at her throat, then issues a panicked, "Jim! Jim!"

"It isn't . . ." Ash says, starting to explain. But there isn't time. The fire is growing. How had no one told her about this?

✺

She thrusts Zach at her grandmother. The baby jostles side to side but he's silent, still not crying. Awkwardly, Goma wraps her arms around the bulky carrier, but she still doesn't move.

"Get him outside," Ash yells before turning to tear a blanket off her father. He slurs something as she tosses it on the burning carpet, leaps on the green and blue tartan pattern like she's doing a jig. Her silver shoes flash and glint, and she only stops when her toes collide with something hard, sending a jolt of pain into her ankle. An empty Jack Daniels bottle. On its side, top off, beside an overturned red metal ashtray. The smell—sour ashes, yeasty booze—is familiar to her beside these new, vivid details of an unknown story.

An unbelievable story.

No wonder, she thinks. No fucking wonder.

Her throat aches as she stamps the smoldering fire. Finally, it's out, and she lurches toward the wall to slide the window open. Relief floods through her as she hears a wailing baby from deep in the dark yard. In the distance, the first strains of sirens stream through the air. Someone must have called the fire department, maybe Goma, maybe Frank. Frank! How can she possibly explain?

Dread fills her as she looks down at the man in the bed. Knowing, now, why he will become what he does. Why he hates himself. How he will wrap himself around this secret like skin over a filament of shrapnel. They all will. Keeping it from her. Death by smoke inhalation, not random, not an innocent accident that was no one's fault.

But not now.

Because she's changed it.

She's altered the future. And yet . . .

She's still here.

She goes to her father, nudges his elbow with the point of her shoe, blackened now, the glitter obscured by soot.

"Jim," she shouts. Then: "Dad!" She doesn't care anymore. His eyes flicker open, then closed, then open again. Sniffing, probably catching the scent of burning; he bolts upright. "Zach," he gurgles, twisting hard off the bed to drop onto his knees. His head swings, searching, and she wonders if he's going to be sick, but he sucks in a breath, digs into the mess of burnt blankets. Digs and digs, sobbing, still drunk, and she lets him, frozen by pity and anger yet distanced, too.

Far away.

Because she's somebody new.

Not his daughter, it feels like. Not anymore.

She hasn't been sent back home, hasn't been snapped up in a flash of blue to churn back through whatever wormhole has swallowed her. Hasn't been delivered to her proper time. This might be the last time she has to see him like this.

Good riddance. She turns away. The sirens are getting louder.

In the living room at the back of the house, the sliding glass door is wide open, letting in a scouring breeze. Ash follows the sound of Zach's crying to the far end of the yard where Goma stands, bouncing him up and down, the car seat crooked on the ground. Behind her, the creek rushes out of the mountains, tumbles toward the big lake.

"Is he okay?" Ash asks.

"I think so." His crying pauses; they listen as he drags in a long breath. "That's good," Goma murmurs. "Clear it out."

At the far end of the street, red lights swirl onto a peaked roof; a horn blares as a fire truck swings around the corner.

"They're almost here," Ash says.

"Who are you?" Goma asks. "How did you . . ."

Ash shrugs. "Walking home from the bar, I smelled the . . ."

"No," Goma says. "That's not it."

Ash doesn't speak. She looks over at the driveway, toward the road, and sees a crowd of people gathered near where

Frank's Jeep had been parked. He's gone. That's for the best. But her heart sinks too. She's come to an end point. She's done what she came here for.

"If you hadn't come along..."

"Yes," Ash says.

"He would have died."

"He did." The words slip out. Suddenly, she feels so tired. All week, she's been alert to the summons, hopeful for a shift, everything in her tensed for days, convincing herself that this was her way out. But now nothing's happened.

"What do you mean he died?" Goma says. "Where's Jim?"

"No, no. He's fine. He'll be fine. Better, probably."

"Better than what?"

Ash crosses her arms. The situation is still unfolding: the arrival of fire trucks, an ambulance pulling into the driveway to throw red light across the rose-coloured siding of the house, deepening the crimson glow.

Behind Goma, the woods and water are like a curtain, the night sky sealed shut. Even the moon barely a crescent, not showing any light. At least that's the same, the cycles of night and day, the seasons.

THE LONGER SHE'S there, the colder it is. Especially the nights. Tonight there will be another frost. Through the thin soles of her ruined shoes, she can already sense the coming icy crunch of the grass.

"Mrs. Hayes?" a man calls, and the two of them turn to see a fireman in his bulky, ochre uniform, approaching. Ash waits for him, but Goma isn't done with her.

"Tell me how you knew."

He's coming closer. It's her last chance. Is this how she finds out? Right here, right now. Ash opens her mouth and lets words sputter out as the man's heavy black boots narrow the distance.

"I know many things," she says. "Your own husband was an alcoholic. Your son is struggling, will struggle, but maybe less . . ." Ash swallows, pulls back from the swirl of possibilities of a different future, tries to remember the details already painted in. "You're afraid that the world is going to war, you're hoping that Jim and Teresa have another baby before you get too old because your knee . . ." She's rambling. She reaches out and touches Zach's flushed cheek. "This guy, Zachary Alexander Hayes, will grow up now, will maybe change the world, will maybe be an artist or an astronaut. Who knows." Goma's staring at her.

"I wish I knew other things," Ash says.

"Mrs. Hayes, the ambulance. You'll need to let them . . ."

"Like the winning lottery numbers. But time travel doesn't seem to let you choose."

"Time . . ." Goma repeats, as Ash gently takes Zach out of her arms and turns to the fireman. Behind him, a paramedic in a blue uniform rushes forward, carries Zach back to the ambulance.

"Mrs. Hayes, can you tell me . . ." the fireman starts, then swivels his head when he sees Jim stumbling through the open sliding glass door, padding across the lawn in his sock feet.

"Ask him," Goma says, and he hesitates, then turns away, leaving them alone.

"I'm from the future," Ash says, bluntly now. "By way of a madman's house."

The doctor is in her head but she can't talk about him out loud, afraid she might call him out of the shadows, give him form, unless she's killed him, of course. And maybe that's why she's still here. "An evil magician, maybe. Or maybe a wizard. Yeah, more like a wizard, but he calls himself a doctor."

Again, she's babbling. She wishes she had a drink, more of Frank's bourbon, to tamp down this nervous energy spitting in her veins. But no, not now, not when she's seen . . . Windows seem to be bursting open in her mind. Elation; freedom. True freedom, not the doctor's lie. It feels so good to tell someone the truth.

"Okay," Goma says, but Ash sees the doubt in her face.

"I know your name is May Eleanor Hayes, short for Maybelline, which you've always hated. I know that Alf was the love of your life, that you met him while you were out picking blueberries and his car had broken down and you knew how to fix it because of your Uncle Milt who was a mechanic in the Second World War and taught you things. I know that Zach's remains would have ended up in that orange and black vase your grandmother brought from Ireland over a hundred years ago and which has somehow remained intact except for the chip in its base. You know the one?"

Goma's mouth has dropped open. She blinks twice then shifts her gaze from Ash toward Jim who's speaking to the firemen, hands cupping his jaw as if he's holding his own head on. Even from a distance, Ash can see the shock on him, the dull comprehension. If she hadn't come along . . . But she did. She did it. She saved her brother. A laugh explodes from the team of paramedics clustered by the ambulance door, examining Zach, and both Goma and Ash turn to look and then she feels Goma's fingers curl around the wrist of her mutilated hand. It hurts, she realizes. A sharp sting she usually ignores.

"What is your name?"

Ash hesitates. "Ripley," she whispers.

Tears fill Goma's eyes; they shine in the many throbbing lights. "Ripley. Ripley." She sucks a breath in through her nose, blinks hard. "I'm sorry, but I'm not sure I can—"

"There are more things in Heaven and Earth . . ." Ash starts, but Goma simply stares at her. She does not join in. Ash's voice peters out as she finishes the quote, then mutters, "Shakespeare." What else happened in that scene? Leigh played one of the guards one summer at Theatre by the Lighthouse. Wasn't it the part where Hamlet was swearing them to secrecy about seeing the ghost of his father, the murdered king? Seems fitting, she thinks, as she feels the churn of fear and grief and sheer utter exhaustion—and love, yes, of course, love—and all of it tempts her to step into her grandmother's arms. Goma, alive and warm, even if she does stiffen slightly when Ash steps close, stooping over slightly to hold her grandmother, oh so familiar, smelling of Oil of Olay face cream and the spiced pears of her favourite perfume and how her heartbeat thuds through the soft skin of her neck. All she wants to do is crawl into Goma's bed, beside her, and go back into the comforting blackness of sleep, but she can't. She blinks back tears. She's a stranger, after all. This Goma has not had Ash's whole life to get to know her. This Goma doesn't know her at all.

She lets go, slips away from Goma's touch. "I love you," she mutters, before she jogs through the darkness of the yard to the hedge and then the right-of-way and out to the road, the river's roar receding as she moves. She's ready now. She's ready. She needs to get to where she has to go. There's one more thing she can try.

39

ASH RUNS ACROSS the road, leaving the chaos of flashing lights, Zach now loudly howling at the centre of the circling officials. They will want to talk to her, but she does not want to talk to them. She'll let Goma explain, create a truth that works — "I smelled smoke; I found him" — and leave Ash out of it.

No wonder he drinks, she thinks, as she kicks a stone on the sidewalk, sends it pinging off the hubcap of a parked car. This has been the story all along. They've kept this secret from her for her whole life. She recalls a vague memory of her father taking anger management classes when she was a kid, seeing a therapist for a while, something about court, even, but she'd always assumed that it was normal grown-up stuff, had never in a million years imagined that it was because he had killed her baby brother.

And her mother. Why had her mother stayed with him after that? How could she have ever forgiven him?

Love does funny things, Ash remembers Goma saying once. She'd asked her about Leigh, about where Leigh's mom was, if Goma had ever seen her or knew her. Ash had been obsessed by that story, took ownership of it, had imagined that she and Leigh were actually sisters, that she'd been slipped into Zach's home to replace him, to save Frank from being a single father to twins.

Love might have done funny things to Frank and the Invisible Woman, but as far as Ash's parents were concerned, she knew that the word was a lie. They don't love one another. She's known that fact her whole life. But they insist on pretending, on keeping the truth a secret, so Ash has learned to do that, too — and now she's learned that this isn't the only secret they've gotten very good at keeping stashed away.

✺

Equal parts pity and rage tumble through her, over top of the sting of seeing, and leaving, Goma again. Frank, too. Gone, and she doesn't know where he disappeared to, but it doesn't matter. It does, but it doesn't, because it can't. She knows where she's heading, and it'll take her a long time to get there, but her body shuffles steadily forward, heavy and drowsy, and sad, so very sad, even despite this victory. She did it! She saved her brother! But in doing so, what has she altered? She can't think about that right now.

All she can do is move forward, carry the load of her knowledge, the whole damn mess of it, hoping that the desperate last-ditch effort she's heading toward, a grasping-at-straws plan, a leap of faith, will put her back where she belongs. Into the right time and space. Her own room, her own bed, Leigh just a quick text away.

If she still exists, that is. And will her brother be there? Will she know him? Or will she have to pretend she does because she'll have slipped into the body of a stranger?

Still, though, he's alive. And maybe Frank is, too. Maybe she gave him enough to think about — although she doubts it — to pause his knee-jerk reaction to enlist. But, then, she might have interrupted other things too, the worst of them being the meeting between Frank and Leigh's mom, whatever the hell her name was. She fishes for it once again, getting closer she can tell . . . Angie? Amber?

Will she be going back to a world without Leigh?

Another terrible thing to add to a world that already feels like a wasteland on the other side of the veil. Her parents' quiet hatred for one another.

California constantly burning.

White supremacists. COVID, which killed her grandmother. Conspiracy theorists.

Trump, refusing to admit he lost the election.

When he shouldn't have been in the White House at all.

When they should have had their first woman president. She and Leigh had sobbed on that terrible election night and then had to listen to Jeremy Bletcher in ninth grade social studies going off about how it was the best possible outcome: "Her emails!" Followed by rants about Pizzagate and the need to decipher the latest Q drop.

And he wasn't the only one. All those vile red hats.

That.

That's what she's going back to.

If she gets back, even if everything's both different for her yet the same, she'll just have to make the best of it. Take what has happened to her—time travel!—back to college with her and try to understand it. Press it into equations, slowly unravel its impossibility.

And if she doesn't make it home?

"C'est la vie," Ash says out loud, her voice filling the quiet street, the same one she keeps travelling. Between Main Street and her high school, Goma's house in between. She will take her chances because staying here, hiding out from the doctor and doing this over and over and over again should he keep catching her is no kind of life, is it? And what if he is dead? Then perhaps she's shut that passage home.

She's nearly reached the pool hall when a vehicle slows, creeps up beside her. Muscles tightening, ready to run, she lets out her breath when she sees that it's Tammy, leaning across the passenger seat, grinning at her through the open window.

"We've got to stop meeting like this."

You've got no idea, Ash thinks as fear drains out of her body.

"Where you heading? Need another lift?"

"Out past the graveyard?"

"This time of night?"

Ash shrugs.

Tammy's eyebrows lift. "Are you a sucker for punishment? Do we need to have a talk?"

"I like it out there."

"Are you living rough?"

Ash doesn't answer. Tammy stops the car. "Get in."

THE REST OF the town slides by, the gas station where a truck sits rumbling as a man fills the blue newspaper box with copies of the Sunday edition, the cemetery.

Is she giving up? Possibly. But when you can't figure out where you fit, with all the many versions of yourself, some of them secret, some out in the open, what else can you do?

Try to sliver through the narrowest gap.

Try to find a way back to the beginning.

Start all over again.

"Turn here," she says, pointing at the doctor's road. Her road. The road to her childhood.

HIS HOUSE IS a lump of darkness, perched on its hill. Her stomach clenches at the sight of it. What if she went back? What if she took her chances? Her stomach drops like the hull of a boat hitting a whitecap.

"Here?" Tammy asks.

Ash shakes her head. "End of the road, please."

"A bit late for the beach, isn't it?"

Ash shrugs. "I'm fine," she says. "Really."

Tammy sighs, continues driving, gravel crackling under the tires. "If you need a place to stay . . ." she says, but Ash doesn't respond.

There are no lights along the road. The for-sale sign is a black square at the property that her parents will buy. Will they still do that? Maybe she's all that's left of her former life. A broken piece, come loose from the whole. But then shouldn't she have disappeared? A sharp, wiggling pain moves through her head.

Tammy turns into the clearing at the trailhead, pulling off the road which cross the railroad tracks, eventually becoming a dirt track that Ash would—will—sometimes wander, picking raspberries, her dog Ripley crashing through the woods to scare off any bears, both of them wearing bright orange vests in case of hunters. If only all danger could be avoided as easily.

"I'm not sure I should let you out here," Tammy says, as her headlights light up the mouth of the path.

"Well, I'm going," Ash answers, pulling on the door handle. She needs to stay clear, focused, in order to do what she came here to do. She climbs out quickly, shoes crunching the cold ground. In the distance, far off down the road, she sees the twin sparks of another set of headlights. Has the doctor seen them?

"Wait," Tammy shouts, as Ash darts toward the woods. She pauses, looks back. Tammy holds a silver wand, pointed at Ash like she's casting a spell. It spins through the air, and Ash catches the small flashlight.

"I'm keeping my eye on you," Tammy calls as Ash plunges into the trees.

40

SHE KNOWS THE trail. She doesn't turn on the flashlight, wanting instead to let the night drape over her, hide her, in case those headlights are the pursuing doctor. Her eyes adjust, turning the darkness to a mottled, grainy grey, and she moves quickly along the path, tripping lightly over tree roots, catching herself, feeling the rise of the granite slope under her tread at the halfway point. Soon, the forest ends, and she's on the beach, the surf crashing onto the sand. It's a sound that steadies her, a sound that's calmed her mind many times in the past; often this beach was the place she'd escape to when her parents were fighting, when all she wanted to do was be free of their bristling hatred, sit on a log and plot out her life, flinging texts back and forth with Leigh if the service was good enough. Sometimes Leigh and her dad would drive out to get her, and they would go for Chinese food at the restaurant in the next town over.

Her sneakers dig into the sand. It's hard to move fast. When she's gone far enough, she stops to look out at the water. The moon is a slender crescent, as fine as a lit filament. The water looks oily and black like its namesake: Ore Lake.

She didn't expect she'd remain lost.

In time. In circumstances.

After saving Zach.

Her only choice to return to the doctor's house and what? Live out her life with Lucille if he's dead and surrender if he's alive? Allow him to rape her over and over? Have his baby? She shudders.

She would rather die. And in dying, there might be some hope. Maybe in dying, she'll wake up where she belongs. Who knows anymore?

✵

THE LONGEST NIGHT

Above the water, in the inky blue-black, a billion stars and planets pulse, the diaphanous ribbon of the Milky Way unravelling at their heart. Here she stands, staring backwards into time. She thinks of that first night, of the cold. Maybe she is already dead. Maybe this is her afterlife. Not heaven or a simple vanishing, but a sort of drifting, reliving events that have both nothing and everything to do with her, pulled, as the doctor had once explained, to the gravity of her life's deepest pain.

Fifteen years from now she and Leigh will have to read an essay for school arguing that the world might be nothing more than a computer simulation run by a technologically advanced future society. They will team up to write a response. The whole exercise will tangle up her head, but she and Leigh and Frank will have one of the best nights of her life sitting around their living room, eating a Hawaiian pizza with the fireplace channel turned on, discussing it.

She cannot bear the thought that she might have erased that, dug up the seed that would create that single night. She wipes the heel of her hand against her wet eyes. It's time.

Ash drops the flashlight and steps into the cold lake, immediately feeling the weight of her jeans. "Here's looking at you, kid," she mutters, then pushes forward into the tension of the water, into the embracing spread of the stars.

41

FIRE WAKES HER, and Ash is back. Napping on her mother's yoga mat beside the woodstove, a book splayed open on the hardwood planks. A familiar scene, easily imagined. A log settles into place, pops and crackles. Her fingers clutch fabric and grit, and shadows shift through her eyelids.

Birds. Crows cawing. White blobs of gulls blur across the flimsy light of dawn. She's grasping the damp edge of a blanket — not the yoga mat — and a palmful of sand. Slowly, slowly, she pushes herself up. Her body feels sloppy, loose, and there's an ache in her head but still, she's hopeful. Maybe she's woken at the beach; maybe she just needs to walk —

"What the hell is your problem?" Frank demands, and her eyes snap fully open, focus. He's staring at her, perched on a length of silvery driftwood, a stick in his hand.

"How did you . . ." Ash starts, but a coughing fit stops her. She chokes and gags, then turns away from the smoke of the fire to drag in a deep breath of cool air.

"I took off for two minutes because I had to drive my sister home from the show. But I went back because you were acting so fucking weird. And then I saw you get in that van, so I followed you. Thought you were just going for a swim, but who the fuck swims in . . ." He jabs the tip of the stick into the sand, spins it so it stands there on its own. He crosses his arms, pushes his hands into his armpits. "You're lucky I was here."

Ash doesn't feel lucky. She feels confused and sad and stuck.

Lying back down, she turns onto her side. Her wet jeans tug and bind as she pulls her knees up to her chest. She covers her face with the blanket.

"Unless you don't agree."

✶

Through holes in the tattered hem, she sees how he's looking at her, palms clasped on his knee, leaning forward, waiting for an answer. Most people won't walk into that room so readily, the one where the truth hides. Once, when she was a kid, Ash's mother had found her focused on sliding the point of a protractor under the skin of her fingertip, staring at the rising bead of blood. Ash saw her mother see what she was doing then quietly, carefully, step backwards out of the room, swinging Ash's door closed as if she was in a film spinning in reverse. Like the moment hadn't even happened.

"You obviously went in on purpose. Fully clothed like that. What's that bad?"

Ash moans, shoves away the blanket. Her head hurts from the cold water she must have inhaled, and she wonders if he has anything—an Aspirin, more bourbon. She scoops up a handful of sand and lets it drain between her fingers, thinking. It's tempting. All those words, the explanations, clustered in her mouth. The truth. Instead, she says, "Can I have a cigarette?"

"Thought you don't smoke."

She shrugs. When he gives it to her, she presses its tip against the coal of a log, pulls it to her mouth to suck the heat into an ember. Maybe it will help. Probably not, but at least it's a distraction. Frank lights his own with a Zippo, shiny and silver, the engraved words flickering in her memory and the firelight. Carpe Diem, 2000. A gift from his father. Leigh owns it now. Uses it to start fires at the beach, like this one, that will burn as they sit and stare out at the lake and talk about the future, about New York.

The sky has taken on that pale blue of early morning, membrane-like, like it's so fragile it might rip. The smoke she's breathing in hurts her tender lungs, but she keeps doing it, watching as the first golden crescent of the sun peeks over the trees on the far shore, turning the water to a spread of chrome. This lake is small, not like the big one, Lake Superior. Ash should have gone there, crossed the highway to Black Beach. Let the legendary cold take her more quickly as she swam for the far horizon, the blank line she used to look out at, wondering, what's out there? What life will I have? She doesn't wonder that anymore. How can she? She is living inside a box. Alive and dead at the same time.

"We used to steal these sometimes," Ash mutters. "Your smokes."

"My smokes? I just gave you one."

"In your apartment over the bakery. It smells all the time like sugar and cinnamon and the people, the Schmidts, give you first dibs on day olds but Leigh says it's making her fat."

"Who?"

He's leaning closer, listening hard, but Ash shakes her head, staring down at the burning ember. Her wet shoes are propped by the fire, steaming and hissing.

"Did you say Lisa? I don't know anybody named Lisa."

Draw it into your lungs, Leigh used to tell her. But she doesn't bother. She isn't willing to invest the time into making it look natural. Maybe later, in New York, if there is a later. But, honestly, it's gross, and hardly anybody smokes anymore. If they do anything, they vape. Frank's an exception, and her dad.

Why bother with those stupid science fiction things, Frank said. Tobacco is a plant.

With a million additives, Leigh always answered, nagging him to quit or at least buy organic.

Ash stabs the last half of the cigarette into the sand. Her hands stink, she realizes, when she pushes them into her hair, straightening it, feeling the scratchy grit against her scalp. There's sand everywhere: down her shirt, stuck to her wet pants. She's freezing cold, and she starts to tremble.

"Hey," Frank says. He gets up and pulls the green wool blanket off the ground where it's fallen, shakes it out and drapes it over her shoulders. It's the one from Leigh's car. An emergency blanket, meant for winter, for when your car goes off the road and you get stuck, and you have to use your cell phone to call for help.

But not here. Not in this reality.

In this reality, you'd be stuck, all alone, having to wait for rescue. For someone to hopefully find you.

Never leave the vehicle, they always say, and Ash remembers a story she heard about two kids in Montana who were high on meth and ditched their car in a blizzard. They didn't know where they were and they thought someone was chasing them, so they got out and they ended up freezing to death in a snowdrift a few feet from the highway, a few feet from their car.

"We should get you out of here," Frank says. He's sitting on the ground with her, wrapping her in his warmth. She leans back into him, head turned, cheek resting against the hardness of his chest. It should feel weird, but it doesn't. It's Frank. Frank, who she has always loved. Frank, who's dead. She starts to cry, and shake — at least there's this, at least he's here — and he squeezes her tighter, rocking her, back and forth, back and forth.

"Maybe to the hospital," he whispers.

"Shhh," she says. Then, when he tenses, "It's okay. I'm okay."

Such a simple lie. She almost laughs. But she doesn't want this moment to end, to get up and bustle off somewhere else, looking for another avenue, another solution to the impossible problem that has no answer.

"Hypothermia?" Franks says. "You're pretty pale. And then there's this." Gently, he lifts her hand. Against her white flesh, the scarring is pink where her skin was pulled closed. The black sutures fell out a long time ago but the whole area still hurts, a throbbing she's grown to ignore. She pulls her hand away, burrows it under the blanket, sends it into hiding.

"Do you want to talk about what happened? I mean, I get it. I've been there. I know the . . ." His voice fades.

He does get it; she knows that. His sister had talked about his fragile moods, how he never knew how to take care of himself, how going off to war was heroic but also stripped his nerves bare. Highly sensitive, Barb said. Ash shifts, twists to look at his face. His gaze is stuck on the fire, but slowly, slowly, his eyes slide down to meet hers, and he's staring at her, into her, as if hunting for the secret that she's holding back. She holds her breath. Should she, can she, will she . . . No no no, but yes. Yes. She lifts her mouth to his.

"Is this—"

"Shhh," she says again and her lips land on his, and it's weird but it's not. It's sweet and then hungry because of all the waiting, when she didn't even realize she was waiting, when time was spinning in reverse until she could arrive right here, right now, when it can actually come to be that they're kissing, hard and deep and delicious, even while her head screams at her to stop, so loud that Frank must hear it because he pulls back. He grips her upper arms, holds her away from him.

"Is this a good idea?"

What is an idea but the sparking of flimsy neurons, the collision of particles in a certain pattern? Chaotic. Ever changing. Anything possible. Magic. She has magic in her, the doctor had said, and she needs to not think about him, erase him, annihilate him, scrub him out of her. She needs to start again, and what better way than with love. To finally—*finally!*—consummate this love that's always been in her, her eternal, constant feelings for Frank that she could never, ever act upon or even confess to her best friend. It's a gift, isn't it? It's her truest destiny, if there was such a thing, and maybe?

"Yes," she answers, pressing against him. "Yes, it is."

42

THEY WAKE IN the sand, the fire burned down to dull coals. The sun is high and bright, scattering its glitter across the lake. A dog sniffs at Ash's face, licks her chin. Ripley, she thinks, heart leaping, but of course it isn't. Another dog, a different dog, a chocolate lab with a greying face, Ash sees when she sits up, the blanket a flimsy shield over her naked breasts. There's a whistling from up the beach, and the dog runs to a woman who disappears into the trees, the dog following. Ash shakes Frank's elbow.

"Wake up."

"Bet you're glad you didn't die now," he says, grinning without opening his eyes.

"Bet you are."

"What?"

"Never mind." A pang of grief that quickly melts away. She has his smell on her, can still taste his lips. He isn't dead; he's here, with her. Her mouth twitches into a smile. More and more, that future, the other reality, feels disconnected from her, like a TV series she's quit watching, mid-binge. Frank sits up, loops his arms around his shins and squints at the shiny water. The skin of his upper arm is smooth and pale, marked only by a small constellation of freckles, and Ash says, "Where's your tattoo?"

He blinks. "What? How'd you know ... What time is it?"

Ash looks up at the sky. "Maybe eleven."

"Oh, shit! I was supposed to go to the recruitment office, I had an appointment after ... Wait, how did you—"

"Allison," Ash blurts. The name of Leigh's mother appears in her head. Allison and something about the tattoo parlour. She cups her face in her hands, suppressing a groan. What has she done?

✳

"Oh my God, weird girl. You've got to start talking. Is that your name? You're Allison?"

Ash cracks her fingers open, peers at him, hoping she's wrong. "Your girlfriend."

Frank lifts his hands, palms out. "Whoa. I know we just . . . got better acquainted, but aren't you moving a bit too . . ."

"No, isn't she . . . Don't you have a girlfriend? Maybe someone you just—"

"No." He shakes his head. "I told you that. Between lady friends. Remember?"

Ash doesn't speak. There are no words. A tinge of red spreads over Frank's face, a blush.

"But I would like to see you again, Miss Allison," he says, leaning toward her, nuzzling his warm lips into the crook of her neck, the dampness of her hair. She squeezes her eyes closed, stabilizing herself within the rush of memory, the story Leigh told her comes back: how Frank and Allison met after he got his tattoo, on the sidewalk outside the shop. It was all very fast. Right away she got pregnant, but he already had his orders, was already scheduled to head off to Florida for basic training. She stuck around for a while, generally acting odd. Nobody was really surprised when she left. Barb moved back from out west to help raise Leigh with their mom, Leigh's late grandmother. But now, none of this will be happen. Despite her best intentions, she has done the unthinkable. Annihilated Leigh.

She groans and presses her face into her hands. It's too much. It's like trying to maintain balance in the eye of a tornado. Only this, she finally decides, her body helps her decide, and she reaches for him like a shipwreck survivor embracing the shore.

AFTERWARD, Ash feels his body relax, his breath deepen. She lifts his heavy arm off her chest, stands to pull on the damp jeans, then stumbles toward the edge of the forest where she quietly throws up. The vomiting from withdrawal should be over by now. It's been days, several full days—and who knows how long on the weird railroad track—since she last drank the doctor's special tea in the gold vessel. But the calculation is clear to her; she doesn't need to use her nine fingers to count off the days or scratch the tally into the sand. Not when it had all been mapped out for months and months on that calendar in the doctor's kitchen.

Not when his intention had been clear and he always got his way.

Not when she'd given Frank that name, spontaneously, without premeditation.

She's Allison.

And Ash, now Allison, is at least a week late.

Probably, she's pregnant.

And probably, the baby is Leigh.

Or one version of Leigh.

And not Frank's either, but the doctor's. Has that always been the case? Yes, if she's really Allison—the woman who refused to be recorded, who slipped away one morning, to go where?

Leigh hated her mother, without even knowing her. No one knew her; she appeared and disappeared like a phantom. Frank, himself, said he sometimes questioned whether his time with her that winter was even real, but then, at the end, an infant. His daughter, with her mother's jet-black hair.

He told Ash about it that night they watched *Casablanca*, when Leigh had stumbled out of her room to join them but fell asleep with her head in Ash's lap, her feet in Frank's.

He'd just broken up with someone—Tina, maybe?—and he was unusually open. A green bottle of Moosehead loose in his hand as he talked about his past that night. He told Ash things he'd never before said, like she wasn't only a seventeen-year-old girl, like she was an adult, a grown woman, but when his eyes popped up to meet hers, she saw them widen in horror at what he was confessing to her, then jump away. His dad-self was back. Bedtime, he said firmly, but none of them moved.

"Hey," Frank says now, crouching beside her. She hadn't heard him get up, get dressed, walk over, attach to her like a shadow. She sinks into him, and he holds her as she stifles her tears, self-conscious, her mind scurrying to figure out how to explain, find a story, tell him what? What now? *What the fuck now?*

"Breathe," Frank says, so she does.

One-two-three-four-five.

She can't solve it all right now.

Five-four-three-two-one.

Can't think too far ahead. Must focus only on this one moment and what she needs to do. Back home, under different circumstances, simpler if still highly problematic, she would have an abortion. Of course! That would be her choice to make — for as long as it's still legal. But here, now, she can feel her best friend's spark inside of her, that microscopic entity building its cellular structure toward becoming someone she loves.

"It's going to be okay," Frank says. What is he thinking, she wonders. The trauma of 9/11? In history class, they talked about it, and Leigh brought up other countries and what they'd been through, and Ash nodded, but they hadn't been there, had they? They hadn't seen those people on the television screens, in real time, holding hands, leaping together to their deaths.

Here, now, Ash has fallen. Into this strange past, as Frank's lover. They could be happy, couldn't they? The future yawns ahead, fractured and uncertain. Maybe it isn't herself she needs to kill, Ash realizes suddenly. Maybe it's him. The doctor.

Maybe she's still here because she hasn't done it. Hasn't popped the veil of his existence like popping the shimmering bubble around Glinda the Good Witch of the North, with her irritating saccharine sweet voice and her perfect blonde, blue-eyed looks. How had Ash not thought of this before? Erase his power, set things right. But, how?

Of course she hasn't killed him. How naïve to think that one jab of an ordinary knitting needle would be enough. In her head, she hears him laughing.

Fury rises in her.

All he's done to her, taken from her, and now this.

Now this.

"You okay?" Frank asks.

First things first. A place to stay, to figure out what she's going to do next. With no money. With only her desperate, down-on-her-luck need.

You can stay with me, she can picture Frank offering, but she can't insert herself like that, fully disrupting the gears of time.

"Can you take me somewhere?" she asks.

"Anywhere."

She'll give it a try. Spin a sad story.

Then, lay low. Grow Leigh.

That's it. That's all she knows to do right now.

PART THREE

"We are all swept up in the river of time against our will."

—MICHIU KAKU

43

"I've always loved the first snow," Mrs. Montogomery says one afternoon. Ash looks up from the floorboards. She leans the broom against the dining room table and walks over to where Mrs. M. is holding back the curtains in the front window. Outside, white flakes float to the ground, growing thicker and thicker, forming a veil, bringing Ash back to that same whiteness that had swallowed her life. How long ago now? She has no idea.

Quickly, she turns away. Mrs. M.'s eyes follow as she returns to her task. Sweep, scoop with the dustpan, repeat.

"Sit yourself down, Ally. It's time for a chat. I'll get you a cup of peppermint tea."

Ash flinches. She does not want either tea or a chat. She talks to as few people as possible, avoiding the other women in the house — Molly, Astrid, Charlene — and sitting silently through Mrs. M.'s compulsory evening Bible study and parenting lessons.

Sometimes she stays in the living room for the evening news. How can she not? It's fascinating, watching George W. Bush with his lopsided sneer, promising vengeance. Fists clenched on her knees, Mrs. M. mutters her frustration, ". . . ignorant white man-child." Ash once heard her hiss and longed to tell her about Obama, but then she'd have to tell her about Trump, endorsed by the leader of the KKK, Breonna Taylor, George Floyd, the tiki torch rally in Charlottesville, so many other things. It's hard. So hard not just to speak about how the world will keep on changing, a giant kaleidoscope twisting and turning into shapes you can't predict. The Black Lives Matter movement. The spreading dark blot of climate change, the internet catching fire with conspiracy theories. #MeToo: a hashtag she can now use to tell her own story, whenever they arrive at the advent of Twitter.

✳

In the living room with Mrs. M., Ash sits stiffly on the horsehair sofa. She doesn't know how to relax anymore. She feels as if at any moment the front door could fly open, and in will burst the doctor, Lucille behind him, come to claim her and his baby. No matter where she is, there's a front door like that, ready for him to break it down. Except sometimes in her own room. In her room, inside those curved glass windows, the skeleton key turned in the lock, she feels safe. A bit chilly, but safe. Even though, sometimes, the remembered piano melody haunts her sleep, pressing on her like the heavy body of an unwelcome animal.

"Normally I only rent it out in the summer," Mrs. M. told Ash the morning she showed up with Frank: sand in her hair, clothes dirty and damp, spinning a story about being a runaway from an abusive father who had nowhere else to go.

"But if you don't mind the cold," she said as Ash took in the view: the big lake a gleaming steel on that mid-September morning, the grey brick of a freighter crawling toward Duluth, and closer, the school yard where she and Leigh became best friends, skipping double Dutch, leaning against the chain-link fence as they talked about everything: Frank's latest girlfriend, their plans for the future.

"It's perfect," Ash breathed, and Mrs. M. agreed that she could stay, rent free, if she helped with the house cleaning and cooking.

"I don't know how you're still finding any dirt in this house, the amount of work you've been doing," Mrs. M. says now, setting down Ash's tea on the coffee table before lifting the dish of ginger candies to offer her one. Ash shakes her head; Mrs. M. settles into the recliner.

It's true. Ash works all the time. Keeping busy to tamp down her feelings, a nervous system set to hypervigilance, and distract herself from the constant itch to go see Goma. Polishing the mahogany banisters until they gleam. Cleaning the china in the display cabinet. Dusting the antique brass wall sconces throughout the house. Awkwardly peeling potatoes or making bone broth for the freezer. Like some sort of twisted Cinderella story, without a prince who can save her. Not even Frank, whom she wants nothing more than to cleave to, let him make their decisions — rent an apartment for the two of them to build a nest, quit his job at the gas station and join the military so he can support his new family, a child he doesn't even know about yet — but she can't. She has more than herself to take care of: all those years up ahead, Frank and Leigh's whole lives.

The mug sits on the table in front of her, steaming. It smells spicy and sweet, but a normal sweet, like honey blended with the plant in Goma's garden that attracts butterflies. Wild bergamot.

"Something you want to get off your chest?" says Mrs. M.

Ash's stomach drops. She focuses on the warm vessel now in her hands, the milky, hot tea, trying to calm down. Of course, this day was coming. She didn't confide in Mrs. M. right away, or Frank, past telling them she had to hide out from that fictional father. That was enough for Mrs. M., soft-hearted, open to all manner of strays, and Ash settled quickly into the house, doing her chores, going out with Frank, asking questions more than offering opinions, needing to feel like she had control, like she could contain the chaotic force of her strange existence, the coming child. Part of her has been hoping that the fuse that is her out-of-time appearance, her pregnancy, might just extinguish itself, set itself right.

But of course that won't happen. And does she want it to? She isn't sure. She isn't sure of much, most of all, right now, what to say. Mrs. M. taps her fingers on the wooden arm of the chair. Ash takes a sip, her mind scurrying into the search for a story, kicking herself for not thinking this through in advance. What is she supposed to say?

I've come from the future. I've been impregnated by an evil doctor, but the baby is actually my—will one day be my—best friend.

What about Frank? Mrs. M. might ask.

Ash would shrug. He's just a guy I've fallen for who'll turn out to be my best friend's father, or at least think he's her father, and he is a great father. But, just in case, let's hope to hell she never wants to know if she's more Scandinavian than Spanish and decides to have her DNA done, because that's a thing where I come from. Honestly, she'd say, leaning forward to lock her gaze onto Mrs. M. Who knew?

But that doesn't happen. Instead, Mrs. M. waits. The grandfather clock in the dining room ticks out the seconds. Ash heaves a sigh. Her breath ripples across the surface of the tea.

"How did you know?"

"Been around the block a few times, my darling. Underneath this youthful exterior"—she pats her hair, cut close to her scalp, greying at the temples—"is a wise old crone."

Ash smiles; she holds the mug in front of her, pressing it against her bottom lip. Hiding behind it, wondering what to say. The story, the true story, moves inside her, impacting Leigh, no doubt. How good it would be to flush it out, purge her system, drain his trickery, his toxins, and of course, her own shame.

Things she beats herself up about in the deepest night.

Why didn't she scream her face off for her parents to let her back inside?

Or fight the doctor, kick and bite and, yes, even kill him. Sneak out of her canopy bed at night to steal Lucille's knitting needles earlier. Consciously skewer his throat.

It's easy to blame herself, because she's pushed away the visceral memory of how he kept her there: the teas, their flavour, how much she hungered for their delicious poison. The mundanity of each hour collapsing into the next with her inside them but barely. Holding on by a single, frail root while her head tipped and nodded, following the doctor's sun, held upright by the trellis of Lucille. All of this is true, but having compassion for herself feels like weakness, and the fight is not over yet. She must still steel herself.

"Is it Frank's?" asks Mrs. M.

Tears fill her eyes. She wants to tell the truth, but how can she? She's building the foundation of Leigh's life. One false move and she could knock everything apart: send Frank running scared, land Leigh somewhere completely different, turn her into someone else like—worst-case scenario—the doctor's protégée.

Pull it together, Hayes. Leigh's voice in her head.

Ash lets out a sigh, then nods. "He doesn't know yet," she says.

Mrs. M. settles back into her chair as if released. "Why not?"

Timing. She needed to sleep with him again, more than just on the beach. Which she has, of course, out at the cabin, on that thin uncomfortable cot that ceases to matter when she presses herself into the heat between them, her whole self erupting with pleasure. Every time, on top of him or underneath, caught up in vivid sensation, she thinks to herself that she is erasing death. She is erasing his death on that bed with all of this life, she thinks. Erasing her own death, too, overlaying what the doctor had done to her. Finding happiness. Finding Frank.

Even now, thinking of him, her heart fills.

"There now," Mrs. M. says. "I see. I see you love him."

Ash can't help the smile that tugs at her lips.

"So you should tell him. He seems a good sort, like he won't abandon you."

I'm the one who'll abandon him, she thinks. Will she, though? The Invisible Woman had, but Ash is no longer sure of anything.

"He'll do what needs to be done," says Mrs. M.

"What do you mean?"

"Take responsibility. You're lucky, you know. Most of the girls who come through here are on their own. The men want nothing to do with them. Their options are very limited."

Ash nods. She does not want to think about options.

"So, you'll give him a chance? Let him do right by you? Even . . . ?" Mrs. M. mimes sliding a ring onto her finger. Ash looks down at her hand but all she sees are the ugly scars, the parts of her that the doctor stole.

"You'll tell him?"

She doesn't want to. Not yet, not so soon. But it isn't that soon, is it? Two months or so along, although she isn't exactly sure how to do that math, and it's not like she can just ask Siri or Google it on her phone. Still, Leigh's birthday is June 11. The timing more or less matches up. And, more than that: this reality is here. The baby growing despite everything—the vow she and Leigh took, how much she hates the doctor, her presence, here, in 2001, having slipped inside the mystery of Leigh's mother's vanishing.

Mrs. M. is right.

It is time.

Time to tell him.

Time to open that door, step through. Because what choice does she have?

None.

None at all.

She's stumbling through darkness, feeling her way forward. At least with him knowing about Leigh—the baby who will become Leigh—she won't be so alone.

But she won't marry him. Not until he's set on a better path, one that does not involve the futile war, fought under false pretenses, the shattering of his own sanity, Leigh's broken heart. Probably not even then, because how can she do that to him? Bind him to her, a person so untethered.

"Allison?" Mrs. M. is leaning forward, her dark eyes studying Ash's face. Ash blinks, brings herself back to the room. She nods.

"Good girl," Mrs. M. says, shifting forward in the chair to stand, her empty tea cup drooping in her hand.

"Please don't say that," Ash mutters.

"Say what?"

"That." She nods toward the vanished words. "As if I'm five years old."

"Well, you've got a lot more growing up to do, starting with owning up to the father of your child."

Ash cringes. *The father of her child.* She curls her arms around herself, sinks back into the couch. Mrs. M. lowers herself again into the chair, watching.

"Ally?"

She looks up.

"It's going to be okay. You aren't alone."

Ash smiles, stays silent, because of course that's exactly what she is. Alone and lost and living someone else's life. Thinking about who she used to be—the young woman with the green lock in her hair, who wanted to be an astrophysicist, who was in college, who volunteered at the planetarium, who had her whole exciting life ahead of her—is like thinking about someone else. Ash. Not her. Not Allison.

Sometimes she asks the others in the house if they've met anyone else in town with her name. "Allison who?" they ask, and Ash fumbles, unsure, but it doesn't matter anyway, because they just shake their heads.

Molly works in the coffee shop beside the tattoo parlour, so Ash will sometimes stop in to keep watch on the place where Frank actually—in some other reality—met Leigh's mysterious mother the morning that Ash tried to . . . not kill herself, not exactly, more like swim back up through the black hole that had swallowed her. She'll sip a mug of hot chocolate, watching as people examine the designs on display in the window, go in and out, in and out, emerging with bandaged skin and brave smiles. One day it occurs to her that maybe instead of there being somebody *not her* who was Allison, that this was another way she'd been Allison, in another timeline: right there in the coffee shop, bumping into Frank when he came in with his freshly inked bicep. So many possibilities blur in her mind, making her dizzy. She's dizzy now, so she fishes a hand through her hair to squeeze the back of her neck, that watchful eye, the slight ridges of the tattoo.

In, one-two-three-four-five. Out, five-four-three-two-one. Attentive to the sensation of her body on the couch, of being held, even if it's only by gravity, another force everybody takes for granted.

44

ASH ISN'T SURE how to tell him.

She wonders how the other Allison, the Invisible Woman, broke the news.

Frank had already left town by then; he was down in Florida for basic training. That version of Leigh's life unfolded with him far away when she was born and during her first couple of years. This time will hopefully be different, although what will that mean for who Leigh is? Still, she can't send him away, encourage him to do the thing that will kill him. It's too much. She needs to focus on the one thing, telling him, but she's nervous, aware that telling Frank means she'll be staying put, at least for a while — committing to her body's inevitable processes.

It's a relief, then, when she doesn't have to look too hard to find the words, when the news comes out easily, impulsively, at the cabin.

Their Friday night tradition: a movie at the theatre if anything good is on, then a pizza and a fire at the cabin and maybe making love, if they feel like it, which they usually do. Tonight, the fire is in the pot-bellied stove instead of the outside firepit, because a cold sleet is pinging off the cracked windows. It's that in-between time of late autumn falling fast into winter, the first few snowfalls have quickly melted, a lacework of ice clots the pebble beaches.

They are stretched out together on the narrow cot, legs intertwined beneath the scratchy wool blanket, Frank's arm under her neck. Breathing together, listening to the wood crackling, the dampness in the logs hissing as it turns to steam, and it's Frank who breaks the silence. "Is there something you need to tell me?" he says. "I feel . . ."

✵

Ash holds her breath. She waits for him to go on, both wanting him to and not. Her secret self squirms inside of her, yearning for release. He lifts a lock of her hair, the one dyed green back in 2020, the colour long since grown out. As it feathers against her cheek, he says, "You know you can tell me anything."

If only. If only that were true. She can't, *can't* risk him avoiding her in the future, making up some reason to stop Leigh from being her friend: that girl's father is an alcoholic, maybe. And yet, there's another piece of the puzzle weighing on her, something else she needs to talk to him about.

"Can you promise me something?" she says.

"Anything," Frank answers. He rolls onto his side, facing her, his eyes bright, and she squirms a bit under their intensity. He's eighteen, just turned, greedy for love and life and she is eighteen-and-a-half going on one hundred and seven, it seems. She focuses on his body, his warm belly against hers, the damp heat of his groin, his penis, soft, when moments ago it had been . . . Desire flares in her. *Focus, Hayes.* She takes a deep breath, concentrates on gathering the words.

"That you won't enlist. That you won't go to war."

He pulls back. She knew he would, of course he would, but the recoil still hurts.

"Oh my God, you can't make me . . . How can you . . ." He heaves a sign, then twists away from her, leaving the bed. She hears the stove door open, a log stuffed in, the embers crackling and snapping. When she looks again—all of it, the whole explanation, the whole truth caught in her throat—he's standing there, staring at her, his skin gleaming in the firelight. But then he turns away to rustle on the counter for his cigarettes and lights one by pressing it against the hot metal of the stove.

Before he can gather his thoughts, argue for what he feels he needs to do, she blurts it out: "I'm pregnant."

His mouth drops open. His face like when he saw her and Leigh dressed up for the last spring formal, looking amazing. She remembers how quickly he adjusted, held up his phone to take their picture, his hand slightly trembling. It's true: Leigh had looked stunning that night in the filmy navy-blue dress encrusted with tiny sequins that Barb and Suzanne had bought for her.

Now, Ash fumbles for words. "I'm sorry. I . . ."

Why is she apologizing? She has nothing to apologize for. It takes two to tango, Mrs. M. is always saying, even though Frank is not her dance partner, and the doctor wasn't either, since she didn't choose to foxtrot or anything else with him. Ash wriggles up to sitting on the bed, fighting against the fatigue spreading through her body. She wishes she could just sleep; she's been so tired lately. Barely made it through the movie. The dark theatre. The jazzy opening music of *Monsters Inc.*, which she saw five thousand times as a kid.

Frank drops his full cigarette into the stove and comes over to her. Side by side, thighs pressed together, they sit in silence. Ash can barely breathe, waiting for what he might say. This scene in the drama of her new life hasn't been sketched out for her in advance, apart from Leigh telling her the basics. Eighteen years old, Frank already committed to the trajectory of his life by the time Allison told him over the phone. And once he found out about the baby, that the future wasn't just about him, he doubled down on his commitment to fight. She's imagined him for a long time, in that phone booth, his beautiful auburn hair a thin fuzz on his crewcut head, receiving the stunning news about Leigh. He isn't there now, though; he hasn't yet enlisted. Gently now, he picks up her hand, cradles the scarred curve of her amputated finger.

"I'll always protect you."

"I don't need protecting," she mutters.

"I don't mean like that."

"Like what?"

"Like a macho dude. Or maybe I do. I don't fucking know. I just know . . ."

Ash nods, bites her bottom lip, hard, to hold back tears.

"When was it, do you think? That day—"

"Yeah," she says.

Frank had saved two lives that day on the beach, although Leigh wasn't yet a life. Only a cluster of cells she could—or Allison could, other Allison, other her—have decided to terminate. Maybe, in another version of this reality, that's also happened, but Ash doesn't want to think about that, about her life without some version of Leigh.

"How far along are—"

"Ten weeks, give or take," she lies. It's more like twelve.

"And you're sure you want to go through with . . ."

Ash lifts her head to look him square in the eye. "Yes."

". . . it," he finishes, weakly.

"Not it. Her. A girl."

"A girl," Frank says. His eyes dark green against his blanched face. She can see his fear. Gently, she touches his jaw, cups his chin.

"I love you," she says, for the first time. He heaves a breath, drops into her, his face against her shoulder, hiding like a young boy. She slides her arms around him, pulls him close, and she feels his hot breath against her neck before he tips his head up.

"I love you, too," he tells her, and he sounds, for the first time, like the adult Frank whom Ash has always known.

Only after they've made love again, and she's lying again in Frank's arms, alert and awake despite the deep craving for sleep, does she realize that they didn't return to the conversation about him enlisting. Oh, well, she thinks, choosing to relax into this pleasure, this closeness. There will be time for that.

"WHAT DO YOU think of Leia?" Frank says later. Ash nearly chokes on the cold pizza crust she's been chewing. She stands naked in front of the stove, warming her bum against its throb of heat. Frank's watching her from the bed; his gaze keeps dropping to her belly.

"Leigh?"

He shakes his head. "Leia. As in Princess—"

A laugh spurts out of her. He grins, his face crowded by shadows in the crisscrossing light from the jumping flames. She turns to look for a bottle of water, eyes smarting.

"Yeah," he says. "Too geeky."

"What about just Leigh," Ash says. "Maybe short for Ashleigh."

"Ashleigh," he repeats. Turned away from him, Ash presses her fingertips against the edge of the wooden counter, carefully, so as not to get a splinter. The moment swims around her, impossible, its air like the thin atmosphere of a strange planet.

"Ashleigh," he says again. "But we'll call her Leigh."

She pulls in a deep breath and turns to cross the cabin, holding out the water bottle. Frank ignores it; instead, he touches her belly, the shallow bump that's forming, that sometimes freaks her out. To have Leigh growing inside her, when the one person she wants to tell it to—how it feels sometimes like she's a cocoon holding a transforming caterpillar, like the one they'd watched, waiting, in the terrarium in their fourth-grade classroom—is Leigh herself.

"I like it," he whispers, leaning in to kiss her stomach. Ash releases the breath she's been holding. Another box checked, she thinks, from a distance, trying to hold at least a little bit back, not to be seduced by this, by love, by Frank, by family. Trying instead to stay focused on her careful construction of the known past, that scaffolding that supports her life, with a few inevitable and, yes, intentional, changes.

Lives saved. *With what consequences, Hayes?* Screw that. What she sees: her parents not losing their son, she not losing her brother, her best friend not losing her dad — maybe, if she succeeds in convincing him. But what else might it mean? Her own annihilation? Someone else's? Who knows.

The future is always the future, it seems. Unknown.

45

THE BABY GROWS. Christmas comes and goes. Frank's parents want nothing to do with her, which is fine, since it means less need for deception, fewer lies. Barb is excited, though, and as a gift, through Frank, she gives Ash a book to chart Leigh's progress. Ash wonders about 3D ultrasounds, posting TikTok videos, sharing filtered Insta selfies of her and her baby bump with all the relevant hashtags. Here, she doesn't even have a Hotmail account. Instead, she shrinks into secrecy, refusing to allow Frank to photograph her, professing to have a superstition of cameras, an undiagnosed delusional fear. No record of her face needs to haunt her eventual future.

But it doesn't matter. Nothing she says or does matters: the baby grows and grows.

The size of a pomegranate seed, an acorn, an avocado pit, a peach.

Forming the doctor's features, Ash thinks, in the middle of the night, in a sickening panic that pulls her up out of sleep: his dirty blonde hair, wolf-blue eyes, overbearing height. A Leigh who might look completely different from her Leigh. It makes her ill to think of the deception she's crafting, but she tells herself she's setting the world right. It's the proper thing to do. She is Allison, and Allison is her.

But then why doesn't Frank recognize her in the future?

Maybe he does. Maybe he just hasn't ever said anything. Maybe that's the reason she's always felt like they are connected in a way that goes beyond just her being Leigh's best friend.

And now he'll never see her for who she is, up there, up ahead in the future. Once she goes back—because she will go back, she has to go back—she'll show him who she is. Except she

✳

can't, can she? Because up there, up ahead, he's dead. Unless . . . Unless she's able to alter that, too, save him like she saved Zach.

So far she hasn't had any luck. He's firm on his new plan: see that she safely has the baby, set them up in an apartment, enlist, head overseas. Do what must be done, for his wife, his kid, his country.

It's noble, she sees that.

And she would respect his choice if it wasn't for the deception that, from her perspective, a visitor from the land of hindsight, it's easy to see. The liars' faces professing to have secret evidence about weapons of mass destruction upon which they're basing their war.

Saddam's regime was hated, she heard an Iraqi author concede, on some video she'd watched, but if the U.S. hadn't invaded Iraq because of a lie, tens of thousands of people would still be alive.

How can she tell him all that?

She can't.

She has to keep quiet.

Quiet with her warnings, and with her questions, too.

There are a lot of them. First and foremost: where is the path home?

When she isn't cleaning house or helping Mrs. M. with the cooking or going out with Frank, she tries to think of a way to find some answers. Goma, of course. Goma, who learned who she was the night she rescued Zach from the fate he'd encountered in her own past. Goma, who spent Ash's life attempting to train her: how to stay calm, where to look for ways out, not to accept food or drink from strangers — if only she'd listened to that last one — not to mention her repeated warnings about staying indoors when it's too cold outside. Ash wants to talk with her, but she doesn't know how . . .

Knock, knock.

"Hey, Mrs. Hayes, remember me? Your time-travelling granddaughter?"

And, anyway, what would be the point?

She's stuck here for the foreseeable future, building Leigh, and as the weeks and months creep by, bringing them deeper into 2002, the baby's weight helps bind her to the gravity of this place and time.

Still, she goes to the library, the only repository of knowledge she can find, because there isn't any easy access to the internet. She understands better the T-shirt her mom's high-school friend Lisa mailed her for her fortieth birthday, that they laughed about over the phone. *I miss my pre-internet brain*, it said. Without it, and without the tether of her phone, Ash's existence feels slower, more solid, as if she's more fully aware of her grounding in the physical world. She's calmer; she enjoys the slower pace of reading.

The library is in the basement of the post office. It smells of sour paper and lemon floor cleaner. She browses the stacks and pulls out whatever interests her although the pickings are slim. The librarian shows her how to use the card catalogue, and she flips through looking for certain topics.

Worm holes: nothing.

Portals: nothing.

Time travel: bingo, but just a few kid's novels with dog-eared corners, most of which she's read, and a few movies on huge, boxy videocassettes in cardboard sleeves with stickers on them that say Be Kind, Rewind.

Then, one day, she treads down the wet stairs in her winter boots and pushes the heavy glass door open to see something new: a fat computer monitor, surrounded by a clutch of women, eyes bright with excited interest.

"Here we go," says Linda, one of the few people of colour Ash has met in town apart from Mrs. M.

The modem shrieks and squeals, and everyone laughs. After it's set up, and the others drift away to make it available to the patrons, Ash comes out from behind a long shelf of paper-back romances and sits down on the creaky office chair. A search engine stares at her. *Ask Jeeves.* Into the open bar, she types: Freedom technique + women. It's a start; there's a lot she needs to know.

But the first, second, third, tenth, twentieth search leads her nowhere. She surfs through an internet full of brick wall and parchment paper backgrounds, ignoring the flashing Click Me buttons, until one day she remembers that she still has his note. Pulpy, faded from going through the wash in the pocket of her jeans but still legible. Her hands tremble as she types his full name into the search bar, afraid that tapping it into existence on the keyboard like this might summon him. Dr. Reginald Alfred Dennison XVIIII. It's a shock what comes up, but somehow not a shock, too.

The first image takes nearly two minutes to load. It's on the website of a museum in Kansas. A sepia print showing a white-eyed man in a floppy hat, holding the reins of a horse-drawn carriage. A sign on the side says Dr. Reginald's Soothing Elixirs in large green letters. Beneath, in smaller cursive: for feminine complaints of all kinds. The next, a Technicolor image of a man in bright teal scrubs, gloved hands, a glint in his eyes that sends shivers up the back of Ash's neck. Then, again, wearing white robes, hands pressed together in prayer, encircled by women dressed entirely in lavender and yellow. And, again, in a khaki wool uniform and a service cap, standing in front of a group of white-clad nurses wearing veils, with bold dark grey crosses centred on their chests. The same man, over and over, throughout time. The ancestors, Ash remembers him saying, with that tight, pleased grin.

Stunned, she settles back into the hard seat, staring at the boxy tent behind the nurses, the hint of the landscape at its edges nothing but a dark flatness, no man's land, and that's where she is when a hand curls around her shoulder, and she nearly screams. Heartbeat hammering in her chest, she twists around quickly to see that it's only Goma. Standing behind her, blocking the glaring fluorescents. Ash melts with relief. She presses a hand against the thumping in her chest.

"I'm sorry, I . . ." Goma starts, but then her eyes drop to Ash's belly, the bump covered with a protective hand.

"What's going on? I thought . . ."

Ash stands up.

"Are you finished?" a boy asks, readjusting a heavy backpack on his shoulder.

Ash leads Goma toward a long table beside the shelf full of encyclopedias with gold lettering on brown leather covers. They sit facing one another. Ash picks at the fraying varnish at the edge of the table, trying to find words. What to say? The doctor . . . What? Immortal? Her head is spinning. Finally, she asks, "How's Zach?"

"Good," Goma says. "Fine. Just fine. And Teresa's pregnant again. But I guess you know that because I'm guessing that's . . ."

Ash nods. "Me. Yeah. Me."

Goma stares, eyes wide, then gives her head a quick, small shake. Her fingers twitch toward Ash's abdomen. "And this? Is this allowed?"

"Allowed?" Ash smiles. "There's not some sort of overseer."

Goma nods. "Maybe not, but I expect it's a bit of a problem. How did this—"

"It's a long story."

"I have time."

Weakly, Ash smiles. Eighteen years to be exact, until COVID comes along. Could Ash stop that, too? At least give a warning. She presses her lips together, breathes hard through her nose. Goma leans forward.

"I didn't expect to ever see you again. I mean..." She shakes her head, a quick, jerky movement like she's reorganizing her thoughts. "This you, this version of you, but then, when Teresa told me she was pregnant..."

Ash nods.

"I've started reading." She fumbles for the bag, slumped against her ankle, pulls it up onto her lap and begins tugging out books to set them on the table. *The Nature of Space and Time*, *The Golden Bough*, a hefty, red-covered tome called, simply, *Poisoning*.

"But I think I'm too much of a dunderhead. I can't seem to wrap my head around any of this"—her fingertip bounces off the cover of the top book—"or what you told me, or what I should do about it."

"You're not," Ash says. "You're definitely not a dunderhead."

Goma wriggles forward in her seat, eyes appealing. She looks like she wants more, to get closer, and so Ash lets her pick up her hand.

"This, for example," Goma says, pressing her fingers into the heart line beneath the missing finger. For a moment, Ash thinks she's going to try to read her palm like she used to do, when Ash was a kid, like she will do, far off in the future.

Instead, she says, "Who did this to you? What happened in that house? How can I let this happen? Your parents are so excited, and yet here you are, in some deep trouble."

Ash doesn't speak. There's a lump in her throat. Already, only here for a few months, and already she's disappointed her grandmother.

"Oh, I don't mean that way," Goma says. "The baby, you pregnant, although Lord knows we need to talk about . . ." She hauls in a breath, sits back in the chair, lets go of Ash's hand. "Maybe we can start at the beginning."

"It'll take a bit of time."

Goma nods. "Are you hungry?"

"I'm always hungry."

Goma smiles. Together, they walk over to the desk, where Goma sets down her stack of books. The clerk takes them without comment, this assortment of strange reading. As they move through the door, Ash sees her turning them over in her hands, examining them, as if deciding whether or not they belong.

46

GOMA TAKES ASH to the Lakeview Diner. Her grandmother likes it—the classical music that the owner plays, the colourful hand-sewn curtains on the windows—and she'll eat lunch with her anti-war group here every Sunday for most of the rest of her life, Ash knows. Have they started yet: the protests, quiet vigils disrupted by threats lobbed by drivers with Bush-Cheney bumper stickers?

She doesn't ask. Be careful, she tells herself, and caution keeps her quiet. It's one thing to babble out a confession about being a time traveller in the middle of the night, when you've broken in to save a baby and expect to soon be returning to your own time and place. It's another to deliberately elaborate on the whole story, fill in all the details. Goma knows, yes, or at least the Goma from her other life does. But has this knowledge helped her? She isn't sure what to say, what not to say, and so she stays mostly silent as they slide into a booth and order grilled cheese sandwiches, a plate of French fries to split.

"Freedom fries," the waitress mumbles, and Ash rolls her eyes, then asks for a glass of chocolate milk: the sugar for her, the calcium for Leigh.

"You're worried," Goma says, "that if I know too much, things will change. That it?"

Ash nods. Partly, yes, but it's also that she doesn't want to disclose anything, tell the truth of the doctor, what he did to her. Explaining all that means an eventual confession: the baby is not Frank's. When the baby *is* Frank's. That is what she must believe.

Goma reaches out a hand, lays it flat on the tabletop. Those carefully manicured fingertips, done every other week by an aesthetician named Emile who makes house calls. Ash squeezes her eyes shut, willfully absorbing her tears.

"I don't want to know," Goma says. "Nothing about the future.

✶

Only how you came here, how I can help you get back. Because things have to be—"

The server sets down the sandwiches, interrupting. Pickles are skewered into the bread with yellow cellophane-flagged toothpicks, and the sour vinegar smell churns Ash's stomach. She nearly laughs out loud, remembers Leigh throwing up at a sleepover after eating an entire bag of dill pickle chips. It's her, all right. It's her.

"I can help you. You can trust me." She picks up the red plastic ketchup bottle. "Earlier you mentioned a madman's house? Something about a doctor who was also a wizard? Where was that? How did you end up there?"

Ash blinks. Turns to look out the window. The restaurant is up on the slope of the mountain, and she can see across the white swath of lake ice to the open depths farther out. She wonders if her parents ever look out there and wonder if that's where she is, if the enormous lake has swallowed her whole. Inside, Leigh kicks, and Ash cups both hands over her abdomen, leans back against the padded vinyl of the booth.

"Winter," she says, quietly. "A cold night. I got locked out of my house."

Goma chews, swallows. "With your parents; where you live with your parents."

Ash nods. "Jim and Teresa," she says. "Yes."

"Okay, and then?"

Ash slumps into the inevitable and gives her some details: the snow, the fox, the old cell phone that wouldn't work. Lucille. The teas. But she leaves out the things she cannot give voice to: her severed finger, his medical theories, the treatments, the crazy train track, the calendar on the kitchen wall, the turkey baster, the trip to the Arctic when he . . . Despite her caution, Goma still asks: "And the doctor, is it him then who—" She points at Ash's belly.

"No," Ash snaps. "The baby's Frank's." She's said too much. Her head feels woozy and light. Not hunger, but something else, the eye on the back of her neck prickling, a pressure on her skull like she's floating up, nudging the ceiling, her vision shrunken close to the sides of her head, narrowed. And then the music changes, and Ash's gaze snaps around the room, looking. Is he here? Has he found her? Does he know about . . . Her hands cup her belly. Her breath is caught in her throat.

"Are you all right?"

"This music . . ."

"Yes?" Goma waits, but Ash doesn't speak, can't.

"It's quite melancholy, isn't it? Eric Satie. My English teacher in high—"

"You know it?" Ash is astounded. It's a composition of this world? Was the doctor simply playing a familiar song? Is she crazy?

"Breathe, dear," Goma says. She pulls a long breath of air into her nose as if to show Ash how it's done, but words come rushing from Ash's mouth.

"It won't make any difference, telling you, because I can't do anything. Not until the baby . . . and maybe even then I . . ."

"Okay," Goma says, shaking salt on her side of the fries. "But we can talk about it, can't we?"

Ash doesn't answer. She doesn't want to. She's come too close to the awful details, feels like they are stalking her mind, stirring things up. That, plus the terrible music which finally, blessedly, comes to an end.

"Aren't you going to eat?"

She shakes her head. She isn't hungry, feels deeply cold as if she's trembling under her skin. Goma watches her as she clenches her hands against the smooth edge of the vinyl seat, focuses on the feeling of her butt on the seat, gravity holding her, the smells of melted cheese, and grease.

Ash is tired, too. Still hasn't recovered from staying up nearly all night a few days ago to help Mrs. M. with Astrid's labour in the birthing room at the back of the house, two bedrooms turned into one long room, the windows overlooking Mrs. M.'s huge herb and vegetable garden. It was a trip to see it happen: the tiny, squalling infant slipping into the world in a wave of interior fluids. We all come from that, Ash marvelled as Mrs. M. lifted the baby onto Astrid's chest, the pain of her thirteen-hour labour erased in an instant. So small, so vulnerable. How careful we must be with children, with the remains of that fragility inside ourselves. But it's hard, handling another helpless life along with everything else. Keeping it together to do everything she needs to: clean and cook at Mrs. M.'s, be Frank's girlfriend, constantly monitor what she says, stay alert every second of every day in case the doctor decides to kidnap her again.

If he's still out there, that is. Not knowing is somehow even worse.

Counting, she sucks in a breath, *one-two-three* . . . So she can't manage Goma also, the effort to tell her things without revealing too much information. How to involve her in planning her escape while also protecting the future. It's simply too much. She needs to stall for time.

"I promise you, Goma. I promise that after the baby—"

"Goma?" her grandmother asks.

Ash's heart drops. *See?* Tiny bits of future information fall from her like dandruff; she sloughs it off unintentionally. Just the other day she slipped and said something about the presidency when she and Frank came across Charlene, the new woman in the house, watching *Home Alone 2*, and Trump was on the screen. They'd both stared at her until, finally, Frank had laughed, assuming she was joking, and Charlene said, "The future's so bright I gotta wear shades." Yes, Ash thought. Bright as a nuclear bomb. But she'd said nothing, relieved when they moved on. Now, Ash heaves a sigh.

"Can you just take me home?" she asks. It hurts. Hurts to be sitting there, watching Goma wipe her hands on a napkin, thinking about those fingernails continuing to grow in the fancy rosewood coffin that Ash's parents had chosen. Her nail polish a colourful purple dust on the casket's champagne silk lining, she imagines.

"Ripley . . ."

"It's Allison now."

Goma studies her. Ash wants to curl up and hide. She pushes the palms of her hands against the slippery polyester of the maternity slacks that Barb had given her in a box of second-hand clothes. Ugly, but something to wear, to get her through the days, and that's all that matters.

"Is your name even Ripley?"

Ash shakes her head.

"Is it Madison?"

"No." Ash has heard this, how that was almost her name but then, a few weeks before she was born, they went out looking at properties and the realtor was pushy, irritating, on her car phone half the day, and had the same name.

"Snapped her gum the entire time," her dad said, when they told her the story.

Expectantly, Goma looks at her. Ash squirms. "If I tell you, you have to—"

Goma holds up her hand, palm out, taking an oath. "I promise I won't influence your parents."

Ash nods. "It's Ash."

"Ash . . . Ashley?"

"Yes."

"Second on the list. Middle name May?"

Ash nods again. "Please don't say anything."

Goma mimes zipping her lips closed.

Her sandwich is untouched, most of the fries, too. Everything looks so greasy. The server comes to take away their plates, to package Ash's food to go. She'll reheat it later, give it to Frank.

"So, Ash, and who is Frank?"

"It's Allison."

"Okay. Under cover. Got it. Did Frank come with you?"

"No. He's . . ."

How? How can she explain who Frank is? If she tells Goma, it might impact Future Her's friendship with Leigh. Goma might keep them apart, afraid to see Frank, afraid to let something slip, and if she does let something slip . . . none of this might happen.

"I can't. He's just"—she shrugs—"a guy."

"But you've said he's the father of your child. And he's here. And you're here. And, what then . . ." Her eyes pop up to Ash's face. "Oh my God, you're not thinking of staying?"

They stare at each other. Ash does not yet know what she will do. Not anymore, not as her heart's expanding, feeding Leigh but also anchoring her in her relationship with Frank. She crosses her arms. The chocolate milk has bloated her stomach, made her feel slightly ill.

"You can't."

"I can do what I want."

Goma emits a sharp burst of laughter. "Oh, my girl. I've got news for you. Nobody's that free. We're all bound up by circumstances, by time, by tragedy, by genetics, by sheer damn luck, a whole mess of things we can't control. Governments that don't do what we want. Wars. You better get easy in the reins. Stay here, and you'll hobble more than your own life."

This, Ash knows.

Of course. Of course she knows.

But how can she leave? How can she even try to leave? Go back to the doctor's house like this, with unborn Leigh, to look for the tunnel home? What then? What will he do to keep her here, to keep Leigh? And what if she does manage to escape? Will she go back as a teenage mother, carrying Leigh's double, or will Leigh simply disappear, absorbed back into her body? And after she has Leigh? What then? Her whole being aches just thinking about it, about leaving. Right now all she can do is siphon whatever courage she has into the baby growing inside of her. After she's born, will she have any left to do what needs to be done: leave, wriggle back through the worm hole to find her own time. She is not sure.

"It's not that easy," Ash says.

"Of course not," Goma says. "You've told me nothing about the doctor, but I suspect he holds the key. Am I right?"

Reluctantly, Ash nods.

Goma presses her hands together in front of her like she's ready to say a prayer.

"Okay, then, so you came here somehow, you can go back again then, too. We just have to figure out how. And in order to do that, you need to tell me what's what. All of it, not just the bits you pick and choose in order to stay comfortable. Okay?"

Ash stabs a fork into the soggy flesh of the pickle, pushes it across her plate, away from her. "Can you please just take me home?"

WHEN THEY ARE outside Mrs. M.'s house, Goma says, "Hang on a second."

Ash stills her hand on the latch of the car door.

Goma clutches the steering wheel with both hands. Ash watches her gaze swim across the windshield as she searches for words.

"Do you know what compartmentalization is?" she says, finally.

"No. I mean, yeah, the word, but—"

"It's this thing that happens when you're living through hard things that you can't really face. Like, with Alf, my beloved. On the one hand"—she flips her right hand over so her palm faces up—"he was my best friend. Smart, creative, hilarious."

"Yeah," Ash prods.

"On the other, a raging, unpredictable drunk."

She laughs, but of course it isn't funny. Ash has never heard Goma talk about her husband, her own grandfather, like this. Like Ash is a stranger, like they're two adult women, sharing truths. Except Ash hasn't been sharing hers, not all of it.

"Tendencies not unlike, if I'm honest . . ." Her gaze flickers over to Ash, then away. "Your father's. Although, to Jim's credit, he hasn't had a single drink since that terrible scare with Zach. But if you hadn't come along . . ." She looks at Ash, eyebrows raised. Ash nods. "With that unfathomable loss, it seems to me that in your time and place, there's a possibility that you might have learned . . ."

Ash shakes her head, teeth grit. She is not listening. She does not want to talk about her father.

"Compartments," Goma says. "It's what we do. To manage. So, what I'm trying to say is that if you tell me what you need to tell me I will store it away so securely that it will never threaten anyone or anything. I'll use this ability I have, fostered from living with your grandfather, to hold both you"—she points at Ash—"and future you, my expected baby granddaughter, both together and apart. Might as well use my powers for good."

Ash doesn't answer. "Do you understand?" Goma asks.

Of course she understands. It's what she does all day, every day, placing her past from twenty years in the future into a tightly lidded box, trying to stay in the here and now, careful, always so careful, to keep the container secure. What a relief it is to be in this car with Goma who at least know her, who she is, even if Ash hasn't told her all—

"You have to tell your secrets to somebody, and I'll be damned if I let you sacrifice your whole life for the sake of . . ." She turns to look straight at Ash. "What are you? In college back there? Up there. Up ahead. Studying something?"

Ash nods.

"What?"

"Astrophysics," Ash whispers.

"Whoa," Goma says, and pats Ash's knee. "Not sure where you got those smarts."

They sit in silence for a moment.

"I'll tell you; I will. I just need time," Ash finally says. Goma looks down at Ash's hand, unconsciously cupping her belly.

"I understand," Goma says. "But don't leave it too long. I'll write down my phone—"

"I know your phone number," Ash says.

"Well, yes. I guess you would."

Ash gets out of the car, and as soon as she's able, she's in her bed, erasing the difficult afternoon with a nap.

47

THE BABY GROWS. The size of a papaya, a turnip. They call her Peach Pit, Little Bit, Munchkin, but the name that sticks, that they use most often, is simply Leigh. Of course, it is surreal. To be growing her best friend, whom she's known her whole life: how her face crumples up when she laughs, the prickle of red in her pale cheeks and high forehead when they've ridden their bikes a long way or spent too long at the beach, that scar she has on her arm from the bite of a feral cat she was feeding in the alley behind the bakery and tried to pick up when she was nine.

All of these things that exist but do not, that have rolled in on themselves and been sucked into the vacuum of Ash's own body. Clouds of particles caught in the drift of decreasing entropy until the combustion of Frank's sperm — she makes herself think Frank's, convinces herself it's Frank's — and her egg knocked time back into a forward flow. Growth instead of disintegration.

The baby grows; the days pass. The winter's snow load shrinks to crust, then dirty puddles, then a lacey blanket of frost on the rooftops before they're hit with another blizzard.

Ash loses herself inside the blur, making salads in Mrs. M.'s kitchen, walking to the supermarket for groceries, sorting the mail.

At least once a week, Goma tries to call her, but she avoids answering the phone and asks the others to tell anyone other than Frank that she isn't available. It's my crazy aunt, she says, and spins a story, another lie, the details of which evaporate from her mind as soon as they're spoken, like a swallowed aspirin leaving only a bitter tinge. They do what she asks. Ash is shielded from Goma when she never once thought in her whole life she would need to be. But, at least for now, it's protection:

✻

from the pressure to come clean, to explain, to alter her current circumstances, to plan for a future two decades ahead when she can barely see in front of her own face. She wishes it didn't have to be this way: that she could walk across town and step into her grandmother's soothing embrace, but she can't. All she can do is answer what her body demands: grow the baby. Insist that Frank stay with her for now. Lay the foundation for the future to come one minute at a time, hoping it will be mostly the same but also better, so much better, because she doesn't want to return—*but how can I not, how can I stay, how can I leave*—to what she left. That hollowed-out grief, waking up every morning with a hard nut of pain caught in her throat when she remembered that Frank was dead, Leigh so sad it was as if she had brain damage, couldn't make words, could only cry. The rest of her life might be different—Zach, alive, her parents possibly happier—but those people, while she loves them, they aren't her family anymore. This is her family. Her family is right here. In 2002, the year that she'll be born.

IT'S EARLY APRIL when Ash turns onto the sidewalk from the path in front of Mrs. M.'s house, heading out to buy some sour cream, to answer a particular craving, and yet more diapers for Astrid's baby girl. The night before she dreamed she'd given birth to a small boulder that cracked open like a geode to reveal the red, glaring face of the doctor, his overly shiny blue eyes. She nearly dropped him, the man in miniature, squalling Ash Ash Ash, but how could she? He was her baby. She felt forced to hold him, feeling inside of her the hollowed space where his entire body had been. In the morning, she remembered it, but didn't. Let it pixelate as dreams do, let it evaporate into only a feeling, and that feeling she pushed aside or tried to, but it all comes rushing back with the fear when she hears her name called.

She doesn't falter. That isn't her name anymore.

"Allison, then!" Goma shouts. Ash stops but doesn't turn around.

"We need to talk!"

"Everything all right?" Mrs. M. calls from the front porch. Standing there, staring at Goma, silver trowel hanging from a gloved hand.

"I'm okay," Ash tells her.

Goma won't stop. Not until Ash convinces her that she is okay; she has it all under control. Her plan: have the baby, go from there. That's enough right now. She crosses the road and gets into the passenger's seat of Goma's car. Mrs. M. hasn't moved. Goma gives her a slight wave, and the woman steps slowly into the house, although Ash knows she'll watch through the front window for a while, to make sure. This thought helps Ash settle as Goma twists in her seat to face her. Her eyes are stern, jaw set. When she speaks, Ash feels like she's fifteen, caught reading in her treehouse when she was supposed to be in bed.

"Listen to me, young lady. I don't know what kind of a predicament you've gotten yourself into or even if you are who you say you are. Jim thinks you're a luna—"

"You told him?" What might that do?

"No! Of course not! Only that you—" She shakes her head. "It doesn't matter. What matters is you drop into my life, tell me all these things you can't possibly know, rescue Zach, then . . ." —she lifts a hand, spins it in a circle— "all these crazy things— time travel, a wizard doctor—and then you won't even talk to me?"

Ash presses her face into her hands. A sudden, sharp pain wriggles through her head. Can time travel give you an aneurysm? She remembers something like that, in a TV show, a movie, a book, a YouTube video, somewhere in the thickets of information waiting in the years up ahead. Goma touches her wrist, draws her arm down.

"You can solve all this by being up front with me. Let me help you."

But then there's Frank, at the far end of the street, headed to her house, the distant smudge of him in his usual dark shades — black winter jacket, green army pants, marked by a blot of crimson hovering at his core. As if he's been violently injured, is confidently walking it off.

"I have to go," Ash says, making sense of the bright red. Only flowers. *It's only flowers, Hayes.* She squeezes her kneecap, feels the smooth fabric.

"No," Goma says. "You'll sit right there and listen to me."

Her scolding voice, angry at Ash for stealing the pennies, one at a time, from her grey bulldog piggy bank. The lesson that stuck with her: honesty is more important than money. Her stomach drops. Sheepish, she shrinks in her seat, crosses her arms.

"There is a fine line between waiting because it's the right course of action and avoidance. Why are you avoiding me? Why can't we hash out a plan, try to figure out how to get you home?"

Home. What is home for her? This is home. That other home is only darkness, despair. For her, personally, and for her country, the broader world, the planet. Here, all people talk about is recycling. Up there, most of the west coast is on fire. Not to mention Australia. Those images of charred koala bears. She shudders. Stares down. Maybe if she stays . . . If she gets into government . . .

"Ash," Goma says, gently. "You cannot stay."

"Why not," Ash whispers.

"Because you're already here. Not yet born, but you will be. And what about school, your dreams, your parents?"

Leigh, Ash thinks. Grieving, needing her.

"Zach, me."

"You're . . ." Ash blurts, but stops herself in time. Panicked, her eyes leap to Goma's which widen, eyebrows raised, and Ash covers her mouth with a curled fist.

"I'm sorry," she croaks. "I didn't mean, I don't . . ." A wail builds in her chest; she has to swallow it lest she make everything worse. "I can't—"

"Stop," Goma says, her voice calm. "Take a breath. In, one-two-three-four-five. Good. Out, five-four-three-two-one." Her voice is soothing. Ash reaches over, lets Goma clasp her hand. Feels her: that soft firm grip, guiding.

"There now," she says. Ash feels calmer, but then Goma starts again. "I need you to let me help. You don't belong here. I want you to take me there."

Where? The future? Does Goma think she has some sort of machine? A spinning blue phone box? A steam-punk contraption fuelled by burning coal?

"His house. The doctor's house."

Ash's mouth gapes open; she stares at Goma.

"I've been studying. You told me how it started. The snowstorm, his strange house. Clearly, the answer is there. Earlier you said he poisoned you. Maybe with a clear head, I can get a good look and . . ."

Ash is shaking her head, has been since Goma began to explain. No no no. Goma squeezes her fingers.

"Honey, I know you're scared, but you wouldn't even need to come in with me. I'll go. You'll just be there to make sure I come out."

"And what if you don't?"

"Then leave me be, drive back here, get Jim—"

"How much does he know?"

Goma sighs. "Not all of it. Nothing about time travel. To him you're just a lost girl running from some imaginary"—she makes air quotes with the fingers of her free hand—"*villain* that his bleeding-heart mother is looking out for."

Ash is relieved but then Goma continues. "Going out there is a risk, of course, but—"

"No," Ash says. Frank is closer now. His outline coming clear. The red clarifying into a clutch of roses. Is there something to celebrate? Has she forgotten something?

"It would help us, if I can just get a closer look, for thresholds, boundaries, talismans, suggestions of the way. I've joined this computer bulletin board where I can ask questions. I'll know what we're dealing with then; I can help you return to your life. Let me help—"

"My life's here." She fumbles to hook her fingers around the latch of the door.

"Ash, please, you can't possibly think you can—"

But she isn't listening. She shoves the door open, drawing Frank's eyes. He stops walking to watch her climb out of the car, cross the street to him. His eyes are on the car and not her.

"Zach's doing great," she says as she approaches, adjusting her face to an expression of pleased surprise, hiding the churning anxiety that Goma has stirred up, the horror.

"Are those for me?" she asks, gesturing at the bouquet in his hand.

48

FRANK WANTS TO do a day trip. To celebrate their seven-month anniversary. That's what the roses are for, that sit in a cut glass vase in the dining room, their colour throbbing like a location beacon as Ash lowers herself onto the bench in the foyer the next morning to tie her shoes. In a flash, he's down there, doing it for her.

"I can do things for . . ." she starts, but then he's knotting the laces on the hiking boots his sister donated to her, which barely fit her, but they're all she has.

"You okay?" he asks, leaning back on his heels.

"Fine," she snaps, as he takes her arm to help her up. She resists.

"You seem like you're mad at me."

All of these people wanting things from her. Even Mrs. M., bugging Ash to drink herbal teas she's concocted (never again!) and succumb to an examination which Ash keeps refusing — *I feel fine* — wanting to never go there again until it's absolutely necessary, sprawled on her back with somebody between her ankles, probing inside her body. Now, she's nagging her about a birth plan, learning to breathe right, toning her vaginal muscles or something. God, how she misses talking stuff over with Leigh.

"I just think we have bigger things to think about than a seven-month —"

He nods sharply. He thinks she means the baby, Ash sees, but she's also hurt him. And there's fear on his face. He's afraid. She presses down on her irritation, reaches for his hand.

"But it's sweet. Where are we going?"

"A surprise," he mutters, turning to leave the house.

✳

Outside, he opens the passenger door of the Jeep for her. A cup of herbal tea in the cup holder steams its calming peppermint scent. Next to it, a coffee for Frank. When they're settled, he hands her a CD case.

"Music for the road," he says, and she takes it, sees a sketch on the front. Her, sleeping. Her stomach churns. "Too creepy?"

It's drawn over text, on a page torn out of the Narnia book. Words — "'This must simply be an enormous wardrobe,' thought Lucy . . ." — run under pencil lines detailing the crease of her breasts, the folds of the blanket, her face, half hidden by the pillow, features unrecognizable. She always thought this was a creative choice and not one done out of impulse, with no other paper around. As a child, she stood with Leigh in her bedroom and stared at this same picture how many times? How many times before Leigh grew up, her curiosity about her mother replaced with anger. She looks up at Frank. He must read the swell of liquid in her eyes as deep pleasure, because he smiles, moves confidently. Takes the turns toward the highway that runs along the edge of Lake Superior, heading west to Duluth. She cracks open the jewel case and slides the disc into the player and Nelly Furtado croons the lyrics about being a bird, flying away. A song she heard many times as a child, belting it out with Leigh until one day Frank barged into Leigh's room and asked her, please, to turn it off. Her heart aches like a strained muscle as she sings along.

THEY GO FIRST for lunch at an Italian restaurant where Ash has lasagna, but the heartburn starts almost immediately. Frank pulls over at a convenience store to get her some Rolaids and comes back with a map drawn on the back of a receipt, but he still won't tell her where they're going.

They drive up the hill and turn into the East End, a neighbourhood full of the mansions that Leigh has always loved.

Frank's eyes flip between the hand-sketched map and the road while Ash watches the houses slide by—one with stone lions perched at the end of the path up to the massive front door, others with huge pillars, turrets, or Tudor details, another that looks like a white stucco Mexican estate. She remembers seeing big houses like these on the news when she was a kid, the real estate signs marked with bright red Foreclosure stickers, the places abandoned with everything left behind. For a moment she thinks that maybe Frank is taking her to one of these opulent places that went up in the early 1900s when only the wealthy could afford to build on the rocky terrain, but he drives them further up the hill and turns down a street that isn't as fancy, finally swinging the Jeep into the driveway of a place nearly fully blocked by overgrown cedar hedges. She smells woodsmoke when she gets out, and looks around, spotting a sliver of the lake through a gap between two houses on the other side of the road. Chickadees burst from the branches of the hedge as they move by. A dog barks, crazily, on and on, after Frank presses the doorbell. He reaches for her hand, and Ash's heartbeat speeds up. What if there's an Allison after all? What if Frank has brought her to her long-lost family? The door swings inward. A man with a long grey beard stands there, staring at them, before extending a hand to shake Frank's. The dog—a tiny Chihuahua with bloodshot eyes—bounces at his ankles, and the man nudges him away with a slippered foot.

"Here to see Elsbeth?"

Frank nods.

"Come in, come in, come in."

They step forward awkwardly, trying not to get in the way of the dog.

"Crowley, zip it!" the man scolds, then sweeps his arm out to gesture at a door marked with an ornately drawn hand, fingers pointing up, a blue eye staring out from its palm like the one on the back of Ash's neck. Where is she? She looks sideways at Frank; he's smiling. If this is a trap—*why would it be a trap?*—that would mean that Frank's in on it, in league with the doctor. She slows down.

"I'll keep it," she says, when the man offers to take her jacket. Franks steps ahead of her to open the door, revealing a dark stairwell. Ash hesitates.

"You okay?"

She doesn't answer.

"My sister came here last year," he says. "It's just for fun."

He slides a glance over to the bearded man, now holding the spitting and snarling dog. They are far from the doctor's house; there's no reason to be suspicious.

"Go on now," the man says.

Slowly, Ash moves her pregnant bulk down the stairs, descending into a room lit by strands of lights, the bright squares of ground-level windows. In the corner, a dim floor lamp illuminates a woman dressed in purple velour track pants, a long black cardigan. Her head is shaved, and as they move closer, Ash sees the white marks of scars in her short bristle, scattered around her ear like a constellation. Her sparkling eyes are circled with heavy eyeliner, and her laugh lines crinkle as she reaches both hands out to Ash. Reluctantly, Ash slips hers into the woman's grip, and Elsbeth holds them gently, thumbs stroking, staring intently into Ash's eyes.

"You must be Allison?" The question in her voice triggers a prickle of sweat in Ash's armpits, but she nods, glances over at Frank, who is slipping away, moving toward a long leather couch in front of a coffee table covered with books and magazines. Elsbeth beckons her to a round table, a heavy glass ball in the centre, like the one the Wicked Witch looked into in *The Wizard of Oz*, watching everything as it happened, seeing beyond, into past memories.

Her pulse has quickened. Everything in her says to leave, get out, get away, but what can she do? Make up some story, another lie, about her strictly religious father, how he beat her when he found her reading *Harry Potter*—wait! Has *Harry Potter* even been published yet?—and instilled in her a fear of sorcery, irrational, just like her paranoia about having her picture taken? Or something simpler? Nausea, feeling faint... Panic blurs the options, and then Elsbeth is speaking.

"Go on, then," she says, so Ash sinks reluctantly into the hard chair, spreading her legs to better accommodate the squirming bump that is Leigh, already so big, bound to be a hefty baby. Part of her wants to know. Wants someone to look at her clearly, tell her everything's going to be all right, that there's a path ahead even if she can't see it.

Elsbeth removes the crystal ball. In its place, she spreads a black placemat, embroidered with glittering stars and the moon in its eight phases. She pulls a deck of cards from the pocket of her cardigan and starts to shuffle them.

"Allison," Elsbeth says. Is it her imagination, or does Ash see a wrinkle of confusion in the woman's forehead? She drops her gaze, cups the space from her missing finger in her left hand, and nods.

"Okay," she says, still shuffling. "And you have a question?"

"Actually..." Why not? What can it hurt? What are the chances that this woman is an authentic psychic? "I have a lot of questions."

"What's the most pressing one?" She sets the deck down on the block of fabric. "Don't tell me. Just hold it in your mind."

Leigh. Will Leigh be all right. But then there is the question of home. Will she stay? Will she go?

"When you're ready, split the cards into three piles."

Will she destroy everything she's ever known?

"Take a deep breath, if that helps. Clear your mind."

She draws air into her nose, smells incense, musky patchouli, then exhales as she cuts the deck. Elsbeth picks up the piles, slides them back together and begins again to shuffle but the cards tumble out of her hands, fanning out on the table, dropping to the floor.

Her eyes jump up to Ash's face, then away. Embarrassed, Ash sees, and Elsbeth grunts as she bends over to pick them up. She sorts them again into a single stack, shuffles, then lays down the deck.

"Let's try that again."

Once more, Ash divides the deck into three piles. Elsbeth gathers them up and begins again to shuffle and again the cards erupt out of her hands, this time launching across the carpet.

"This has never happened to me before," she says. She stares at Ash like Ash might harm her. Like it's she who's the villain, not the victim. Abruptly, she stands up, and calls over to Frank, who's behind her, whose reaction Ash can't see.

"Of course, you don't have to pay," says Elsbeth. Ash stays seated. In front of her, on the table, a single card stares up. A naked man, hanging upside down from an ankh by one foot. Arms outstretched, palms nailed to what look like green lily pads. Ash reaches out to push it away, touches the card's background, its illustrated grid of blue and yellow. Elsbeth turns toward her movement.

"Stagnation," she murmurs.

How do you think you can live a normal life?

"Stuck in illusion . . ."

When nothing about you is normal at all?

" . . . And by the looks of this"—Elsbeth gestures at the cards scattered everywhere—"there's great energy which will need to be dispelled before you can freely find your way."

All of this she says kindly. Even so, they are then quickly escorted upstairs. Frank goes ahead, moving across the front porch, keys in hand. Ash steps onto the welcome mat, and the woman's fingers close around her wrist.

"You don't belong here, do you?" she hisses, before Ash wrenches free, runs toward the Jeep.

"THAT WAS WEIRD," Frank says, as they drive east for home.

"Totally," Ash answers, then turns away, leans against the locked door. She stares out at the blur of forest passing by. He turns the music down, the heat up.

How can she hold him hostage to this, to her strange, unnatural existence?

It's impossible.

What will happen when she and Leigh—other she, the she-to-be-born in June—meet, become best friends? How will she ever explain her resemblance to Teresa and Jim's daughter? Would Teresa be suspicious of her, thinking . . . She shudders. She and Frank and baby Leigh will have to move away. Never come back.

Look for what's possible, Goma has always said.

She's right, except the possibilities are very narrow.

Ash needs help.

To figure out what to do, to make a plan.

To fully trust her grandmother, as she had in her other life. She wouldn't have hesitated back then, would have gone to Goma in an instant to ask for advice. Trust yourself, Ash; learn to calm your nerves, Ash; think things through; hunt for paths out; learn about portals, magic, marked thresholds, because of course she knew.

Goma knew.

But how?

Because little her, the her whom Teresa will—fingers crossed—give birth to in a few months hasn't gone through this before.

Unless she has.

Unless...

The shock of the sudden understanding makes Ash jump. She knocks her forehead against the glass, feels the hardness of her skull bone.

"You okay?"

But she doesn't answer. Can't answer. Mind scurrying.

A loop.

Could it be that her entire life is a time loop?

That she, Goma, all of them simply keep living this again, again, again, again?

Like that *Buffy the Vampire Slayer* episode when she keeps running into the magic store's basement to fetch a zombie hand for a customer until she realizes she's stuck in a loop and figures out how to break the repetition.

Slay something. Kill a demon. Untangle the mystery with her team.

But Ash has no team.

Except for Goma.

"Penny for your thoughts?"

She draws in a shuddering breath, feels Frank lightly touch her knee.

"I don't..." Ash starts.

Because Frank... is Frank caught, too? Stuck on repeat? War, death, war, death, war.

"... think you should enlist."

It's their first fight. The first time they've returned to this topic since the night at the cabin when she'd told him about Leigh.

They hammer through the first bit, "Yes, I should; no, you shouldn't," until the heat abates, and he breathes out, almost whining, still a teenager, "But why?"

She stutters around the truth, finally stating, simply: "Things are not as they appear."

"What the hell does that mean?"

Ash struggles for words; a fish, out of its element, gasping for air.

"You don't think I can do it."

"Of course, I do! You can do it; you can do anything," she lies. Frank is into science fiction, Dungeons & Dragons, special effects. If he were her age, in her time, he'd be learning to code, building elaborate digital landscapes, trading Bitcoin, never mind the complications.

He never should have gone to war.

His gaze pulses on the road straight ahead.

"You don't believe in me."

"I do. I do believe in you, baby," she says. He is a baby. Here, they're pretty much the same age but she feels eons, decades older.

"Why shouldn't I go? We were attacked. It was an attack. Why shouldn't I be part of the response? I'm not a coward."

"Of course you're not! I didn't say that! You fought hard for your whole . . ." She stops, shakes her head. "It isn't . . . There are things that you—"

"What are you talking about?"

She doesn't answer. The heartburn has returned. A knife in her throat jabbing at that burning wound of sorrow.

"Anyway, it's a path, right? I could go overseas for a while and then to college. I could become an engineer." He looks over at her. "You think I want to work at a gas station for my whole life, be that, only that for our . . ." He flips his knuckles, gesturing at her belly.

That was the plan, she remembers. For him and Allison. Her. Other her. But it had never come to be. Allison gone and Frank too damaged; too ill; on disability for the rest of his life.

"She won't care," Ash mutters. "She'll love you—"

"No, but I care," Frank says. "I care. I want to be something bigger, something more. I want to serve my country."

It's as if she's told him who he'll become, and he's arguing for another chance at it, at the same choices he'd already made: to be a hero, to pledge himself to a broader cause. She's relieved when they enter the long tunnel through the Silver Creek Cliff and darkness falls over them. How tiny. How tiny their lives must be if they are indeed caught in this repetition, ants on a Möbius strip.

Can she do it? Compartmentalize. Separate her future self from this past. Allow Frank his own path. Her eyes smart. The Jeep is filled with a hard tension; finally, she turns to him, as they get closer to the spot of light.

"I'm sorry," she croaks. "I'm just scared. I just don't want to lose —"

"Of course, you are," Frank blurts. "Of course, and you won't, I promise that you won't. I will always be here for —"

She bursts into tears as they emerge, her eyes dazzled by the sudden light. Weeping, for him, Leigh, future pain, broken countries, so much death, her own lost self, so much, so huge, that Frank pulls over at the scenic viewpoint and holds her, rocking her until she is empty. When she stops, eyes stinging, face wet, he says, softly, "Look."

Ash twists to see a pair of eagles against the lake's white and steel blue, dropping fast in their courtship dance. Clutching bright yellow talons, spiralling, joined, in freefall. Trusting what they know to do.

49

ASH KEEPS TO her room over the next several days. Frank is busy at work, picking up shift after shift to make money for first and last month's rent on the apartment she wonders if she'll ever see. She leaves the turret only to do her chores and eat meals, mostly in silence, with Mrs. M. and the others. She feels Mrs. M.'s eyes on her, studying, attempting to see into her mind. For so long, Ash has thought that only she could give her secret away, only her words, her actions. She hadn't counted on being pinpointed by the same sort of magic that had landed her here in the first place. Elsbeth, the psychic: *you don't belong here,* echoing exactly what Goma had said, and neither of them are wrong. That's the shitty part. They're absolutely right.

Even though belonging, weirdly, is what she feels most of all. Braided to this time and place by Leigh's sturdy roots. But she doesn't; she is far, far from home. She's not in Kansas anymore.

In the living room at Mrs. M.'s, Ash sits down to wait for Astrid to get off the phone. She needs to call Goma.

It's time.

Time to lay out all the details, set them out like the artifacts in the curio cabinet back home: the muskrat skull, the ashes of her brother in the orange-black vase, the fossilized sea shell, the—

She starts, shoulders jerking in surprise.

The opal!

Glowing like a miniature nebula, inside its own glass box, in the curio cabinet.

So much like the one nested in the doctor's chest hair.

Somehow taken from him, in another version of this reality that she keeps living over and over again.

But why? Does it hold his power?

✳

Can it help her get home? Had it helped her?

Surely even if she's killed the doctor, the opal is still there, somewhere in his house unless — her head swims; she wraps her arms around herself; how could she have been so stupid? How could she not have realized this before?

Unless Lucille has buried him with it. She can imagine that.

Strange Lucille taking days to dig a big enough hole. Using all her strength to tip him into it.

A shiver surges through her.

Zombie hand, looping railway track, Möbius strip.

"Ally." Her name, spoken by Astrid, breaks her out of her thoughts. "I said I'm done."

She groans, gets up, and stretches the spiralling cord to sit down at the table, then Leigh kicks hard, a blow against her liver or appendix, some tender, invisible organ. Ash lowers her head into the nest of her arms. Mrs. M.'s warm hand presses on Ash's back.

"Getting ready," she says. "The baby. Exercising her new muscles."

Ash sits up. "I'm okay."

She has to be. Has to do this. Needs to tell Goma everything, get her help, make a plan, investigate, even if the thought of it, of going back there, to that house, implants a hard knot of fear beside Leigh.

On the third ring, her father answers.

"Hello?" he says a second time, as Ash fumbles for words: "Mrs. Hayes, please?"

"Can I ask who's calling?"

"Allison." She starts to spin a story. "I wanted to ask her—"

But it isn't necessary. The phone clunks down. Onto the wooden table with the attached seat. The gossip table, her grandmother called it. Ash pictures it. How Goma will sit there to talk to Ash. The look on her face as she listens. She pulls the handset away from her face. What is she doing? Is she crazy? Crazy to think of agreeing to go back there, to the doctor's, intentionally returning like some sort of obsessed Nancy Drew. Why would she do that? How can she?

The voice erupts into Ash's ear. "Ash? Allison! I'm so glad you called. Hello? Hello?"

She holds her breath. Hovering between actions, already knowing which way she'll turn. She wants that. Only this: here, now, her feet on the ground, the landscape as seen through her limited human perception, this world as one of many. Locality.

Even if there are a million hers, particles ricocheting into every conceivable path, this her, right here, right now, wants only this: to simply try to talk to her grandmother.

But it's hard.

"I have to . . ." she starts. Her mouth is dry.

"Please let me help you."

Ash doesn't move, wanting to hang up but not wanting to. Needing to. Knowing she can't.

"Tell me why you called."

"I . . ." The opal, stuck in her mind like a moon that never really disappears, is only hidden by the sun.

"I'm coming over," Goma says, and hangs up, leaving Ash standing there, tears hot in her eyes.

50

GOMA PICKS HER UP, and they go to the park beside the high school where she and Leigh will meet for playdates as toddlers, hide out in the hollow red slide as teenagers, backs pressed together, staring at their phones. Goma sits beside her on a bench facing the lake as Ash tells her what happened: locked out of her house, the drugged teas, the treatments, the inseminations, the surreal and horrid trip to the Arctic. And, especially, the opal.

Goma listens, steadily, Ash alert to her breathing, her every twitch. It's hard to pull out the words. They are sticky, coated in thorns, bound to her insides like burrs. Goma's hand is lain on top of hers on the planks of the bench, and Ash feels her heat, even in her absent finger, as Goma plucks the truth out of her, one bit at a time. When Ash is finished, she looks down at the bump of Leigh, pushes the toes of her boots into the frozen mix of sand, snow, cigarette butts.

"It's not your fault," Goma says. "Listen to me, and always hold this close: what he did to you is not your fault. He's a monster."

Ash collapses sideways, into the warm crook of Goma's arm, and pulls in a deep breath—Goma's pear perfume, the fresh smell of distant open water—and tells her the rest.

"So," Goma says, when she's done, "he's wearing the opal, but it's also—"

"In our curio cabinet."

"How?"

"Replicated, I guess? From a previous loop?"

"Wouldn't there be more of them then? If time is indeed circling . . ." She presses her fingertips against her brow, rubs the furrowed skin.

✳

"Maybe, unless..."

"Go on."

"Previous loops had different outcomes."

Goma heaves a sigh. "Oh, sweet Jesus, how are we even talking about this like it's possible?"

Ash doesn't answer. She recalls the paper about life being a computer simulation, the simplicity of its threaded argument: if one thing is true, then this; if another, then this... If the world has advanced into technological maturity, then, yes, we're probably just part of a huge video game. Maybe that's what's happened to her. A thread in the story. Some twisted programmer having a bit of fun.

"You're sure it's the same pendant?" Goma asks.

Ash nods. "Pretty sure."

"But not a hundred percent?"

She shakes her head.

Goma turns to face her full on. "Maybe he stole it from your house. Maybe when you were drugged, he went —"

"Please don't say that." She can't think about that, about him in the night — what? — murdering her parents?

"Well, this is a bit far-fetched, Ash. A loop —"

"Goma, I'm here in 2002, when I'm actually about to be born. I'm not making this up. I can tell you things —"

"But you won't." Her eyes give a pulse of warning.

"No," Ash says. "I won't."

They stare out at the far horizon, a solid thread between the slate grey lake and the lighter overcast sky, and slowly start to hatch a plan. Go to the doctor's, give Goma a look around, let her try to figure out where the portal might be hidden, perhaps get the opal. It's frail, barely a plan at all, but it's all they have. Ash will stay in the car, guarding herself and Leigh, Goma's tiny revolver on her lap, loaded, ready to use if she has to. She doesn't want to do it, none of it; wishes Goma could go by herself, but of course that isn't an option either. This is her mess, and somehow she has to fix it. Her biggest fear, though, is that what he said is true: that all roads lead back to him, and that he is a dead end.

51

THE DOCTOR'S YARD has been tidied. The wrecked Grinch hauled off the lawn, leaving a shadow of dead grass. Only the nativity scene remains, or part of it: tumbled down cedar logs shedding their bark, straw a thick mat spread over the beaten earth floor. She'd wanted to curl up in there, that first night. To climb inside the now-missing cradle and sleep. Maybe that would have been better. Her hand, the one mutilated by the doctor, presses the gun's smooth barrel against the dome of her belly as the car comes to a rumbling stop at the top of the gravel driveway.

"Not too close," Ash says, and Goma shifts into reverse, lets the car slide back, closer to the road.

"You okay," she asks as she cranks up the emergency brake.

No, Ash wants to tell her. Her entire body is tingling, shivering, telling her to run. Goma reaches into the back to tug on a blanket that's piled next to Zach's car seat, and Ash wraps it around herself. It isn't cold out. It's a warm spring day, yet her veins are full of slush.

"I don't think I can do this," Ash murmurs, and Goma snaps a look at her.

"Of course you can. You didn't do anything. It's him who should be scared, the animal, if he's still in there, in his dirty den." She makes a sound like a growl. "You can hold your head up high. Anyway, you'll stay in the car, and I'll . . ."

"That's the plan?"

Goma nods. "Like we said: I'll look for marked thresholds, suggestions of portals, magical stuff."

"Magical stuff." Ash's voice sounds flat. They both know she is very new at this, has been frantically digging through every resource—the library, listservs—to try to learn. Ash has told

✸

her some of the things that Goma will teach her in the future—portals, familiars—but, in truth, most of the time she wasn't really listening.

She's also explained the images of the doctor she'd seen on the very slow internet, but that isn't any help. Sure, the doctor might be immortal, and therefore likely not dead from Ash's flimsy stabbing, but that doesn't point them to the pathway for her to get home. It only tells them that he has power, a lot of it, which Ash and Goma already know.

"What if you don't—"

"Wait one hour and no more," Goma says. "Lock the doors. Can you shimmy over into the driver's seat?"

She pulls the latch, pushes the door open. The hinge squeals. Ash flinches.

"I love you, my girl," Goma says, and Ash says, "Wait."

It should be her. She is the one who doesn't belong here. She's been so fixated on making sure Leigh is okay and Frank survives, and caught up, too, in the flood of love she feels for them both, that she hasn't given enough thought to her own unborn self. If Goma goes in and never comes out, she won't ever know her. She feels a howl build, an urge to scream. *Come back!* But Goma marches purposefully up to the front door. Does she even have a weapon? A small, secret switchblade to puncture his liver if he gets too close? Fear bristles the tiny hairs on Ash's arms. Goma should have taken the gun, she thinks, setting it on the dashboard before awkwardly hoisting her thick abdomen over the cup-holders and the emergency brake to drop into the driver's seat. Easier to get out and walk around, of course, but she's not setting foot on this ground. No way.

Goma's on the front step. It's cluttered with cardboard boxes that weren't there before. The leg of Ash's old pink jogging pants drapes out of one of them, its cuff stained with dark mud. Goma glances down, then crouches to get a closer look at the engraved letters on the door's wooden threshold that Ash herself had touched, had examined, when she tried to escape the first time. Then Goma stands, tries the knob, but of course it's locked. Ash holds her breath when she pushes the doorbell, sinks down into the seat. She holds both hands over the back of her neck, elbows covering her face, fingers concealing the eye that doesn't seem to work, which has maybe faded away, since Frank's never noticed it. It takes a while, but then the door opens. And there he is. Hale and hearty, as her grandmother might say. Ash lets out a tiny cry. He's dressed in paint-splattered jeans, his face hovering in the black crack like the moon. Her heart beats hard. She shrinks lower, the steering wheel pressing painfully against her breasts.

"Be careful, Goma," she murmurs as the doctor smiles that sweet grin. The one that made Ash trust him. That, and the teas of course, shoved at from the very beginning by Lucille.

He steps back into the darkness of the house, opening the door wider. The wisp of Lucille behind him, a tiny light glinting off her glasses. Goma steps inside. The door closes. Ash can hardly breathe.

52

"I TOLD HIM I was a real estate agent," Goma says, half an hour later. Ash has spun the car into a U-turn, then gunned it out of there, tires spitting gravel. But they aren't running; there's no need. Only Goma had emerged from the house, the doctor a shadow, watching from the door — *I shouldn't have come! I shouldn't have come!* — as Goma walked jauntily down the driveway and climbed into the passenger's side. Ash feels the prickle in the back of her neck, half expects to be rear-ended by the blue van by the time they reach the stop sign at the main highway.

"A client of mine was interested in his house, I told him. He said he wasn't selling, but I asked could I take a look around anyway, just in case." She swivels in the seat to face Ash full on. The forest slides by, smears the windows with darkness. Night is coming on.

"He didn't seem nervous at all," she says brightly. Her brow is oily with sweat, accentuating the glow on her face.

"Are you all right?" Ash asks. Goma ignores the question.

"They were in the midst of painting a room, him and that bubbly little —"

"Lucille," Ash says.

"Anyway, I asked him about all the boxes just to make conversation, just while I was looking around, and he said he's a collector. Asked if I thought there'd be a market in town for a shop of rare collectibles and antiques. Better to do that in the city, I told him, and he said, I like it out here, tucked into this pleat. That's the word he used. I think he meant time. A pleat of time." She pauses, then mutters, "Maybe he's a time lord."

Ash whips a glance at her. "What? Like in *Doctor Who*?"

"I know, it's ridiculous. It's all beyond the pale."

✷

THE LONGEST NIGHT

She shakes her head. Doubt, again. Ash has seen it before. When she told Goma about the polar bear, the railroad loop, she'd said, "Wait. Maybe a dream? A drugged hallucination?"

"He seemed quite gracious," Goma says now. "Insisted I have a cup of tea before I could wander around, and Lucille had just baked cookies. Nutty and delicious." Her eyes flicker to Ash, bright but uncertain. "I tried to . . . Honestly, Ash, he seems like such a—"

Ash slams on the brakes, the rear of the car fishtailing as she aims it for the side of the road. Clutching the seatbelt, Goma goes silent, understanding opening her face. She stares at Ash, frightened. "Oh my God, I wasn't . . ."

"Make yourself throw up," Ash says, checking the rearview, seeing nothing but the empty road. He would not be following because he's already followed, some sticky part of him sloshing around in Goma's belly.

"Do it!"

"How—"

Ash shoves a finger in her mouth, demonstrating. "Get it down your throat, tickle that little thing at the back. Go on!"

Goma flings her door open, does what Ash says. "Deeper!" Ash shouts, and finally a cloudy green liquid spews out of her, steaming, chunky with some sort of nuts. Ash presses her palm against Goma's spine.

"Once more," she says, looking over Goma's shoulder. The next mess is a heap of what looks like mushy bread and bright red jam. And on top, a coil of inky black viscous bile. "What on earth," Goma mutters, and they both stare at it before Ash tells her to shut her door and hits the gas and they leave it behind.

GOMA'S DIFFERENT AFTER that; slower, heavier, more somber. Her face pasty, forehead a matte pale pink. They stop at the convenience store, and Ash buys a banana and a small carton of chocolate milk to coat her stomach, get her blood sugar back up.

"He knew who I was," she says, as they continue driving. "Called me Goma. Told me to give you his best. Congratulations, he said, and Lucille—"

"His flying monkey," Ash mutters.

"Pardon?"

She shakes her head, but Goma says, "Like in Oz?"

Ash nods. Goma's gaze drifts as she continues talking. "Well, she couldn't stop smiling, like some sort of Stepford wife. You know that story."

"No," Ash says. Goma reaches out and strokes her forearm even as Ash grips the steering wheel, foot over the break as they coast down the hill into town. Goma's fingers move up and down, up and down, like when Ash was little and couldn't get to sleep. She isn't surprised that he knows. Terrified, yes, but not surprised. It's like he's put a tracker on her. Inserted a microchip into one of the sutures on her hand. Maybe she emits some sort of signal, whatever it was that made the tarot reader's cards explode out of her hands. She and Frank could move. They'll have to move eventually. New York City. Hide inside that vibrant metropolis. But then, she'll be giving up on ever getting home, sacrificing her friendship with Leigh, altering everything she's ever known.

"He seemed to mean it," Goma says. "Maybe he's given you up. He seemed like a very charming..."

Ash pulls away; glares at Goma. "That's how he does it. That's how he convinces you. Did he show you the basement? The treatment room?"

Goma nods.

"That's where he..."

She can't say it. Not again. Not twice in one day. "All in the name of fixing me, making me better, all explained in a soothing, quiet voice while I was hella cooked on those concoctions."

"Pardon?"

"Drugged. I mean, drugged. Like you just were."

She turns toward Mrs. M.'s place, then pulls over to the side of the road, across from her future (and past) elementary school.

"Well, it seemed like a professional set-up," Goma says, as Ash shuts the car off. "Peaceful, even, with that painting of the old wooden door. What do they call that? Trompe Loyal?"

Is Goma doubting her? Can Ash not even trust her? In a small voice, she says, "You believe me, right?"

"Oh, honey, oh my God, of course." She shakes her head, sharply, then rubs both palms against her forehead.

"Fuck him," she hisses, and Ash gasps. She can't remember ever hearing Goma swear. A pleasant heat rises in her chest at seeing Goma this way, enraged at the doctor for his trickery, his manipulation, his silent poisoning.

"He's so sneaky, and so very convincing. It must have taken you so much strength to get yourself out of there. I can't imagine. I don't know how..."

Goma's voice fades out. Clearly the drugs are still in her system. Her pupils slightly shrunken, her head moving loosely on her neck. The feeling comes back to Ash: that easy, warm flow like all you had to be was a plant, following the yellow heat of the sun. She turns the key in the ignition to drive Goma back home. There, she'll call Frank to come get her. A solid dose of normalcy will do her good: him and her, and isn't *Firefly* on tonight?

"I saw sigils too, carved symbols. The word from sigillum, which means seal. In the threshold, the same as the ones in the frame of the painting."

"In the basement?"

"Yes. Mandala-like, that field at the centre. The distant house." Her words are clipped. Ash remembers that. How hard it was to make words.

"And the girl in the foreground," Ash says.

Goma clears her throat, presses the hand holding the balled Kleenex, strange seed at its core, against her clavicle. "No girl."

"No girl?"

She shakes her head. "Tall grass. Lit golden by the setting, maybe rising, sun. Striking."

"And the snow?"

"No snow."

Changes. More changes she doesn't understand. She signals, swings into Goma's driveway, her mind pulling away to thoughts of her life, her normal existence, beyond the container where she stores the details of her actual, bizarre reality. It's how she's been surviving, after all. Maybe she can sneak Frank up to her room tonight. The cot at the cabin has become too small and, anyway, she can't stay out all night; Mrs. M. won't have it. That's part of the agreement, with a curfew of eleven o'clock, too. As if having sex will alter anything; it's not like she can layer another baby on top of Leigh. A yawn overtakes her; she can't stop it.

"And I heard something."

"The humming," Ash says.

Goma nods. "Just the furnace, he told me."

Ash nods, trying to stifle another yawn. She's so tired.

"Pretty loud furnace," Goma mutters, and Ash remembers the sound, throbbing up through the floor as she had lain in that bed. Bed. She needs sleep, urgently, right now. Leigh needs her to sleep.

FRANK IS NEARBY, playing pool with a friend from work. He says he'll be over soon to pick her up, and Ash swallows the last of her peppermint tea, finishes the toast and raspberry jam Goma made for her and wipes her mouth. They've been talking about the rest of it: the opal a slight hump concealed by his shirt; Zeuxis, the cat, who wasn't around; even the piano music which

Goma says she can still hear in her head. There is not very much to go on: no obvious gaping holes signposted as the way back to 2020, to home, and Goma is slurring her words, head nodding as they sit at the table.

Ash helps Goma into her bed, eyes smarting as she remembers her grandmother before they took her to the hospital and she was put on the ventilator, so sick it was like her bones had been sucked out of her fragile, papery skin. She kisses her—already asleep, breathing heavily—then returns to the kitchen to clean up, turning to drop her napkin into the trash under the sink. Only one thing else is in the garbage bag: a red-and-white box of Basic cigarettes, flipped open, almost entirely full. Her father's continuing battle to quit. She wonders if he's actually done it this time. Just in case, she reaches in to pull out the smokes. Even though she wants him to quit, it'll be a gift for Frank; they can use the saved cash.

53

THE BABY GROWS. The size of a coconut, a cantaloupe, a pineapple poking at her bladder, her sciatic nerve. She cannot get comfortable. Mrs. M. relents and lets Frank spend time with Ash in her room after his shift finishes at four in the afternoon, or eight in the morning if he's working nights. They sip herbal tea and sit and stare at the heaps of stuff that Barb has been gathering, sourced from yard sales and classified ads and from a friend of hers who had a baby the year before. The boxes remind Ash of the doctor's house, and, just like she did there, she feels drugged and distant, uncertain how to dig through to figure out what she needs. What does she need? Frank is clear on this: an apartment, a place of their own. Money. Yes, money.

"I saw a few ads," he tells her one day, sitting in the hard and creaky rocking chair in her room. "There's a place in a house that backs onto Devil's Fork Creek. It's a basement. Why don't we go—"

"I can't," Ash says.

"Why not?"

She shrugs. She's used the same excuse so many times: Mrs. M. needs her here, she has to bake bread, clean the bathrooms, help the other women. Frank levels a stare at her, waiting. Finally, he says, "Is it me? Do you not want to—"

"What? No! God, no! I love you!"

"You do?"

"What do you mean?"

"I mean you seem pretty happy here." He swings his arm out in a wide gesture: the bed she's lying on with its white iron frame, the dresser with crystal knobs and sticky drawers, the curved windows letting in an oily light. "It seems like you've got everything you need to make a nice little nest, just you and Leigh."

✳

Ash swings her legs off the bed, sits up.

"I've been holding off waiting to enlist, but I'm starting to wonder why. Maybe I should have just gone on with my life. I'd be over there now, helping to set some things right, making a difference instead of busting my ass at a stupid, demeaning... for somebody who..." He chuckles, dryly. "For nobody. Miss nobody." His voice cracks. "Oh shit," he mutters.

Never before has Ash felt such a strong desire to lay it all out, explain everything, the whole painful future, the entire chaotic present. "I want to tell you something," she says, squeezing the edge of the mattress with both hands.

He looks at her. It's sad Frank, but twenty years younger. Without his green eyes hunting for something to say to his daughter to make it all right, because they'd shared every sadness, hadn't they? When they put down their cat Yoda's mom, Crystal, after she was hit by a car; when Frank's parents died within a few months of each other; when Leigh's first crush, Marcel, dumped her for somebody else. All of it, he'd shared with her, except for the deepest darkness inside his heart, the damage done by that war. That, he'd held inside, so it spread like an untreated cancer, taking over his life.

Ash clears her throat, searches for words.

"I have a friend whose dad died. They were really close, just her and him. Her mother... I don't know what happened," she lies, "but she wasn't around. Anyway, he died."

She hesitates. How much truth can she—*fuck it, Hayes; tread lightly, Hayes*. Voices collide in her head. Beneath them all, Leigh, molecules gathering inside of her like an infant star: bones, blood, flesh, that steadily beating heart beneath her own.

"He killed himself."

Frank's face pinches, an echo of empathetic pain.

"He'd been in the war."

"Which war?" he asks.

Ash's mind swims back, back. What wars does she know: Afghanistan, Syria, all the many mass shootings which feel like war: Sandy Hook, Orlando, Las Vegas.

"Iraq?" Frank asks.

"Iraq..." she mutters, trying to remember tenth grade social studies. She did an essay on the Rwandan genocide while Leigh did...

"Desert Storm," she blurts. Frank cocks his head, forehead furrowing.

"That must have been hard."

Ash nods.

"More into the Ninja Turtles than global conflicts, I bet." He starts humming a tune, gazing at Ash, trying to lighten the mood, she supposes. He watches her, expectant, but she can't join in, doesn't know it. He drops his gaze, goes silent. A blankness hangs between them until he lifts his head, crosses his arms.

"I'm sorry for your friend, her dad, but of course there's a cost. It isn't like I don't know that there might be a cost."

But what if it's for nothing, Ash thinks. And based on a big lie. They sit there, staring at one another, Leigh invisible between them. Ash pulls in a long breath. There's no way around it. "If something happens," she says. "To me, I mean. Promise me—"

"What's going to happen?"

"Promise me you'll stay with Leigh."

He squints at her, suspicious.

"Just in case," she says.

"In case of what?"

Ash shrugs. She doesn't know how to answer. It's looking less and less likely that she will ever get home. Nothing is coming out of Goma's research. The other day she'd called to say she found something, but it was only the definition of one of the carved symbols. A rune called Dagaz. Marking liminal spaces, thresholds between worlds. The time of Dagaz is June 14 to the 28, Goma told her, with Ash's birthday, the summer solstice, right there in the middle. But it didn't mean much to her: she tried all the thresholds—the front door and the garage, even the sliding glass door off the dining room—and none had returned her to her proper time and place.

"Do I need to be worried about you?" Franks asks. "Are you thinking of—"

"No," Ash says. "No, no, no." She presses her lips together, gathering courage. "It's just . . ."

"Yeah?"

Fuck it.

"We're going back there. To Iraq."

Frank's mouth opens. He stares at her. "How do you . . ." He leans forward, hands gripping the handles of the rocking chair, his voice hushed. "Are you in the CIA?"

"What?" They've been watching *Alias*, waiting whole weeks between episodes. She shakes her head, suppressing a laugh.

"Seriously, what's in Iraq? How do you know—"

"Nothing. That's the point. I did an . . ."

Essay, she was about to say. And what else? Fell down the rabbit hole of research into what actually happened after you helped me—you, with your messed up head and your bit of shrapnel excavated from your own body. The whole thing had made her so crazy: how long the government had known that a threat existed, how much they dismissed it. The same way Trump's government has been dismissing domestic terrorists. She ranted about it all to Leigh before Leigh had asked her to stop, not wanting to know about the statistics from the *New York Times*: forty-four thousand soldiers wounded, one in five coming back home with depression, brain injuries, PTSD, like Frank. What's done is done, Leigh had said. "Nothing can make my dad different."

Ash stopped talking about it and helped Leigh with her stuff: making an anatomically correct heart with papier mâché that lit up with an interior strip of LEDs. They skipped school on Fridays for Future. They took the vow that's now been broken.

"Promise me," Ash says.

"You seem to know a lot. How—"

"Just—" her voice rises. She can't help its edge of panic. "Promise me you won't enlist, that you'll stay with Leigh."

"Why are you still talking like this?"

Ash shakes her head. She's reached her limit. Nothing else can be said.

"I can't do it," Frank says.

"Pardon?"

"Ally, I can't."

He stands up and comes to her, sits close beside her on the bed, their thighs touching.

"Nothing's going to happen to you, and enlisting is the best bet for us. Do you know how much we'll have to borrow for the hospital?"

"I'm having the baby here. It's already been arranged."

"What if something goes wrong, and we need to get an ambulance?"

He slides his hand onto her knee, squeezes it, reassuring. "Nothing will, of course. Nothing. But there's first and last, too, and diapers, and the Jeep, and all of the rest of the stuff—"

"I know," Ash whispers and leans against him. He puts his arm around her, pulls her close. Daylight swells in the curved window, golden, the sky slowly transitioning to the rosy hue of dusk. The days are getting longer.

Is this how her mother had felt?

Ash, her second unexpected baby, holding her in time and place? Grief from Zach's death, and then an infant, and her own established life keeping her where she was: job, husband, house being built, years going by, and then a teenage daughter with expensive ambitions.

Everyone is, in a way, trapped, Ash thinks: by the era they are born into, the random occurrences of history, their own past traumas. She happens to live in a time when people think that accidents don't happen: the pandemic must be a grand scheme designed by governments instead of a mutation of nature, but everyone—Frank, her parents, Leigh, Goma—is contained just like she is: within their own timeline, their own circumstances. Hers just happens to have been twisted up—the chaos of life meeting the doctor's evil power.

He's somehow above it all.

While they are all swimming in the choppy sea, the doctor is surfing the waves.

There's nothing more she can say. What will be will be. Her body ragdolls against Frank until finally he says, "Sleep now. We'll talk more later." He leaves her in the quiet peace of the turret, staring out at the darkening sky.

54

THE BABY GROWS. The size of a meteor, a small planet, or so it feels to Ash.

The days are getting nicer, spring spreading out, but all Ash can do is waddle between the rooms of the house, out onto the front porch to sit with a book from the shelf in the living room. She's chuckling at the neuroses of Bridget Jones one afternoon when the phone rings and somebody yells, "Ally!"

It's Goma, her voice eager. "Can I come over? I've found something!"

Ash sighs. It's taken her an eternity simply to get from the creaking wicker chair on the verandah to the phone. All day she's been feeling off: rumbling gas, cramps, whispers of pain, her pelvis shifting, but it's a full three days before Leigh's birthday, enough to change who she will be, so Ash tells herself it isn't time, these aren't contractions, refusing to believe the warning tremors and subnivean shifts.

You cannot come out, Leigh, she mutters, and partly, she knows, she means *ever*. Because the truth is, she's terrified.

Goma says, "Do you know what trompe l'oeil means?"

Ash lowers a hand to her belly, covering a shudder of pain. "No," she murmurs.

Goma pauses. "Are you okay?"

"Uh huh," Ash breathes, even though she isn't sure.

"I didn't ever thank you, for our trip out there. I had the most horrid dreams that night, did I tell you? Of . . . Nothing. Just . . . a vacuum. Like being dead, maybe."

"Goma," Ash pleads. She can't take it: the image of her grandmother's face — over-rouged, hair shellacked, uncannily still — pops violently into her mind. But Goma doesn't seem to hear her.

✳

"If it weren't for you, I would have . . . The doctor showing his power, I suppose."

She remembers the black thing on the ground that Goma threw up. What would it have done? And will her baby come out coiled in those inky strands. Her throat tightens, but Goma goes on—"it's French for deceives . . ."

Ash can't hear anymore. Something is happening, a hot vine cinching around her abdomen as Goma talks on and then it squeezes, and Ash screams and feels warm water seep into her underpants. She drops the phone, hears "Ash, Ash, Ash," as Mrs. M. rushes up beside her. Her face hovering close, asking things that Ash can't answer as she's led, stooped, both hands gripping her rippling belly, toward the stairs.

"Stand up tall now. Don't bow down to this pain. You let it do what it needs to do but don't surrender to it."

Her voice is warm, smells spicy from her favourite ginger candies. Ash does what she's told, hand on the wide wooden banister, climbing the stairs—one, then the next, then the next, then the next—to go to the birthing room. On the landing, she catches a glimpse of Charlene peeking through the gap of her door.

"Bring me the sheets from the laundry, and put on the pot to boil," Mrs. M. commands. Charlene floats by, barely solid in Ash's peripheral vision, but Ash casts her voice into the woman's wake, "And call Frank!"

In the room, all she wants to do is lie down, but Mrs. M. won't let her.

"First, we walk awhile," she says, leading Ash the length of the long room and back, from the bed to a cabinet and chair on the far side, sometimes looping through one door, down the narrow hallway, and in through the other. Around and around. "Breathe," says Mrs. M., and she tries.

One-two-three-four-five.
Five-four-three-two-one.
As Goma taught her, back, before, long before, in the time when she was little.

Backs turned to the door, Ash hears when it opens.

"Just leave them on the bed," Mrs. M. says but when they turn, Ash sees through the fog of her pain that it is not Charlene in the doorway, holding the sheets. It's another woman's face, smiling, bright. An obscene, scarlet, stupid joy lighting her up. Lucille.

EVERYTHING HAPPENS so fast.

The huge, dark shadow of the doctor falls on her from behind.

A fat mitt muffles her mouth and nose.

A searing odour spins her head.

Blackness, thick and clutching.

The last thing she hears is Mrs. M. screaming, then the thunk of her body hitting the hard floor. Down, she goes, into darkness, dropping like a stone into the sea of her pain.

55

SOUND WAKES HER. Squalling. A shriek fills the air. Footsteps pound, and then her arms are tugged up, her limp body pulled against Frank's heaving chest. She knows it's Frank because she can smell him, hear him—"Ally! Ally!"—then there's the blur of him when she blinks open her heavy, heavy eyes. Beside them, a towel, blood soaking the fringed hem, and a baby, naked, squirming, writhing. Beyond, the dark shape of Mrs. M. whom Ash can't let herself look at, laid out on the floor. Through the thin glass of the room's window, a siren bleats, coming closer closer closer, splitting the hard cap of Ash's head, pain ricocheting as she heaves herself onto her knees, arms swimming through the muddy, clinging air to gather her infant to the planet of her breast.

✳

56

BUT THE SLIPPERY, squalling newborn will not latch. Not then—before the paramedics arrive, Ash dopey from whatever chemical-mystical compound the doctor had pressed into her face—and not later, when she's back home, a new terrified mom. In the hospital, she denied, first groggily, then lucidly, knowing anything about what had happened, spinning a story for the crisply uniformed policewoman—not Suzanne, thank God—who stood beside her bed, blocking the window's sun. Maybe one of the resident's angry boyfriends, Ash theorized.

"We're all teenage moms," she told her. "We've all fucked up."

The woman's pen paused on her notepad; her eyebrows lifted.

"I don't know anything," she repeated, and then hollered, "Where's my baby?" Partly to push the cop out of her room, partly because she was afraid the doctor would come back to snatch Leigh away.

Why did he come in the first place? He didn't take Leigh; he left them all: her, Frank, Mrs. M., although she's still sunk inside a coma. The uncertainty is almost worse. Ash's imagination fills in the blank: that he implanted something inside of Leigh, a spell that will cause her own life to loop, a beacon bringing her to him. Ash feels like now she will be stuck, spending the rest of her out-of-place existence waiting for whatever he did on Leigh's birthday to come clear.

Worrying about her always.

But then, she's already starting to realize: that is parenthood.

She makes it back home, Frank by her side, staying with her in the turret while Mrs. M. remains in the hospital. When she manages to sleep a couple of hours, she dreams about the koi fish in the doctor's aquarium, their flashing bright bodies piled

✷

like firewood on the soggy carpet in the living room. Trying to pick one up, swaddle it, but a hand lands heavily on her arm, pulling her back, and there's Lucille, face warped and wobbly, staring at Ash as if through water. It's Ash who's underwater, though, fists hammering against the walls of the glass aquarium, and she wakes coughing and choking, heart hammering in her chest, and has to get up to check on the baby.

Over and over again.

Even as Leigh won't latch.

Waves her miniature, miraculous fists, squalling for milk that she won't take from Ash. It's as if she knows. She can picture the conversation with Leigh, in her other life, how it might have gone: if your only choice for food was to breastfeed from me, would you do it?

The expression on Leigh's face. Scrunched up, disgusted.

The two of them bursting into laughter.

The other women in the house—Moira, who's been there since April, and Charlene, who was locked in the cellar that night until Frank found her after calling 911—try to help, but they know just as much as Ash, which isn't much. It's Goma who finally comes to help her put Mrs. M.'s lessons into practice, showing up a couple of days after Ash arrives home with the baby. She teaches her and Frank how to properly do the things they've never learned: warm a bottle, check the formula's temperature on a tender wrist, burp the baby, correctly change a diaper, and she helps Ash bind her breasts to stop the milk. One day, after Frank has gone off to work, still believing that Goma—whom Ash calls May in anyone else's presence—is just a friend, they sit on the verandah and talk. Leigh suckles the bottle's nipple greedily in Ash's arms, her eyes swimming around the sky, already shifting from a surreal bright blue at birth (like the doctor's) to a light green (coincidentally like Frank's).

Can love do that?

Work such magic?

She believes it.

Goma sits on the wicker loveseat while Ash is in the chair, an afghan spread over her knees, Leigh's head warm and soft against her bare arm.

"I've been doing some more research," Goma says.

Ash doesn't answer, stares down at Leigh, feeling the bind of invisible threads braided between them. The love she feels for her daughter is shocking, atomic, like the hot stable core of a new star. How? How can she ever leave? Especially now. Now that the worst has happened: the doctor came.

Came and rejected Leigh, gave them both a pass, because only a boy would do for him. Ash moves on the creaky chair, lifting Leigh to her shoulder to get her to burp. She gives a large, bubbly burp, and Ash smiles.

Very Leigh, Ash thinks, remembering the three of them, her and Frank, too, having belching competitions around the Formica table in their tiny kitchen.

Goma laughs with her, and then they are silent. A boy walks by on the road, tugged along by a large German shepherd who's sniffing the grass on the curb, the spots where Mrs. M. planted sunflower seeds. The dog brings back another dream: dogs like that one rustling through the underbrush behind her house as her parents and the police hunt for her body. Eventually, they found her, or what passed for her, in Ash's subconscious: the remains of an enormous inflatable spread over a slope of rock. Leigh, on her knees, weeping, her tears soaking the candy-skull printed fabric of that old favourite nightgown lost in the doctor's house.

"I know it's not easy," Goma says. "Won't be easy. To try. To leave."

She's leaning forward, stroking Leigh's forehead, the fan of her fine dark hair, with a fingertip. Leave? she thinks. She will never, ever...

THE LONGEST NIGHT

How much time has gone by for them? Her parents? How is it for Leigh, older Leigh, her Leigh, with so much loss. Still, Ash is here, embedded in the strong thatch of her tiny family. How can she go anywhere?

"Trompe l'oeil," Goma says, settling back. The chair crackles beneath her shifting weight. "Used to create the illusion that something flat is actually three-dimensional, but what if the doctor has gone further than that?"

Ash waits.

"What if he's used his magic to give the impression that a three-dimensional doorway is two-dimensional when it actually is a door, right there in front of you?" Goma's eyes are bright. She's waiting for her reaction, Ash can see, but Ash's head is tangled up. Baby brain has dulled her mind. And how can that be? How could Ash have spent so many hours on that treatment table staring at the fake window, the fake door, watching Zeuxis use the cat door, when all the while it was actually the way back home?

"I know it sounds nuttier than a peanut parfait, but listen to this: 'trompe l'oeil is an artist's trick, it's a painting in two dimensions that conjures three.' Sounds just like the kind of trickery the doctor would enjoy. And you know what else?"

"What?"

"Zeuxis."

"The cat."

"That's the name of the originator of trompe l'oeil. According to my new Albanian friend Petra on this art history listserv . . . the amazing world-wide . . ." Goma shakes her head, getting back on track. "Zeuxis painted grapes so realistic the birds tried to eat them."

"Really?" Ash says.

Goma nods. "It's worth a shot," she says, and right then a smell wafts up, the diaper dirtied, and Ash is saved from agreeing to anything. She carries Leigh inside, and anyway, Ash thinks, what does Goma expect? That they'll trot on over there, let themselves in, interrupt breakfast for supper... "Don't mind us, we're just here to test a theory that the way home was staring me in the face all this time..."

When she's done, she tells Goma she needs to help with the cooking and then go with Charlene to see Mrs. M. even though she's still unconscious. Goma stands at the open door. The bright sun behind her casts her face into shadow so Ash can't see the disappointment spread over her features. For that, she feels relieved.

57

THE BABY GROWS.

    The size of her small, hot body, her own little universe.

    The size of her cosmos-swelling first smile.

    The size of her eyes, absorbing both her parents.

    Ash and Frank spend hours staring at her, passing her back and forth.

    Her tiny heart pulses between them when they kiss goodbye, when Frank has to pull himself away to work. They are bound, the three of them, she and Frank twin moons around the planet of their daughter.

    And then, Mrs. M. wakes up.

✵

58

THE CALL COMES in the wee hours. Frank is working a night shift. Charlene calls her name through the crack of her door, then agrees to sleep in her bed, to keep watch over Leigh. Ash drifts her fingers over the heat of her daughter's head, slips on the dirty sparkling silver shoes she was wearing the day before to work in the yard and heads outside. The hospital isn't far — it's the old one, with the basement regularly flooded by the lake, not the new one out on the highway that they'll build when Ash is fifteen.

"Stable," the nurse told Ash on the phone. "She came to consciousness an hour ago, frantic to talk to you." The stars are spread thickly overhead as she hurries downhill, gravity pulling her, excited and nervous and carrying a sense of dread. What did Mrs. M. see? What does she know? How will Ash's life change again?

It's 4:12 a.m. when she walks in through the Emergency entrance and tells someone she's been called. The nurse meets her at the elevators, because visiting hours don't start for another few hours. The name on the plastic pass pinned with a silver clip to her top is Marika Patel. "It isn't protocol," she tells Ash when they step out onto the third floor. "She was insistent, though, so I made a judgement call."

Mrs. M.'s room is dark. Only a slight amber glow from the outside streetlight, the haze from the washroom nightlight, the tiny green polka dots on the machines. In the shadows, Ash makes out Mrs. M.'s face, her mouth sagged open. She looks better: oxygen tube out, the iodine-stained bandage no longer wrapped around her head. Only the IV is still attached, and a heart monitor that beeps more rapidly when Mrs. M. opens her eyes.

✳

"Where's your babe?" She digs a hand into the mattress, struggles to sit up.

"Allison's come to see you," says Marika. "You asked for her, remember?"

"Of course," Mrs. M. snaps. "Where's Leigh?"

Her eyes drill into Ash's.

"With Charlene, back at the house. She's—"

Mrs. M. cuts her off with a heaved breath; her eyes close and she sags back into the bed. Ash exchanges a glance with the nurse who says, "I'll get you a warm blanket."

"Always cold," Mrs. M. mutters, as Ash sets her hand on her wrist, rubs her thumb, searches out the steadiness of her pulse. Her throat is tight when she speaks.

"Mrs. M., I'm so sorry. This is all my—"

"People like me ... take the hit," Mrs. M. mutters, and Ash feels hollowed out, a sudden lack of substance sinking her into a chair. People like me. Does she mean Black people? Shame surges through her. Of course, she's right. She thinks of the terrible murder of George Floyd, the children at the Mexico–United States border, separated from their parents, left to fend for themselves in cages. And here, now, in less than a year, the bombs that will be dropped on Baghdad despite millions protesting around the world, leading to thousands of Iraqi deaths in the first few months alone. Even as a time traveller, there's nothing she can do to stop it, to stop any of it. Inside the helplessness—and the guilt, too, sitting there, staring at Mrs. M.—a prickle of anger starts to grow. Toward the doctor, how he uses women, what he's done to her, how he's hurt Mrs. M. But it has nowhere to go, except into protecting Leigh.

The room is chilly. Summer is coming late. The nurse doesn't return; finally Ash gets up and goes into the hall to find her, and Marika apologizes and opens the blanket cabinet. She hands Ash a folded, fat square of white-and-blue flannel that Ash wishes she could wrap around herself, then adds another because she must see it, must see the fatigue and wear on Ash's face, and the fear and worry, too.

Marika touches her arm. "She's going to be fine. I think she turned a corner today."

Ash nods, and lets out a held breath. She's relieved, of course, but as the minutes tick by, she starts thinking about how Leigh will soon be hungry, will wake up wailing, needing to be fed. She flashes a look at her watch. 4:48. Maybe Charlene can feed her? She wishes she could whip out her phone, send a text.

Mrs. M. is awake and sitting up. One leg half out, hand gripping the chrome IV stand. "I thought you left," she says, as Ash drops the blankets at the end of the narrow bed.

"Do you have to get up?" she asks. "Use the bathroom or . . ."

Mrs. M. shakes her head, then flinches. She is breathing hard. "I thought you left. I was worried. I have to tell you—" She stops; Ash watches her chest rise and fall. The blue gown sags around her shoulders.

"Should I call the nurse?"

Again, Mrs. M. shakes her head, presses her fingertips delicately against both temples. Her hair is frizzy and wild, sticking up in clumps. Ash steps forward, plumps the pillows behind her, tries to encourage her to lean back into them, but Mrs. M. pushes her away.

"Just listen," she says, staring hard at Ash. Brown irises clear against the murky reddish tint of the whites. Slowly, Ash nods, sinks into the bedside chair, trying not to remember the details: the doctor's baseball mitt of a hand cupping her face. That acrid stench in her nose, drilling into her head, shoving her down into oblivion. She is afraid of what Mrs. M. is going to tell her. That she is wrong to think that the doctor's given up on her. That there is a cost. Because he and Lucille just left, somehow satisfied.

"That man," Mrs. M. says. "That night." She's twisted sideways on the bed, the sheets tangled around her legs, the pillows askew. A deep purple bruise saturates her cheek, edged in amber. Ash's fault. She feels sick. She presses a palm onto her belly, against the rising nausea. "He was there to—"

"Have you told—"

"Girl!" Mrs. M. snaps.

Cowed, Ash nods, but she's also noticed how Mrs. M.'s lips are sticking together, the ribbon of dry, pale skin. She should get her some water, some ice cubes, or those foam things to suck on, and she glances behind her at the door, wanting to step out there, to get away.

"Leigh wasn't alone," says Mrs. M.

Ash feels a weight sink fast into her belly.

"Leigh first, then a boy." Ash stares. Starts shaking her head, steadily: No.

"Smaller, like he was hiding behind his sister, but there he was. I thought it was the afterbirth, but then out he popped."

No, Ash thinks. *No. I would have known. I would have felt . . .*

She scoffs. *Crazy old lady.*

Mrs. M. watches her.

A mistake. The knock on the head.

Mrs. M. sucks in a breath. "That girl, that woman, massaged your belly to help you deliver, they made me help you . . . I'm sorry I didn't know. I should have been able . . ."

Her voice fades away. There is only the beeping of the machine. Ash cannot speak. A rushing has started in her ears like she's been clobbered, is about to pass out, is actually underwater. "I don't . . ." she starts, but she doesn't what?

She doesn't what?

"I picked up your girl," Mrs. M. says. "Laid there on the floor, tossed aside. He'd cut the cord, and he bundled up the boy, and the two of them . . . Left. I screamed, Ally. I tried to stop him. I did my all, but he came back, and that's when he..."

The beeping speeds up as Mrs. M. remembers.

Ash wants to move, to comfort her, to pull the blanket up, tuck her in, help her rest, as she'd longed to do at the end with Goma. Only able to say goodbye over FaceTime, observing the last flicker in Goma's eyes as if watching a documentary about someone else's grandmother.

"He just kept saying, 'He's mine,'" says Mrs. M. "'He's mine.' I can still hear him, still see him, face beaming before he clocked me. 'He's mine.'"

Still as stone, Ash sits. Eyes shut. Gone numb. Flooded with cold anesthetic.

Another baby. A boy. Leigh's twin. A baby, Ash's baby, whom he's stolen to do what with? Raise to become a monster like him? Her son. Out there, all alone, cooed to by crazy Lucille, growing up believing that she is his mother.

How could you not have known, Hayes?

But what can she do? Nothing. She can do nothing, lest she risk everything.

Her voice when it emerges doesn't sound like hers, and why should it? She isn't her, not anymore. She is now someone completely different. Not Allison, not Ash, but someone she doesn't even know.

"You need to lie back now," she says to Mrs. M.

"What? You have to call the ... I have to ..."

Ash pulls open a blanket but it's now cold.

"... the police. I can tell them ... I saw, in those evil—"

Mrs. M. is breathing heavily, tumbling down into exhausted sleep.

"... evil people. Who was he, Ally? I got this bad sense of—"

"It's okay," Ash says. It's all she can say. She's become an AI, an android, Siri answering an easy question. "Everything is going to be all right."

"All right?" Mrs. M. bleats as Ash spreads the second cold blanket over her.

It's a lie. Or course, it's a lie. A slim part of her wishes Mrs. M. hadn't told her. Maybe part of her knew—how could she not have known?—but then again, she has become used to letting her body keep things from her, lock knowledge away, hide it in the tender pleats of her cauda equina. And now she's being made to feel it, the pull of that other small body, her son, and comprehend the full extent of what the doctor's taken.

Not just her finger.

Not just her body.

Not just her agency, her sense of safety.

Her entire old life.

But more.

So much more.

"You need your rest," she says.

And like a robot, she stiffly turns, and leaves the room.

59

AND RUNS RIGHT into Goma.

Exiting the elevator.

Colliding with her familiar scent and warmth. Hands clutch Ash's elbows to stop the full impact of their bodies.

"Oh, I'm so . . . Ash?"

All her defenses slump and then she's melting, *I'm melting, I'm melting, who would have thought a good little girl like you could destroy my beautiful wickedness* . . . into Goma's arms.

In the quiet hospital chapel, Ash blows her nose. The tissue is crumpled and soft, pulled out of Goma's purse.

"Mrs. M. woke up," Ash says. "Are you here to see her too?"

But they don't even know each other, do they, Ash thinks, recalling the protective glare Mrs. M. had given Goma the day Goma came to speak to her, before Frank arrived with the roses for their anniversary.

Then the trip to Duluth. That updraft seizing the tarot cards, sending them flying. The hanged man staring up at her. She feels like that. Powerless. No way out.

Had her instincts at the lake been right?

How long ago that night seems. The night she saved Zach, the action that was supposed to correct everything, to send her home in a flash of blue light.

How naïve she's been. How stupid to think she has any options at all, that she's been outsmarting the doctor, that's he's given up on her. She lets out a groan.

Goma squeezes her knee. Her eyes are on Ash while Ash's float around the room. The alter. The artificially lit stained glass window of a heavily robed Jesus, palms turned out, looking sad. It's so quiet that it feels like they're inside some sort of vacuum: the hush a heavy presence, swallowing her, humming like the

✷

constant noise in the doctor's basement, which had sometimes anchored her, helped her sleep.

Maybe she should just go back. Be the other baby's mother. Leave Leigh with Frank. Is that what's supposed to happen? Then Goma's words fill the silence: "I came here for you, Ash. You were born."

"Oh, for Christ's sake," she says loudly, too loudly. Too much. She wants to curl up, dial back time to that straw-filled manger, lie down there, and sleep. All these babies when she never wanted any at all. *Life goes on, Hayes*, the voice in her head says. Leigh? Somebody else. Somebody wiser than the two of them combined. She stands when Goma reaches for her hand, allows herself to be led.

To the elevator, the second floor, a large interior window flanked with life-sized paper cranes stuck to the pale green walls, each with a cap on: one blue, one pink, the tyranny of assigned gender, Ash thinks, then sees her name, her own name, scrawled in black marker over one of the cribs: Ashley Maybelline Hayes. But it's empty.

Thank God, she thinks. She doesn't have to see herself, outside of herself; what good could that bring?

"You must be with your mom," Goma says.

"Can you check?" Ash asks, relief giving way to fear as she imagines Lucille dressed as a nurse. Scrubs decorated with tiny rainbows and Scottish terriers. They could take everything from her, including her own new life. Nothing will surprise her now.

Goma leaves her staring at another baby whose fists are squirming through the air. Ash's body tugs at her, a restlessness luring her back to Leigh.

"Cute as a bug, you are," Goma says, coming back. "I can already see her in you. A right match, right down to your . . ." She lifts her hands, taps her own pinky. Ash's mouth drops open.

"What do you mean?" she chokes. "Is she missing . . . Was she born without—"

"Only one little finger, just like you."

"But I wasn't . . ." She swallows. Had she not told Goma? Had she just left it this whole time as frostbite? "The doctor did this. He cut it off."

They stare at it each other. Finally, Goma speaks. "What does that mean?"

Her throat burns.

"Ash?"

She shakes her head. All she knows is that things are changing. And that the doctor has taken her other baby. Is he also missing a finger? Where does he belong?

"Ash!"

She spills, tells Goma everything that Mrs. M. told her, and as she speaks the knowledge grows. She can't stay. Not there, floating around the bright halls of the night hospital, nurses giving them scolding, sideways glances and tapping at their watch faces, or even up the street, in the house with Frank. Not when her son should be held against her, against her skin. Maybe he would feed easily; maybe that part would be simple with him: nourishment, providing food. Her face is hot and soaking wet, nose running. Goma is out of Kleenex, pulls a folded washcloth off a cart and Ash wipes her eyes with the scratchy fabric.

"You know we can't leave him there," Goma says. "We have to go, Ash. Now. Who knows what the doctor might . . ."

They move. Ash follows. Lets Goma lead her. Stops resisting. Lets her decide what they need to do. They exit the building, climb into her car. Ash isn't thinking anymore. She stares straight ahead. The soft grey gauze of dawn is tangled in the trees, spread over the lake. It's come so early. It isn't even six in the morning. The longest day of the year. Solstice. The day that she was born. Happy birthday to her.

60

THEY DRIVE. Car spitting dust on the edge of the road Ash has walked too many times.

Past the ice cream parlour, pool hall, high school, where she sees Tammy's maroon van pulled up outside, sees the daughter, a black shape walking to an idling bus with a giant instrument case for some sort of band trip like the ones Leigh had gone on: Chicago, once to New York. It's so early; they must be going far... Her own right foot pushes at a pretend gas pedal on the floor, trying to accelerate them faster toward the doctor's house, to get them there before any more time can slip through that hourglass. The scene erupts into Ash's mind, springing from the edge of her consciousness: Dorothy locked in the witch's castle, the sand streaming fast, counting the seconds until she'll die.

"Breathe," Goma says, and Ash does, but it makes her feel things: the threads tying her to Frank, to Leigh, growing taut and strained, ready to snap. Part of her wants to reach out and take control of the car, spin them back around, return to what's become her normal life.

But she cannot let the doctor win. Not like this, not when another life, her child's life, is at stake. They press on, the car straining up the hill, past the cemetery, the tinder of a violent anger catching fire in Ash. She wants to crack his bones, spread him out flat like a butterflied chicken, hammer him to a wall.

"Open the glove box," Goma says. The bullet-pocked stop sign throbs red in Ash's peripheral as they turn onto Ore Lake Drive. She does what Goma asks, sees the pearl-handled revolver.

"I'll back you up," Goma says, as Ash pulls out the gun.

"What's the plan?" Ash asks, staring down at the tiny weapon. Will it be enough?

✺

"Maybe we should have brought Frank," Goma says. Sharply, Ash shakes her head. Of course not! How would she explain?

How will you explain another baby, Hayes?

She doesn't know, will figure that out later . . . or Goma will, because Ash isn't stupid. She knows she might not come back from this. She squeezes her hands into fists, hardens herself, holds her breath for a moment as if to still the fibrillation of her revolting heart.

"Just us," Ash says. Her and Goma. The way it's always been, she knows down deep: loop after loop after loop.

Goma cranks the steering wheel to send them up the slope of the doctor's driveway, quickly twisting the keys to extinguish the motor, the headlights. Likely it doesn't matter. The doctor probably already knows they're there, can see into his own crystal ball or, like an animal, sniff at the air, detect their scent.

The house looks like a grey box, a yellowing cedar wreath lopsided on the front door, red ribbons hanging from it, picked to threads by birds. Ash looks over at Goma, but Goma is staring at the fringe of trees beyond the roofline, a jagged zipper against the soft pink of the dawn sky.

"Dagaz," she whispers. The rune representing boundaries, liminal spaces.

"Do we have a plan?" Ash asks. Goma clutches the steering wheel, hands at eleven and two.

"One thing at a time," Goma says. "We have to try. Get in, get your babe, and try the painted door. Okay?"

"The door."

Goma nods.

"Okay," Ash says, although she's terrified. She feels the cold prickle of sweat under her clothes. But she has to do this. Get moving. Get her baby. Go home. Back to her own new family, because she's pretty sure that Goma must be wrong. But Goma will not be satisfied until Ash tries. Maybe she'll even get to kill the doctor, and then return to what has become her life.

"We've got a weapon. Surely that will help. Surely he's not so powerful—"

"Let's go," Ash says. She does not want to talk about the doctor's power. She does not want to lose her nerve.

"THIS WAY," Ash says, gesturing for Goma to follow her. Her silver shoes—sparkle dulled by months of wear, escape after escape—crunch on the gravel, then go silent on the grass and dirt around the side of the house.

The back door slides open easily. Ash pushes forward through layers of heavy velvet curtains, trying not to sneeze. The dining room table is set for a celebration. A silver candelabra holding gold candles, wrapped gifts on the sideboard where Lucille dug out that flip phone a million years ago, blue and green balloons clustered in the ceiling's corners.

Zeuxis is curled up where Ash's plate used to be. The cat lifts her wide face to look, then stands up on all fours, tail straight up, and steps over to Ash, purring. Ash listens, hears the hum of the basement, the eerie plunk and trill of the eternal piano music, and Goma breathing behind her. No voices, nothing else. Nothing, as they creep slowly into the kitchen, stop to look at a baby bottle on the island and the golden vessel the doctor forced her to drink from, sending them both to the Arctic. Beside it, a mortar and pestle holds a scattering of noxious-smelling herbs. Ash glances over at Goma, and in that instant of connection, an infant's cry rises from the basement.

Ash moves fast. If she could, she would fly; she's surprised that she can't. Her blood pounds, body propelling her toward the squalling, which grows louder as she gets closer, as she blasts into the basement treatment room.

The trio of them, at the far end, near the pink salt lamp,

which is glowing like an amniotic sac. Wiggling infant hanging at the centre, the doctor's hands in his armpits. Leigh but not Leigh: the same dark hair, but this baby has the splotch of a strawberry birthmark on his cheek, shaped like a comma, like the break between connected thoughts. The doctor and Lucille look over, their faces wide and white. The opal glows in the hollow of the doctor's throat, throbbing, blue white, as if lit by internal combustion. A spiral of green fog coils from the doctor's mouth toward the baby's gaping lips.

"What are you . . ." Ash cries, running forward. She's forgotten everything; the revolver tumbles to the floor. Her hands grasp the infant's naked legs and, quickly, he's tangled between them. He howls, high-pitched, as the doctor hollers her name — "Ashley May!" — while he expands, growing rapidly taller, so tall that his head bumps the ceiling.

The same ceiling she stared up at as he assaulted her. The same ceiling she clung to when she left her body, rising into the cold stillness of imaginary outer space.

Fury fills her as Lucille pulls on the baby; Ash lets him go, not wanting to hurt his fragile limbs. Lucille stumbles backward from the sudden release and bounces against the trompe l'oeil wall, gripping the infant. As Ash watches, she begins to rock him, cooing into his red face, trying to quiet him, but he is roaring, enraged, as he should be. Ash spins back to face the doctor.

But she's staring at his stomach, the buckle of his belt. He's become a giant, the buttons on his shirt the size of her curled fists, the opal a pink-white nebula throbbing in his chest hair. Her heart pounds, her neck hurts as she stares up at him. When he speaks, his voice shakes her blood.

"Ash! What are you doing, Ash? Once again interfering, trying to destroy something you do not—cannot—understand. You've made your choice! You've given it all up, all of your potential power and joy, so take one last look . . ."

He spreads his enormous hands, gesturing at the room as if they are somewhere special. Not in his room of horrors, but in the centre of Paris, although that would not have been enough. In a flash she realizes she doesn't care about any of it anymore: New York City, the fantasies she's built, which seem to just keep getting interrupted by real life. All she wants is love. Frank, alive, her best friend back, her parents, somehow happy, however that might come to pass.

"Ash," Goma says, close behind her. She feels the cold barrel of the revolver against her elbow. Ash takes it, and as Goma slips back, she holds up the gun. Trembling, she aims it at his belly. The doctor laughs, that dry chuckle she grew to hate, that has no humour in it at all.

"Oh, my smart, stupid girl—"

She pulls in a breath, stabilizing herself, pleading with the random universe for this to work. Remembering Frank's face that day at the gun range when she hit the paper man right in the heart.

"— do you really think that will hurt me at all?"

"No," says Ash. "But this might."

She aims the gun and fires.

The bullet hits the opal.

It is as if the universe gulps.

A shockwave of blue and white light explodes out of the shattered gem. Fragments fall like galactic debris. Through the sparkling chaos, the doctor seems to be turning to nothing, only wispy arterial veins, the points of his limbs outlining his form, standing out like a constellation. Lucille changes, too: hair turning white, body beginning to rapidly fray, like a braid slipping loose in water, and there's Ash's baby boy, a solid mass, strung like a fly in a web, wriggling, about to—

"Goma," Ash shouts, but she doesn't need to. Goma is already there, plucking the baby out of the chaos of disturbed energy, pulling him into her safe arms. Ash watches her retreat. She's still holding the gun on the doctor, who has not completely disappeared, who is still present, but shorter now, shorter than Ash, shrinking fast. As the mist of energy dissipates, and she sees him: face splotched with liver stains, hair falling in clumps like the reddish fur from the fox stole. His eyes, though, are the same. Blue like the hottest fire, the hottest sky, summers that have broken all records. He smiles his thin, sharp smile, holds up both hands, palms out, placating, gurgling words she can't make out. She's in control. All of her choices, even when she felt like she didn't have any, have come to this.

"Go on now," Goma says, from the far corner of the room.

Is it time? Time for them to go?

Back to Frank, to baby Leigh, to her life, and now a second baby.

That life. The life that is not hers.

She looks over at Goma and sees Goma watching Lucille. The hummingbird has lifted off her arm; it's hovering near the window painted on the trompe l'oeil wall, which is not fake at all, but real. The window is real, and the door. Zeuxis, ears back, tail twitching, stares up at the blur of the jewel green bird as it slips through the opened window.

"Go!" Goma says, and it's as if the word blasts the back of Ash's neck. The eye blinks. It sees her grandmother, blowing her a kiss over Luke's — somehow she knows that the baby's name is Luke — fragile head, and Ash is overtaken by a drowning wave of grief and then fury. Fury at everything unfair, unacknowledged, simply swallowed, shoved down. Shut down. Frank's suicide, Goma's death, running out into deep winter, barely dressed, instead of shouting at her parents to . . . her parents. Why would she shout at her —

Most of all, though, the doctor. Fury at him.

THE LONGEST NIGHT

She screams. A piercing, vengeful shriek that snaps through the lolling piano music as she drops the gun and goes for him. Strengthened by adrenaline and rage, she muscles what's left of him toward the wall. He's frail, his head flops and jerks like it's empty, made of nothing but air and skin, no brain or bone. She pushes him back against the painted door, which swings easily on its hinges, putting her inside a long dark room where the humming groan of whatever is at the heart of the house grows louder and louder as the doctor thins in her grip. Transforming to the flimsiest fragments, like dry seedpods crushed in autumn, like filaments of ancient bone, until finally her hands are empty of anything but a fine grit that Ash wipes on her pants.

She looks back. Can she return? Far off in the distance, as far as the tiny girl in the field in the painting, Goma stands with baby Luke. She blows Ash a kiss. She waves goodbye, steps backwards into invisibility, and Ash's heart crumbles in her chest.

Between worlds, she is. At the core of choice, a tachyon particle travelling to where it needs to be. Despite the quake of her broken heart, she must push on. She moves into the room's farthest corner, which isn't a corner at all but the opening into a tunnel that grows narrower and narrower, squeezing her as she moves on. It closes tightly, like a cocoon.

Black as a cocoon, too.

The humming continues, never altering, its constant white noise somehow soothing, like blood rushing inside the womb, making her tired, so very tired . . .

Whatever happens, she's saved Luke, demolished the doctor, set things right even if it means . . . A cold wave of grief crests inside her. Too much, it's too much; she stops moving, curls up where she is, lets herself succumb to the cradle of sleep.

61

ASH SWIMS INTO cold. A cold that sucks up all the air so she struggles to draw in breath, thinking *there's something back there, something she needs to* . . . Under her head is an icy hardness, and her cheeks sting. She gropes over the roughness beneath her, feeling for where she is, and then there's a soggy warmth in her face, a tongue slopping over her lips. She rips her frozen eyelashes open to a soft gaze.

"Ripley!" Ash worms her arms around the big dog's neck, squeezes her thick fur, holds on as the dog's damp nose snuffles her neck. She uses the animal's sturdy body to help her get to her feet, then scans her surroundings: she's on the front porch of a completely dark house. Ahead of her is a long sloping driveway that ends at a road. Her breath blasts in a fog in front of her face. *Where is she?*

Ripley turns to start walking; Ash stumbles down the broken concrete steps to follow, unsteady with confusion but also cold, really cold, so cold she knows that if she doesn't get warm soon, bad things might happen. At the bottom of the driveway, she looks back at the house. It's the one up the road from her place, she realizes. A shell of a place that's been abandoned for her whole life and is slowly tumbling down. The bungalow's long, black shape looks like a redaction, cancelling out a forbidden thought. An enormous tree grows through the roof, limbs spread across the shingles, bare of leaves because it's winter. The branches are crooked, eerie against the full, fat moon. Ash stands there for a moment, clenching and unclenching her hands, trying to get them warm, feeling the strange bite of her fingernails in her palms, her little finger missing since birth, but *why is that strange?*

Her body aches as if she's been chewed on, spat out. She's seriously underdressed for the weather: wearing only a pale

※

purple rain jacket, jeans with a baggy elastic waist, her bare feet clad in ridiculous silver sneakers. Clothes she doesn't recognize. But that's the least of her worries. Every part of her is starting to sting and burn and ache: face, hands, even her bones. She knows that she's beginning to freeze.

Up ahead, Ripley barks, so Ash starts to run.

Fast.

For her life.

THE DOG KEEPS her going, and, soon, there's her house. Relief washes over her when she sees it: the familiar structure tucked inside the grove of tall pines, moonlight shining on the silver sailboat weathervane that her mother bought on a family vacation in Wisconsin. Ripley trots ahead, leading her, as Ash's breath waves a shimmering white flag in front of her face.

The door is locked. She bangs and bangs, and soon the light snaps on and her father charges into the mudroom. She expects he is drunk but why? Why would she expect that? He does not drink, never has. Apple juice in place of champagne; sweet tea instead of beer. The lock clunks as he flips it open.

"Ash? What are you . . ." he starts, but she pushes past him, burrowing into warmth she hasn't felt for eons, it seems.

The woodstove crackling in the living room.

Orange light jumping in the slim gaps around its iron doors.

Ash's father opens the top of the stove to slip another log in, and behind her she hears the sound of the couch easing under Ripley's weight.

"Did you hear the cat? Did the dog have to go out?"

His eyes hover on her face as he waits for her answer. Clear, attentive, like Goma's. Memories flicker: her father, laughing as he set up the tent trailer this past summer on the edge of the Rainy River, and on the dock, casting her line to get it out farther, then turning to watch Zach net a mooneye. One of only a few weekends she had off from her job at the museum where she'd been taking every shift she could to save for her and Leigh's move to New York, stalled by the pandemic, but still the plan.

Now, her mind stumbles. Why did she go outside? She can't remember. She feels heavy and still cold, the chill not yet loosened.

Finally, she mutters, "I just wanted to see the stars."

"Okay, but next time use the spare key. It's good you let Zelda in though. Not a good night for—"

"Zelda," Ash murmurs, her gaze sliding to the cat who's cleaning herself in her bed by the stove. She stops, looks up at Ash with her wide yellow eyes and their gaze holds. Something stirs in Ash, but she cannot pin it down. It slips away like a mist burning off as Ash's father steps closer.

"And, uh, that's not exactly the footwear I'd recommend for our winters."

Ash looks down; her ankles, bare, are flushed bright red where they emerge from the sneakers. She does not even recognize these shoes: dull silver, once sparkling. That, she remembers, but not where they came from, when she'd decided she wanted them. Aggressively, she kicks them off; he reaches out to clasps both her shoulders.

"You okay?"

She flinches. She can't help it: his sudden, heavy focus, the weight of his grip. Again something twists inside of her, a memory she can't catch, doesn't want to. He lets her go, steps back, dipping his head to look into her face with concern.

"Ash?"

No, she's not. A dark bird flaps wildly in her chest and then she's crying, mind stuttering over possible explanations, finding none. He reaches for her again, pulls her into an embrace.

"Missing Goma?"

She nods, her head pressed against his solid chest. That must be it.

"Me too. Firsts are hard. Especially Christmas."

They stand like that for a couple of minutes, and then he pulls back, lifts a lock of her hair and tugs on it like she's little. She expects him to ask her where the green went, green like the witch's skin in *The Wizard of Oz*, but why? Ash has never dyed her hair that—

"Time for bed, huh?"

—colour. That's Leigh's thing.

Leigh! Her breath catches in her throat; an enormous wave of pain destabilizes her. Only Ripley notices, gazing at her as Ash slumps onto the couch.

"You're sure you're okay?" her dad asks, and she nods. There's nothing he can do to help her, she suspects. She needs to navigate this weird confusion on her own.

"Well, don't stay up too late, and load the woodstove before you come up," he says, already halfway up the stairs.

"Okay," she croaks. He must be right. It must be grief. She lies back on the couch, letting the feelings come. When the tears stop, she gets up slowly, her body heavy with a deep exhaustion. From what? Ice skating yesterday? Christmas shopping with Leigh in Duluth? She hopes she isn't getting sick.

Ash puts another log on the fire, then leaves the door open to let it fully ignite while she gets a glass of water. When she comes back the flames are flickering into ribbons of orange, the light catching in the glass of the curio cabinet.

It holds her eye like scrying. How does she even know that word? Goma, of course. Goma.

Ash steps close.

Everything inside is familiar yet somehow different. Like someone's come along and rearranged the items, swapped a few of them out for other objects.

But no, they're all there, everything that she remembers.

The hunk of glittering purple amethyst from when they'd driven around Lake Superior. A raven's skull she found in the woods behind their house.

The abalone shell holding her father's AA chips.

The fox fur stole that Goma gave her, stretched along the bottom shelf, with the gold eyes that seem to glitter. And on the top shelf, the blown-glass vase with its heavy lid.

Ash grows very still. She stares up at it. Zelda stirs, circles her bed, then settles again. Memory moves like a creature under thick snow, scampering through its secret tunnels. Alive under the surface but invisible, disappearing as soon as you try to unearth it.

That vase was Goma's.

Doesn't it hold something important?

Someone? Someone's remains?

Carefully, Ash climbs on a chair to reach the top shelf. Inside is an envelope, the paper hardened into a permanent curl, molded against the vessel's form for a long time.

She pulls it out by a yellowed corner. Her name is on it: Ashley May.

How has she never found this before? The vase has always been here. Ash can't remember not seeing it, perched on that top shelf, its orange and black glass glowing in the flickering light when sunset filled the room, or the fire was roaring behind the mesh grate. But it's so slim. Easy to miss if you didn't look. Why did she look?

She puts the vase back exactly where it was, in the round clearing in the dust. The dust lies evenly on all of the shelves. Nothing has been moved around. Nothing has changed for a long time, despite her uneasy feelings. She closes the woodstove, shuts off the light by the couch, and carries the letter upstairs. Ripley follows, her claws clicking on the hardwood, and jumps on the bed. Ash closes her door.

Her hands are shaking; she doesn't know why. Carefully, she slides a nail file into the envelope's top seam and splits it open. She pulls out a sheet of Goma's stationary. Pale lavender, bordered with a fine gilded thread of gold that loops at each corner. The ink is blue but faded to the colour of a late-day summer sky. At the top, the date: June 22, 2002. Ash was one day old. She reads.

Dearest Ash:
You are safe.
Focus on what you have, grieve what you've lost, settle into each moment as a new miracle. I'm so proud of you, and I love you, always and forever and beyond.
Your Goma

What the actual... When wasn't she safe? Is this a mystery she needs to now try to solve? No, says a voice in her head. She holds the letter against her heart. Minnows of memory flash in her mind, but they do not stay. They swim off into a murky darkness, those green and distant depths. She sets the paper down on her bedside table, glances at her phone, but she's too tired to check it. Sleep is seizing her. She snuggles under her quilt — tea stained, slightly ragged, a source of deep comfort — and she sleeps, a deep sleep, the best sleep she's had in a long time until the morning sunlight wakes her up.

It is December 22, the day after the solstice, a time her grandmother would have called liminal, in between. From now on, the days will start getting longer. Through her pillow, her mattress, the wooden walls and floors, which her father hammered into place himself, Ash hears the clunk of a log tumbling into the woodstove, the crackle of the carefully tended fire, and the soft rumble of her parents' voices like a train that's carrying her, steadily and safely, home.

62

ASH'S CELL IS plugged in, fully charged, beside a steaming cup of coffee that her mother must have brought for her, God bless her. She wriggles up in bed and turns the phone toward her. On it, there's a single notification, sent the night before, at 11:16 p.m., when she was locked out of the house.
Hello?
It's from Leigh.
She takes a slurp of the coffee, sweetened with maple syrup, and sends back a waving hand emoticon. Instantly, Leigh responds.
omg I thought u were ded!
SRY.
It wasn't that long, was it? All she did was fall asleep. It happens. She sends back a snoozing face.
Still on for later?
Later. What's later?
?, she texts.
The party?
Ash fishes around her head and the memory slowly grows, images of the many times that Leigh and her family have come over on the holidays for her family's annual open house. Smaller, this year, because of COVID, but Barb and Suzanne will be here, of course, and Mrs. M., who runs the house for teen moms where Ash's mom volunteers as a pro-bono nurse. It's a tradition. How is it that it feels like something new? She sends back a thumbs up.
Leigh sends an emoji of a warthog blowing a kiss.
Ash responds with a dozen hearts.

✹

SHE DOESN'T KNOW why she's so nervous. It's just the Olsons: Leigh and her twin brother, Luke; and their dad, of course. Frank. She's spent thousands of hours with them over the years if not more, has known them since she was a baby. But it feels as if there's been a seismic shift inside of her: continents aligned to form a whole new landscape. Like some hidden revelation, maybe a dream she doesn't remember having, has changed her thinking. Her heartbeat jumps in her neck when the doorbell rings. Zach goes to answer it while she helps her mother pour cheese puffs and chips into bowls, spreads dessert bars out on a floral-patterned plate.

Leigh comes into the kitchen. Behind her is Luke, his hair longer than the last time she saw him; the twins look startlingly similar, except for Luke's birthmark.

"My kids!" Ash calls. It's what she calls them. It's what she's always called them. They pile their bodies against hers, and she's swallowed into the embrace, emerging from it, laughing, to catch sight of Frank. Quickly he looks away and accepts a cup of punch from Ash's mother, then says something to Zach. Ash sees the edge of his tattoo under the collar of his dress shirt, over his heart. An infinity symbol, she knows, that he got one drunken night at community college when he was learning how to build websites. It was designed to cover the cursive lettering of Allison, the twin's mother's name, the Invisible Woman who stole his heart until Tasmin came along when the twins were four.

An ache spreads through her, more grief she doesn't fully understand. She reaches for something sweet, a turtle square made from Goma's recipe, but right then her eyes lock with Frank's. He lifts his cup in a silent toast. In memory of Goma, she thinks, since the two of them were also close, but it's unusual. Normally, he ignores her, and even now his smile is sedate, distant. Ash gives him a shy grin, standing between Leigh and Luke.

Heat swarms into her cheeks, reddening them, she'll see later in the picture that Tasmin snaps. *Never gonna happen, Hayes,* a voice says in her head. She hears it, understands it, even as the pulse of sadness moves again in her heart. Some things, Ash knows, are never meant to be.

ACKNOWLEDGEMENTS

Thank you, reader, for bringing Ash's story to life in your own imagination! Writing is a collaborative art!

Thank you to all who've helped usher this story into the world: my tireless, always supportive agent, Samantha Haywood; Naomi K. Lewis, editor extraordinaire (whose short story "Flux" helped plant the seed that grew into this book); Kelsey Attard, the acquisitions board, and the rest of the team at Freehand Books for taking on Ash and her unusual journey; and copyeditor Elisa Petrovich for the final sharp-eyed polish.

Research sources for this book include: *Physics of the Impossible* by Michio Kaku; the article "Some Black Holes Erase Your Past" by Robert Sanders (in UC Berkeley News); Iraqibodycount.org; various online media and personal sources related to the impact of 9/11; *Foundations of Modern Cosmology* by John F. Hawley and Katherine A. Holcomb (the source of "[a]ny particle that crosses the event horizon is doomed, since it must fall toward the infinite crush at the centre," which Ash recounts in Chapter 14).

The quote "trompe l'oeil is an artist's trick, it's a painting in two dimensions that conjures three" that Goma recites in Chapter 56 is from Julie Myerson's review of the novel *Trompe l'Oeil* by Nancy Reisman in the *New York Times* (June 25, 2015).

Ash's recollection of the meaning of superposition as "just a term for something we don't understand" comes from *Quantum Mechanics and Experience* by David Albert, as quoted in Anil Ananthaswamy's *Through Two Doors at Once*, a book that contributed greatly to my understanding!

Deepest gratitude goes to:

My husband, Jason Mills (by now inured to my three a.m. stumblings to get to my office when a story is simmering), for reading and comments and 24 years of support, love, adventures, and animal-kids. My mom, Laura Carter, for her insights and edits and constant support of the value of a creative life.

My nephew, Mitchell Agema, for information related to tattoos, and Jody Baltessen and her son Hunter Ward for help with a colloquial term for being really high (zooted?? Who knew?!).

My Minnesota in-law aunt, uncle, and cousins, the Carsons, who provided hospitality and answers to questions (when they might not have even realized they were being asked!). All mistakes related to Minnesota details are, of course, my own.

Donna Besel, who invited me to co-host Wild Writing in the Boreal with her in 2018, where the fire of this book was stoked and my path towards my business Wild Ground Writing Retreats began.

All of the writers who come on Wild Ground retreats and share their incredible stories, creative yearnings, and deep connection to the written word. They strengthen my love of the process and craft of storytelling, provide me with enriching community, and deepen my conviction that this is our birthright as human beings. We all have the right to creative self-expression. Enormous gratitude to my co-facilitators who put heart and soul (baked oatmeal and hilarity!) into our retreats: Anita Allen, Ariel Gordon, and Donna B.

The Manitoba Arts Council, for financial support and a boost when this book really needed one, and Margruite Krahn who helped me keep the fire stoked (literally!) when I spent a frigid February week on retreat with a draft at her historic Herdsman's House in Neubergthal.

The Winnipeg Public Library, who hired me as Writer-in-Residence for the 2020/21 term to work on this book and provide teaching/critique, and the Saskatchewan Writers Guild for hiring me as Virtual Writer-in-Residence, which helped fund the writing.

And, finally, how can I fully express my gratitude to the women who have helped me stand, even during the most difficult times: my mother, Laura Carter; my sister, Carey Carter; my cousin, Caitlin Chisholm, and my late Aunt Linda; Amanda Walker, Patti Train, Julie Intepe, Conni Cartlidge, Liz Page, Ariel Gordon, Erna Buffie, Crystal Van Den Bussche, Kerry Holmes, Dr. Marianne Johnson; my sister-in-law, Amber Mills, and mother-in-law, Joy Mills . . . and anyone whose name will come rushing into my head at two a.m. after the book has gone to print . . . You all mean more to me than you know. Thank you.

LAUREN CARTER is the author of five previous books, including the novel *This Has Nothing to Do with You*, winner of the Margaret Laurence Award for Fiction in 2020, and the short story collection *Places Like These*, a 2023 INDIES Book of the Year Awards Finalist. She holds an MFA in Creative Writing from the University of Guelph and offers supportive writing instruction in unique locations through her business Wild Ground Writing Retreats. She lives north of Winnipeg, in a riverside home on Treaty One territory, in the heart of the homeland of the Red River Métis.